# PAPER SPARROW

Magda Palmer

Copyright © 2025 Magda Palmer
All rights reserved.
The Amazon Endure typeface was designed by 2K/DENMARK in 2025.
Template ID: ST-414D415A-25-A01
Printed in The United States.
ISBN: xxx-xxx-xxxx-xx-x

## DEDICATED

To those who refuse to be folded and for the hope of flight.
To the fragile who are stronger than they know, and for the courage required to rebuild a soul from its own ashes.
To the quiet fighters and to anyone who has ever had to piece themselves back together, only to discover they were a mosaic al

# CONTENTS

DEDICATED .................................................................................................. iii
ACKNOWLEDGMENTS ................................................................................. i
Part 1 ............................................................................................................... 1
    CHAPTER 1 ................................................................................................ 2
    CHAPTER 2 .............................................................................................. 13
    CHAPTER 3 .............................................................................................. 17
    CHAPTER 4 .............................................................................................. 23
    CHAPTER 5 .............................................................................................. 32
    CHAPTER 6 .............................................................................................. 41
Part 2 ............................................................................................................. 49
    CHAPTER 7 .............................................................................................. 50
    CHAPTER 9 .............................................................................................. 70
    CHAPTER 10 ............................................................................................ 83
    CHAPTER 11 ............................................................................................ 94
    CHAPTER 12 .......................................................................................... 104
    CHAPTER 13 .......................................................................................... 120
    CHAPTER 14 .......................................................................................... 130
    CHAPTER 15 .......................................................................................... 137
    CHAPTER 16 .......................................................................................... 154
    CHAPTER 17 .......................................................................................... 166
    CHAPTER 18 .......................................................................................... 182
    CHAPTER 19 .......................................................................................... 195
    CHAPTER 20 .......................................................................................... 203
Part 3 ........................................................................................................... 215
    CHAPTER 21 .......................................................................................... 216
    CHAPTER 22 .......................................................................................... 225
    CHAPTER 23 .......................................................................................... 237
    CHAPTER 24 .......................................................................................... 251
    CHAPTER 25 .......................................................................................... 264
    CHAPTER 26 .......................................................................................... 275
    CHAPTER 27 .......................................................................................... 288
    ABOUT THE AUTHOR ......................................................................... 299

Paper Sparrow

## ACKNOWLEDGMENTS

A paper sparrow is fragile, but with the proper support, it can soar. My heartfelt thanks to the friends who were that support, encouraging me to write through the pain and offering the honest critique that gave these pages strength. And to my husband, my anchor: you built the quiet space-both literal and emotional-for this bird to find its wings, tolerating two years of all-night writing sessions with grace and love. Thank you for being my shelter.

# PART 1

# CHAPTER 1

*The year is 1943, the location is Woolooware, a suburb in Southern Sydney, in New South Wales, Australia.*

Marj pushed a twin baby stroller along the dirt road, now and then yanking the oversized iron wheels out of holes left by dislodged stones from occasional traffic. Powdered dust disturbed by the preceding baker's horse and cart settled on her hands. It irritated her eyes and attempted to invade her throat, but Marj deprived the cloying grit of that victory because her mouth was shut tight, and her jaw clenched. She didn't feel like the pretty blonde with baby blues who had queened church dances before she married Albert.

Albert was away on training duty with the Australian army because the government, the military, and the people were deeply alarmed when Singapore had fallen to the Japanese, who also bombed Darwin. In addition, German and Japanese warships and submarines had entered and were still entering Australian waters.

Albert had rented a house in the bush, twenty-four kilometres south of Sydney, to keep Marj and his children safe. Not much in the way of neighbours, but there was a lavender farm with plum trees, the Murphy's who had a pet cockatoo, and a widow who grew potatoes and collected butterflies. They were all within shouting distance.

Marj had walked for an hour to the nearest grocery shop, then laboured for an hour and a half to return with the week's heavy load, which she'd crammed into the baby cart with her youngest children, Sylvia and Bertie. Albert was a good husband and did his best, but Marj felt short-changed because she'd been brought up to expect a comfortable life as the only daughter of doting parents.

The babies were gurgling a language understood only by them. They sounded happy, so Marj didn't investigate, which was just as well because if she had discovered the cause of the frivolity, she couldn't have done much anyway. Sylvia and Bertie had mixed melted butter with poo from one of their nappies and were smearing the repulsive muck in each other's hair and on their clothes. The related heaven-high stench soon made the oppressive heat of the day intolerable. It was all Marj needed to amplify self-pity and her unsolicited dislike of Peggy, their eldest child. She reminded Marj of a sparrow, constantly chirping and naturally friendly. Up close, sparrows are afraid of humans. Nobody wants sparrows anyway.

Peggy had skipped ahead; she'd caught up with the baker who had stopped to deliver bread to the lavender farm.

'Hello, Mr Baker, Mummy's going to vote because she's twenty-one.'

'G' day Peggy, what's that you say?'

Peggy chanted the words to her melody, repeating the lyrics as she skipped around the stationary horse-drawn cart.

'Mummy's going to vote because she's twenty-one.'

'Are you sure your Mummy's twenty-one, Peggy?'

'Yes, Mr Baker, Mummy's going to vote because she's twenty-one.'

Marj had caught up. The baker removed his hat in salutation.

'How are the young 'uns? Nice day, Mrs Piper. No secrets with kids around, ay? Peggy at school yet?'

Marj smiled sweetly.

'Next year, Ronnie, next year.'

'Peggy's as pretty as her mum. Hope you don't mind me saying.'

Marj acknowledged the words from Ronnie with a nod. He meant to pay a compliment, but it wasn't.

The wafting aroma of crusty loaves stacked on wooden shelves in the baker's roofed cart almost eclipsed the stink from the pram.

'Crikey, Mrs Piper, the kids' carriage is a bit full.'

Marj thought the little man might have meant 'foul' instead of 'full'. She suspected he wasn't referring to her groceries and that he was holding back laughter.

'How about I leave your loaf in the shade on your veranda? Here's something for you to sweeten your day.'

Ronnie offered Marj a paper bag concealing something fresh to nibble, then took off.

The iced finger bun was sweet, and she didn't have to share it. Peggy had skipped ahead again and was singing, well, sort of singing.

Marj pondered another time on this same road when she and Albert had been strolling behind a dancing Peggy. The child had jumped on a stick which had sprung to life as a menacing brown snake, hissing as it spiralled up her leg. Peggy stood stationary. She bent down and lightly touched the reptile's face with a bunch of leaves she was carrying. Then, astonishingly, it uncoiled and slithered into the thick scrub. Peggy then continued bopping along unperturbed. Marj noted Alfred's admiration for the child's natural communication with nature.

They reached the entrance to Murphy's residence. Their cockatoo perched on the gatepost. Peggy skipped faster because she knew the bird would try to make her talk to him. Too late, the bird was shaking with excitement.

'Ello say ello to Cocky. Go on; please say ello to Cocky, poor Cocky, say ello to Cocky.'

Peggy stopped and went to the bird.

'Oh, alright. If you don't swear. Hello, Cocky.'

The cockatoo jumped up and down on the post, flapped its wings madly, then screeched.

'You bloody drongo, I hate you, you ugly cow.'

Peggy, upset by the exchange, ran away. Marj smiled.

The cocky quietened down, slowly working up a jig while pleading.

'Poor Cocky, please say 'ello to Cocky, poor Cocky, please say ello to Cocky.'

Peggy gingerly came back.

'If you promise not to say nasty things to me ever again.'

The cocky lowered his head, pretending shame, imploring.

'Say ello to old Cocky.'

Peggy gave in, 'OK, Hello, Cocky.'

Then it started all over again. The cockatoo ranted, raved, and cursed. Peggy ran away, then came back and tiptoed beside the stroller, touching it with one hand. Marj ignored her.

They reached the rented house, and Peggy, now over the Cockatoo episode, ran forward and opened the wooden gate. She helped guide the stroller along the path up the ramp Albert had built over the steps leading to the veranda. Just about every house in Australia had a covered porch. Their presence enhanced the entrance's appearance and encouraged the circulation of fresh air throughout the hot, tin-roofed homes. Verandas also served as a great place to relax and chat with passing neighbours. Marj slumped into the nearest chair. While she recovered, Peggy half-carried, half-walked two-year-old Sylvia to the outside tub, undressed her, and gently hosed her clean. She returned to see that Marj had wiped the putrid mess from Bertie and wrapped him in a clean towel.

'Mummy, can I have a banana?'

'Get me a cup of tea and a biscuit. Then clean and save what groceries you can. Put them away, remembering the meat must go in the icebox under the house. And close the icebox door. Next, rinse the dirty baby clothes and leave them soaking in the tub.'

Peggy carried out the tasks, then asked.

'Can I have a banana, Mummy?'

'No. Go to the outhouse and shut the door behind you.'

Peggy knew this was the ultimate penalty if she displeased Marj. Conditioned to never knowing what she had done wrong and to accepting punishment without question, she trudged back down the ramp along a rough path to a small bush structure topped with a corrugated iron roof. Near the entrance, she moved swiftly, pressing herself against the far wall to prove she was inside because Marj had followed her. Peggy shut her eyes tight in fear.

The walls shook as the door banged closed, and Peggy heard the big log used to secure it slam into hooks on the toilet's outside walls. The only other time she'd known this door to be locked was when they spent a weekend away with Grandma Maggie and Papa Pilgrim, Marj's mother and father.

Marj's footsteps faded into the distance. Peggy eventually spread an old newspaper on the floor, to be torn into squares for toilet use, and sat on it, knees up to her chin, hands hugging her shins. A deep sense of despair and loneliness welled up inside her. There were no tears as she had already learned the value of concealing her feelings, but the walls bore witness to her tiny body convulsing as she rocked herself to sleep.

Peggy woke to see a spider about the size of a doorknob high on the wall. Her web looked like a crocheted tablecloth, but more beautiful. It sparkled and quivered against the grey fibro wall. Peggy thought the spider must have followed a pattern like one she'd seen in a knitting book because the same design was repeated over and over again, but sections were cleverly larger as the web grew. Peggy spoke to the spider.

'Spider, why are you happy in this outhouse? It's cold. Perhaps you don't feel the cold. But it's not a sweet scent. Maybe you can't smell?'

The wind blew leaves and dust under the door, causing the bundle of newspaper squares meant for wiping one's bottom, hanging on a hook, to flap. They settled when the wind stopped, each sheet held firmly by a straw-coloured string threaded through a hole in the top corner. Peggy lifted the first square and saw the one underneath had a photo of a dark sea cushioning a big boat with soldiers on board.

Peggy was frightened because soon it would be night, but maybe her soldier dad would come home early and save her.

'That's what soldiers do, Spider; soldiers save people from terrible fates.'

The little girl stood up and tested the door, but Marj had jammed it tight. She called out, saying she was sorry if she was naughty, but only her friend, the blue-tongue lizard, heard her. He had entered through a hole in the wall Peggy hadn't seen before. Now she knew where he sheltered when it rained. The four-year-old unhooked the wad of paper, laid it over the rim of the wooden toilet seat, and leaned her head on it. She slept; her shoeless feet warmed by the lizard who covered them.

Marj was feeding her babies the following day when she spotted the Dunny Man in his flat hat walking towards the outhouse carrying an empty pan. Back he came, balancing the spilling container on his leather-padded shoulder. She hoped he hadn't seen Peggy. Albert was due for his three-day leave and should be home soon, so Marj crept down the path and silently removed the log jamming the door; what Albert doesn't see, Albert doesn't know.

She bathed, settled Bertie and Sylvia, then looked in the mirror. She needed sprucing up. Marj dressed and primped, curled her flaxen hair with hot tongs, powdered her nose, smeared a few drops of cochineal on her lips, pinched her cheeks till they were pretty-pink, set out her China tea set, then sat comfortably sipping from a glass of water to wait. The train would have dropped him off about half an hour ago, but it was a long walk, and it was incredibly uncomfortable while wearing army clobber and carrying a backpack.

She knew her husband idolised her, just as her father did. She cracked a grin, remembering Alfred's confession of his premarital sexual experience. When he was fourteen, he met a girl who helped her mother, a cleaner at the plumbing and drainage business office where he apprenticed. They had flirted, met secretly, fallen in love, and vaguely planned to marry. The girl decided they should become intimate, so they formed a pact that she would show him hers if he showed her his. He had obliged, opened his fly, and let it hang out. She had lifted her skirt, dropped her knickers to her ankles, and shown him a triangular patch of hair. Albert had sworn to Marj that there was nothing more to it.

Albert had no doubt Marj was utterly innocent, so he hadn't asked her for a confession. But if he had, she would have handled him the same way she'd always done with her father and half-brother Lincoln. Tear-filled eyes wide open, hand to heart, and an expression of unbridled hurt accompanied by an almost inaudible gasp for breath.

Then Marj pulled back to the moment because Albert was singing. He got closer, his rich, baritone voice colouring the humid air.

***Little Grey Home In the West:***
*'When the golden sun sinks in the hills,*
*And the toil of a long day is o'er,*
*Though the road may be long,*
*In the lilt of a song*
*I forget I was weary before.*

*Far ahead, where the blue shadows fall,*
*I shall come to contentment and rest,*
*And the toils of the day*
*Will be all charmed away*
*In my little grey home in the west.*

*There are hands that will welcome me in,*
*There are lips I am burning to kiss,*
*There are two eyes that shine*
*Just because they are mine,*
*And a thousand things other men miss!*

*It's a corner of heaven itself,*
*Though it's only a tumbledown nest,*
*But with love brooding there,*
*Why no place can compare*
*With my little grey home in the west!'*

Albert stepped through the open gate, threw off his backpack, bounded up the path and ramp, lifted Marj in his arms, and carried her to the babies' room. He tenderly put her down. They laughed and cried, kissed and hugged, then took a child each and returned to the porch, the perfect picture of an Australian soldier with the love of his life and their children.

Albert wondered at the loveliness of both Bertie, with his carrot-top mop, and Sylvia, nicknamed Silva, for her white-blonde hair. But one was missing.

'Where's Peggy?'

Marj replied carefully.

'She's in the outhouse.'

Albert and Marj exchanged stories and dunked biscuits in tea while Silva and Bertie rolled about in the playpen on knitted rugs. Albert began to worry about Peggy.

'She's been there a while now; I'm going to get her.

The cement path to the outhouse was cracked and splitting from the weather, with weeds pushing through. Albert reached the building, pulled aside the hessian-covered door frame, and saw Peggy asleep on the dirt floor, her body leaning on the pan closet, her head resting on the closed lid. He lifted and carried her to the house, noting how cold she felt. Marj met him, her blue eyes spilling tears as she looked empathetically at Peggy. Albert put the child down on the rug beside Bertie and Silva, motioned her to stay, then put his arm around Marj, who leaned heavily on him. They went inside, where Marj confided.

'She's evil that one. No wonder nobody wanted her; the devil drives her. If you don't recognise that, then you are less intelligent than Murphy's Cockatoo. That bird knows her for what she is and swears at her when she tries to talk to it. What's worse, she's telling the world our family secrets. She gossiped about me to the baker, who became familiar and laughed at my age and then said she's prettier than I am. My dear husband, please punish her before you go away. Please do this for her good; she's a liar and a mischief-maker. I believe she's jealous of our own two children, who are babies and can't defend themselves. Please, Albert, help me turn her into the sweet child we thought she was and know she could be.'

Albert held Marj close to him and thought about this adopted child who had upset his precious little wife, even preferring to sleep in the outhouse rather than in the sanctuary of the loving home they had provided. He decided to talk with her immediately. He settled Marj on the bed as soon as she stopped crying.

Marj implored her husband.

'Albert, please don't tell her she's adopted. I want to do that, mother-to-daughter, when I feel the time is right. It is kinder to let her believe we are her true Mummy and Daddy.'

Albert stroked her hair and asked Marj to stay where she was while he sorted Peggy out.

'Please, Daddy, can I have a banana?'

'So, you preferred to sleep in the outhouse, and you weren't frightened? Now you're hungry? Why do you cause so much trouble for your mother?' God-fearing Albert silently agreed with Marj that Satan must possess this four-year-old child who preferred to sleep in a toilet and had no fear. Albert was sure this conclusion was correct because the sign was there. Her body was icy.

'I'm hungry because I've had no lunch and no dinner, and no breakfast, and I was frightened and cold, and I don't know why Mummy made me sleep all night in the outhouse.'

Albert's temper and righteousness flared.

'How dare you tell such terrible lies about your caring mother!'

Unable to control his rage, the large man in the soldier's uniform grabbed the first thing he saw, an electric cord. He bellowed.

'This will hurt me more than it hurts you.'

The child ran in fear; he cornered her and whipped her till she dropped in pain, exhaustion, and in shock.

Albert stormed out of the house, furious, angry, and guilty. He had never witnessed it, but according to Marj, Peggy was a cunning and spiteful child who needed a severe hand, no talking to, but physical punishment. The bible advised, "Spare the rod and spoil the child." That was the way he knew. The nuns had often beaten the devil out of him and had made him eat their apple cores until his throat hurt if he told a fib. But they'd also taught him to sing, play the piano, and practice forgiveness. In the future, when he was released from army service, he would teach Peggy to sing and play the piano as soon as they could afford to buy one. But for now, he had to find a way to occupy her active mind. The next day, he pulled the wool from a pair of army socks and taught her to knit, using big nails to replace the knitting needles.

Before meeting Albert, Marj was to marry a man who died after suffering an epileptic fit in the bath. Marj's ever-doting mother, Maggie Pilgrim, took her on a luxury cruise between Sydney and Melbourne to distract her from the overwhelming sense of loss.

Albert was the ship's plumber and a dashing six-foot figure. His dress uniform enhanced his charismatic personality. His laughing violet-blue eyes were never dull, and his head of wavy, golden-brown hair was reminiscent of ripe corn in a field. Marj was the prettiest thing Albert had ever seen, a bunch of forget-me-nots in human form, an earth angel with a pearlescent complexion and a face framed with softly curled fair hair. It was love at first sight, so Albert proposed; Marj accepted, and they wed almost immediately.

Marj's cousin Emmaline had married a pilot who died in action soon after their wedding in the same period. Society shunned single mothers, and Emma was pregnant, so Albert offered to adopt the unborn child rather than have its paternal grandparents eventually take it to Russia when the war was over. The family agreed for Emma's sake. But it was the same outcome because after arrangements were in place, Marj vehemently insisted that Emma have no contact with her child. Emma's heart broke, but she had no alternative but to bend to this harsh decision. Emma's mother was secretly relieved because the stigma of a fatherless child would be gone, and their spotless reputation would stay intact. They reasoned that without her child, Emma would have a chance for a new start. Moreover, the family swore never to reveal Peggy's true parentage to her.

Emma's one condition to this arrangement was choosing her baby's Christian name, her only gift to the child whose conception and birth were proof of her deep love for her husband, Danyal.

Emma chose Magda, an abbreviation of Magdalena, in honour of the biblical Mary Magdalene. This was significant because St. Mary Magdalene was the Patron Saint of women, and it was on her feast day that Emma conceived joy for the second name to attract happiness and light.

To ensure secrecy, Emma, Albert and Marj moved to Melbourne. Emma, on the pretext of an extended holiday to heal from her husband's death and the Pipers to stay with Albert's frail mother. On 19th April, Magda Joy took her first breath and was later that week dubbed the prettiest baby born that month in the ***Jessie McPherson Hospital*.

Albert had an acquaintance employed at a newly formed government Child Welfare Office. He advised Albert to name himself and Marj as the natural parents on the birth certificate as a precaution against Emma claiming her child at some future date. Being a Lay Pastor and hoping to become a Justice of the Peace in the future, Albert didn't want to perjure himself, so Marj's father, Charlie Pilgrim, travelled from Sydney to the Melbourne Registry Office. There, he signed legal papers naming Marj and Albert as the newborn's natural parents. Under Marj's instruction, Charlie Pilgrim broke their promise to Emma and registered her child as Margaret Joy. But, for a reason known only to herself, Marj decided all would know her as Peggy.

Albert and Marj returned to Sydney twelve months later with their 'firstborn'.

***Little Grey Home in the West**, composed by Hermann Frederic Löhr and D. Eardley-Wilmot, featured in the 1938 film "Sweethearts", starring Jeanette MacDonald and Nelson Eddy.

** **The Jessie McPherson Hospital** had humble beginnings in December 1930 in a Melbourne church hall. It was founded by a pioneering group of female doctors who recognised an urgent need for a hospital to treat the city's unmarried and married women who had fallen pregnant to men who died for their country and cause from the beginning of WWII. The hospital was named by the then State Premier, Sir William McPherson, who donated £25,000 to build a hospital in memory of his mother, Mrs Jessie McPherson.

# CHAPTER 2

*Year: 1944.* The location is Rockdale, a suburb in southern Sydney, New South Wales, Australia.

Emma suffered because she longed to see the daughter she'd given birth to five years before, the baby she had held in her arms only once, the daughter she relinquished to Marj and Albert. After all, children of single parents were stung by society stigma. Although Marj had refused any contact with Emma's family since the adoption, Emma had secretly hoped to accidentally bump into the Pipers somewhere, anywhere, in the hope of setting eyes on her lost daughter. Now that dream had ended because she and her new husband were leaving for Canada. Harry was to join EATS (The Empire Air Training Scheme), a policy designed to train Royal Australian Air Force pilots to transfer into the Royal Air Force. Yes, to her parents' dismay, Emma had fallen in love with another pilot—not comforting, since a pilot's life expectancy during WWII was tragically four weeks! Emma lived in fear that misfortune would repeat itself, but she loved and cherished every second for as long as fate allowed.

It was the day before the couple began their transfer. Emma was finalising her travel preparations while Harry was in the garden relaxing with Emma's parents, Ivy and Joe. He suggested an extended holiday for Ivy and Joe in Canada as a sweetener before revealing a plan he'd already set in motion to give Emma something she had long desired. Harry had invited Marj, Albert, and their family for afternoon tea the next day.

On hearing this, Joe didn't know if he was alarmed or amused, but it was an issue with Ivy. She was secretly ashamed to be part of a society that separated a mother from her child because the father was killed in action fighting for his country, or was it for another country, England? No matter, it was the same outcome. They agreed to go ahead with Harry's plan because it was well-intended and too late to change. Besides, it was unlikely that Emma and Harry would return to Australia, and if they did, many years would have passed.

Ivy and Joe were stunned because they hadn't expected Emma to divulge the family secret, not even to her nearest and dearest. It was a taboo subject. Ivy, Marj's mother's sister, was aware of the difficulties Marj could cause, so she sought the minister's urgent help. He visited the Pipers and convinced Marj that all would remain faithful to the arrangements made at Peggy's birth. Her children would be visiting their Auntie and Uncle, who are moving to another country.

Emma's mother and father decided to keep Emma in the dark about the Pipers' upcoming visit. It was to be a special farewell memory of Australia. Still, to allow her to look her best, an hour before the Piper family's arrival, Harry suggested Emma dress appropriately for a surprise afternoon tea party.

She looked as he knew she would, gorgeous, soft, and feminine. Ivy was afraid Emma might burst into tears at the unexpected, but she longed to meet her daughter, so Harry took his wife for a walk and gently told her who their guests were.

So as not to cause inconvenience to Ivy and Joe, Harry had previously paid for caterers. Ivy, expecting an elegant affair, was amused when a knock at the door revealed a jovial man wearing a candy-pink striped bowler and matching waistcoat. He introduced himself and his three-person staff. They decked the trees in coloured balloons, then set up a trestle table stacked with delights fit for a Mad Hatter's Tea Party.

Harry and Emma returned; Emma held tight to her husband's hand, barely containing her excitement.

There was another rap on the door, and Joe ushered in Albert, carrying Bertie, with Marj, Peggy, and Sylvia following behind. The little girls were delightfully dressed: Silva in pink, Peggy in yellow, matching bows in their hair, long white socks trimmed with lace extending from white shoes. Ivy was immediately afraid for Emma, but there was no need to be. Peggy, holding Silva's hand, looked straight at Emma and smiled widely.

'This is Silva, and I'm Peggy. You're pretty,' then hurriedly glancing at Marj, 'So is my mummy.'

There were seconds of perplexed silence because the child had shown fear of Marj when she complimented Emma, and now it was out in the open that Marj had broken her promise to Emma that she would not change Emma's child's name.

Harry saved the day. He stepped forward with a balloon for each child.

'I'm Uncle Hazza. Look at something I can do.'

He opened his mouth and wobbled a false front tooth. The children gasped.

'When it falls out, you must put it in a glass of water by your bed, and then during the night, the fairies will take it away and leave you sixpence.'

Harry pushed the tooth out at an angle, and the children screamed and laughed, asking him to do it again and again.

Joe sat at the cake-laden table, taking mental photographs of the granddaughter he had thought he'd never meet. He was content because he was now sure Emma had married the right man —a wise person who would always see to her needs, as he had today. Marj, Albert, and Ivy joined Joe while Harry steered Emma toward her child and her niece, the latter resembling Albert. Who did Peggy bear a resemblance to? Her father's high forehead, cheekbones, and bright eyes. She also reminded Emma of Lincoln, her deceased cousin, and Marj's half-brother.

By late afternoon, the party was over. The caterers had cleaned everything, leaving balloons and leftover food. Peggy and Silva sang *Twinkle, twinkle Little Star*, then voluntarily disappeared inside, where they fell asleep on Emma's bed. None of the adults wanted this precious once-in-a-lifetime event to end, so Harry came up with another idea.

'Marj, would it be too much to ask you and your family to stay and take breakfast with us tomorrow? Emma and I leave late afternoon, and we have little chance of ever meeting you and your family again.

And I'm sure you must have a good reason for calling the little one Peggy instead of her birth name- Magda Joy.'

To his surprise, Ivy chimed in.

'Please do, we have two spare bedrooms, and Joe will make our traditional Burns recipe Scottish crumpets for breakfast. Peggy has been known as a nickname for Magda, hasn't it, Jo?'

Against her will, Marj enjoyed her Aunt Ivy and Uncle Joe's hospitality, and upon the promise that this would never happen again, she agreed.

Evening came, and Harry slept on a lounge settee while Emma slipped into bed beside Peggy and Silva. Harry opened one eye to observe a whispering trio tiptoe past during the night, steal leftover cake, return to bed, then giggle till they fell asleep.

Emma woke earlier than the girls; she listened to their soft breath, then studied their faces. She prayed that when Magda required her birth certificate sometime in the future and saw that she—Emma— was her natural mother, she'd remember this time together and understand that Emma had parted with her for the most selfless reasons. She kissed her forefingers and gently placed them on Magda's forehead.

'Be blessed, my little one; I love you as I love no other.'

Emma was quiet after they left. Harry worried until she brought him a cup of tea with a note on the saucer which read, 'Thank you, my angel, she is as she should be. My heart is still.'

***"Twinkle, Twinkle, Little Star"** *is a famous English-speaking lullaby. The lyrics are from an early-19th-century English poem titled The Star by Jane Taylor.*

# CHAPTER 3

*Year: 1946. The location is Jannali, a suburb in southern Sydney, New South Wales.*

Albert's time in the army had ended. Although fallen arches spared him an overseas duty, he managed to obtain a low-interest loan to buy land and build a family home at Jannali, a more populated suburb of Sydney. The military did well by him; he had signed up as a Plumber and Drainer and had come out halfway through an architect's course, which he had continued to study through correspondence. He now owns his own business and was a local council member on an advisory level in building and planning.

Peggy was seven years old; Silva was almost five, and Bertie was three and a half. Baby Beth had been born just over a year ago. Marj was happy because she indulged in playing the pretty female with a sweet baby, which Beth certainly was.

When Marj smiled, Beth smiled. As young as she was, this beguiling coquette charmed people by lifting the edges of her skirt in a flirtatious manner while toddling toward them. Beth was a fair version of Grandma Maggie, even to being small in stature and slightly plump. She resembled a Kewpie doll on a stick sold at the Royal Easter Show. The children loved Beth but loathed washing her dirty nappies. Worse still, they had to distribute the solid contents around the established clumps of rhubarb; then, about a month later, eat the same stalks cooked and covered with custard! They vowed never to eat that stuff when they grew up.

The daughter of Mrs Miller, next door, was Peggy's schoolteacher. It was common gossip around town that the milkman, the baker, and the postman stood accused of upsetting Marj, yet none had met her! Albert was spreading doubtful truths that the powdered variety was healthier than fresh milk and boasting that his and Peggy's homemade bread was tastier than the baker's. The corner shop owners and the butcher down the street had never met Marj and said they wouldn't know her if they fell over her. They all said that the eldest Piper child was a well-mannered, responsible little girl who constantly trudged back and forth, carrying the heavy shopping for her family.

The jovial butcher confided to Mrs Miller that once Peggy came to purchase the family supplies, he sang the chorus of the Peggy O'Neil song to her, thinking she'd like that.

***Peggy O'Neil***
*Is a girl who could steal any heart*
*Anywhere, any time*
*And I'll put you wise how you'll recognise*
*This wonderful girl of mine.*

Peggy had asked him to please never sing that song again because she was not a thief. If anyone were to tell her father that she stole a heart, he would beat her severely!

Mrs Miller told her daughter that she was worried about Peggy because she often saw the child sitting on a rock at the back of the house, crying while nursing a cat. And she was considering selling her home because she was distressed by the Piper children's screams when being punished by their father, who had told her he believed in corporal punishment. Albert Piper was a big man, and they were small and too young to defend themselves.

Peggy told Miss Miller that her father had told her she could no longer play her recorder in the school band and must leave the church choir because her lips were the wrong shape for singing. Peggy had to stand instead of sitting at a desk like the other children during school hours and could no longer play sports. Her legs and arms were red with welts, and her blonde/red hair, although neatly ribboned, was thinning. Festering sores covered her chin.

There was no law as yet against extreme corporal punishment, but Peggy's teacher decided to try shaming the perpetrator in the hopes of curbing his actions. She also wanted to find the source of Peggy's low self-esteem. Surely that had nothing to do with her home life, because her father was the local Justice of the Peace who, when the occasion arose, sat on the court bench as a magistrate, a position that called for integrity and common sense. He was also a Forest Ranger and a Lay

Pastor with the Baptist Church. All posts were calling for compassion.

The teacher wanted to help her student, who was not protected. She made an appointment by posting a letter to speak with Peggy's parents.

Albert stood tall in the classroom doorway, smiling broadly. He introduced himself, stepped forward, lightly shook the teacher's hand, and thanked her for inviting him to discuss Peggy's progress. He apologised for his good wife's absence and explained that this hot weather affected her delicate health.

'Mainly asthma brought on in the first place by fear of living in the bush while I was away soldiering. Now, what's that Peggy been up to?'

'On the contrary, Mr Piper, Peggy has done nothing wrong, and there are no issues with her studies. I've called you in. She has unattended skin problems, welts on her body, and possible back pain, which is obvious because she often chooses to stand in class rather than sit. Peggy has dropped out of the school band and is limping too heavily to play sports. Mr Piper, I believe children who cannot partake in sport lose the advantage of peer communication and are less healthy than those who take fresh air and exercise.'

For a moment, Albert was silent, caught off guard by this stranger who knew nothing of his child's wickedness or how to deal with her. But he was aware of increased scepticism and serious debate aimed at prohibiting the physical punishment of children. Albert was careful and knew his reputation might be at stake. He answered without hesitation.

'Peggy likes to spend time with animals, loves them so much she doesn't want to eat meat, and even climbs trees to be with possums. That's how she hurt her legs. Yep, that's it, and she jumps over rocks too broad for a girl. A fall between them could have hurt her back. Peggy's got a cat she found in the bush, and we reckon that's where she gets her sores. So, in future, to protect the other kids and make certain they can't catch them, I'll paint the sores with gentian violet. Until she's better, she'll sleep on the covered veranda with Lassie, our dog, who also has sores. I've stopped her singing and playing the recorder as punishment. Peggy's a sly one who is always upsetting my wife when I'm out working. Never in front of me, only when my back is turned. And my dear little woman is expecting another baby.'

'Did you adopt Peggy? My mother, your next-door neighbour, has told me that your son continues your name, yet Peggy, your eldest daughter, was not named after your wife.'

'The wife doesn't talk to her family because they're all jealous of her.'

Albert answered the teacher's question illogically to avoid the issue of Peggy's adoption. He decided Miss Miller was guessing. She had no grounds for that thought, as a legal document had been lodged at the Melbourne Registry Office naming Marj and Albert as Peggy's natal parents. There was no coming back from that, but Albert was on high alert because the degree of physical punishment a parent or carer could use on a child was gaining momentum as a legal regulation. His ailing confidence returned.

Then the teacher asked Albert.

'Why does your daughter wear a woollen polo-neck jumper every day, all year round? And I'm worried about her hair. Are your other children attacking her, Mr Piper? And surely there is no truth in gossip that this seven-year-old child is making and baking the bread for your large family.'

Albert looked the teacher straight in the eyes and replied.

I help her with the weekend bread making when I have time. I'll try to stop Peggy from coming to harm. She wears that polo neck jumper to hide her long neck. My wife thinks it is good training for her future sense of style. She is concerned that Peggy may become conceited because people are always telling her she's pretty. It's best to tell her she's plain and that she's inherited my big honker.'

'Mr Piper, your "honker" as you call your aquiline nose, has a prominent bridge, whereas one can only describe your daughter's nose as straight-edged and small.'

'Yes, but tell her otherwise often enough, and she'll believe it; she's afflicted with a vivid imagination.

'Blessed Mr Piper not afflicted. Imagination matters. It is the root and birth of all creative and innovative thinking. Good day, Mr Piper.'


That night, Peggy's cat died while giving birth to conjoined kittens. Unlike Marj, Albert loved cats, so before his wife woke the following day, he went outside, lined a box with a new hessian bag, and decorated it with Flannel Flowers. He posed the dead cat in a sitting position with her stillborn kittens and placed the tiny coffin on Peggy's favourite rock. He was pleased. The early morning sun streamed through the trees, directly floodlighting Peggy's feline friend in such a way that it appeared she and her kittens were about to ascend. He woke Peggy and told her to say goodbye to Woollie, whom the angels were winging to heaven.

Albert watched while she stroked her best friend. It struck him that although Peggy saw death for the first time, she understood it because, in solemn silence, her tears, shining like crystals in the morning light, were dropping on the still, furry body, linking the child and cat with ethereal chains. His eyes opened, and for the first time, he saw before him the tragedy of Peggy's life and his own brutality, flamed by Marj. Despite his army experience, Albert remained a naive man who still believed that, as he had come through with merciless nuns as mentors, Peggy would come out positively with the same treatment.

'Peggy, it's time to go and let Woollie and her babies sleep forever.'

Peggy stood submissively, her hands supporting her aching back.

Even then, he saw himself not as a tyrant but as a righteous man who worked hard and provided food for the table, clothing, and shelter. Peggy touched her cat for the last time, then turned towards Albert. He saw her bruises, her welted legs, and sympathised, looking at her gentian violet dyed chin covering a wealth of sores; he wondered how much it had hurt when Marj tore out a clump of her hair. Of course, it was an accident. Marj had lost her balance and grabbed the first thing for support, which happened to be Peggy's hair. Peggy caught his gaze and felt his sympathy, but he was slowly losing hers.

*In 1921, **Harry Pease**, Ed. G. Nelson and Gilbert Dodge wrote the waltz "Peggy O'Neil," published by Leo Feist. The song became very popular. The lyrics are about Peggy O'Neil (born Margaret O'Neil, 16th June 1898 in Gneeveguilla, County Kerry – 7th January 1960 in London), an Irish American vaudeville actress.*

# CHAPTER 4

*Year: 1948. Guardian Angel, pure and bright, watch me while I sleep tonight.*

Albert and Marj had sold the Jannali house, making a healthy profit. That allowed Albert to purchase a large parcel of land and employ a surveyor to determine roads and separate blocks. On these, Albert designed and built to suit each buyer's needs. On blocks not included in a house-and-land deal, he built move-in-ready homes, which kept Marj happy because she had the job of choosing flooring, features, and appliances. The family lived in a spec house on site until there was enough money in the kitty to buy a large, sloping, waterfront block of land on the Georges River in a suburb in southern Sydney.

Albert drew up Cape Cod-style plans for this family home, comprising a large kitchen, a separate dining room, a covered back veranda, and a giant lounge room. It featured an open fireplace between two massive plate-glass picture windows, taking in the ever-changing view of the river as it ebbed and flowed. The entrance foyer seated a broad, winding staircase that led to bathrooms and bedrooms, the latter designed to fit snugly behind the steep roof, each with an extended gable. A front veranda ran the entire length of the house and introduced its main entrance. A garage, workshop, an extra toilet and a washroom would fit under the main dwelling into the slope of the land. Albert submitted his plans to the local council, and they passed them—no trouble, no changes.

Employed labourers and the older children cleared and prepared the site. The ceiling of the first washroom was a reinforced concrete slab upon which Albert pitched two tents. One served as a bedroom for Marj and Albert, and eleven-month-old Olivia. The other became a shared bedroom for the children and a dining/lounge room. It was summer, so food was cooked on a barbecue and served with salad. Sweets were almost always cold banana custard or fruit in season.

The children nicknamed pineapple the "barbed wire fruit". It deserved its nickname. Albert, still bound by the creed of frugal nuns, "waste not, want not," insisted they skinned the fruit's rough exterior so thinly that prickles remained, which punctured the inner flesh of their lips and caused the acid juice to penetrate and burn. Pineapple was another undesirable food that the children would never eat when they grew up.

There was a shortage of building materials and labour due to the post-war influx of migrants needing housing.

Undeterred, the Master Builder, a title Albert now proudly carried, chiselled the massive sandstone blocks found on the land into big square chunks. When placed and cemented, they made impressive walls for the second floor. He constructed another reinforced slab for the ceiling, replaced the tents with two rooms, a temporary kitchen and another bathroom, much needed for the growing family. Workers and mud-covered adventurers were allocated the first washroom, now on the lower level. Great, the family didn't have to live on barbecued food, and no one had to wait for yonks to have a shower. Peggy or Albert and Peggy made bread again, so Marj didn't have to be upset by the baker, who, she complained, was disrespectful.

Every afternoon after school and on weekends, while their father was hacking away at sandstone, Peggy, Silva, and Bertie were child labourers manufacturing cement bricks. It seemed never-ending, like circus performers on a tightrope: the children balanced on dangerously narrow scaffolding planks, lugging heavy bricks from the ground to the next floor one at a time, the planks getting longer and higher as the house rose to the clouds.

Albert partitioned off more rooms for the family to occupy. The "Worker Bees" (as Grandma Maggie called the children) continued to toil, now stamping cement tiles for the roof. Finally, the Piper mansion was complete. With lace curtains and painted gutters, it was the prettiest home in the street. The children swam in the river at the bottom of their yard. Peggy, Silva, and Bertie made pocket money by cracking the shells of oysters that flourished on the mangrove trees, sliding the fleshy creatures into jars filled with vinegar, then selling them to the local fish shop. Peggy wrote poems and drew pictures that she entered in competitions held in the children's Sunday papers section. Peggy often won five pounds. Sometimes she wrote a poem for Silva, who put her name on it, and she gained five pounds. With their earnings, they bought presents for Marj and Albert, books for

Grandma Maggie to read, a new collar for Lassie, ribbons, and bubble gum.

Bertie learned to steal the pretty things Silva and Peggy bought from their hard-earned oyster and poetry money. Silva punished Bertie.

The three children began using logic. They discussed and wondered why their father, the school teachers, and the church told them never to tell lies, while their mother seldom told the truth. They wondered why the police allowed parents to beat their children until they couldn't move when they learned at school that it was England's shame that boatloads of convicts suffered the same treatment.

The children learned through painful experiences which of them would be their mother's next victim. Her tyrannical bouts usually followed the medical discovery of one of her phantom pregnancies, jealousy over whatever or something horrible nobody else experienced. They discovered the ominous sign and called it "the fisheye", a descriptive name for an expression that suddenly flashed from her sharp, pale blue eyes at the next to be accused and consequently flogged. These children were like all others. They accepted brutality and near-slavery as part of everyday family life.

Marj told Albert she was too delicate to look after their children, so Livia was officially given to Peggy to care for, while Silva and Bertie oversaw Beth's welfare. Peggy cooked the evening meals, and Silva and Peggy made breakfast and school lunches. Now they had even less time for school homework.

Lucy was born and fast became Marj's favourite because she looked a bit like her. Beth was Albert's pet because she wanted to be a doctor when she grew up, which had been Albert's secret wish when he was a boy. Beth had learned to manipulate Albert's affections. Marj didn't like Livia because she looked like Albert's mother, which meant Lucy and Beth's longish, thick blonde hair was set in rags for special occasions, while Livia's lion-coloured hair was chopped short and never curled. Silva and Peggy made it up to Livia by saying she had beautiful legs and often sang a song they learned at school called "Red Silk Stockings and Green Perfume."

It was Peggy's 11th birthday, and Albert asked what she would like most. Peggy requested that he play Manuel de Falla's "Ritual Fire Dance" on the piano, that he sing The Egg Song, never to have to wear yellow again, and that she could please be called by her proper name, the name Auntie Ivy and Uncle Joe said she had, "Magda."

Marj flashed her `fisheye' at Peggy, then turned to Albert and put her hand on his arm.

'Albert, although I never wear yellow, it is my preference for her, and the name Peggy is an endearment because that awful name Magda is a Jewish name short for Mary Magdalene, who the Bible said was a sinner and prostitute.'

'What is a prostitute?'

Peggy's question gave Marj the reason for an asthma attack, so there were no birthday presents. Instead, Albert told Peggy she would leave the table and wait in her room for punishment because she'd upset her mother.

Immediately after the belting, Marj decided Peggy was developing stooped shoulders and begged Albert, for the child's sake, to do something to stop her from becoming a hunchback. Albert needed to please Marj, so he thought back to the orphanage nuns and remembered a punishment given to a boy who wouldn't stop picking his nose.

Albert found a broomstick, forced Peggy's elbows back as far as they would go, then placed the broomstick across her back, wedging it in place between her bent elbows. Albert repeated this physical cure for a week. He administered it immediately after Peggy made breakfast for the family and had eaten hers. Late afternoon, he removed it to prepare dinner for the family, then again until she went to bed at night. Marj sent Peggy to school like that with a note from Albert explaining the reasons for the broomstick cure, but Peggy was afraid of being laughed at, so instead, she sat in the bush all day, sometimes singing The Egg song, often changing the words and tune.

***The Egg Song***
*'Maxwellton's braes are bonnie*

*where stands the Grand Hotel*
*and 'Twas there I'd an egg for my breakfast*
*and I knew as I opened the shell*
*That it was an egg of the Old Brigade*
*though it had changed and altered*
*There it stood quite undismayed*
*and in accents low, it faltered*
*"I'm humming! I'm humming! I'm not new-laid, I know."*
*So, turning to the gasping waiter, I said, "J – J – J – Joe!*
*"I don't believe this egg has been laid for months and months and months*
*its calling-up notice has been delayed for months and months and months*
*I think perhaps it was laid by some extinct dodo*
*ten, twenty, thirty, forty, fifty years ago."*
*And then, a small chicken popped out and cried, "Parlez-vous?"*
*and in my best French, I replied, "The same to you!"*
*"My mother," it said ", lived over there*
*with Mademoiselle from Armentieres"*
*So, we pushed it through the window*
*we pushed it through the window*
*we pushed it through the window*
*And the waiter went to the grocer's shop to find the fellow*
*who'd supplied him*
*with his father's sword, which he'd girded on, he slew that egg which ran beside him*
*There it lay*
*till the next day*
*and when the dustman came to take the bits away*
*Eggshells he saw! Eggshells he saw!*
*So, he wrapped it up in his tarpaulin jacket*
*and thought for his tea it would do, would do*
*he ate it, and early the next morning*
*his widow, his club money drew.*
*So, Rule Britannia! No matter what you've paid*
*eggs are never, never, never quite new-laid!'*

That weekend, Peggy heard a distressed rooster squawking and screeching while the next-door family laughed loudly. Even with the broomstick pinning her arms tightly behind her back, she climbed on a workbench close to the fence. She saw the children standing on a tree stump, holding a white rooster down with their feet. Mrs Curry was standing at the back door laughing while their father, Mr Curry, was chop-chopping the terrified bird's head off with a blunt axe. The head fell to the ground, and the children jumped off the bird's body, which fell off the block, ran headless a short distance, then fell over and was still. They all whooped with laughter and kicked the bird's head to each other as though it were a football.

Peggy shouted.

'Why did you do that, Mr Curry?'

He replied.

'Animals don't feel pain, ask the butcher. Tonight, we'll have chook for dinner.'

Deeply disturbed by that hideous spectacle, Peggy promised the headless bird that she would never eat flesh again, even though she usually slipped her meat under the table to Lassie, the family dog, and she had never tasted poultry. Except for Marj, who ate ham, lamb chops, or steak, the rest of the family ate neck chops, minced steak, and sausages, sometimes a roast on the weekend.

Peggy believed the dead rooster had become an angel whom she called "White Feathers." She told the Sunday school teacher about White Feathers, and the teacher said that if the bird had transformed into an angel, Peggy would see a sign. It happened! On the way home, the wind dropped a white feather at her feet.

Peggy could hear Marj and Albert talking to someone at the front door. She peeped around the corner and recognised the tiny lady with the long white plait who lived in the house across the road. Albert saw Peggy and beckoned her to join them.

The lady smiled at Peggy and said to Marj,

'I'm sure you'll allow your daughter to come for afternoon tea. I've seen her looking over the fence at the statues in my garden, and I'd like to share their beauty close-up with her. What is her name?

Peggy got very excited and almost said Magda, but Marj quickly replied.

'Peggy.'

The lady smiled and held out her hand to Peggy.

'Hello Peggy, I'm Mrs Loveday, and you are invited to afternoon tea. Come.'

Three times a week, Mrs Loveday called for Peggy, and three times a week, Peggy sat like a lady, sipping tea from a delicate China cup while holding the saucer. She never took a second biscuit. Sometimes the two sat in silence, listening to music they later discussed.

The garden statues looked like Mrs Loveday because she was a model for her husband's best friend, an artist and sculptor. He sometimes stayed in a two-story studio specially built for him in their garden.

During her afternoon visits, Peggy was encouraged to touch the statues and discuss the different textures of the materials forming them. Sometimes she and Mrs Loveday ventured upstairs in the artist's cottage and studied his paintings, the shading, the lights, the lines, and the angles he chose to portray his subjects.

The best days were when they put cushions on the lion-headed cement benches and sketched the statues with charcoal sticks on butcher paper. Sometimes they added a daisy chain of whatever flowers were in bloom and drew the exact figure again, later discussing over tea and a biscuit if the garlands changed the sculpture's character and personality and took away from the artist's work of unadorned beauty.

When Mrs Loveday felt strong, the two wandered through her garden. They searched for exquisite surprises such as clumps of tiny green orchids, which hid in damp, sheltered spots or spectacular profusions of wild, creamy-white, star-like Flannel flowers. They bloomed in mass, their grey, woolly-stemmed branches and leaves covered in downy hair. Peggy was puzzled when she learned that Flannel flowers did not belong with the daisy family but were kin to the celery, parsnip, and carrot groups, yet they were not to be eaten or planted near fruit or veggies!

Then came the intoxicating scent of orange blossoms. In ancient times, Mrs Loveday said that orange blossoms featured in Bridal bouquets in China and India to ensure the couple would have many children. Peggy thought that was because oranges were healthy.

Blossoms had a short life, and many fell to the ground or were blown elsewhere by the slightest breeze. When the remaining flowers eventually produced fruit, Mrs Loveday taught Peggy to make Pomander Balls.

They took a ripe orange and wrapped it in a long red ribbon, which they knotted after pulling it tightly, then used a knitting needle to pierce holes in the skin, into which they stuck whole cloves. That done, they tied the remaining ribbon into a bow, pushed a length of thick cotton under it, joined the ends with a secure knot, dusted them with powdered cinnamon, and then hung the Pomanders inside to dry.

They were a delightful couple: the erudite, still lovely elderly lady, and the raw child developing artistic skills and a unique way of looking at the world.

Peggy's newfound interest in fine art and sculpture led her to design something herself, so she fashioned a silver ball from Mrs Loveday's foil. She was enthused by her lovely project, adding silver sheets from the lining of discarded cigarette packets she found on her way to school. Her secret wish was that the silver ball would one day be the plaything for her own little girl.

Then Mrs Loveday got sick. She gave Peggy a cup and saucer to remember her by. A short time later, she died in her big, four-poster bed. Peggy placed the precious keepsakes beside her silver ball and the emptied Vegemite jar containing a white feather on her bedside table.

The next day, when Peggy was at school, Albert melted the silver ball down because he ran out of solder. Peggy cried, and Marj gave her the fisheye.

She said it was the least a daughter could do to help her father with his work and that she was an ungrateful child who must learn to appreciate how lucky she was and how hard life was for children less fortunate. Albert added that the nuns used to make him scrub the wooden floors with a toothbrush, so Peggy was put to work on the back veranda with an old toothbrush, soap, and a bucket of cold water. She ate bread soaked in water for dinner that night because poor people ate that. The evening saw her sleeping on the bare boards; Albert covered her with a rug.

***The Egg Song*** - *an amusing medley written by Greatrex Newman (1892-1984), music arranged by Wolseley Charles (1889-1962). The latest recording is known to have been sung by Clive Clarke in 1982. https://youtu.be/wLIFmgaRDsO.*

# CHAPTER 5

***Year: 1951. The locations are Oatley and Sydney. The world begins to open for Peggy.***

Peggy prepared for secondary school. She passed the state exams for the highly regarded Fort Street Public Girls' High. Still, Marj said she wanted everyone to know they could afford a private school, so Peggy had to sit another exam at the Grammar School for its principals to decide which classes were most suitable for her future. The outcome included special studies in English, French, Latin, and Art.

The school was divided into clans, each named after a talented person, animal, saint, or famous scholar. Students were assigned their dynasty and received a badge to be worn on their uniform beside another showing school identification. This practice encouraged group loyalty and allowed individual students who excelled in sports and scholarly competitions to gain popularity.

The clans, also known as houses, were fiercely competitive, which qualified Peggy as an asset. She was unbeatable in spelling bees and short-distance running, and was a dependable field hockey centre-forward adept at swiftly distributing the ball in any direction. She gained respect but was barely tolerated by classmates, who decided she would never move in their social circles. She was a builder's daughter, and that was new money.

Silva chose to attend a different private school because she preferred a green-and-gold uniform to Peggy's royal blue and white. Silva took a backseat in everything. She loved cooking, nurturing children, adored Labrador dogs, and was a perfectionist in her appearance.

Bertie wasn't old enough to do anything except stay at his public school. His carrot top had changed to a mop of thick, fair hair. His casual personality, good looks and football agility appealed to the opposite sex. They fancied him, but he pretended to ignore the attention.

One afternoon, the children were on tenterhooks because Marj was flashing her fisheye, silently promising retribution for nothing. She declared that the cupboard under the stairs had to be emptied and cleaned. Peggy, Silva, and Bertie worried that they would be in trouble at school for not having time to complete homework, but that would be nothing compared to the punishment at home if they did not meet domestic duties.

The children began cleaning the deep, dark, forgotten area by removing everything. First, they found empty cardboard boxes stuffed with junk, newspapers, and ancient Christmas decorations. Next, boots still coated with dried mud, a musty blanket once prized by their elderly dog Jake, who Bertie had found as a puppy tied up in a sack and drowning in the river. Then a lost cardigan, parts from long-dead vacuum cleaners and two large, framed pictures they'd never seen before.

Except for Livia, who was still too young to work, the children dragged the pictures out into the lobby and then stood them up against the wall. They were different shapes, but both were very large with beautiful, gold-embossed surrounds. The oval frame held a photograph of a young girl with long curly hair wearing a blue net draped around her bare shoulders. The rectangular picture framed a photo of a little boy dressed in old-fashioned clothing, holding a violin. He was standing next to an Irish Wolfhound that looked as though it needed a hair comb.

They fell about laughing. Marj heard the uproar and investigated. Their mirth's objects were portraits of herself as a child and Lincoln, her older half-brother. Marj didn't know the Lincoln abomination existed. Her mother must have hidden it as a precious item. She thought Lincoln had finally disappeared from her life after the earth covered his coffin many years ago.

Lincoln was the son of her mother's first marriage and the daughter of her mother's second marriage. Lincoln was a child prodigy—a violinist of great talent who didn't mind covering for Marj's lack of skill when they pretended that she, too, was a musical genius.

For a fleeting moment, she once again basked in applause. She remembered tiptoeing on stage, a four-year-old angel in soft blue and pink organdie with hair fluffed out and curled, having been set in rag ties the night before, her violin tucked under her chin and pretending to move her bow on the strings while Lincoln played unseen in the wings.

It was Lincoln's fault that all that stopped. He was stupid enough to trip at school, which injured his spine. Even as he gradually went blind and before paralysis set in, he still played his violin to even more praise, but her pretend career had ended, and life became all about Lincoln.

The children watched their mother's reaction in silence, sensing her mood, waiting for the telltale fisheye. Fear set in as they didn't know who it would land on, knowing that person would cop their father's fury when he returned home. Bertie and Silva were terrified because Marj had not picked on Peggy recently, so one of them might get the icy daggers.

Peggy, Silva, and Bertie cleaned the house twice, peeled potatoes, and made Irish stew to win favour. They got spines in their hands from pulling small, pear-shaped Choko-squash off the vine hanging over the fence. They disliked this mild vegetable/fruit, which tasted like boiled cardboard and prickled their lips as pineapple did. They added chokos to the list of foods they would never eat when they grew up. They collected wild oranges from the tree growing in the bush and juiced them into two tall glasses. They climbed the big tree in Mrs Miller's yard with her permission and picked fresh figs, which they displayed on the kitchen cabinet —a big deal because Peggy had learned that ancient Romans poisoned their enemies by injecting figs with poison. Hopefully, Marj didn't know this, and their hard work would spare them punishment for laughing at the pictures under the stairs.

The atmosphere was thick, so oppressive that they were even afraid for Lassie's safety, their tiny, long-haired dog. They fed her and tucked her out of harm's way in their father's workshop downstairs. Finally, they set the table with a glass of orange juice beside Albert's place, and the same, plus a small vase of flowers, where their mother sat.

All was silent. Albert's car was pulling into the drive. Marj was stalking the room, running fingers across shelves, then blowing imaginary dust into the air. She doubly inspected dishes that had just been washed and dried. She was smiling, just smiling. Their father was at the door, his usual happy self.

'How are my little wife and lovely children? It's a lovely night. Share this bag out after dinner.'

He threw a full paper bag on the table, and the kids were swooping on it when Marj held up her left hand.

'Look, Albert, no rings.'

Everyone froze.

'Where are they, Marj?'

'I don't know because somebody stole them.'

'Who stole them?'

The children held their breath. Someone was about to get the fisheye.

'Silva did. I saw her trying the rings on when I took them off to clean the bathrooms.'

Silva fell to her knees, clasping her hands in prayer.

'That's not true, Daddy, I cleaned the bathrooms, and I haven't taken her rings.'

Silva got the fisheye, and Albert shoved her into the back bedroom, the children called 'The bashing room'.

Peggy, frightened for Silva, who seldom got bashed, appealed to Albert.

'Daddy, that's not true. Mummy put her rings in the empty biscuit barrel. Look and see for yourself.'

'Albert, she's calling me a liar.'

Albert, who didn't look in the biscuit barrel, was attacking Silva while shouting.

'Your turn next, Peggy, for calling your mother a liar.'

Silva was screaming.

Albert yelled for her to quit screaming, or he'd stop her for good.

The noise was terrible. Marj grabbed a pillow off the settee and bolted into the bashing room, slamming the door after her.

Bertie ran outside, and Peggy opened the bashing room door.

Silva was writhing on her back. Marj was attempting to suffocate her screams by sitting on a cushion placed over her face. Albert was flogging Satan out of her with his thin leather belt.

'Thief, you'll never steal again.'

Peggy found mighty strength and dragged her mother and the pillow off Silva's face.

Marj still had a spoon from the dining table in her hand; she jumped back on Silva and tried to gouge out her left eye.

Peggy grabbed the spoon and pushed Marj off Silva for the second time.

Marj rolled on the floor.

Albert hit Marj by mistake.

Marj punched Albert, who shoved her aside.

Albert was circling his belt above his head, gathering speed to whip Peggy, when Bertie returned with a fence paling and began thumping Albert on the head.

Blood was everywhere; it was over.

Albert, accompanied by Marj, drove himself to the hospital for stitches. Peggy walked Silva and Bertie to the Police Station. She reported what had happened because she hoped the police would protect them and did not want Bertie to go to jail. He was only saving his best friend. The police called the children liars.

'Albert Piper would never do anything like that, he's our mate.'

Later, Albert's police friends told him of his children's accusation. They warned that such talk could be dangerous for his reputation.

'Be careful, Al, kids will be kids, and they have loose mouths.'

Albert was worried. He'd worked hard to become the good citizen he undoubtedly was proving to be. He studied herbal medicine and treated the district free of charge for their aches and pains. He provided free or almost free plumbing services to the elderly, delivered speeches at council meetings, and shared leadership as a Lay Pastor in the Baptist Church. The only thing Albert was a bit ashamed of was having to sneak to his masonic lodge meetings, but what was a man to do? Marj did not believe men should keep secrets from their wives.

He often said to Marj regarding idiots attempting to bring in child welfare laws.

'These interfering, godless people don't understand that children carry the original sin that has existed since Adam and Eve consumed the forbidden fruit in the Garden of Eden. Can't they see that this world will become a place of darkness if laws are passed forbidding cleansing of the soul through bodily pain?'

When alone, Albert reasoned that someone must have reached Peggy, since she had begun protecting her sisters and brother at her own cost. He spoke out loud to himself.

'She stood in front of Silva to protect her while he punished Silva for stealing Marj's rings, and she shoved Marj away when she was holding the pillow over Silva's face. Peggy snatched the spoon out of

Marj's hand when she threatened to dig Silva's eye out, which was a stupid thing to do because obviously, Marj was surely only pretending, and it was Peggy's fault that her head was whipped by the electric cord when she stood between it and Silva.

I have done my duty. I taught Peggy to play the piano and to sing. I have shown her how to say goodbye to a dead pet. I have led her to forgive. She teaches at Sunday School and sings in the choir. I believe that if I have been a touch heavy-handed, I have done enough to be awarded forgiveness.'

That night, Albert waited until Marj was asleep, then made two cups of coffee —one for himself and one for Peggy—so Marj wouldn't know she had it, and Peggy loved the stuff. He went to her bed and woke her up.

'Peggy, I must speak with you. I've made a mug of coffee.'

She appeared in the kitchen. Albert touched her arm; she pulled away instantly and stepped back.

'Peggy, sit, you must listen, understand, and forgive.'

'Forgive what, Daddy?'

That forced him to consider his savagery at Marj's bidding.

'Peggy, I do as your mother bids because I love her. She is my little wifey.'

Albert saw no flicker of change in Peggy's blank expression.

'I am her husband, so I must do as she wants; otherwise, she'll have an asthma attack.'

He felt an oncoming river of tears and realised he loved this child. Yet, he had ignored her suffering; he had not understood her protective nature and had underestimated her bravery.

'I am sorry, but I must do it. I know you understand and forgive.'

# Paper Sparrow

Until Albert said those words, Peggy had always felt sympathy for her father, understanding that he was a victim of three women. His war-widowed mother sent him to an orphanage to avoid bringing him up while accumulating a string of houses. There, the nuns ruled with wet canes and other abominations. His wife, a spoiled and vindictive petty tyrant, used femininity and her dominant wifely position as a supreme weapon. Yes, Albert was a trained puppet, but he was also a human born with the capacity to choose his actions. He was a big man who decided to commit violence against his children, who could not defend themselves. She perceived his tears were for himself and that he felt no shame for his unjust brutality. Until this talk, she liked and loved him, but now the love was gone.

Albert went to bed, but Peggy stayed up. She was restless and wide awake, so it seemed the perfect time to do homework. No children to look after, no cooking, no cleaning, all was quiet. She sat at the kitchen table and studied for about half an hour. Then she put pencil to paper and sketched, for the second time, a portrait of Livia crying. The original was in charcoal on butcher's paper, worked on in art class at school. Peggy was excited and proud when her teacher awarded her first place. But when the prize-giving day arrived, her artwork was missing; it was later found partially torn and screwed up behind a toilet seat. Consequently, first place went to another girl called Nannette, whose gang sneered at Maggie.

'Where is your artwork builder's daughter?'

Maggie put aside her drawing and returned to her homework, then felt another's presence. Her eyes lifted from the books directly to the face of a beautiful young man who was looking around the door that opened onto the side veranda!

He had bright blue eyes, olive skin, and lightly curled dark hair. He looked like and dressed as the boy in the photograph with the big dog. But he had grown up! He smiled, and Peggy smiled back, quite at ease. Then panic set in. This person is not a natural person, so perhaps he was a ghost! He was beautiful. The scriptures say that Satan can appear as a lovely being to tempt us. This apparition must be the devil! Peggy was terrified and started screaming.

'Daddy help, the devil is here, help, it's the devil.'

The person disappeared, and Peggy ran to the stairs, only to meet Albert descending. He asked where this devil was. Peggy replied that the devil was at the back door, but he disappeared when she called for him. Surprisingly, Albert didn't punish her but listened intently. She described a face that resembled the boy in the old photograph found under the stairs. It suddenly dawned on Albert why Marj could not abide Peggy; she looked a little like Marj's deceased half-brother, Lincoln.

# CHAPTER 6

*Year: 1952. Fly sparrow, fly.*

Three weeks to go, and Peggy was about to turn thirteen. The big house was carpeted and furnished very nicely, thanks to Grandma Maggie and Papa Pilgrim selling their home and donating the money to Marj. When she wanted a new car, Grandma handed her a big, old biscuit tin crammed with so much money that when the lid lifted, the notes flew out all over the floor! Then Grandma & Papa had nowhere to live, so they moved in. Papa was in a comfortable bedroom upstairs, but Grandma's clothes hung in a cupboard on the veranda, and her bed was a sofa in the big lounge room where she read books late into the night. Possibly a mental escape from the harsh life she'd lived with Cockney-born and bred Charlie Pilgrim.

He had entered the workforce as a twelve-year-old cabin boy on a sailing ship. In a short time, he had the envied position of ship's cook. Like so many other English sailors, Charlie jumped ship in Sydney and then found work as a cook at Boys Town Orphanage. A couple of years later, he successfully found a better job as a Caretaker in an elegant city building with a luxury apartment. He married Grandma Maggie, and that was their home until 12 years after Marj was born.

Charlie Pilgrim was a man with no soft edges. He boasted that he once didn't speak to his wife for 7 years because she accidentally scorched the collar of his best shirt. He crowed that she still cooked his meals during that time and ironed his shirts, never daring to burn them again. Newspaper reporters and radio announcers crowned this shameful man as the most popular political speaker in * *Sydney's Domain!*

Grandma could read teacups, so Peggy asked her to read one for her birthday. Grandma Maggie came from a long line of Scottish Maggie Burns. She obliged, but this had to be "secret woman's business" because Charlie Pilgrim and his fish-eyed daughter considered such a practice devil-inspired.

The kettle whistled. Grandma's big China mug had milk and sugar, waiting to be flavoured by hot tea. For the first time since Mrs Loveday's death, Peggy used her China cup and saucer. No milk or sugar in this cup. It would only hold water and the telling tea leaves. The ritual began.

Peggy swilled hot water around the empty teapot, tipped it out, then took two pinches of tea leaves, dropped them in the pot, and blew lightly on them while wishing for good reading. The water was re-boiled and poured immediately on the dried leaves. Grandma sat opposite Peggy, who filled both cups with the steaming liquid. They linked hands before Grandma Maggie spoke.

'Please grace this reading with good advice for the consultant's passage through life.'

They sat in silence while Grandma Maggie sipped, and Peggy drank, leaving tea leaves and a small amount of liquid in the cup.

'Peggy, please take the handle of your cup in the hand you prefer to write with, then, while thinking of your future, rapidly move it in a circle three times clockwise. Now slowly turn the cup over to rest on the saucer. Lift your hand away, and we shall wait until the liquid drains.

Peggy, please give me your teacup. These pictures reveal a public career. You are a child of fate, born to communicate but not face-to-face or person to person.

There is much study of literature, languages, music, and cultures. Creative arts are in the blood that pumps through your veins. Your communication abilities will lift you to heights that may cause envy. The advice here is to tread softly with others, as though you wear feathered shoes. Then you shall travel with little harm because those who are jealous will see you leave soft footprints and will not wish to rule.

We see you surrounded by people, but you will prefer to walk alone for many years. The sum of this action will rescue you in times of need.

In midlife, you will do something that attracts many people who want you to lead them. It would be best if you stepped back from this position. Stay with your arts.

Opportunities will be constant, as will the unconditional love you'll receive from your chosen family, whom you have yet to meet.

In Scotland, based in Glasgow and Edinburgh, we ask that you contact the Begley family, who are married into the Burns. These Burns are your direct bloodline. Their talents are where you inherited yours.

You will spend the richest years of your life in other countries, as that is where your spirit resides. You'll climb many stairs and fall some. But, before long, your flag will fly above this planet.'

'Should I ask a question, Grandma?'

'The answer may not be forthcoming, but go ahead.'

'Will I marry a nice man?'

'Who else would you attract?'

'Will I have children?'

'Aye... but this is where your private life must remain undisclosed.'

Grandma motioned Peggy to stop asking.

'Peggy, I am sad because I shall not read for you again, but I consider myself blessed that this opportunity has come. Remember, do not fear. A hard-working, exciting, enjoyable, and successful path lies ahead. It is vital to keep your council and your private life to yourself, and always tread lightly. Finally, you will be welcomed by the highest and humblest. ***May the road rise to meet you; may the wind be always at your back.'*

Peggy resolved to carry a feather to remind herself to always proceed with caution.

On Tuesday, 15th April, four days before Peggy's birthday, she was alone in the kitchen preparing the family's evening meal when she heard a dull thud outside, followed by a yelp from Lassie.

Perhaps their little dog had hurt herself, so she quickly placed a glass bowl of freshly made banana custard on top of a kitchen cupboard where it would be beyond the reach of little Beth, who had a passion for sweet food. Then, she stepped onto the veranda.

Marj was standing close to the old milk churn, which held umbrellas and Papa's walking sticks. She was scrutinising the hats and coats hanging from the wall hooks.

Peggy asked a question.

'Is everything OK, mummy? I thought I heard a bump and Lassie yelp.'

'You imagine things.'

'Then you're not hurt? Would you like a cuppa and a biscuit?'

'You won't give up, will you, little sparrow? Get back in the kitchen, get out of my sight.'

Marj snatched a stick and advanced toward Peggy, who stepped back in a panic, then tripped against the cupboard. The bowl full of custard toppled and broke in half on Peggy's head. She fell to the floor. The pain was excruciating. Fear, custard and blood temporarily blinded her. Marj was above, thrashing the stick furiously. Peggy raised both arms to escape, grabbed a cupboard shelf to pull herself up, and the cupboard fell on them both.

Marj was out from under first, mercilessly beating the escaping Peggy while hissing,

'Get the hell out of my house and never come back. Your soul was bought by Satan when you were an embryo. The proof is your ugly face, your beaked nose and your vile neck. Wait till my Albert comes home. I promise he won't stop beating the evil out of you till you're smashed to smithereens.

Extreme fear, emotional trauma, shock, and the promise of increased physical pain triggered self-preservation. Peggy's acceptance of parental aggressiveness was over. She found courage, ran outside, and Marj in pursuit, still wielding her weapon. Peggy had a second thought. She turned, bolted back into the house, upstairs to her bedroom. She grabbed Mrs Loveday's cup and saucer and the jar holding the feather, then, dodging her lifelong antagonist, fled from the property, but didn't escape Marj's final words.

'He thinks you'll be the swan of our family. You'll never be a swan. You're a sparrow. A rotten, plain little sparrow who hangs around hoping someone will love it, but nobody ever will. Get out of my house, sparrow, hop it. Run, sparrow, run. And don't think you can fly to Emma for help; she doesn't want you either. She's in Canada.'


Seven houses up the road, Mrs Page was watering her front garden when she saw the bedraggled girl approaching. There was an urgency to her, yet she was dragging her feet. Up close, a thick, yellow substance intermixed with blood had coated her hair and was trickling down her face. Mrs Page had heard talk regarding the Pipers and their savage punishments, and this was proof. She stopped Peggy in her tracks by walking gently toward her, took the cup, saucer, and jar, and then guided Peggy inside her home.

Bankrupt of energy, frightened, and not knowing what to do or where to go, kindness caused Peggy to break. Her words, between sobbing and gasping for breath, exposed the caustic relationship between her parents and their children.

Mrs Page inspected the head wound, found it clean-cut, assured Peggy that she was safe under her roof, then suggested that Peggy shower and shampoo her hair. The petite English lady was about the same size as Peggy, so she selected fresh underwear, a skirt, a top, and a cardigan from her wardrobe. Diana Page handed the clean clothes through the partially open bathroom door. Not long after, Peggy presented herself as a crushed and fragile adolescent. In adult clothing, she appeared a little older than her years, as Mrs Page had hoped.

She pondered the dire situation. First, she must find a safe refuge for Peggy. She was homeless through no fault of her own, but by the actions of a psychologically unsound parent. The situation was urgent; there was no time to find foster parents, and those interested in taking in teenagers were few. Peggy couldn't stay with her because the law demanded two parents to foster, and she was a widow. Also, it was too close to the home from which a parent had evicted her. Peggy needed legal guardianship immediately.

Child welfare would interview the parents, who would whitewash their actions, leaving no choice but to admit Peggy to the notorious Parramatta Girls Training home and reformatory, the only place in the Sydney metropolitan area that housed homeless children. It was a jail that accommodated 200 older girls, many of whom had committed petty or significant crimes. Mrs Page had this knowledge because she was a child welfare officer who worked on a casual basis. She made a wise decision to take Peggy to the rectory of the local church, which she knew Peggy attended.

Without discussing her plan, she put twenty pounds, a comb, a handkerchief, lipstick and a tiny phylle of perfume into a handbag, along with a pencil and notepad with her name, address and telephone number written on the first page, then packed a small suitcase with two changes of clothing, two nightgowns, and underwear.

The Reverend Cameron had known Peggy for many years and considered her to have a well-developed sense of empathy, so he and his wife introduced Peggy to the Matron of a post-operation recovery hospital/Rest Home. Matron agreed to take responsibility for her if she worked and followed strict rules.

Peggy couldn't leave the grounds, even to sit in the park opposite, without permission from Matron or the Duty Nurse. But that was fine because here she was safe from Marj and Albert. She had a room to herself with a chair and a small table on which the jar holding the white feather and Mrs Loveday's China looked grand. Her bed was narrow, but not to worry—Peggy was so skinny that some said you could see the wind whistling through her!

Off duty, she bought her food from the shop opposite but was allowed in the staff dayroom to help herself to a maximum of three cups of tea daily, accompanied by two biscuits or a slice of cake. On duty, she ate breakfast of gluey porridge sprinkled with brown sugar, toast spread with jam, a mug of coffee, and a sandwich. A welcome change from the same brand cereal swimming in hot powdered milk she'd eaten for as long as she could remember.

Three months later, Peggy decided to take one last look at the house where her family lived.

She stood on the crest of the hill and saw it nestled in the valley. It reminded her of the gingerbread houses she and other church members had baked as gifts for Aboriginal children at La Perouse last Christmas. She wished she had the cute photo of one of the girls and herself, taken when they were both about 7. Marlee was wearing white stockings and Peggy black stockings, which gave the impression they'd swapped legs!

Peggy looked back at the house, with its protrusions of balconies and bedrooms, each with a separate, sloping roof jutting out of the more extensive top that capped the three-storied residence. It was a proud sight. She and her siblings had personally made both bricks and tiles from hand-churned cement. She remembered how she, Silva, Bertie, and Livia worked, their hands made rough and burnt by lime and other building materials. How tired they were at the end of each day. She remembered the time when little Livia fell off the plank and lost her two front baby teeth.

Peggy sat on a stump by the side of the road and fashioned a gum leaf into a whistle. She recalled the many times she'd rested high in the fork of a tree, sucking the same leaves she'd sprinkled with sugar after bruising them with a rock. Then, suddenly, in front of her was Papa, her mother's father.

He saw her. Charlie Pilgrim knew Marj had kicked Peggy out of the home, underage, with no money, clothes, or anywhere to go. He knew she must still be desperate and frightened about her fate, but he walked on and ignored her.

Peggy jumped up and ran after him.

'Papa, please say goodbye to me. I broke the custard bowl by accident, please.'

Peggy touched his arm. He whacked her hand off him with the contempt he used when swatting a fly and stared at her with the same `fisheye' expression his daughter so often used.

Peggy stood still and held his stare; the sun was setting behind him, and she had her first vision. She knew that the next time she saw him, he would be in his coffin, eyelids shut tight, hiding those unseeing eyes forever.

They walked separate ways, he on his voyage into time, while she walked toward tomorrow and her future, knowing there must be a better way to live. She was not afraid. The wind was at her back, Grandma Maggie had seen it in her reading, and she could feel it.

*Speakers' Corner was established in the eastern end of The Domain near the Art Gallery of NSW in 1878. The Government closed Hyde Park in Sydney as a public speaking venue in 1874.*

**A Celtic Blessing**: *"May the road rise to meet you, may the wind be always at your back. May the sunshine warm upon your face, may the rain fall soft upon your fields. And until we meet again, may God hold you in the palm of His hand.'"*

# PART 2

## CHAPTER 7

*Year: 1954. The hospital was not a regular hospital & the Hootenanny*

The hospital wasn't a significant health care institution with specialised medical staff and equipment. It was a small Nursing Home for those needing short-term post-operative care and a full-time residential care facility for the elderly awaiting their journey to the good lord.

There were three private rooms for post-operative care, two wards for mature men, a mix of short-term and permanent residents, and one for older women, primarily permanent residents. There were eight bathrooms with lavatories, an emergency operating theatre, a morgue, a laundry with an old donkey-burner that had to be regularly stacked with coal, a kitchen, a staff room, a reception lounge, and an office containing a locked drug cupboard.

Peggy had worked there for just over a year as a nursing aide, assisting residents with daily activities, including personal care and hygiene. She made beds, filled water jugs, served meals, and hand-fed those too feeble to feed themselves. In addition, under supervision, she monitored patients' health by taking their pulse rates and temperatures. Her job was a way to earn a living and was agreeable because she liked helping those in need, but it wasn't what she wanted to do for the rest of her life. She dreamt of working in the arts, not in a hospital where her nostrils objected to a pungent mix of churning odours from bedpans and cleaning disinfectants. Sometimes her head swam with the mildly rancid, sweet, and musty scent of old age—harsh servitude for a girl who hadn't yet turned fourteen.

Peggy often spent off-duty time visiting those who were alone. Matron thought this was comforting for her patients and a valuable learning curve for her young charge. Peggy had an incredibly soft spot for Florence, a fragile lady who enjoyed having her agonisingly cold hands massaged vigorously with a mix of lavender and olive oil. Florence was a lightweight, so Peggy was able to lift her out of bed and sit her in a comfy chair while she plumped her pillows and straightened or changed the linen. During these times, Florence hardly spoke, which Peggy understood because what did she have to talk about in her present state?

One afternoon, Peggy was reading aloud to Florence when a well-presented, mature man in a Service uniform, who claimed to be her nephew, Aubrey Austin-Webb, entered her room. Peggy bookmarked the page, then rose from her chair, intending to give them privacy, but a quick turn of her patient's head and a flash of panic from normally serene eyes triggered an alarm, so Peggy stayed firmly by the bed. The man recognised the situation with a faint smile, then stooped close to Florence's face and spoke.

'Aunt Flora, do you remember me, Aubrey, your sister's boy?'

Florence showed no sign of recognition or welcome to her visitor, instead focusing on Peggy. Unperturbed, Aubrey lowered himself into a nearby chair and motioned for Peggy to sit.

'Did you know that our Flora was an English Music Hall Star? We are in the presence of a supreme drum musician who became world-famous when she performed in a Scottish Show at the theatre of all theatres, the London Palladium, the premier venue for promenade concerts, variety shows, and pantomime.

Without waiting for an answer, Aubrey stood tall, spread his arms high and wide, then theatrically whispered.

'Imagine this. The lights went down in the Palladium auditorium. The seated audience, transfixed by the luxurious red velvet curtains as they slid open, revealed a purple-and-pink heather-covered mountain on the grand stage. Dimmed lighting showed the silhouette of a marching army on the horizon. A bright star appeared and shone on a proud, Lone Piper at the foot of the mountain. His reed was chanting a centuries-old, mournful tune composed in memory of a lost boy in the tunnels under Edenborough Castle.

A dramatic pause.

'The spotlight surrendered to a blaze of back-lighting on the peak of the mountain, awarding stardom to our Flora, an earth goddess standing as still as a tree with no shadow. Tartan socks were clinging to her long, shapely legs. Her lower body wore a short kilt topped by a white frilled bodice under a glittering, sleeveless waistcoat. She had auburn curls crowned by a tartan bonnet, its excellent feathered embellishment almost brushing her raised arms, which held sticks, patiently waiting to beat the drum attached to her waist.

Seconds later, the auditorium exploded with the thrill of a full Scottish band. Flora's hands blurred as she swirled her sticks furiously, then dropped them to produce a bright overall sound that resonated with the tune of Scotland the Brave.'

Aubrey caressed Florence's arm, which she moved out of reach. Unperturbed, his other arm swooped grandly, indicating Florence.

'Now, this is part of Palladium history, and I tell it as it was.'

He leaned forward, splaying his hands on the bed for balance, lifted his head, and his eyes stared into space, scrying this past event.

'Flora slowly and deliberately descended the mountain, her drumming thundering above the bagpipes ramped up the unofficial anthem. The tune of the patriotic song hit its zenith when she reached centre stage. There, her final drum roll shook the auditorium.

As the principal player should, Flora turned and faced her audience. She waited for applause, but the emotionally annihilated audience, overwhelmed by Flora's beauty and talent, was silent until…'

Aubrey, in military posture, assumed the position of attention: shoulders back, stomach in, chin up, chest out. In a salute to his upcoming statement, he flicked his hand to his forehead and continued.

'I repeat until a deaf and dumb man in the front row led a standing ovation when he shouted, 'Long live Scotland.'

Florence half smiled, then moved her hand to touch an exquisite gold egg embellished with red enamel, which she wore on a fine, twisted silk rope around her neck. Aubrey glanced at the egg.

'Florence was sought after by nobility of all nationalities; an Indian Prince gave her that Fabergé pendant in the hope that she would become his.' 'But no, she didn't have time for marriage. Flora was too busy being driven from one theatre to another, playing her drums and supporting the *Suffragette* movement in public appearances. Yes, she was one of the many who fought for gender equality.

But that is not all. Florence was also a "*Canary Girl*", a brave soul who worked in a factory handling toxic chemicals, making weapons such as shells and bullets, risking her life and limb to supply ammunition to the frontline during WW11. Canary Girls were so-called for two reasons: the toxic chemicals and sulphur turned their skin orange/yellow, and secondly, they were in constant danger of being blown up and killed, as was the fate of the little birds used in underground conditions by miners to detect toxic carbon monoxide.

The free world should pay tribute to her. We need to remember and honour these women as we do soldiers. They were warriors, daughters of Zeus, who, without their efforts, we may have lost the Second World War. Life as we know it would have looked very different. I salute her.'

Aubrey softened his pose, bent to Florence, and touched his forelock.

'Financial problems hit our family hard during and after WW11, so we migrated to Australia, supposedly the land of plenty and great opportunities…but that is another story, including my mother's sad break with Flora. I've searched and found her and have come to pay my respects.'

The narrative finished; the gentleman's stance folded in exhaustion. Florence had fallen asleep. Peggy tucked her patient's cold hands under the blanket and excused herself.

She returned with the visitor's book and watched him sign himself in (which he hadn't). Peggy suggested that he should sign out when he left. She wrote in the report book that Florence had a visitor who said he was her nephew, but she didn't appear to recognise him and felt uneasy in his presence.

Peggy wished the Duty Nurse had reported seeing Aubrey Austin-Webb leave while tucking something into his inside pocket. He had stolen his aunt's Fabergé egg pendant.

# CHAPTER 8

***1953. The locations are in the north Sydney suburbs of New South Wales.***

It wasn't Melbourne Cup Day, but there was another much-anticipated horse race coming up. Lorraine, a Duty Nurse, asked Peggy if she'd fancy a flutter, meaning perhaps she'd like to risk a small amount of money gambling on a horse to win. What fun! Peggy had saved a little money, and she didn't go anywhere to spend it, so why not? Lorraine put a printed form in front of her. Peggy decided she'd squander ten pounds to win on Trixie-Dell, the jockey wearing Peggy's old school colours, royal blue and white. Of course, everyone questioned and even objected to her choice because the horse was an outsider with little chance of winning. But, with beginner's luck, Trixie-Dell came in first at 50 to 1!

Matron was unhappy with Lorraine for potentially leading Peggy astray, but very happy when Peggy celebrated by buying cakes for all and presented Matron, the Senior Duty Nurse, Almeda, and Lorraine with a bunch of flowers each. Then, with Matron in a rosy mood, Lorraine got permission to take Peggy to Sydney while she went to the hairdresser, promising to leave Peggy safe in a major store's music department.

David Jones's basement held a wealth of records for sale. An assistant dressed in black and white asked which music Peggy preferred. She explained that she didn't know much music but was fond of Bach/Gounod Ave Maria, Manuel de Falla's Ritual Fire Dance, and a beautiful Operatic Aria—Pedro the Fisherman.

She was led to a booth, seated, then asked to wear headphones and listen to her heart's content.

When Lorraine returned from the hairdresser's, she was astonished to see Peggy still listening to music. She had already purchased the

Beethoven String Quartet No. 14, Bruckner's 9th Symphony, Wagner's Ring Cycle, and a recording of Gracie Fields singing "Pedro the Fisherman." Lorraine was curious.

'Have you a record player?'

'No, but White Feathers will lead me to one.'

'White Feathers?'

Peggy didn't have to answer because Lorraine's friend from the beauty salon joined them, and the three left for lunch.

Una, who pronounced her name "You – Nah", was at the hospital for post-operative healing and rest. Her doctors and psychologists had successfully softened both emotional and physical trauma resulting from her family's death in a fire that raged through their home five years previously.

Sister Almeda said the opportunity to surgically restore a large, consecutive series of facial burns in which destruction was massive seldom went to one surgeon. Instead, the reconstruction plan for Una had been rigidly adhered to by several specialists. They each gained her trust, cooperation, and confidence by pre-assessment of how much improvement they could expect immediately and remotely.

Physical therapy, counselling, and medication had banished Una's anguish, depression, and nightmares. Reparative surgery had subjected her to 28 operations, and although raw surfaces had healed during the first three months, her skin was still angry. It had darkened between the ridges and lumps left by skin grafts and scar tissue. Una's eyelids, lashes, and eyebrows had been restored or fashioned; her lips were, as she boasted, beautifully shaped, malleable, and perhaps sexy. Una's cheeks were once part of her thighs, and her thick mane of tight ringlets, which replaced straight hair before the fire, mostly hid her disfigured neck, forehead, and ears. Medical artists hadn't yet sculptured them, and this visit was resting in care after a surgeon had rebuilt her nose.

Perhaps the cruellest stroke had been that, only one year before the tragedy occurred, Una was studying to obtain her Senior Nurse qualification. She was aware that a stranger to her appearance might feel uneasy or even afraid, so, with grace and understanding, Una only showed herself at night when she was in for post-operative care. Even then, she carried a tiny bell to ring before she entered a room.

Those who hadn't had the pleasure of meeting this heroic female were advised not to show pity or sympathy unless her conversation suggested they should.

The nursing staff were excited because they were anticipating that Una would join them for supper. Although they were interested in her medically and expected to see swollen eyes and bruised cheeks, which would add another dimension to her unusually florid complexion, it was the lady herself everyone looked forward to enjoying. Una was special.

Then, as though preceding a magical presence, a clear chime split the air. Peggy moved deftly to the door, opened it, and dropped to a deep curtsey as one does for royalty.

Una swept in wearing a white tom-boy shirt with long sleeves unbuttoned at her wrists, fashionably not cuffed. Sleek, tapered trousers just grazed her ankles. She wore ballet flats and held an outsized pair of sunglasses that suggested she'd just come from the French Riviera. Luxurious curls foamed over her shoulders while those close to her face were twisted into ropes and tied back. Dressing hid her nose, but that seemed to add mystery, and she knew it. The unattractive was now spectacular, the essence of elegance and femininity. Her energy was far beyond the physical improvement gifted by surgeons.

Stunned silence, then light applause, which Una accepted with a queenly wave. She had changed much in a few years.

Peggy, being the youngest, the least diplomatic, and the most enthusiastic, commented on Una's sculptured figure, to which Una replied.

'It's all down to yoga. I was tired of waiting to continue nursing training and decided there were other ways to fulfil my life's ambition to help others, but first I had to heal myself. I joined a 7086-day pilgrimage to India, lived in an ashram, and studied the Bhagavad Gita, a 700-verse Hindu scripture. Because my western brain was stretched to encompass another culture, I can now embrace fate and practice self-mastery. Scholars cherish the principles of philosophy and spirituality that the Bhagavad Gita teaches, and its wisdom is woven into Gita Yoga.

Una reached into her handbag, then presented each listener with a pamphlet headed, "Welcome to my Gita World at North Sydney- Join me if you would like to create a kinder and healthier planet by returning to the natural rhythms of life. Allow yourself, through Gita Yoga, to live your life as an integral part of the Whole."

During Una's two-week post-operative care, Peggy's appetite for knowledge about the source of creation was genuinely whetted, so she kept Una's pamphlet to investigate the Gita, its mysteries and serenity, and the young ladies formed a close friendship.

Then came the Hootenanny episode. It was Saturday night in the men's ward. Peggy was on the evening's final bedpan run while Almeda was dispensing medicines. They were surprised to find the men showering and sprucing up as though they were waiting for visitors. Yet visiting time was over, and it was almost lights out in the ward. A few men were singing, supposedly in harmony with another strumming a ukulele. Others were shaving, and the air was heavy with Old Spice cologne. Almeda was gorgeous, looking like an angel in her stiffly starched white veil and pale blue uniform, so Peggy was not surprised when one of the men said they dolled up for their Ward Sister.

Almeda thanked them, then advised it was time to remove their dressing gowns and pop into bed. Peggy noticed that most men had forgotten to remove their slippers, but reasoned they must have cold feet. Peggy and Almeda plumped up the pillows of those who were either too feeble to do it themselves or wanted to be spoiled, then bid them goodnight and pleasant dreams.

The ladies were mainly a gentle lot. Peggy and Almeda worked as before; Peggy filled the bedpans, and Sister administered the medicines. Most patients needed to be propped up on extra pillows to help them breathe easily during the early morning hours. Knitted shawls were draped around their shoulders to keep them warm. Peggy moved the vases of flowers from the ward to the nurses' desk, pulled curtains around each bed, and dimmed the ward lights.

A male patient was waiting at reception. He said some of the men were having trouble sleeping because the light in the staff room was shining through the open door of the ladies' quarters into theirs. Almeda closed the ward door.

The Rest Home was in sleep mode, all was still, and silence reigned but for the radio playing softly in the Day Room. It was 2 am. Almeda was writing reports, and Peggy was working on flowers, changing their water, sorting the fresh from the dying, and rearranging the vases to brighten the ward for the coming day. Then, they heard a great thump and running feet. It came from the ladies' ward.

Both nurses moved swiftly and discovered the door was locked from the inside. Peggy kept guard while Almeda rushed to retrieve her key, which hung on a hook near the drug cupboard.

Peggy heard muffled men's voices and ladies' whimpering.

When Almeda unlocked the door, they found a dishevelled mess. Bed curtains were dragged to one side, and some of the ladies had fallen out of bed, silently mouthing 'help'. Blankets were either on the floor or hanging off. Ladies who had access to sheets were holding them so tightly against their faces and bodies that their knuckles were white, most were staring with wide-open eyes, and three ladies were standing in the doorway of their bathroom holding onto each other and weeping!

All the windows were open, yet Peggy and Almeda had closed them before lights out. There'd been an intruder, so Peggy shut and locked the windows while Almeda settled the patients. She tried to coax the ladies into telling her what had happened, but they were in a state of shock, so getting a word out of them was like asking a statue to sing.

There were no broken bones, and everyone was back in bed, so Almeda gave mild sedatives to help them sleep.

Peggy was heating milk for those who wanted cocoa when she felt a tap on her shoulder. She smelt Old Spice cologne and turned to face a patient from the men's ward.

'Hey, Nursie, we want hot cocoa too,'

He winked at Peggy.

'Those kittens sure looked like frightened mice when we Hootenanny Cats grabbed them!'

Peggy didn't know what he meant. This man often rambled, which made one think he was slightly off the planet, so she replied without thinking.

'I suppose they did. I'll make the ladies first and then bring yours in. How many cocoas?'

While Peggy was delivering the men their hot drinks, Almeda came to check if they were settled, then asked if they'd seen an intruder.

'What intruder, where? In here? We've been asleep, yeah, we've been asleep. We woke up when the lady's lights came on. OK, that's right, Cats?'

The men nodded and concentrated on their cocoa.

Almeda checked their windows and found that all were shut except one, so she closed it. Peggy gathered empty mugs, then locked the window and dimmed the lights.

While double-checking the ladies who were still unsettled, one patient asked that their door be left open so they could see us and know they were safe.

Peggy sat in a chair by the ward entrance, folding linen. Almeda stayed in reception and wrote the nightly report.

The relief staff had come on duty, but Almeda and Peggy waited for Matron instead of leaving. They needed to recount in detail the previous evening's extraordinary event, which robbed many patients of their speech and left them with no appetite for breakfast.

The Day Staff read the report whose details were as clear as mud. All agreed that something awful must have happened in the early hours of the morning, but what?

Matron flushed with annoyance at having to leave her breakfast. She looked great in her white dress and shoes, a white veil with red edges and a red cape. Peggy thought,

'She doesn't have to spend time combing her hair when she can shove that veil on.'

It didn't take many words for Matron to decide the incident was severe enough to report it to the police. She remarked that her Senior Nurse should have done this as soon as the dreadful thing happened, but reasoned that, on the other hand, the comfort of her patients came first, so perhaps Almeda did do the right thing.

The Detectives took Almeda and Peggy into the staff room and asked questions over and over again. Finally, one Detective asked Peggy how old she was. She told them she was going on fourteen, and the minister got special permission for her to work.

A detective found one of the male patient's slippers outside the ladies' ward window. On confrontation, the owner confessed that he and the men had waited until the ladies were asleep. They climbed out of their window and through another window into the ladies' ward. They then snuck over and locked the door, after which they jumped on top of the ladies and had sex with them. The man said it was a harmless ending to their Hootenanny, seeing the females were too old to get pregnant!

The next day, newspaper headlines read.

**Mass Rape following a Wild Hootenanny in a Nursing Home staffed by a 14-year-old girl and one senior nurse.**

*Police Sergeant Patricia Walker said victim statements were incredibly graphic. Their relatives demanded to know why the Duty Nurse in charge did not immediately report the assaults. Sergeant Walker added, 'It is a sign of our times that predatory men are free to roam at night with ample opportunity to enter a hospital ward through unlocked windows to enjoy forced sexual intercourse with fragile old ladies.'*

*The horrified daughter of one victim said that "The enormity of knowing cowardly perverts, on record, saying their heinous behaviour was just a bit of fun, is a terrifying example of the direct result of skeleton staff through monetary greed. She added that "Although her mother suffers dementia and remembers no facts of the actual violation, the shock of being intimidated, bullied, ravaged, and spanked when she objected hasn't been lessened".*

There was a staff meeting that evening. There would be more trained nurses and lower wages. Matron said she didn't want Peggy there anymore because she was too young. Peggy wasn't allowed back in the wards as a nursing aide, and she should pack her things and be out in 5 days. At that time, Peggy would receive her wages to this day, plus the three weeks' holiday pay owing to her.

Peggy had a stash of money saved from her win on Trixie-Dell, cash leftover from her previous salaries, and the promise of three weeks' holiday pay. She needed somewhere to live and a job, one without bedpans and the musty smell of collective old age. Peggy was clueless about finding either, worried, but perversely elated because suddenly there was freedom from rules. Life promised to be better because now she could choose to go where she pleased and do what she wanted. She was a teenager who'd never been to a party, a dance, or a movie theatre.

Peggy took a bus ride to Sydney, caught a ferry from Circular Quay to Milsons Point, then disembarked. Just a hop, skip, and a jump away, Sydney's iconic amusement park loomed. She joined a mass of people edging towards the entrance, the open mouth of a giant effigy of Old King Cole's face, his glittering crown of transcending lights promising thrills and fun.

Street artists took advantage of the slow-moving crowd and earned money painting individual faces to resemble lions, tigers, dingoes, and butterflies in neon colours. A man had his balding head and face transformed to resemble the comic superhero, the Phantom, and his girlfriend became the famous green lizard. Peggy had a flannel flower painted just above her knee to honour the memory of Mrs Loveday. Observing the recreated humans, she noticed an interesting phenomenon: they adopted personalities and body language that matched their masks!

On the other side of the entrance, a clown was selling balloons. Peggy bought one, then asked where the merry-go-round was. The clown, holding out an oversized, gloved hand, kindly offered to guide her.

'Our ears will lead to something bigger and better than a merry-go-round. I am taking you to a carousel. Like a merry-go-round, it turns in a circle, but unlike a merry-go-round, which spins faster and faster, hoping to dislodge those on its deck, a carousel has synchronised motors that cause magical steeds to float up and down to the rhythm of bell organs.

This was a very serious clown. Peggy tried to make him smile, but without luck, until they reached the carousel ticket office, where he suddenly sprang into life, bowed low, laughed like a hyena, pinched her bottom, and ran away!

Peggy climbed aboard a dappled pony that almost immediately began bobbing to a slow waltz, then quickened to a rocking-horse gallop as the music climbed up-tempo. She felt the wind on her hair fly as her steed circumnavigated a spiralling galaxy of lights. It sped past an inner circle of woodwork panels, set with large mirrors in Art Deco frames. They reflected children sitting in swan-shaped seats, an elderly couple in a Cinderella carriage and Peggy on her journey. Too soon, they slowed to a stop. Peggy dismounted, then left *Luna Park, not wanting to lose the magic by entering the Haunted Castle or the Hall of Mirrors.

Walking around Kirribilli, fear and doubt replaced the joy of freedom. What was going to happen to her? Where would she start looking for somewhere to live, and how could she find a job? She sat on a park bench, watched a family picnic, and wondered why Marj and Albert didn't have them. She was fascinated by a flock of Ibis with their predominantly white plumage, black legs, bare heads, and long down-curved bills poking into the grass, searching out tasty morsels. A fallen white feather was within easy reach. She scooped it up. This was a good sign, but it was time to return to her room in the nurses' quarters.

While meandering to the station, a sign in a shop window caught her attention. It offered houses, apartments, and bedsits for rent, the standout notice being.

**BEDSIT** in a quiet house in Kirribilli.

**Rent, inclusive of all bills,** is to be determined based on the renter's responsibility.

**Date available**-Immediate. A youthful, working female preferred.

* This accommodation consists of a shared toilet.

* It is newly refurbished and comes fully furnished.

* Open plan dining lounge with a fitted kitchen.

* The bedsit is in good condition, within a short walk to the ferry and near the bus stop to North Sydney station.

Peggy remembered Grandma Maggie's teacup reading.

*"Do not fear, for we see good fortune which will rescue you in times of need,"* and *"you need to keep your council, your private life secret."*

Peggy was sure Grandma Maggie and White Feathers were with her, so she entered the real estate agent's door.

The estate agent asked questions that seemed tailor-made to suit Peggy's needs.

'Where do you live now?'

'In the nurse's quarters.'

'Are you happy being a nurse?'

'I'm a nursing aide and have been working for a year.'

'Why do you want to move?'

'I need a place away from the hospital and Rest Home, a place that I can call my own.'

'Would you be happy paying eight pounds per week?'

'Yes, but I'd like to pay less. What does "Rent, inclusive of all bills, to be decided according to the responsibility taken by the renting person mean?'

'Inclusive of all bills' means there are no extras, such as electricity or gas, to pay. The house owner will drop the rent if the shared toilet and kitchen are kept clean and no parties are held.'

'I've never had a party, I've never been to one except when I was about five years old, I don't want to have a party, and I'd be happy to keep the toilet, kitchen and my room clean. Is there a bathroom?'

'This is a modern house; you'll have your private shower. I believe the owner may drop the rent to six pounds.'

'It's getting late, and I don't go out at night. May I come back tomorrow, please?'


Back in her soon-to-be-vacated confined space with its narrow bed, one chair, and an excuse for a table, Peggy experienced the elation of a captured wild bird if its cage door were accidentally left open. Being a tad superstitious, she was excited but didn't dare start packing until she knew the Kirribilli bedsit was hers. She opened the bag she kept her money in, emptied it on the bed, and was counting it when Lorraine breezed in.

'Hello, you lucky thing, I've found a job for you. Well, if you want a job, that is and if you don't mind working in a coffee shop.'

'Where is the coffee shop?'

'They have two, one at North Sydney and one at Kirribilli.'

Peggy put her palms together and steepled her fingers in a silent thank you for a few seconds. Lorraine was at a loss until Peggy jumped up off the bed and hugged her.

'Yes, I want to work in a coffee shop. I want to work, and I need to work near Kirribilli. Even North Sydney.'

'They're Hungarian People, friends of mine, they'll work you hard, but you're OK with that because you've worked the shittiest job in this hospital for about a year!'

Peggy was delighted.

'No more bedpans, no more lifting, no more ironing, and starching my work clothes.'

'Where will you live?'

'I'll show you. Are you working tomorrow?'

'Morning off.'

'Come to Kirribilli with me, Lorraine, please.'

Lorraine drove Peggy to Kirribilli, first to her friends who owned the coffee shops. She introduced Peggy to Elec and Pippi Deri, the married couple who owned the business and Elec's brother, Andras. There was instant rapport, which was important. The Deri family wanted to treat staff as extended family. Peggy was to start work in a week. There would be two full days beginning at 6 am at Milson's Point for the breakfast clientele, finishing at 3 pm, and three days at North Sydney, hours 10 am to 4 pm.

Pippi preferred Peggy to wear anything she owned in black under a white apron that came with the job. It was piped with green, embroidered with a red tulip on each of the two pockets to hold an order pad and pencil. The wage was enough to pay rent and save a little, and she could keep the tips. They didn't open at night, and if they did, the family would do that job.

Pippi would train Peggy in the art of waitressing, while Elec would teach her all he knew about serving, presentation and preparation of the simple edibles on the menu. Also, because Café Gerbeaud hosted an English-style afternoon tea for specific clients, Peggy would train with a lady who prepared afternoon tea for the Governor-General of Australia when he was in residence at Admiralty House, Sydney.

Business arrangements over, they enjoyed coffee and "Pogacsa", a Hungarian scone which was the most delicious food ever. Peggy wondered what Mrs Loveday would have thought of this Hungarian trio dunking food in their coffee and dancing their fingers on the table in time to gypsy music in the background.

Then Peggy and Lorraine drove to the estate agent, Aimie Norris, who showed them the house with the bedsit. Peggy signed a document at the office stating she would stay for at least 6 months. She paid a month's rent of six pounds per week in advance, which was refundable upon leaving if the bedsit was still in good condition. Aimie would meet Peggy at 2 pm the next day with the key, show her around and introduce her to at least one of the other people in the house.

Peggy was leaving her room at the hospital for the final time when the emergency light above her door flashed, signalling all hands on deck. Why would she be called to the wards when she hadn't worked there for almost a week? Peggy concluded this was a mistake. She ignored the call, picked up her suitcase, the small bundle of thank-you cards she had made for the staff, and her personal nurse buzzer. She took one more look inside the matchbox she'd called home. Her emergency buzzer flew into action again. She switched it off and walked towards the dayroom. Almeda came running towards her.

'Peggy, hurry, Florence needs you.'

Peggy hesitated.

'Matron has given you permission as a visitor.

Peggy and Almeda slipped through the drawn curtains around Florence's bed and entered without noise. She felt their presence and said in an almost inaudible voice.

'My earth angels are here. Welcome, I've been waiting, now I'm ready.'

Florence slightly turned her head to Peggy.

'Please, my bible is in the bedside drawer.'

Peggy opened the drawer and took out the book. She wondered why somebody shrouded Bibles in black leather. It was wrong. A book advocating decency and peace should stand out in a jacket of multi-coloured cloth from a non-violent source, surely.

Almeda moved to the opposite side of the bed; Peggy put the bible on Florence's chest, warmed both her hands, then laid them on it. Florence, concentrating on the curtains, spoke clearly.

'I see a beam of white light, in which your holy feet are shining jewels. I hear the rustle of angel wings. I come to you humbly in reverence.'

Florence sighed, and all was still, so still, so silent, peaceful, and beautiful. Florence had gone. Peggy covered the cold hands with a rug and saluted this lady she knew to be extraordinary. Almeda and Peggy left without saying a word.

The duty nurse wrote in the daybook, *"Almeda and Peggy were with Florence at her passing, 12.27 pm Monday.*

Accompanied by Almeda, Peggy entered the staff day room, placed her cards on the table alongside her buzzer, then turned to face her ex-colleague. They touched hands for a moment, then parted.

\* The **Bhagavad Gita** *is the most treasured and famous of India's spiritual texts. It was written in the third or fourth century BCE as part of the Mahabharata epic.*

\*\* **Luna Park** *is an iconic,* heritage-listed *amusement park located at 1 Olympic Drive, Milsons Point, New South Wales, Australia, on the northern shore of Sydney Harbour.*

# CHAPTER 9

*Kirribilli heralds a new way of life, a new way of living.*

In the taxi to Kirribilli, Peggy pondered the finality of death. Florence saw her oncoming death as a long-awaited passing from mortal to eternal life, obviously a beneficial belief because she happily embraced her fate. Previously, Peggy witnessed oncoming death as frightening, painful, sometimes tragic, lonely, or as a merciful relief. Importantly, she saw that when at death's door, nearness obliterated fear, and a belief in some form of afterlife affected the ease with which life slipped from a body.

She'd read divergent beliefs associated with life after death. Reincarnation was based on the tradition that Buddha remembered his past lives. Christianity, Judaism and Islam believe not in reincarnation, but an afterlife promised as a reward for following those religions' rules. This suggests that scripture beliefs are a psychological tool created to control the masses. Revival of life is unproven because those who have died have not returned to enlighten those still living.

Then, thinking about a specific hospital experience, Peggy was puzzled about when life leaves the body. This was particularly in reference to a young man who appeared alive because his heart was beating, and he was breathing. He was on life support in the recovery ward, yet it was certain he would not survive because his brain had stopped functioning. His open eyes, covered in a rough film of jelly-like substance, were staring at nothing. He was stiller than still. His many relatives were in the early stages of grieving, all sitting and waiting. Abruptly, his mother jumped up from her chair, put her mouth to his ear and screeched.

'Say hello to mama.'

In response, the stiff body of this "braindead" person convulsed and gyrated. His mouth didn't open, his lips didn't move, but a mighty rattle reverberated around the room, after which he fell silent forever.

Death should be accepted and have no sorrow because it is a natural happening that all must face. Life is real and everlasting because it is measured in achievements, glory, tragedies, failures, and success. Although death has no performance, the end of life is as physical as the beginning. Compared to the shortest life, death is fleeting and leaves no shadow; does it exist only as nirvana, a transcendent state in which there is neither suffering, desire, nor a sense of self? Is death the final goal of life? Then death is a significant happening equal to and as mysterious as a region of space where gravity is so strong that nothing—no particles or light—can escape its pull.

The taxi stopped outside the estate agent's shop, and Aimie Norris was waiting. It was precisely 2 pm. Peggy's study on the character of death shifted to anticipation.

Awareness of her new surroundings heightened—a range of emotions, many conflicting, cluttering her thoughts. Panic set in, and her memory blurred. She'd only had a glimpse of her bedsit. She had seen a bed. Was there a chair and table to display Mrs Loveday's China and her many feathers, which had multiplied from the original one she had when her deranged mother demanded she leave the Georges River house?

What if Miss Norris had changed her mind and was about to tell Peggy she thought she was too young and therefore not wanted, as Matron had done?

Miss Norris had said she would introduce Peggy to at least one of the other two people in the house. What if one of them, like Marj, fabricated lies about her? Peggy's stomach wanted to join a circus.

She had reached her destination. The taxi driver had collected her bag and had opened the door. Anxiety had clouded her clarity of thought; she wanted to ask him to wait until she was certain all was well, but Miss Norris had stepped up to the cab. She was smiling, showing the palm of her hand with two keys.

'Welcome to Kirribilli, Miss Piper.'

Peggy had never been called "Miss Piper". She almost laughed, then felt giddy with relief when Miss Norris welcomed her. A strange, serious mode took over, and she politely answered.

'Thank you, Miss Norris. I'm delighted to be here and am looking forward to meeting my housemates.'

Aimie Norris was happy. Her wish was answered; her mother would love this young woman.

'One of your housemates is my mother, who means the world to me. She owns the home but doesn't need all the space. She's young at heart but not so young in the legs. She uses a stick when walking. My mother takes great pleasure in sharing morning or afternoon tea with her paying guests. She has a young dog. I like the idea of her having a pet, but a puppy worries me because it needs training and may get under her feet and cause a tumble.'

Peggy fondly remembered her afternoons with Mrs Loveday. Then in her mind's eye, she evoked White Feathers.

'Yes, yes, yes, thank you, my angel, who led me here. Thank you, White Feathers.'

She answered Miss Norris.

'This is the best news ever! I like taking tea, but only on Saturdays and Sundays, depending on my working hours. I am excellent with puppies and will do my best to train and keep them from getting under your mother's feet.'

'His name is Benjamin.'

Alone, Peggy looked at her empty suitcase on the double bed and at the generous cupboard in which her clothes were hanging. Her record player and records were on top of the extensive set of drawers holding her other belongings. Her China cup, saucer, and the jar of feathers were very much at home on a bedside table. Her shoes looked neat on a rack in the lobby just inside her entrance door. The soft carpet caressed her bare feet.

While the kettle was boiling, she stacked her suitcase on the shelf in the broom cupboard, then realised she had no tea or coffee. Too bad, she'd go shopping tomorrow. She opened the cabinet under the sink to discover a jar of dandelion coffee, a bottle of coffee essence, sugar, and a packet of *Bex. Further investigation proved more goodwill from Miss Norris with a tin of Sunshine Crackers and a bottle of milk in the half-sized fridge.

Peggy flopped on the luxurious bed and spread-eagled her arms and legs. Such luxury after having endured the physical restraint of the narrow, hard bed in the nurse's quarters. She imagined she was on a bed of sweet-smelling moss. Then a great idea flew into her head. She would invite Mrs Norris and Benjamin for a cuppa and a biscuit or two.

Mrs Norris called him Benji, an intelligent, eager-to-please, medium-sized black-and-tan 4-month-old puppy. It was love at first sight for Peggy. However, she kept her emotions under close wraps because she'd spent her childhood continuously falling victim to a jealous female. This green-eyed monster might also afflict Mrs Norris. She may be so obsessed with Benjamin that she may fear Peggy would steal him or that the puppy might grow more attached to Peggy than her.

But this was not the case. Over tea and biscuits, Mrs Norris proved herself to be free of such pettiness. She was a fascinating, I-am-as-you-find-me lady, the very essence of elegance with a bit of wildness thrown in, not unlike Grandma Maggie. She had an almost naughty twinkle in her soul-searching, chocolate-brown eyes. Her face was framed by wispy, delicate-as-gossamer silver hair held with a buckle at the nape of her neck. Her temperament was as soft as a slipper, and empathy flowed through her words. Mrs Norris was a natural psychologist who, upon reading Peggy, decided to step lightly. She asked no personal questions but walked to the displayed China and nodded approvingly. She commented on the stack of records.

'I also like Ave Maria, is that **Nellie Melba* singing? How delicate is this cup and saucer, Peggy? Do you drink from it?'

Peggy told her about Mrs Loveday and the statues modelled on herself in her garden. She spoke of their walks, searching for native orchids and flannel flowers; the times they sketched and painted; and the pomander balls made from fresh oranges and cloves—the quiet times when they listened to music and visited the artist's studio.

Mrs Norris wanted to know more about this young lady.

'Did you sculpt anything, Peggy?'

'I formed a silver ball.'

Mrs Norris was aware of an invisible wall that suddenly separated them, so she suggested taking Benji for a walk to relieve himself. She held his leash out to Peggy.

'Would you do the honours, Peggy?'

That night, Peggy knew peace, but before she slept, she thought of her siblings. She asked their angels to protect them. No doubt, Marj and Albert were still punishing them for being born with the original sin. She decided to update Mrs Page on her new address.

Elec and Pippi Deri's business in Milson's Point was Café Ruszwurm, after the oldest café in Budapest, where Elec was born. The North Sydney café was named Gerbeaud after a prestigious European tea room where Pippi's father was a celebrated pastry chef.

Like their Hungarian namesakes, Ruszwurm and Gerbeaud were famous for their sweet delights. There were strudels with apple, apricot, sour cherry and sweet cheese fillings, marzipan mice filled with chestnut puree, and ice cream. Every morning at 6 am, before the first ferry arrived at 6.45, it seemed happiness was on the menu at Ruszwurm. The patrons nicknamed it "Rusty Worm". They packed the place, breakfasting on savoury Pogacsas, pastries and coffee while exchanging pleasantries.

Days at Café Gerbeaud were quite different, as it catered to young mothers, their mothers, and single would-be socialites. They were inclined to treat Elec, Pippi, and Peggy as servants. They were too condescending to leave a tip, or perhaps, being primarily Australian-born, didn't know about tipping, as this was a European custom.

Peggy preferred the light atmosphere at Rusty Worm but didn't mind Gerbeaud because there was something precious about the place, including the clientele whose snobbishness amused her.

Gerbeaud didn't cater to the style of people who stuffed their faces with snack foods sold in the ordinary cafes and Milk Bars in the area.

Its menu boasted traditional elegance, such as canapes, cucumber sandwiches composed of paper-thin slices of crustless, white, buttered bread, and little cabbage rolls with sour cream. The main course was Túrós Batyu—a deep-fried pastry served hot, topped with fresh curd cheese sprinkled with a hint of sweet paprika, and chilled sweet-sour cherry soup.

Patrons couldn't get enough of Hungarian specialities. Two favourites were the Gerbeaud Cake with its layers of shortcrust pastry smothered with almond jam and walnut filling, topped with rich, dark chocolate, and the cake named after the Hungarian Prince Paul III (1786–1866). It was a cognac-spiced buttercream, liberally sandwiched between five layers of almond meringue, dripping with cognac butterscotch icing. Yum.

Maggie's favourite —the insanely delicious, addictive, cake-like Hungarian scone called pogácsa —was so popular that Pippi and Elec once joked they would have a riot on their hands if they hadn't baked enough.

The display cabinet flaunted so many delectable treats that some people took up to 10 minutes to choose just one, then almost immediately wolfed it down and came back to try something else.

Pippi's father provided the recipes, and Andras found pleasure following the great man's footsteps as a specialty pastry cook.

Andras cherished a girl whose family were Armenian from Turkey. Her culinary weakness was Locum. This rose-scented pistachio confection, known to the English as "Lumps of Delight", was invented by Arab apothecaries around the ninth century.

Love is sweet, and Andras wanted to show his devotion to his Karine by including Locum on the menu. Sydney had become a fast-growing hub of mixed nationalities, so Elec and Pippu decided to add it to their list of goodies, but they would market it by its more exotic name, Turkish Delight.

One morning, Peggy found the first two Turkish Delight batches sitting in shallow, rectangular dishes covered with wax paper. Beside them, instructions for packing.

*"First, dust a cutting board with freshly sifted icing sugar, then lightly oil two sharp knives. Empty the jar containing the bag of icing sugar and cornflour mixture into a wide bowl. Next, line the two airtight containers with wax paper, and cut six sheets to fit inside each. Now begin the surgery. Peel off the wax wrap covering the sweet. Next, gently run the tip of one of the slippery knives between the sweet and the wax sheet lining the dish, then carefully turn the Turkish Delight onto the prepared board. Now take the second sharp, oiled knife and delicately cut the sweet into squares measuring no more than 1 inch. Drench each cube separately in the cornflour mix. Bring the airtight containers to the drenched sweets and place each cube, one at a time, in rows. Cover the base with the previously cut wax paper when the base is full, then begin another layer; repeat until finished. Lid the container, and as you close, press the centre to expel air, then fix it tightly, adding the dated sticker to the top right corner. Do not freeze, but store in a cool place for up to one month."*

Turkish coffee was on the menu. For an entire week, during the launch of this new sweet, each cup of coffee had a sample square of Turkish Delight slipped onto the saucer. Naturally, people went potty over it, but one lady complained that the sample was decidedly too small, in fact, stingy. She demanded that, as she and her daughter were regular patrons, they should receive a more acceptable offering—triple the original size would be appropriate. Peggy took the complaint to Elec, who shrugged.

'If she wants it, she can have it, but only once. Please tell Madam that this is a courtesy which I cannot repeat.'

Peggy delivered. No sooner had the lady pushed the colossal Lump of Delight through her lips than her head jerked back, her hands flew to her face, and an obnoxious noise sprang from her throat. Her outstretched fingers were pushing against the sides of her face, causing it to resemble a leering gargoyle. Her false teeth, glued together with Turkish Delight, had come loose from her gums and were unsuccessfully trying to escape her distorted lips!

The bizarre picture was hysterically funny, but no laughing matter. The gummed-up woman was now hysterically thrusting her fingers into the sides of her mouth, forcing it to stretch in a contorted straight line almost to her ears in a tortured quest to remove the amalgamated mass.

Elec didn't wait; he telephoned for an ambulance, an emergency dentist, and Pippi.

The ambulance and a vehicle embellished with a large red mouth and white teeth came wailing up the street. They attracted a small crowd who pressed themselves up against Café Gerbeaud's display windows, while the more curious individuals edged their way inside.

Peggy wished she had a tent to encompass the unfortunate woman, but lacking that, she moved her to a chair, with her back to the growing audience.

The lady's daughter, who had previously asked to be out of the limelight, became a star of the scene and led the paramedic and dentist to their patient.

On inspection, the ambulance man mumbled.

'These teeth resemble a carnivorous plant that has caught an exploded victim.'

Then to his patient.

'Eating with dentures isn't like eating with your regular teeth, madam.'

The lady spluttered through clenched teeth, so her daughter replied.

'Obviously.'

The Dentist turned to the audience.

'This regrettable situation happened because Madam used her front teeth to bite into a tactile sweet, which unfortunately adhered to the material in her dentures. Consequently, when Madam tried to free her dentures by snapping open her mouth, the action dislodged them from her toothless gums, which may not have been the case if Madam had had at least two teeth to grip the dentures.'

The daughter, again trying to hide her face, pleaded.

'Please, to be toothless is a social shame.'

A man in the audience spoke.

'I'd like to lay a bet that the false wooden teeth worn by the ancient Japanese would have had the same effect as day-old gluttonous rice pudding.'

A person in a school uniform chimed.

'False teeth are part of history. We've just learned that teeth pulled from corpses of dead soldiers at Waterloo were mounted onto a base of ivory and worn as a status symbol among the elite in the 1800s.'

The lady begged through her stuck teeth.

'Angel of Mercy, help me.'

The dentist spoke to his audience.

'Madam could have avoided this situation if Madam had used her side teeth to bite, then maneuvered her tongue to coax the food to the back of her mouth.'

The woman's daughter was indignant.

'Idiot, mummy had to bite with her front teeth. The elephantine proportions of the Turkish Delight made it unacceptable in public to pop it into the back of one's mouth.'

The lady hissed through her stuck teeth.

'It was massive.'

To which her daughter added.

'Mummy would have had to open her mouth as large as the gap between your ears.'

An onlooker spoke.

'Or the space between expectations and reality.'

Then the ambulance man.

'Or ***Jayne Mansfield's booty.'

A woman in the audience was offended.

'You're thinking of sex when a victim of Turkish aggression is suffering?'

The dentist faced the audience.

'Ladies and Gentlemen, let this be a lesson. All foods, even if you don't have dentures, should be moved to the back of your mouth on both sides. Or in the front corners.'

The ambulance man wanted action.

'As my patient cannot open or close her mouth, the situation is getting desperate. The only way I can think of helping her without operating is to force her mouth open as far as possible at the corners. Then we could rock the whole bang lot until the teeth either break or slide into a position where we can grab them.'

An onlooker offered advice.

'Or she could take a big breath in and hold it until someone belts her on her back, then she'd hoick them.'

'Cuddle a Koala Idiot. My mummy doesn't know how to hoick.'

The dentist did some heavy thinking.

'If we did the latter, we'd have to submerge Madam's head in a bucket filled with water, so Madam's dentures would float. Otherwise, they may drop and break before we can catch them.'

'Stop calling my mother, "madam".'

The onlooker asked.

'Did she just say, Stop calling her mother madam?'

'I most certainly did. Stop calling mummy "madam". She has nothing to do with brothels and is not the President of the United States.'

Another onlooker was offended.

'Fair go, he was using his gentlemanly manners. Then again, he could have meant she was bossy or uppity like you. Lady, have you tried sucking the gooh between your teeth until it dissolves? Second thoughts: what about gently chewing, like a cow with cud?'

'Dimwit, her teeth are immobilised.'

The ambulance man addressed Peggy.

'Have you any vinegar? That may dissolve the glug.

'It's not glug. It's Turkish Delight.'

A fisherman, stepping out of the crowd, offered to help.

'I've got fishing gear; we could ease two separate lines between her choppers, then she could suck while you cut. That should do the job.'

The daughter held her mother's head while the dentist inserted the fishing line and began sawing. Pippi had a big towel under the lady's face, while the ambulance man rubbed ointment on his patient's lips, gently massaging and stretching them. Suddenly, pandemonium broke out as the cemented teeth flew into the crowd. Somebody caught them, held the skeleton-like grin high and shouted.

'Finders keepers.'

There was a cacophony of applause, whistles, congratulatory phrases, and general discord. The dentist took a bow, the ambulance grabbed the teeth, and the fisherman raised the toothless lady's arm in the air, imitating a boxer who'd just won the fight of his life and a world title.

The ambrosial confection known as Turkish Delight became a source of public anxiety. Pippi and Elec were concerned about Café Gerbeaud's excellent reputation and Andras's reputation as a pastry cook. A nameless person sent the story to a local newspaper, suggesting that the editor demand that a sensory panel of professional tasters test the guilty sweet from the same dated container.

The verdict came in that the ingredients of the heavenly recipe did not cause the problem. Rather, it was the fault of the preposterously large order placed by the affected customer, who attempted to devour it while wearing false teeth. The referees also found that the customer had personally demanded Café Gerbeaud supply her with the whopping sample. Additionally, when the customer consumed the correct first portion in the proper size, she had no cause to complain; therefore, Gerbeaud and the pastry cook were exempt from blame.

The panel of tasters' findings attracted publicity, often with comic sketches featuring false teeth. Café Gerbeaud swarmed with people ordering Turkish Delight while laughing and clicking their teeth.

\* ***Bex*** *was a potent compound analgesic that was popular in Australia for much of the twentieth century. It came in APC (aspirin–phenacetin–caffeine) tablets or powder, containing 42% aspirin, 42% phenacetin, plus caffeine.*

\*\****Dame Nellie Melba GBE*** *(born Helen Porter Mitchell; 19 May 1861 – 23 February 1931) was an Australian operatic soprano. She became one of the most famous singers of the late Victorian era and the early 20th century, and was the first Australian to achieve international recognition as a classical musician*

\*\*\****Jayne Mansfield*** *was an American film, theatre, and television actress. She was also a singer and nightclub entertainer as well as one of the early Playboy Playmates.*

# CHAPTER 10

**The year is 1954. "The real voyage of discovery consists not in seeking new landscapes,** *but in having new eyes"-Marcel Proust (1871-1992.*

The move to Kirribilli changed Peggy's life dramatically, comparable to being born again, but not in a spiritual sense. More akin to the metamorphosis in which a tadpole turns into a frog.

Gone was the time she'd obtained sanctuary at the rest home as a thirteen-year-old ward under the draconic rule of a matron who financially exploited her. Through the most insufferable duties as a nurse's aide, Peggy paid penance that was hardly due. She had softened that state by refining her writing ability, illustrating poems, reading, and listening to classical music.

Entering the workforce at thirteen years of age seemed Dickensian in social injustice. Still, Peggy's lack of tertiary education would not have taught her that some parents and the workforce currently treat children and teenagers as enslaved people and serfs. Ever optimistic, Peggy believed her childhood to have been a valuable apprenticeship in studying and recognising manipulative individuals. Through reading library books, she had learned the consequences of the cruel and coercive control of political parties and reigning kings and queens that outweighed human virtue. Through meeting and caring for the aged, she decided to live a meaningful life.

Peggy had seen the results of miracles, such as the reconstructive surgery on Una's fire-ravaged face and body. But here, the question was more significant than the physical transformation. How extraordinary were Una's medical mentors who made whole her shattered mental state and focused her mind on the unique gift of life?

Was there unseen energy that cosseted Una and led her to India, where she became the beautiful, robust soul through the study of ancient wisdom? Did she, Peggy, genuinely have a spirit friend called

White Feathers, or was he, in her imagination, an invention needed for mental support and strength?

Peggy was mulling over this while sitting in the park near Milson's Point wharf and thought it a good idea to make a shortlist of life rules for herself.

1. *Tell people as little as possible about myself.*
2. *When asked a question, reply with a question about the enquirer; people love talking about themselves. That way, I remain private and safe.*
3. *When asked my age, I reply that I am a working teenager.*
4. *Don't discuss religion or vegetarianism, as they are argumentative subjects.  It was time she went for a walk with Mrs Norris and Benji. Animals were unique beings, asking nothing of you, sincere in friendship, generous in giving and thankful to receive.*

The past year was happy. Peggy had bonded with Mrs Norris and Benji. Pippi and Elec were constant in kindness, and Lorraine had maintained her position as a big sister. Mrs Page was still in touch, but sadly, she was happily returning to the United Kingdom with a Scott with whom she'd fallen in love.

Peggy experienced better fitness through Yoga classes, especially in managing her asthma, sleep, and concentration. Una's wisdom and Gita were learning curbs suited to Peggy's thirst for knowledge of the planet, all living things, other cultures, and the consequences of action and speech.

Born into a god-fearing family, Peggy hadn't considered not having a religion, but now questioned some aspects of the teaching. How could an innocent child be born with the burden of original sin when there are different views on original sin? Peggy decided to find a religion that practised the golden rule, *"Do unto others as you would have others do unto you".*

She discovered that many religions and cultures accepted this rule, but different sects treated it differently; many applied it only to their own kind. Most importantly, one didn't have to believe in any religion to endorse it. It was evident that looking from the outside in was different from looking from the inside out.

The capricious wind at her back had a habit of changing direction, therefore breaking bonds that had once seemed forever. Anticipating change and not trusting her secure lifestyle, Peggy thought it appropriate to show appreciation to the extraordinary people who had opened their hearts and accepted her as family. Mrs Page, Pippi, Elec, Andras, Mrs Norris, and Lorraine were engraved on her *Akashic Record.*

Music and sumptuous food were the frangible threads that bound them together. What better way to show her gratitude than to host a dinner party at Grey Eagles Restaurant, specialising in Hungarian cuisine, accompanied by Gipsy violinists?

Peggy delivered her handmade invitations. Aimee Norris had, regretfully, made previous arrangements, but her other guests accepted. Aimee would look after Benji, so he would not be alone. Peggy booked a table for eleven next to the dance floor at Grey Eagles. She chose Saturday night because she and her guests could recuperate the next day.

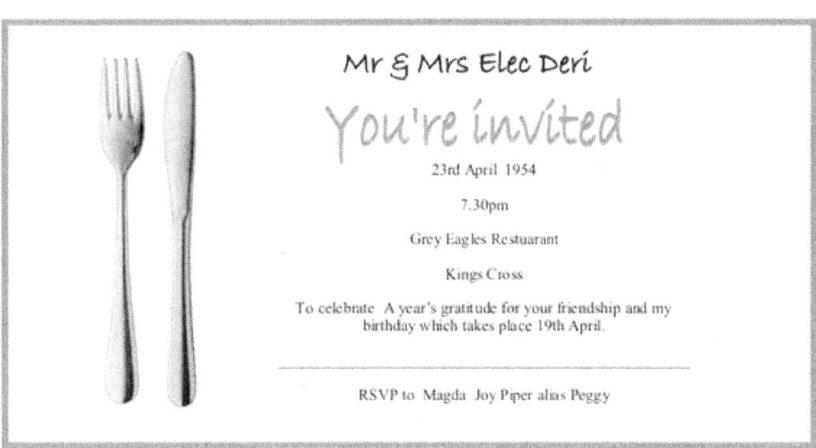

Lorraine and her husband, Simon, drove half the party in their spanking-new second-hand car, and the Deri family picked up Una. Mrs Page came with her fiancé, Rupert.

After seating the party, the maître d' presented the ladies with a wrist corsage and the gentlemen a boutonniere. Place cards gave information on the flower chosen for the occasion and facts about April 19th, 1939.

*" In 1939, April 19th fell on a Wednesday. It was the 109th day of the year and the 16th Wednesday. If you have kept your old calendar, you can reuse it in 2023 because both calendars will be the same! Your* flowers *are the traditional Australian flower for April, the Flannel Flower. Its symbolism is abundance and strength, which I wish for you. Thank you for being my guest".*

Dinner was serenaded by gypsy violinists, whose flirtatious black eyes, mops of dark ringlets, and glittering gem-covered fingers authenticated their identity.

The main course was well received, and as the sweets were delivered to their table, the musicians stopped serenading and took their place perched on a rostrum behind the dance floor. There, they lost their individualism and acted as a collective, vibrating their bows on the strings. It sounded like a chorus of a thousand bees. Next, a proud, single dancer leapt on stage, whirled in a circle, stamped his feet, then heralded a troop in embroidered costumes.

Simultaneously, violins and coupled dancers began a slow, mesmerising Hungarian dance. The company deftly shifted their weight from foot to foot in step with the music, which gradually accelerated. The more mercurial the music, the faster the dancers snapped their feet inward and outward, spinning in an ecstasy of the union to the compelling, syncopated rhythms of the Czardas. Personal improvisation took over as couples wheeled, no two in the same direction, yet the company danced in a labyrinth, perfectly in time. Finally, music and innovation blistered the atmosphere to a frantic finish.

The floorshow stopped; musicians and performers bowed and threw kisses, and Grey Eagles patrons thundered their applause. The lead dancer invited the audience to join, and it started all over again.

Pippi, Elec, and Andras found fire in their stomachs and joined the dancers for that round. Mrs Norris, Lorraine, and her husband Simon,

Karine, Maria, Mrs Page, Rupert, and Peggy passionately stamped their hands on the table. Peggy was confident her party had been an unforgettable experience for all.

When she returned home, Peggy found a red bicycle adorned with ribbons, a recording of Hungarian dances by Johannes Brahms & an envelope containing a card wishing her a happy, belated birthday. Her Grey Eagles cheque was there too, cancelled because her guests had divided the bill.

Two days later, Pippi and Elec told Peggy that Mrs Page had informed them of the domestic violence she had escaped. They asked if she'd prefer the name "Magda" she had signed on their dinner invitation.

Peggy explained that it was her birth name, according to her Aunt Ivy and Uncle Jo, but her mother had refused to let her use it because a biblical fallen woman had the same name. Peggy also spoke of the strong emotional bond with Auntie Emma, who now lived somewhere in Canada.

Elec thought the name "Peggy" should be in the past tense, referring to the people who didn't care for her.

Pippi thought Magda was better suited to her character and to her preference for European appreciation of music and food. But she also suggested that Maggie, a shortened version of Magda, was more suited to the Australian, casual lifestyle. Peggy didn't have to think twice about this. Maggie was the name of her dear Grandma.

Peggy discussed this with Mrs Norris, who wholeheartedly agreed with Pippi and Elec. Discard all things related to unhappiness; welcome the positive. In this case, the positive was reclaiming her true self.


Lorraine was tired of nursing, so she and Simon bought a fruit farm beyond the Blue Mountains in NSW. A country show was in the district, and, knowing Maggie and Maria's love for animals, Lorraine invited the girls and Benji to experience a weekend of country life.

Mrs Norris approved. It gave her young dog a chance to meet other animals and enjoy the freedom of romping on acreage, which wasn't possible at Kirribilli.

Maria and Maggie packed a variety of clothing to suit the events they were attending. Casual, warm clothes and flat shoes for the agricultural show and Blue Mountain sightseeing, sensible gear for exploring the orchard, and something dressy to wear for dinner at the Hydro Majestic in Medlow Bath. Mrs Norris packed Benji's food, his knitted jacket, and his bed.

The Agricultural Show opened with a distinguished speaker who said its purpose was to celebrate achievements and establish a good reputation with contacts outside local businesses. There were prizes for the fastest woodchoppers, the largest pumpkin grown in the area, the finest embroidery, and the yummiest cakes and jams. Livestock prizes went to the bird with the most outstanding feathers and to the champion bull. An exciting new addition to the arts and crafts section was a sand sculpting competition.

Lorraine and Simon were interested in horticulture and the study of grapes and wine production. Farming was far from the girls' minds, so the company split, deciding to meet in the tea pavilion in two hours.

Maria, Maggie, and Benji headed for the baby animal section. An official asked them to keep Benji on a short lead, then asked whether he was on command. Benji proved obedience by sitting when the gentleman asked if he could sit, and on hearing the word "close", he became one with Maggie's left leg, so the three entered the big shed.

Here, a variety of baby creatures were cared for by doting animal mothers. A woman was sitting beside a tiny cow and her calf. She was adjusting a lei of flowers around the pretty animal's necks. Maria asked.

'Hello. Is your small cow fully grown?'

'No, she's still a baby. She's the youngest heifer known to give birth.

'Congratulations, is this her little one?

'Yes.'

'You appear to love her very much.'

'I do.'

Maggie jumped into the conversation.

'Then I'm correct in guessing that this little girl won't be murdered and then eaten. Does the baby take milk from her?'

'He is weaned next week and then.'

The woman kissed the heifer on her neck.

'It's your turn, my little miracle.'

Maria was curious.

'Turn for what?'

The Woman smiled sweetly.

'The man with the big knife. Poppet was difficult to calve, and because she gave birth out of season, she will no longer be in sync with the herd's calf drop. That is more work for me, so it's goodbye, Tootsie. He's off too.'

The woman patted the baby's lower back.

'Calves make great Wiener schnitzel.'

It was best to part company with this pathetic woman and her unfortunate wards. In quiet, the three wandered the flower displays. They bought cakes and jams for Lorraine, Simon, and Mrs Norris. They saw a pumpkin that was almost as big as Benji; vegetables exhibited on plates and in group displays, giant fruit, macadamia nut pinwheels, and market-basketfuls.

The most awe-inspiring exhibition was presented under a brightly roofed marquee. There, individually roped off for safety, were the sand-sculpting artists' inspired works, a far cry from the sandcastles children build on the beach. Each exhibit was wondrous in ethereal beauty and impossible to imagine constructing.

Maria and Maggie couldn't take themselves away from a miniature replica of a Siamese temple. The tip of its pointed roof stood as tall as Maria, about 5'7", and its base was as broad as Maggie was tall, about 5'2". Master engravers had worked on the many turrets, and the windows showed exquisite detail. The doors partially opened to balconies entwined with flowering vines. Elephant heads decorated the walls, and chained dragons flanked each side of the main entrance. Two lions guarded the outside steps to the temple gates. They were incredibly lifelike in Lilliputian size, their manes wild, their teeth sharp, and their eyes that looked straight at you. A little mouse slept at the foot of the female lion.

The sculptors, a mature couple, were sitting on chairs, guarding it, but not well enough. A woman came into view; her child ran ahead and slid under the ropes. She watched as her youngster ran through the centre of the masterpiece, creating havoc, kicking and punching, throwing handfuls of dedicated time to oblivion—a work of harmonious beauty created in peace, ravaged by wanton sacking.

The man leaned toward his lady and put his arms around her

Maria and Maggie thanked the couple for their treasure, then purposely turned their backs on the woman whose child had inherited her inhumane genes.

Tea and sandwiches were hurried because the ring events were about to begin. Lorraine and Simon left Maria, Maggie, and Benji at the entrance because the girls suspected it would not be a pleasant experience. The notice board read, "Eat Beef, Live Better, Breed Beef, Eat Better. Best Beef Cattle Awards."

Half an hour later, they were bored, so they entered the stadium. The grand champion prize bull had just entered the arena, led by a small man. The bull's body was colossal, so massive that he could barely walk. His spindly legs gave the impression they were about to break under his bulk. The beast stumbled, the crowd murmured in alarm, but the egotistic man did not let the bull rest. He wanted his triumphant parade of glory. Repeatedly, he viciously yanked the lead attached to the iron nose ring purposely inserted to control the bull through excruciating pain. Finally, the animal managed a few steps, then faltered and dropped dead. The crowd stood as one and cheered.

An onlooker had to be confused. Why did they cheer? Was it for the member of the animal kingdom who had bred another for its pound of flesh? Or could it be an echo from ancient Rome when people cheered to see the death of a beautiful soul? Was this a form of modern entertainment? Whatever the reason, the crowd's reaction to the demise of a tortured animal was ugly.

Lorraine and Simon's new home was everything one could dream of. A blazing log fire, a kitchen that smelt of freshly baked bread and oversized baths filled with hot water. Everyone dressed for dinner, Benji was fed and settled in a room with the door shut for his safety, and off they set to the iconic Hydro Majestic at Medlow Bath.

They weren't the only people at the table. Lorraine and Simon had invited the Greek family who owned a farm next door to join them. They were Mr Vasilakis, his daughter, Margarita, and his son, Greg.

Spotlights swept the breathtaking escarpment on which the Hydro Majestic spanned. It lent mystery to the panoramic views overlooking the Megalong Valley. The party approached the restaurant along a chandelier-lit corridor decorated with jungle plants and vines home to Australian wildlife royalty, visited by Asian monkeys, and exotic birds.

Maria and Maggie enjoyed a vegetarian meal, while others had whatever they wanted, followed by a cheeseboard and out-of-season fruits. Maggie was happy to drink coffee while the rest enjoyed a glass or two of wine.

Nobody wanted the evening to end. Mr Vasilakis invited them back to his farm for a goodnight drink of brandy, bourbon, or a cream-based liqueur, which Simon and Lorraine accepted.

Understanding the girls weren't interested in an alcoholic nightcap, Greg suggested they might enjoy a hayride on the back of his truck instead. Lorraine was reticent, but as Simon and Mr Vasilakis believed there was safety in numbers, she agreed on the condition that Greg would look after Maggie, who had just turned 15, and Maria, who was in their care. He also pledged to escort the girls back to the orchard.

Margarite took the wheel while Maria, Peggy, and Greg squashed in the cabin beside her.

They drove to the showground, parked the truck, and walked to a make-shift pub. There was laughter and shouted encouragement coming from a congested bunch of people.

On closer inspection, a woman was trying to stay on a bucking mechanical bull. Greg said it was a training device for rodeo competitors. The machine plunged and spun in fast succession. In no time, the rider was thrown off, landing on oversized cushions on a padded floor. She lay winded and laughing, then stood unhurt to the delight of enthusiastic onlookers.

To an encouraging audience, rider after rider tried their luck. Greg had a go and met the same fate as did Maria, but Margarite refused. Not wanting to be a party pooper, it was up to Maggie to win the champagne bottle offered to whoever could stay on longest.

Greg lifted her onto the saddle. He made a knot in the rope, closed her hand around it and instructed her to keep a tight hold.

'The secret is to clutch with your thighs, relax and match your body movements with the changing rhythms of the ride.'

Greg stepped aside, and the bull slowly started to rock and roll. It picked up the pace, spinning this way and that in fast succession. Maggie pretended she was on a ship on a rough sea. She relaxed her body and let one arm free. Maggie kept her hand clenched over the knot and stubbornly gripped with her thighs. She was hell-bent on staying on as the bucking machine jerked and shuddered, spun and about turned. She didn't hear the noisy audience, but she noticed when they stopped and started clapping in unison. Maggie was sore and relieved when someone made a timely decision.

'That's enough; the winner is the redheaded cowgirl with Margarite.'

Greg jumped into the ring and lifted her off. On standing, her legs gave way, so he carried her to a chair where she collected the winning bottle of champagne. They all agreed to save it for Lorraine and Simon. Greg bought a glass of beer each. On tasting it, Maggie pulled such a face that they all laughed. Greg asked the obvious.

'What? Did that beautiful monster-face mean you didn't like it?'

'I'd prefer apple juice or water.'

Greg went away and came back with non-alcoholic wine.

There was something magical about being in a festive crowd for the first time. Unity lent a feeling of false protection, and Maggie's make-believe boat, which had weathered the rough sea on the mechanical bull's back, was in a safe harbour.

Over the past two years, she had cruised in the sheltered bubble of a chosen family and had gained social graces. She had shed the unwanted nickname Peggy and reclaimed her birth name. But Maggie had no experience regarding the world of boy meets girl, so she was vulnerable to predation.

*In theosophy and anthroposophy, the **Akashic Chronicle** is a compendium of all human events, thoughts, words, emotions, and intentions that have ever occurred, past, present, or future. Theosophists believe they are encoded in a non-physical plane of existence known as the mental plane.*

## CHAPTER 11

***What's done cannot be undone. The location is in the Blue Mountains. New South Wales.***

The crowd in the makeshift pub were rowdy, their vulgarity and tomfoolery building by the second. Greg suffered mental agony provoked by predatory rakes breaking into their group, trying to latch on to the girls by garbling inane jokes. He was annoyed. Recently, an unwelcome jackass removed one of Maria's shoes, filled it with beer, and emptied the golden liquid down his throat. To Maria's discomfort, he then insisted on returning the sodden footwear to her foot! The local philosophical drunk had tried logically to discuss the relationship between alcohol consumption and ethical decision-making. The atmosphere here was bound to fizzle his budding romance with Maggie.

Greg searched his brain for a more appropriate venue when a silverback gorilla-sized man, topped by a giant Akubra hat, brazenly placed himself directly in front of Maggie. He fixed his eyes on her face, then outrageously proceeded to rotate his hips while singing the current rhythm-and-blues hit "Earth Angel, Will You Be Mine" in a sugar-sweet, high-pitched voice. His gloved hands simultaneously mimed chords on an oversized cardboard cut-out guitar attached by chains to his torso.

***Earth Angel***
*'(Oh, oh, oh, oh, Wah-ah-ah, oh, oh, oh, oh*
*Earth angel, earth angel*
*Will you be mine?*
*My darling dear*
*Love you all the time*
*I'm just a fool*
*A fool in love with you*
*Earth angel, earth angel*
*The one I adore*
*Love you forever and evermore*
*I'm just a fool*
*A fool in love with you*

*I fell for you, and I knew*
*The vision of your love-loveliness*
*I hoped, and I pray that someday*
*I'll be the vision of your hap-happiness oh, oh, oh, oh*
*Earth angel, earth angel*
*Please be mine*
*My darling dear*
*Love you all the time*
*I'm just a fool*
*A fool in love with you-oo-oo*
*I fell for you, and I knew*
*The vision of your...*

A perfect psychological storm was brewing. It was apparent that Maggie was transfixed, enthralled, and maybe, through her apparent innocence, even attracted to this oaf by his animal magnetism. The blundering Elvis impersonator was brazenly gyrating his sexuality. He was charismatic and talented. Before this, Greg was confident he had Maggie softly, softly in the palm of his hand.

Greg summed up the situation. The danger for anyone wanting to stop this charade was the big guy's followers. They showed loyalty and intentions by their appearance. Sleeveless, black leather jackets decorated with chains and painted skulls, arms touting grim reaper tattoos, and their heads featured flattops, mohawks, and pompadours streaked bright blue and green. When their mouths opened to emit a wailing chorus of *Ohs* to back their performing boss, pointed beards jutted like stabling knives.

The ad-lib floor show had attracted a fired-up audience who were waiting for action, perhaps even the spilling of blood. All eyes were burning into Greg's ego.

He decided that clear thinking, a daring move and raw masculinity were on his side. But before he had hatched a plan, the man stopped singing, passed his guitar to a mate, and held his hand out to Maggie.

'I want to dance.'

'No, but thank you, I don't know how to dance.'

'I want to dance with you. You-me, me-you.'

Greg championed her cause. He vaulted off his barstool, placed himself between Maggie and his pretender.

'The lady said she doesn't want to dance.'

Greg's efforts galvanised the pub. He knew the shock of his action against such adversity had placed him as a hero to the maiden. He stood his ground. The performer looked down at Greg, showed amusement, transferred his hat to Greg's head, smiled, revealing a set of pearly whites, and then addressed Maggie.

'I don't know what he has to offer or if this impresses you, but I've more money than he does, I own my own house and business, and I'm better looking. What'll it be? A dance or?'

He spun into a boxer pose and faced Greg, relaxed, and hooted with laughter, then waved his arms to include the whole crowd.

'Drinks all round?'

The onlookers cheered and demanded another performance. Maria took the initiative and suggested they move on. She'd done her homework on the Blue Mountains' day and night tourist attractions and suggested they drive to Lithgow to see the glowworm tunnel. Greg thought that was a drive too far and said he'd like Maggie to experience the magic of the firefly colonies on such a balmy evening. They were closer than Lithgow, between Katoomba and Leura. On the way there, they could pick up takeaway coffees. He had torches, bottles of apple juice and plenty of petrol in his truck. Maria laughed.

'Can we come too, or is this just for Maggie?'

'Ah, she's the one I'm trying to impress, but that aside, Marg and I will be delighted if you both have a wonderful memory of The Blues by moonlight.'

He touched Maggie's hand.

'Are you impressed?'

Margarite quipped.

'She's impressed.'

Maggie spoke for herself.

'I think you're a sincere person and a great host, so yes, I'm impressed.'

Everyone laughed. Margarite drove while the three crammed into the truck's front seat.

An hour later, the party picked its way up a well-worn track. Their torch beams startled bush creatures, which scampered to a darker place or froze as statues against the trunks of silvered trees. At the slightest movement of the torch, shining eyes were there then, not there. Creeping shadows became longer than themselves, then melted into the void of the surrounding deep. Torches off, and moonlight silhouetted the rocky terrain. The deliciously cool breezes fanned their hot faces, and their city lungs were cleared of fumes and replaced with the potent fragrance of eucalyptus.

Maria's foot slipped, causing her to stumble. Greg steadied her.

'Let's go in single file for safety. Margarite, you lead, I'll follow, Maggie stick close to me. Here, could you give me your hand? Maria, you come behind with your hand on Maggie's back.'

Progressing like caterpillars, they entered either a cavern, an enclosed tunnel, or a canyon; it was hard to decipher which. Margarite suggested they should snuff all torchlights. Greg continued to hold Maggie's hand, which she didn't mind; it felt comfortable and safe. It was too dark to move, so they stood still. As eyes adjusted to low-light conditions, here and there, a diamond winked from deep space. Then magic took over. A slow wave of luminescence increased from a few to a significant volume. It migrated while surging to another somewhere, a strange and hypnotic phenomenon—a silent orchestra warming to a crescendo. The Fireflies flickered and danced in synchronisation. In spontaneous order, they distanced themselves from each other, mimicking stars in the heavens. And now, more like couples at an Elizabethan ball, they flirted and merged, then moved on in measured rhythm, eager to meet a brighter partner. Somewhere there was silent music, its melody only heard by those nocturnal love bugs and the humans tuned to the moment.

Maggie believed this symphony of lights had become part of her being. The memory will remind her that grace and serenity are hidden in places yet to be discovered. Her mind flew to the many times she and her sister Sylva sang the old nursery lullaby "Twinkle, twinkle Little Star", a thought which led to her longing to see Auntie Emma again.

Maria-the-Practical had an idea.

'The night is young because we are, so before tomorrow, we should move on. Maggie, do you still want a hayride?'

Greg answered for Maggie.

'Of course, she does because there's no tomorrow night. You're both back in Sydney, working the next day. Are you thirsty, Maggie?'

Maria decided a ride on the back of a truck wasn't for her. She wanted to sit comfortably in the cabin, enjoying the Blue Mountains in the evening. With Greg's help, Maggie climbed into the back of the truck. She discovered the hay wasn't hay. She had landed on big bags of high-quality rejected chocolate and sugar-coated nuts, destined to feed the Vasilakis pigs. These bags were fun. They acted like big, squashy pillows, hugging your body no matter how many times you changed position. Greg and Maggie laughed until they went quiet. They then toasted the evening with cups of apple juice and settled into their ergonomic chairs. The hum of the engine and the excitement of the evening made Maggie strangely dizzy. Her body felt heavy; she couldn't move and didn't want to, then fell into a deep sleep.

The next morning, Maria thought it was time to wake Maggie, but she wasn't in her room. Maria panicked and called Lorraine, who laughed and pointed to a couch on the veranda. Maggie curled up around Benji.

'You must have had a whale of a time last night. Maggie's sleeping like a newborn baby and hasn't even taken time to remove her shoes!'

Maria explained.

'She fell into a deep sleep during the hayride. Rather than wake her, Greg carried her in and put her on the couch. See how she and Benji love each other.'

Lorraine nodded.

'They say a boy and his dog, but here is a girl and her dog. Maggie, wake up, rattle your bones, have a shower. We're leaving in a second to learn about grape cultivation and wine production. You can come with us, go sightseeing with Maria or stay at home.'

Simon bounded up the veranda steps, looked at Maggie and addressed Lorraine.

'Lorrie, is Maggie OK? She's hardly moved since I went out for a walk around the orchard a good two hours ago.'

Addressing Maria.

'Did she have alcohol last night? Anything to eat?'

'We had a snack at the pub, and no, she only drank apple juice.'

'What pub sells apple juice?'

'Greg had it in his truck.'

'Did you drink the apple juice?'

'No, I had a takeaway coffee and sat in the cabin with Margarita. Maggie drank apple juice when they were on the back of the truck.'

Benji started licking Maggie, who stirred, sat up and sank back down again.

'I'm tired. Hello, good night.'

Simon remarked to Lorraine.

'We must go, but I don't like this. Maggie's underage, inexperienced and, far as I can tell, not worldly. Greg's five or six years older and gives the impression of being a lad around town.'

Lorraine shook Maggie, made her sit up, then asked.

'Did you enjoy the hayride?'

'What hayride?'

Maggie tried to stand but slumped back on the couch.

'Oops, my head's fuzzy and I'm sore from that bull.'

'What bull? Don't tell me she rode that mechanical bull at the showground! Did you have a go at it too, Maria?'

'Maggie won the bottle of Champagne.'

'Did you drink/share the bubbly? What time did you get in?'

Lorraine reached over to the veranda railing and picked up a bottle of Champagne.

'Is this it?'

'We saved it for you and Simon. Maggie and I came home together. I found Benji, and he jumped up beside her. I saw Greg off and went to bed. May I get her a cup of coffee, Lorraine?'

The two girls were sipping their coffees, and Benji was eating his breakfast when Greg and a friend arrived. They brought a bag of doughnuts and had made plans for the day. Maria wanted to go to the lookout at Katoomba, take photos of an unusual rock formation called The Three Sisters, buy mountain devils made of pipe cleaners wearing red capes for her friends, and a Blue Mountain souvenir collar for Benji. Maggie declined, explaining she needed to spend the rest of the day with Benji. They would be roaming Lorraine and Simon's orchard and farm. Greg showed surprise.

'You don't want to go for another hayride?'

'Greg, I apologise, truly I'm quite ashamed. I fell asleep and must have ruined your evening. I'm ever so sorry. The weird thing is, I don't remember anything about the hayride. I only remember drinking the apple juice.'

'As you fell asleep during the hayride last night, perhaps you'd like another ride this afternoon and not go to sleep this time?'

'No, thanks. I'd be a dull company because I'm still tired and my head is in some other place. It must be the mountain air. Apart from that, Benji needs to explore.'

The orchard's serenity and the fruiting trees reminded Maggie of Mrs Loveday. She mused on the game called Twenty Questions, which they sometimes played titled "Animal, Vegetable or Mineral".

When wandering her garden, Mrs Loveday would ask, pointing to a statue.

'Animal, Vegetable or Mineral?'

Maggie answered.

'Mineral.'

Mrs Loveday would then lean against a tree.

'Animal, Vegetable or Mineral?'

'Vegetable.'

'And moss?'

'Moss is a vegetable.'

'And this little chap?'

'A lizard is an animal.'

Once, they came across a fallen log sprouting a wealth of mushrooms. Mrs Loveday asked again.

'Animal, Vegetable or Mineral?'

Maggie answered.

'Vegetable.'

Mrs Loveday carefully picked a tiny mushroom and placed it in Maggie's palm.

'Look closely at this miracle which resembles a little tree; note that it has no roots, seeds, or leaves, so it is not a vegetable. Many forward-thinking scientists consider mushrooms as neither animal nor vegetable, but rather somewhere in between and more closely related to humans than plants!'

Maggie was horrified because she didn't eat meat, and now it seemed her favourite food was a living creature! Mrs Loveday laughed.

'No cause for alarm. Eating mushrooms is not cannibalism. Mushrooms do not have a heart, respiratory system, or blood. Mushrooms are the fruiting bodies of fungi that have a separate domain in Earth's kingdom of life. When our planet was an infant, about 500 million years ago, the first green plants crept from the ocean and put down roots on dry land. Millions of years after that, a part of that group separated. So came the blueprint for animals and fungi. Later, they, too, separated and developed individually. Consequently, animals, plants and Fungi are separate domains in the kingdom of the living.'

Benji growled. He moved close to Maggie's side. Greg appeared, with a rug, a pillow, apple juice and a beer.

They wandered for a while, then Greg asked Maggie if she was still tired. When she nodded in the affirmative, he suggested they rest. He spread the blanket, and they sat, Maggie, Benji and Greg. He poured apple juice for her, a beer for him and a surprise bone for Benji. They toasted their meeting, their lovely weekend, the orchard, the birdsong, and Benji for being a good dog.

Greg handed Maggie another apple juice. He didn't have to wait long before she fell unconscious. He dragged Benji to a tree where he fastened his lead.

Greg stood and looked down at the teenager. She'd been a great candidate for the second time that fateful weekend, Greg Vasilakis drugged and raped Maggie Piper.

***Earth Angel** (Will You Be Mine), Song by Harry Waters Jr. and Marvin Berry, Released: October 1954 Genre: Doo-wop; rhythm and blues.*

## CHAPTER 12

*"The best laid plans of men and mice often go awry", Robert Burns (1759-1796*

Six weeks later, Maggie fell off her bicycle on her way to work. She wasn't hurt but was too dizzy to stand. A passerby guided her to a park bench, then rested the bike beside her.

After a short spell, she recovered and continued to the ferry station. There she opened Café Rusty Worm and prepared for the breakfast rush. To each table, she added serviettes, menus and a flower, then arranged the seating. She turned on the coffee machines and lined up cups and saucers, mugs, and takeaway cartons. While warming the pogácsa, her stomach churned unpleasantly. Puzzling. Hungarian scones were one of her favourite foods.

When Elec arrived, Maggie was still nauseous, so he gave her the rest of the day off, joking that she looked decidedly green and that it was too early in the day for patrons to be confronted by a Martian.

After a late-night out, Maria arrived home to witness Maggie drop her bicycle on the lawn and rush to a flower bed, into which she vomited. Maria took Maggie to the doctor, who discovered Maggie's blood pressure was decidedly low. After hearing about her other symptoms, he asked Maggie if she'd prefer his female colleague to complete the examination.

'Why would I not want you?'

'Then may I ask your friend to be here while I examine you?'

The doctor left the room and came back with Maria, who took Maggie's hand.

'Mags, do you know what this is about?'

Maggie indicated no.

'Maybe I have an unusual illness.'

'The doctor thinks you're pregnant.'

'Now that is unusual, and it's bonkers. How could I be? I haven't made love to anyone.'

The doctor left the room and came back with his female colleague, who addressed Maria.

'Is your friend saying that she hasn't had intercourse?'

'As far as I know, she hasn't. She's all work, art, dog walking and no play.'

'She's underage, which means there will be a serious outcome for someone if she is, as we believe. But it may be a false alarm, probably connected to her menstrual cycle. I'll examine her; please stay.'

'Maggie, are you regular?'

'Regular in what way?'

'In your menstrual cycle. Do you bleed regularly?'

'Do you mean from down there?'

A nod from the doctor.

'Yes, every so often, there's blood. I asked a girl who worked in the chemist's shop if she'd ever heard of this, and she said yes. She told me not to worry. It was a natural occurrence for all women until they got too old to have babies. She sold me pads and suggested thick underwear for when it happens.

'Have you a boyfriend?'

'No, not even a secret one. The only men I mix with are our customers in the cafés, those at yoga and Greg. He's not a boyfriend, although I think he'd like to be. Maria and I met him in the Blue Mountains.'

Maria broke in.

'Yes, he's the son of Mr Vasilakis. We spent Saturday evening with him, his father, and his sister, Margarite. Holy Moses, Maggie, you went for a hayride with him in the back of his truck on Saturday evening, then spent Sunday afternoon with him in the orchard! I think I know what happened. I thought you were having fun, but now I know. I was in the front cabin with Margarite, who was driving. I looked through the back window and saw you both jumping around on big, full bags. Then you drank something and soon after fell into a deep sleep. When we arrived back at Lorraine and Simon's, you were still asleep, so Greg carried you in. He put you on the veranda couch.

The next morning, we had one hell of a time waking you. Then, so tired from the night before, you stayed home on Sunday. We went sightseeing without you. Maggie, after a short while, Greg left us and said he was going back to keep you company. That bastard. It's obvious he knocked you out again with another spiked apple juice. Simon found you deeply asleep in the orchard, Benji tied to a tree, but no Greg. Holy Moses. That rotten Greek.'

The doctor stopped Maria's rampage.

'Maggie, do you remember anything at all about the ride in the back of the truck? About this man's visit the following day?'

'I can't remember anything about the hayride after drinking the juice. The same thing happened the next afternoon in the orchard. I must be allergic to it.'

'How long ago was this?'

The medics examined Maggie, who was vocally upset at the infringement of her privacy. The findings were definite, and the conclusion was obvious. This teenager had been raped on two consecutive occasions while unconscious after drinking drugged apple juice.

Maggie was shaking and wanted to leave, but Maria stopped her. The doctor asked.

'Maria, do you know your friend's parents?'

'No, and I don't want to. Maggie's home life was often violent. She was placed at work by a child welfare officer just before her thirteenth birthday.'

Maggie had been listening, understanding the conversation, but not comprehending the magnitude of her predicament. She was worried about the probability of losing her job and not finding work while having a baby. Even more terrifying was that there was nowhere to go if Aimee Norris didn't want a pregnant female in the house. What if the police returned her to Marj and Albert? Marj had promised that Albert would not stop beating the devil out of her until he smashed her to smithereens, and she didn't doubt he would. What physical effect would this have on her unborn baby? Intense fear caused a panic attack. Pain racked Maggie's chest, and then everything went dark. She convulsed, her body contracting and relaxing repeatedly.

One doctor held Maggie steady while the other gave her an injection. Finally, she calmed, was exhausted and resembled a crumpled doll.

The doctors wanted to admit her to the hospital for observation, but Maria could see that would result in a police interview. She thought quickly, then suggested Maggie may be better off in her bed, where she'd be watched and comforted by herself or by Mrs Norris, who was a close confidant.

'Maria, it is our duty to inform the police, but I'm sure we both agree to hold off for the moment because we must do the best for our patient. She has a hard time ahead, both physically and mentally. She needs medication to stop her morning sickness and keep her calm. We don't need another panic attack. Take this script. Please bring Maggie back in a month for a check-up. Have you contacted the child welfare officer who originally helped her? Unless she wants an abortion, and at her age that can be legally arranged, it is of utmost importance that immediate plans for her confinement in a hostel are in place. Do not choose a refuge. Be sure that Maggie knows her predicament and that she will have a life after this tragedy.'

That evening, Maria told Mrs Norris, who reacted calmly and said she and Benji would comfort Maggie.

The following day, Maggie woke with a clear head and dressed, ready for work. Mrs Norris had already spoken to Pippi, saying that Maggie was not feeling well but offering no reason for her illness. Pippi wished her well and said she must return to work after she recovered.

A telephone call brought Diana Page into the picture. She hoped the offending male would have the decency to stand by Maggie financially during and after the birth, which would stand in his stead if criminal charges were to follow. Diana Page advised that he should be aware that Maggie has a reliable witness to the conditions leading to, during and after he drugged and raped her.

Mrs Norris asked if there was any way around Maggie having to face him. The answer was that it was of utmost importance that she speak to him face-to-face. She must not delay or avoid talking about this unpleasant and challenging issue. For her sake, now and in the future, another person must be present at the meeting when he will be asked to take financial responsibility for the expense of her confinement and for Maggie and the baby six months after birth. Don't tell him this, but if Maggie decides to keep her child, she can take a court order for him to pay maintenance.

That evening, Greg telephoned to ask when Maggie was revisiting Lorraine and Simon. She told him she needed to speak to him on an urgent matter. His following words took Maggie off guard.

'Are you pregnant? Well, what do you want me to do about it?'

'I don't exactly know, but an authority has told me that in all fairness, I should speak to you before the doctor puts this matter in the hands of the police.'

'Meet me at The Great Southern Hotel near Central this Wednesday at 11 am.'

Maria and Maggie were sitting at a small table in the foyer when Greg walked in with Margarite. He was cocky and cheerful, while Margarite gave the appearance of a woman made of stone. They sat on the two remaining seats opposite the girls. Margarite spoke.

'Greg's an attractive man. He doesn't have to drug females to have his way with them. I gather you're saying he drugged you. If so, you need proof. Is this your proof?' Margarite pointed at Maria. Maria spoke calmly,

'Am I "this"? I was already angry, but now I'm seething and offended. You've met your match. Yes, there is proof, and you're part of it. You were driving Greg's truck. I was in the cabin with you. I looked through the back window to see if Maggie was enjoying her promised hayride. I saw Greg give Maggie a drink, then, within a few seconds, she sank into the big bag she had been sitting in. Then I saw him on top of her. I repeat, I saw him give her the drink, which knocked her out. Greg's actions were without her consent. I didn't realise it at the time, but I witnessed the first drugged rape occur.

She was still unconscious when we arrived back at Lorraine and Simon's farm. Greg carried her from the truck to the couch on the veranda.

The following day, she was still in or recovering from the drugged state. She couldn't go sightseeing, so we left her to wander in the orchard with our dog, Benji. A short while later, Greg left us, returned to the farm, and repeated his ugly deed for a second time that weekend.

When we returned to Sydney, Maggie was ill, so she consulted a medic. Testing revealed fruit juice containing a drug in her system. It is on record. And, for your file and as a lesson in decency, Maggie asked the doctors not to report it because she thought it caused her little harm beyond a heavy sleep. But now the situation has changed. Maggie is expecting Greg's baby.'

Margarite addressed Greg.

'You are an idiot, but no worry. We'll hear what she has to say. Then we'll be gone.'

Maggie found her voice.

'Greg, it would be nice if you acted like a gentleman. I'm asking that you help me financially while carrying your child and for a short while after our child is born. I will secure a suitable job where I can work and still care for the baby. I am healthy. The doctor assures me that I'll recover quickly. If you want to be in your baby's life, I won't stand in your way.'

Margarite spat the following words.

'We are not interested in this bastard child, whom it would be wise to abort. I hope you don't expect him to marry you. He's Greek, and you're Australian. Probably of convict stock. Tell me, what do you plan if we don't do as you request?'

Maria answered.

'Police will charge him with carnal knowledge and more.'

'Try it. Both your reputations will be mud. I doubt if either of you could afford the lawyers our family can. Enjoy your punishment, little one, for trying to force yourself into my brother's life.'

Margarite stood up and zoomed to the exit. Greg took his time to stand, smiled at Maria, leaned forward, placed his elbows on the table, and investigated Maggie's face while he spoke.

'You were out to it, princess, so you don't know if it was just me or if my friend who called by had a go too.'

Before Maggie and Maria could answer, Greg straightened, blew a kiss to Maggie, then swiftly joined his sister, who was almost out of the hotel.

Maggie was stunned and struggled to reason with Margarite's aggressive disparity between the guilty and the innocent and between different nationalities.

Maggie had never asked another soul for help. Now, when she did it with legitimate cause, she had been treated like rubbish. How could one female be so uncharitable to another in such circumstances? This baby was going to be a mix of Australian/Greek blood. Margarite's bigotry and prejudice against Australians was racism. Why? She and her siblings were born in Australia. Her family had prospered in this country that had once welcomed them as penniless migrants. Somehow, Margarite had surpassed and betrayed decency more than her brother, who had drugged, raped, and now abandoned her.

Maria decided not to race after Margarite, strangle her and deball her brother, but concentrated on controlling her anger and taking Maggie home, who wasn't crying but had shut down. It reminded Maria of the time when she knew that her parents did not survive the holocaust. Then Maria had a brainstorm she'd put to action for Maggie's future after her ordeal was over. Right now, Maggie needed to walk with Benji along the waterfront.

Diana Page told Mrs Norris that it was wise to know where Maggie stood with Lorraine and Simon on two accounts; Lorraine had been a friend for two years, and Maggie was their guest when the obscenity occurred. Meanwhile, as Maggie had refused to end her baby's life, she would find the best place for Maggie to spend her confinement. It was in Maggie's interest to delay the doctor's report to the law because if they did, she might be forced to spend time in a brutal Sydney refuge for single mothers in waiting. These places were like prisons where females without husbands, even widows and rape victims, were considered little better than prostitutes and treated as such. Baby farming was a well-practised business by employees, and these people relentlessly belittled single mothers to obtain their children for the market.

Mrs Norris had a further conversation with Diana, who gave her Marj and Albert Piper's telephone number and address. She suggested Mrs Norris speak to them regarding financial help. Perhaps, as parents who put out in the world with no financial support and no education on the facts of life, they might feel some pang of guilt. But Mrs Page doubted it. And considering Maggie's legitimate fear of her parents, on no account should she be present.

Mrs Norris and Maria drove to the Blue Mountains. They were greeted and ushered inside by a serious Simon. Lorraine seated herself next to Mr Vasilakis senior because she thought this was an appalling personal situation for herself and Simon. They were new to the district, and their close neighbours were the Vasilakis. She had called in a friend well-versed in the law.

The friend listened while Maria recounted the Saturday evening.

Simon described Maggie's memory loss the following morning and late Sunday afternoon after spending the more significant part of the evening and part of the next afternoon with Gregory Vasilakis. He added that Maggie was unconscious and Benji was tied to a tree after Vasilakis junior left in a hurry when Simon returned.

The friend asked Maria to repeat the doctor's findings.

He questioned Maggie's character and morals, then advised.

'All Australian states rule sexual intercourse with a minor to be carnal knowledge. It is punishable as a crime. Maggie is a minor, while Gregory is an adult. A person who administers a substance to another person without the other person knowing that substance, with intent to cause the other person to be stupefied or overpowered, is guilty of a heinous crime and liable to imprisonment.'

He asked Mrs Norris.

'You did say this female is under the age of sixteen years?'

'Without a doubt.'

The man looked straight at Mr Vasilakis.

'Even if the female were of age, your son's actions would be considered a crime. But as she is underage, it would be wise and beneficial for your son if she were in Victoria and he in New South Wales, or at least if both were in different states. Do not think of Queensland. Queensland law is unforgiving of these acts. I say this to you because you may want to soften the experience this female is about to endure.

He was looking straight at Mrs Norris and Simon.

'It is obvious the girl must choose between an abortion and going through with this pregnancy and its aftermath. But is it not necessary to blacken a young man's reputation for life? Instead, send her to a faith-based hostel. Victoria has many. Tell her that because of possible damage to her mental health while she's carrying a child, it would be best to delay naming her abuser until after the birth.'

The advisor addressed Mr Vasilakis.

'At that stage, she should be utterly traumatised and will want nothing more than to put the incident behind her. The time delay would be enough to allow your son to leave the country if need be. A savvy lawyer could say the victim was the male who was encouraged by a female of loose morals. But frankly, there seems to be little evidence in support of this line of action.

A sticking point could be you, Mr Vasilakis. That is, if you, as the paternal grandfather, put in a claim to the baby, which you may want if the child is a boy, as another male may not be born to carry on the family name. Be aware that you would have to pay maintenance to both mother and baby until the child is old enough to work.'

Mr Vasilakis was silent. He made a point of not looking at Mrs Norris or Maria, but did smile at Lorraine and Simon.

Lorraine's reaction made it clear that Maggie had little chance of receiving fair treatment. There seemed to be even less chance of punishment for this monstrous young man without putting Maggie through more hell than she was about to receive. Then the man asked Lorraine.

'Have you met the female's parents?'

'No, but he is a Lay Preacher with the Baptist Church; a local Justice of the Peace, and heaven knows what else. In addition, he has a string of social titles.'

'There lies the answer to your problem, Mr Vasilakis. He or his wife won't want to be embarrassed socially. There is every chance they may not approach you.'

Lorraine stood.

'Tea and cake, Mrs Norris, Maria?'

Mrs Norris and Maria declined tea and stood to leave. Simon saw them out of the party and commented to Mrs Norris.

'She hasn't a leg to stand on, has she? Has Maggie given you a clue as to what she wants to do with the baby?'

Mrs Norris ignored the last question but said.

'No sympathy there, so I believe it is best not to tell Maggie of this meeting. I'll speak to her wretched parents; she'll need money to survive.'


After the meeting broke up and all participants had left, Lorraine asked Simon to sit with her.

'Simon darling, I'm sure you'll agree Maggie will be better off for this experience. She'll learn there's a price to pay for trusting people. It will help her through life's ups and downs, knowing she lived through it and came out kicking.'

'How would you know the outcome? Are we on the same page, Lorraine? Even when a married couple has an unplanned pregnancy, it can raise many confusing feelings and thoughts. Maggie is young and alone. She has no family or financial backing.'

'We can't help. Our money's in the purchase of this place. We have only just moved here. Tell me, darling, who wants to be out of sorts with their next-door neighbour? We'll need his advice and help in setting up our vineyard.'

Simon physically reeled.

'People are abusive to an unmarried mother. I can't imagine how she feels or what dark thoughts she's having right now. Her immediate future is terrifying. Her fate and that of her baby will be playing on her mind.'

'Simon, I'm glad I married a knight in shining armour, but let others sort this out. It's none of our business. There is a maternity allowance, and if she stupidly wants to keep the baby, there is a government child endowment for after the baby is born. It's not enough to live on, but she'll manage. As I said, it's none of our business.'

'It's very much our business. Lorraine, your friend, a teenage girl, was drugged and raped in our orchard while staying as a guest under our roof.'

Simon left Lorraine to her thoughts. He telephoned Mrs Norris and suggested that he be present when she spoke with Maggie's parents. She asked Simon if he intended to blacken Maggie's name or to support her. Simon assured her that he must be the first or second voice in Maggie's favour. Mrs Norris asked if his wife, Lorraine, wanted to be there too. Simon said they were of two different opinions and best not discussed.

The Cape Cod house was as Maggie had described. It was astonishing to know that a family of children made every brick and roof tile by hand, then carried them one by one up vertical planks to form upper floors.

Albert, a good-looking man with a broad smile and laughing eyes, met them at the door. The oversized room boasted an open fireplace between two enormous plate-glass windows that framed a magnificent view of the Georges River. Afternoon tea was set on a low table.

Already seated was an elderly lady, no doubt Grandma Maggie, whom Mrs Norris knew Maggie adored. A small female entered. Her once-blond hair had darkened and was worn in a tight perm, which didn't soften her sharp features, tight mouth, and pale blue eyes. Tea was served, and polite pleasantries were exchanged, then Albert seeded the conversation.

'Mrs Norris, you say you are a friend of our wayward Peggy. What has she been up to?'

Mrs Norris registered shock. Simon saw red and spoke first.

'Mr Piper, your daughter, who chooses to be called Maggie, is far from wayward. On the contrary, she is young and courageous, but in dire circumstances.

Grandma Maggie, introduced as "Maggie, Peggy's Grandmother", spoke.

'I hope she is with you, Mrs Norris. How can we help?'

Mrs Norris and Simon noted the snatched, cold glance Marj flashed at her mother. Mrs Norris answered.

'She is in my care now, but that cannot last because she has been drugged and raped.'

Albert asked.

'Was she injured?'

Grandma Maggie looked as though she could wipe the floor with him. She answered sharply.

'Of course, she was injured, but not as you would see it.'

To Mrs Norris.

'I believe she is expecting a baby. Perhaps a boy.'

Unexpectedly, Marj showed interest.

'A baby?'

Simon answered coldly.

'It's not a monkey or a mouse, Mrs Piper. I repeat, your daughter has been drugged and raped. She is expecting a baby. If all goes well, the child will be born mid to late March.'

Albert was about to speak, but Simon continued.

'Maggie refused to consider ending the pregnancy. We wish to allow her the kindest refinement. We have spoken with the same child welfare officer who placed your daughter, who was just thirteen at the time, in foster care and work after you turned her out of your home almost two years ago. The welfare officer has booked your daughter into a Church of England hostel for mothers in waiting. This hostel is in Melbourne.'

Marj urgently leaned forward.

'Melbourne! She was born there. What will happen to the baby?'

'That must be and is yet to be decided by the mother. The immediate problem is Maggie's welfare. She will need frugal committed finance, not for lodgings, as the job she has secured while waiting for the birth covers that. She will need some money to live off and a return ticket to Sydney.'

Grandma Maggie asked.

'Does my granddaughter know you are here?'

'No, but I do know she would send you her love.'

Albert looked to Marj, who said.

'Albert, the poor little girl. It's a pity we have no money. But Albert, we should investigate the welfare of the baby.'

Their quest was in vain, so Mrs Norris stood to leave, as did Simon, who placed his card in Grandma Maggie's hand. He then turned to face Albert.

'Mr Piper, I am married to a friend of Maggie's. Mrs Norris and I approached you, hoping for financial help. Maggie does not want to return to your home. She holds no grudge but is wary of you for a good reason. Through our Child Welfare contact, we know that you practised severe corporal punishment, which is at least frowned on and at most considered a near-criminal act. The way I see it, two different men have domineered your daughter through no fault of her own. The first could only prove his masculinity through physical force, while the other used drugs and his penis.'

Mrs Norris and Simon were almost out of the door when Grandma Maggie caught up with them.

'Please. I know Maggie loves pretty things. I do not need my watch; she'll need one now.'

Mrs Norris looked into the warm, brown eyes of Grandma Maggie, who whispered.

'Thank you.'

She pressed a small parcel into Simon's palm.

'Simon, a gift for my Maggie.'

They didn't wait for Albert and Marj to see them out. They just left. Mrs Norris glanced across the street to the home and tranquil garden where Maggie had spent precious afternoons with Mrs Loveday. It would be easy to imagine the fragile lady's ghost and her student still wandering the garden. Mrs Norris gave homage to the teaching of beautiful manners and appreciation of art presented by a wise woman to a child. She had nurtured Maggie's exceptional nature and character, inherited from Grandma Maggie. It certainly hadn't been passed down from Marj and Albert Piper.

Mrs Norris found Maggie with her arm around Benji, sitting on a park bench. They were both staring into space, the dog tuned to the girl's faraway thoughts. Mrs Norris took Maggie's hand in which she placed the white linen handkerchief tied around Grandma Maggie's gold watch, a pair of gold stud earrings and two hundred pounds. There was also a message on a scrap of notepaper.

'How? Have you met her? Did she come here?'

Mrs Norris answered.

'Trust me, don't ask, but know she loves you dearly. And Maggie, so do we.'

She touched Benji on his head.

Alone in her bedsit, Maggie thought about Mrs Loveday and White Feathers. She felt at peace and finally looked at Grandma Maggie's message.

*"My darling Granddaughter. Do not fear this unexpected happening. Your angel, whom I call your spirit guide, has already set in motion an exciting and successful journey through life. It will begin on your return to Sydney. Your immediate time will be lonely, but you are fine with that, as you have always been a loner. I repeat from your reading: It is essential to keep your private life secret, always tread lightly, walk softly, and avoid argumentative people. During your life, you will be welcomed by the highest and humblest. May the road rise to meet you, may the wind be always at your back."*

# CHAPTER 13

*Year: 1954. The location is Melbourne, the coastal capital city of the southwestern state of Victoria.*

The coal-fed, steam-hauled passenger train had just left Albury, the southernmost city in New South Wales on the Victorian border. It would take approximately another 4 hours to arrive at Melbourne's Spencer Street station. The premier royal blue and gold coloured locomotive was snaking its way through the lush Victorian countryside at an average speed of 52 miles per hour on the most extended non-stop rail trip in Australia.

Maggie nestled in the round-ended observation car at the rear of the *Spirit of Progress.* It offered panoramic views and a sense of isolation from chattering passengers. This and all other carriages were fully air-conditioned and luxuriously decorated in Art Deco style with wood veneers. The seats were so comfortable that one could swear they were personally crafted for each passenger. Drawing closer to Melbourne than to Sydney, Maggie was mesmerised by the act of scenery shrinking as it disappeared into the distance. It seemed that the turns and colours ran into each other. They blurred like wet watercolour on absorbent paper, while the gentle rocking caused by wheels on rails quelled her anxiety in the same way a mother cradles her baby.

The hypnotic effect made her think of Una, whose presence radiated tranquillity. Yet, Una had suffered the tragic consequences of the wildfire to her psyche and physical appearance. But against all the odds, Una had come out trumps. So will she. Before this journey, they made a pact to meet in India in future years. But for now, Maggie must face this fearful, unplanned happening that would end with her crossing from adolescence to womanhood while still legally a minor!

She thought of Maria and their last time together.

'Maggie, how about we take Benji to the beach? We'll have a picnic. I need to chat with you. It's important.'

'Tell me when and I'll ask Mrs Norris if he is available.'

'As soon as possible. If the woofer can't come, we could go to a restaurant and chat over a long lunch.'

It was easier to go to a restaurant.

Maria opened the conversation.

'You probably don't want to talk about this or face it, but you must make plans for your return from Melbourne.'

'I'm hoping Mrs Norris and Aimee will let me return to my bedsit. Perhaps Pippi and Elec will have me back at Café Gerbeaud and Café Rusty Worm.'

'Have you spoken to them about this?'

'Not yet.'

'Maggie, you must face this reality. You will be away for many months. During that time, others will take your place in the house at Kirribilli and in the cafés. Business is a business that waits for no one. Apart from that, I believe you have more potential than to spend your life as a waitress, which brings little money, no future, no glamour, and it's tiring.'

'Maria, I prefer waiting on tables to slaving as a Nursing Aide, and I don't know anything else. I have no skills and little education.'

'Listen to me. I am Austrian. My parents were victims of war, so I migrated to South Australia with my mother's brother and sister. Not long after arriving in Adelaide, they each found partners. They didn't say, but there was no room for me. I was fifteen. I found a job waiting tables at a football club, where I earned enough to pay my rent and fares to work, and I had free food. A member asked me if I wanted to lift my lifestyle. She suggested I travel to Sydney, where her business partner would give me a job as an escort.'

'What is an Escort?'

'The job description was to act as a social partner to members of the opposite sex. Meaning to attend functions, dinners, and theatres. If needed, to be their companion for a weekend.'

'Did you take the job? Is that how you got to Sydney?'

'Yes.'

'Do you still do this? Did you have to make love with these men?'

'That's my secret. But Maggie, the purpose of this conversation is not to involve you in such activities. I wish to arrange a proper job that will bring you respect and fair wages. I have a contact who will understand your position and employ you on your return from Melbourne. That is, if she thinks you are suitable, as I'm sure you are.

Her name is Olessya Frank. She is a friend of my aunt, who manages a beauty salon in Sydney. I've taken the liberty of asking if there was a chance of taking you on as an apprentice beautician or hairdresser.'

'Will she want me after I've had a baby out of marriage?'

'Do you imagine you'll have such information tattooed on your forehead? Mags, you will be no different from other teenagers. Yes, she wants to help you. It would be best if you never mentioned it, since this is off the record, but recently someone close to Olessya found herself in your position. She committed suicide. As an apprentice, your wages will be low, but this is an exclusive salon, and the clients will leave generous tips, enough to live on.'

A week later, Maria and Maggie stood outside a big red door in a city building. Maria prompted her.

'You must ask at the reception desk where the office of the Manageress is situated. Tell them you have an appointment. They will buzz her. She will come out to greet you, or you may be led to her office. Whichever way, you should stand still and straight, smile, and then introduce yourself. Say something like, "Good morning,

Miss Olessya. I'm Maggie Piper. Thank you for agreeing to interview me."

Wait for her to lead the conversation. If Olessya asks where you will be living, tell her that the agent you have used for the past year is happy to find you suitable accommodation near the city, or recommend you to another agent. A word of warning, at no stage, mention your pregnancy unless she asks you about it. Then, it only gives scant information. There is no shame; instead, she may be testing to see if you will keep your business to yourself, a much-desired trait in a beauty salon.'

Maggie was all smiles when she met Maria an hour later. Yes, Miss Olessya had assured her that she would be working within two weeks after contacting the salon. Maggie was to drop her a note every month to let Miss Olessya know all was well. Her initial training would be as a manicurist. She will wear a pink-and-white uniform; her hair will be styled before starting work, and she is to grow her nails while in Melbourne. After six months, Miss Olessya and she would decide in which area to further her career.

Maria advised.

'You should talk to Aimee Norris. You will need to tell her when you're leaving your bedsit so she can arrange the refund of your deposit. Also, ask for a reference. Tell her you have secured a future job and ask whether it would be convenient for her to be called when you return.

Maggie, I must drum this into you. There must be no circumstances in which you discuss your rape and pregnancy with anyone unless it is a matter directly relating to the law or for your well-being. The less information you share about yourself, the better, because people are harsh and judgmental. The only exception I can think of is Mrs Norris.'

'Maria, I've been wondering what to do with my bicycle, my record player and records. Can I store them with you?'

'Yes, you can, but only if I have your address in Melbourne because I may move, but I intend to live in Sydney for at least another year.'

'Of course, you'll have my address, as will Mrs Norris, Pippi and Lorraine.'

'I need to discuss your friendship with Lorraine. If I were you, I'd write her a letter of thanks for being so helpful over the past couple of years, and hopefully you'll meet up again someday. Unfortunately, Lorraine is not your best friend. She does not want bad blood with her next neighbour, whose son assaulted you.'

'Pippi and Elec?'

'They are kind people who are sad about your predicament. But again, they are businesspeople who may not wish to be part of your tragedy. To protect yourself from hurt and disappointment, play it safe. Do not discuss your plans unless they ask, and then give only scant details. At the end of your last day of employment, tell them that you've enjoyed Café Gerbeaud & Café Ruszwurm and thank them for treating you like family, which they have. Ask if you may contact them on your return.'

'Mrs Norris?'

Mrs Norris loves you as a daughter. But again, do not burden her with your sadness and fear. Thank her for making your burden lighter. Tell her you are returning to Sydney, where you'll work in a top Beauty Salon as an apprentice beautician. Ask if you may stay in contact.'


The warmth of the carriage and the purr of the wheels had sent Maggie into a light catnap, but she heard a tapping on the door by a smartly dressed gentleman in a Spirit of Progress uniform.

'Pardon me, Miss. Did she wish to eat here, be served in your carriage, or go to the dining car?

'I'd prefer to go to my carriage, please.'

'May I suggest that you may be missing a delightful experience? The dining car is elegance personified, and its cuisine comes from the best menus in Australia's leading hospitals, with an extra touch of deliciousness from our top chefs. I can arrange a separate table if you'd prefer. But before you decide, I'll tell you a story which is the absolute truth involving a bowl of soup and this passenger train which is reputed to be one of the finest in the world.'

The attendant had captured Maggie's imagination.

'Please, do sit.'

'I'd rather stand, but thank you, Miss. When the Spirit of Progress was born, it ushered in a standard of sophistication previously unknown in Australia or elsewhere in the civilised world. Comfort was of utmost importance, and it was in its last stages of refinement. No detail was overlooked by the Victorian Railway Commissioner, Mr Harold Clapp.

He had an engineer road-test the Spirit's travel smoothness on curves by studying a bowl of soup in the dining car. If the liquid splashes or touches the container's edges, they must reduce the curve's momentum or modify it for higher speeds. Another point of interest, his wife, Mrs Clapp, named this classic vehicle The Spirit of Progress.  I've dallied too long, Miss. Shall I book you a table in the dining car?'

On her return to her carriage, Maggie felt the need to open the soft carry case Mrs Norris had put into her hand as the train was pulling out. She spread the contents on the vacant seat opposite.

There was an envelope stamped with Simon's business address containing a card and two 50-pound notes.

*'Dear Maggie, I speak for both Lorraine and myself. Forgive her for being a little shocked and confused. Both our thoughts are for your welfare. We had two reasons for purchasing your return tickets. Importantly, we hope you can return, and we believe a little luxury goes a long way. First-class return tickets on the Spirit of Progress from Sydney to Melbourne were an opulent way to begin and end a chapter that will forever hold mixed emotions. Stay safe, Simon.'*

From Una, a colourful postcard depicting Durga standing on a tiger. Durga, the warrior goddess of India whose mythologies centre around the empowerment of women, and a book titled Van Loon's Lives: Maggie read on the back cover; "*Being a true and faithful account of several exciting meetings with certain historical personages, from Confucius and Plato to Voltaire and Thomas Jefferson, about whom we had always felt a great deal of curiosity and who came to us as dinner guests in a bygone year.*"

A second note, which read.

*Greetings Maggie, enjoy this book. It's fun and one of my favourites. Inside, you'll find a bookmark with my contact in India. She will guide you to me in a few years when you visit, as I'm sure you will. I'll be in India when you return, but I shall wait to travel until you've given birth. I shall post a Birthing meditation for you to become familiar with. Contact me when you go into labour. Think of Durga when you need courage. I do. Till then, Atithi Devo Bhava. Una.'*

There was a bulging envelope. It contained the Café Gerbeaud Pogacsa recipe and a roll of twenty-pound notes!

*'Hello, egy kedves embernek (hello to a dear person). Please accept these three hundred pounds as extra holiday pay. If you don't spend it all, bring us back a present. Pippi and Elec.'*

Then a box of Turkish Delight. It caused Maggie to giggle at the memory of the greedy woman with her teeth stuck together.

*'Hello, Magda, another box is waiting when you return. We'll be married by then. Andras & Karine.*

Now, a wooden box tied with a royal blue ribbon.

*'Know your angel is with you. Believe in yourself, Maggie. Please find in this box jeweller's wax, a carving tool set, and an instruction book. – Tea and biscuits are waiting when you come home. Sincerely, Mrs Norris.'*

A soft parcel begged to be opened. But first, Maggie read the message.

*'Hello, dear friend, I've made these for you on my little machine. Soon you'll need this tent dress, the smock, the maternity skirt, and the trousers. Do not forget to contact Miss Olessya. Here is the beauty salon phone number and address. Please send me a monthly note, and then I'll know you're OK and managing. I believe you will come through, no problems. Mit Liebe, Maria.'*

Another envelope was attached to a small silk bag with long strings containing one hundred pounds.

*'Hello Maggie, I'm so glad we've met. It would please me always to have your current address. You once told me your grandmother read your teacup and said you would be working in Scotland. When you do, contact us at this address. "Us" refers to Rupert and me. We are relocating. If we move to another address, I promise to forward it to you. Regarding your money, keep it all in this bag and keep it secret from others. Do not put your money in the bank. Your account may not be secure while you are in the hostel. Greed often rules. This bag has long strings to tie around your body under your clothing. Please don't wear it in the hospital while being examined or giving birth. I am proud of you. Diana Page, soon to be Diana McLeod.'*

The last parcel was oval, flat, and felt solid with a bone-shaped tag attached to the ribbon. It read from me to you. Benji had given her a photograph of himself! Indeed, this was the most precious gift of all.

Maggie took Diana's advice, rolled, and folded her gifted money, added Grandma Maggie's two hundred pounds and placed it in the silk purse. Then, she went to the toilet and tied it around her waist, and just in time because the Spirit of Progress attendant knocked to inform her they were approaching Spencer Street station, known as the gateway to the Victorian provinces. To Maggie, it was the gateway to the future of the child she was carrying.

She exited the station. A howling wind announced her arrival. She put her back to it and let it choose her course. She wanted it to drive her forward, to stay with her, to blast away chaos. Some say the wind causes havoc; others call it a friend, and others a foe. But to Maggie, the wind was nature's healing tool and the carrier of nourishment. Without it, the planet would still be and go to waste. The wind carries soil to blanket bare rock, seeds for vegetation, and rain to nurture.

But this wind was angry; it was in a cantankerous mood. Herculean gusts swept papers, leaves and debris along the street. Then it dropped to a whisper and pretended it wasn't there. This deception lured the unsuspecting out of the shelter. Then, with enthusiasm, the wind howled like a banshee and pulled at their coats and scarves. Maggie laughed; she'd taken refuge in a bus terminal, which brought her back to reality. She opened her bag and found the number and the bus's posted destination, which would drop her at the hostel for mothers-in-waiting. Then she had an alarming thought.

She would have to ask the bus driver where to get off. No doubt the driver and the other passengers would know that it housed single mothers-in-waiting, and that she was one of them! They would see her as a loose woman, maybe even as a prostitute! No, she couldn't face that. She'd catch a taxi. She decided it would be wise and asked the taxi driver to drop her off a block away from her destination.

Sitting in the cab, Maggie knew that this was the right decision. The driver hadn't blinked an eye or shown any recognition when she gave him the address. About fifteen minutes into the drive, he stopped the cab and announced.

'We're here, little darling. Let me help you get your luggage out of the boot.'

On the street, Maggie thanked him, paid, and gave him a tip. As she was stepping away, he grabbed her arm.

'Hey there, darling, where you're going, you won't get any of this.'

He flamboyantly opened his coat. He was comically stark-naked except for chopped off trouser legs tied with rope below his knees and big boots! His extended penis protruded from a bush of black hair, which matched his black-bearded face. He licked his protruding, thick lips. It was the first time Maggie had seen a penis. It was hideous. The cabbie, his extraordinary get-up and his nakedness were ludicrous.

Hysteria set in. Maggie started laughing.

Affronted, he looked down at his pride and, at the same time, released her arm.

Her counter-reaction was terror. Maggie grabbed her luggage and sprinted down the block, thankful that the wind of change was at her back. Maggie had seen the hostel in a photograph, a large, white house. The gate was open, the door ajar. Her head was on fire, her heart pounding, and panic took control. With blurred vision, she kept running. She made it to the first step of a winding marble staircase and crashed. She pulled herself together and sensed impending doom.

She escaped back to the street, boarded a bus and asked to be put off at a quiet hotel to spend the night.

# CHAPTER 14

*Remember not the harshness of the times but the warmth of things yet to come.*

Standing at the window of her hotel room, Maggie watched dawn break. Damp rooftops spawned fine white mist, which rose to invisibility. Flocks of Birds in synchronised flight swooped and soared on fickle air currents. The waking city was evolving from night to day, from dark to light.

Maggie felt flutters of fetal movement. Was it reacting to her wonder that structurally uninteresting buildings can be foundations for celestial grace? This concept brought new responsibility. Trauma from the past and fear of the future must create discordant energy. There was no way she was going to douse her unborn child with negativity. Fear must transmute positivity and confusion into clarity. She paid her dues and left the hotel.

Maggie crossed the road, reasoning that the bus that brought her to this part of Melbourne must, on a return trip, take her back to the hostel. But time was not precious this morning, and she was in no hurry. The air was inviting, scented by flowering shrubs where calling Honeyeaters were flirting. Coffee and doughnuts were for sale from a vendor on the street corner. Ready-for-work garbed men and women singularly approached the van without so much as a nod in the direction of others whom they must see regularly. Birds were friendlier than humans.

The temperate climate suggested days like this were for wandering through museums and art galleries, walking a dog, or leaning against a sturdy tree, eating an apple. But these times don't last. Soon, the same people will be rugged up. They will be thankful for a mug of steaming liquid to warm their freezing fingers, allowing them to reach for Vitamin C & D deficiency tablets. Brisk walking will replace pleasant strolling. Maggie caught herself and immediately stopped the gloom.

It was time to face her future. She checked the bus number, and yes, it did pick up here, but she would enjoy a walk to the next stop. She had the street to herself, workers had left, and it was too early for shoppers.

Almost to the concrete shelter, and a bus pulled in. Doors opened and out spilled babbling children jostling each other to be near two adults who were placing their charges three abreast in preparation for a journey to somewhere.

Maggie took refuge in a church whose door was open, as it had been in the big white house the day before. But unlike the hostel, this building emanated welcome. She sat in a pew, laid her hands over her tummy, and silently asked White Feathers to protect her child. She submitted to prayer so profoundly that she didn't notice a man in a cassock had taken place beside her.

'Are you a mother-in-waiting?'

'Yes.'

'I believe you were asking for help and protection, perhaps physical and mental strength?'

'I'm on my way to a hostel.'

'I believe life tests us in ways that appear cruel and confusing. But ultimately, adversity is instrumental in forging a fruitful relationship with the divine self. Are you aware that volcanoes are Earth's geological architects and that material from their lethal eruptions benefits our environment? While rivers of molten lava obliterate everything in their path, volcanic material generates fertile soil. The spewed, poisonous gases are enveloped in droplets of water, forming a blanket that shades our planet from incoming radiation. Dinosaurs who survived volcanic fury morphed into birds singing new songs. Yes, creation can be painful, but our world would be barren without its nonstop action. What knowledge do you have of creation?'

'The Bible teaches that God created the world in six days, but Dreamtime mythology tells that in the beginning, the earth lay sleeping. Nothing moved or grew because there was nothing. It was dry and flat with no hills, mountains, or valleys. All living things were underground in a deep sleep. One day, the Rainbow Serpent woke from slumber and came to the surface to see and feel the sunlight. She rejoiced and decided to look around. Wherever she wandered, her body left long, winding tracks, and wherever she had curled up to sleep, there were deep, sometimes wide indentations. When the Rainbow Serpent eventually returned to where she'd begun her travels, she called the frogs to leave their cold underground caverns to enjoy the warmth of the sun. The frogs came slowly because their bodies were heavy from the water they drank before the big sleep. The Serpent was in a playful mood, so she tickled their fat tummies. The frogs laughed so much that the water ran out of their mouths. It filled the Rainbow Serpent's tracks, which became rivers, and the sleep-made hollows transformed to waterholes, billabongs, lakes and oceans. What do you know about the big white house?'

'It is a cold building matching Matron's attitude to the wonder of life, which robs her of empathy. Are you artistic?'

'Yes, I write poetry, draw and paint. My friend Mrs Norris gifted me jeweller's wax and tools to carve it during my confinement. I'll use it to fill in time and to survive the unknown.'

'You will survive, but I doubt you'll have much spare time—fortunately, I may be able to help with your artistic efforts because that hostel looks graciously on our parish. One of my flock is an extraordinary man who teaches Chinese philosophy and wax carving. He concentrates on the form of the human body. Would that worry you? My name is Peter.'

'I'm not into humans, although I'm glad to have met you. I've taken up much of your time. I'm Magda. People call me Maggie.'

'After the biblical woman from Magdala? My time was for you, Maggie. Would you allow one of our young people to escort you to the hostel? It would act in your favour.'


In the Georges River house, Marj was waiting at the gate for Albert to return from work. She opened the garage doors and, as they walked to the house, she linked her arm in his and leaned into his body. He was taken to his favourite chair and offered a cup of coffee. Marj sat opposite him. She took both his hands and looked into his eyes.

'Albert darling, do you realise I've had four phantom pregnancies? The nurse in the clinic told me that these dreadful false alarms result from physical or mental trauma. Albert, the cause can't be the former because you have always been my soldier and protector. I've suffered no physical harm, but…'

'Marj, are you suffering mental trauma? Why didn't you tell me? Who are you shielding from my wrath?'

'Albert, I suffer because we have lost Emma's baby, whom the family put in our care. Granted, that child was almost thirteen when she left and, therefore, old enough to stand on her own two feet. But, Albert, that thought keeps me awake at night. My husband, you sleep soundly, unaware that I sit in the kitchen night after night. Alone. Sipping Tea.'

'My dear, my lovely, soft and gentle soul, are you saying there is a cure for these false pregnancies? How are we to fix mental trauma? We've medically proven that you can't carry another child. Should you consult one of these new-fangled mind specialists?'

'Albert, I have discussed this with myself many times. I know the cure. It came to me in a flash this morning while I was admiring the mural Peggy painted on the wall behind you.'

'Is the answer to your ailing health to bring Peggy back?'

'No, you silly darling husband. The answer is to adopt her baby. We could do this through the courts. She will be a single mother of fifteen. We are legally her parents and the child's grandparents.'

'Marj, I'm hearing that you want to take Peggy's baby legally. Why? Indeed, we would become loving grandparents, and we have every chance of that if we apologise for the harshness we inflicted on her. We could convince Peggy that we have softened our ways and make things right between us. I could build her a cottage on this block, then she wouldn't have to live under this roof, and you would have unlimited access to our grandchild.'

'But Albert, who said I wanted her back? The stigma of an unmarried mother living here in this household or even on this land would be an ugly experience for our pure children. I want her baby. The answer to this problem is a good lawyer.'

'Marj, I am ashamed of the violent and cruel actions I once practised as a parent. I no longer believe that children were born with original sin. Parenting should be like planting a seed, nourishing it, watering it, and trusting it to develop its predetermined shape and characteristics. Marj, are you aware that former residents of orphanages have won compensation in court cases against those who committed corporal punishment? I know you want this child, but please listen carefully. Consider this. If you attempt to take Peggy's baby lawfully, she may respond with vengeance. After your last altercation, the child welfare officer who placed her in care has evidence that we practised physical abuse and neglect. I am a Justice of the Peace and have an envied position on the local council. I cannot take this chance even to please you.'

'Albert, you are breaking my heart and condemning a helpless child to poverty and shame. We must provide and protect this poor illegitimate child.'

'Marj, have you forgotten that Peggy carries this burden through no fault of her own? It would not sit well in court that we showed no compassion and refused to help financially during her confinement. As her father, I have failed miserably. I cannot agree with your plan because it is proven that a mother's agony has no end if separated from her child.'

'Albert darling, you have the donkey by the tail. In this case, the unfortunate mother is not important; my compassion is for the child. Yes, you could build her a cottage on this land or somewhere else, for that matter, but if we don't legally adopt, she may spirit the little thing away, and I'll never again have the joy of a newborn baby. Peggy is only fifteen. I am an experienced mother. It is much to the child's advantage that you are a qualified parent who has successfully raised and is presently educating five healthy children.'

'Does this mean we'll have to track her down?'

'I've already done that. Peggy's in a Melbourne church hostel, and there's only one of its kind. Think of the advantages this baby would have. This lovely home is against a slum. Well-to-do parents oppose a struggling teenager without a job, a steady life, rather than being dragged from pillar to post. Albert, you must have it in your heart to agree with me for the baby's sake. Albert, you know how much I love babies, and I don't much care for another phantom pregnancy. I beg you. Please.'

'How could we handle this, a baby from nowhere? What would we tell our children and our neighbours, my colleagues?'

'Easy. We'll pretend I'm pregnant. I'll secure a cushion under a smock. We'll go for a holiday to Melbourne and return with the baby, saying I had a premature birth. Remember that we went to Melbourne to adopt Emma's baby, and that worked well.'

'Marj darling, please don't get your hopes up. I doubt Peggy will agree to this.'

'She'll have no say in the matter. I've had professional advice and opinion. We are well placed for adoptive parents as grandparents to the child of an unstable teenager. I've good faith that the mother is unlikely to retaliate because she will be at a low ebb and lacks the finances for legal advice and representation.

Her present, full-time job is mentally challenging as it is in the maternity wing of a hospital, in constant contact with new mothers nursing their babies. She lives in a hostel of silence with shame piled on the heads of even the most innocent. She sleeps in a dormitory with other pregnant females who will be in a state of despair. Her labour will be exhausting and an experience she will want to forget. This hospital's mandate stipulates no pain relief, especially during childbirth, for single mothers. The board of directors consider them trollops who have flaunted their bodies to get into their unhappy position. Yes, Albert, circumstances will crush her. Peggy will have no fight left in her.

Albert, understand my need. Our happy place is when we have a baby. God has sent us a gift. Let us take the legal advice and not approach the mother.'

## CHAPTER 15

*What is the price of a child?*

Maggie's room was tightly packed with ten narrow beds, obviously accommodating eight bodies, as evidenced by suitcases stuffed under them. It was a dormitory, cold and foreboding, with no cupboards and no other signs of personal belongings. The only relief from its rancid butter-coloured walls, woodwork and bedspreads were the dark iron bed frames, the spotlessly clean, worn wooden floor and a massive poster of the Virgin Mary holding her infant. It loomed behind the row of beds, adding misery to those who would never nurse their child. Maggie imagined this as an extension of jail, purposely uninviting, rather than a hostel for expectant mothers.

She followed suit and placed her luggage under the nearest of the two beds available, then headed back to the marble staircase.

Maggie saw a teenage girl standing in the downstairs hallway. The woman, who must be the matron, had a firm grip on the girl's shoulder and was tap-tapping the floor with a long, thin walking stick in her other hand. She demanded of her captive.

'Who in God's name are you? Where did you come from?'

The young female was shaking.

'A man had no clothes under his coat. He had a big penis.'

Matron shot back.

'And you're not used to that? You're pregnant. Are you Harriet Brown?'

'Yes.'

'Where is this naked man?'

'On the street, he was the taxi driver.'

'You've come from Perth?'

'Yes.'

'If you've come in today, then you must have come by bus and train exchange.'

'I did.'

'Why didn't you catch another bus here? I advise you not to spend unwisely on private vehicles. We'll have none of your upper-class nonsense here. You'll have to take your nose out of the clouds, Miss.'

'I couldn't find the right bus. Before the taxi stopped, I was going to walk.'

'That would have been a stupid thing to do when you've got a bun in the oven. We need a healthy, full-time baby for adoption. No one wants a premmie. Next thing you'll tell me you travelled first class. More likely, you relocated from second class to the Guard's carriage, where you were having a bit of nonsense. Your room's upstairs, the first door on the right, and your bed is the one without a suitcase under it. As you seem to like the stairs, your job will be to clean them with that Miss, the one standing up there listening to this conversation.'

Matron used her stick to jab-point at Maggie.

'From tomorrow morning.'

The matron was abusing her power over one shaken by her experience with the taxi-driver pervert and exhausted from travel. Maggie waited for Harriet to pass, then began to descend. Matron demanded.

'And where do you think you're going, Miss?'

'I heard a bell ring. I gathered it was a call to go downstairs. Another lady signed me in. She told me the bell was a signal to go to the dayroom. My name is Maggie.'

'Your name is "Nothing" here, girl. We will know you as "Miss", a reminder that you are a fallen woman, an unmarried pregnant female. At this time in the afternoon, the bell was a reminder to be in the kitchen preparing the evening meal with others of your kind. In future, you will only step on these stairs to scrub them as you will do daily from 5.15 am to 7.15 am with the help of the other Miss. The back stairs are your exit and entry to this building. Within this home, you will remove your shoes and stockings, no socks.'

Maggie returned to the dorm and met up with Harriet. Together, they found the back stairs beside a partitioned area just beyond the row of tightly packed beds. A plaque identified the space "Live-in Social Worker. Do Not Enter." They peeked around the room divider. There was a comfortable bed, a small bedside table bare except for a bell, and a dressing gown hanging on a coat stand. Slippers were under the bed. The back stairs connected the sleeping quarters to a rectangular room with a row of showers, six toilets, and four laundry tubs, with no walls between. The ground floor was divided equally into a dayroom with a bookshelf half-stacked with worn magazines and a kitchen with a long table surrounded by an assortment of chairs.

Three young women, at various stages of pregnancy, were standing, chopping vegetables. A mature lady had her back to them, stirring a pot on the stove. One of the vegetable cutters caught Maggie and Harriet's gaze, made an enormous effort to cross her eyes, then put a finger to her mouth, indicating not to say a word. The pot stirrer turned and walked with a waddling gait to the table. She was in advanced confinement. Without enthusiasm, she waved to Maggie, and Harriet then pointed to a humongous pile of flour and margarine. Besides that, the two "newbies" spotted a recipe to make scones, enough to feed at least twenty people. The kneading was laborious, heavy work, so they sat in chairs to complete their task.

Almost immediately, Matron's stick came crashing down on the table, just missing their hands.

'Up, Miss, up. Feet are at the end of your legs for standing. Your posteriors are for resting; you are not permitted to rest them when working. Dinner is at 6 pm, after which you'll be given your itinerary for the week ahead.'

Sleep that night came easily, but by 5 am, the woman who had to be the live-in social worker because she was wearing the dressing gown they had seen hanging on the coat stand in the partitioned room woke Maggie and Harriet. Without a word, she gave them work smocks and trousers. She beckoned them to follow her to the shower room. She sat on a chair, watching. They dared not speak. When dried and dressed, she led them to a washing tub beside a cupboard holding buckets, scrubbing brushes and a wad of soft rags. She demonstrated the amount of cold water needed in the buckets. Loaded with cleaning gear, they followed her to the excellent marble staircase sacred to the hierarchy and, for the first half-hour, scrubbed and rubbed under strict supervision, then were left to continue until a bell shattered the airwaves at 7.15 am.

The woman in the dressing gown returned. She had changed into navy trousers and a shirt. Her black shoes were reminiscent of those worn by the police. She beckoned Maggie and Harriet to follow her back to the laundry. As they passed the shower room, hurried females, eyes down, silently descended the stairs.

After the buckets and brushes were cleaned and stacked away, the social worker pointed to the shower room. She raised her arm, opened her palm with five fingers extended, indicating a quickie. Then it was back to their dorm, where hospital uniforms—smocks, skirts, and caps—were on their beds. Downstairs, they scoffed a glass of water and toast with a promise of jam. Attaching themselves to the tail end of departing hostel girls, they crushed into a little bus which transported them to the hospital maternity wards.

On arrival, they immediately served breakfast to future mothers in various stages of labour and to those who had just given birth. After used trays were returned to the kitchen, they were allowed a weak cup of tea and a biscuit during a ten-minute break. The hostel girls worked and worked and continued working into the early afternoon. Then they were offered a choice of limp vegetables, an ice cream scoop of potato resembling concrete, or a sandwich. Everyone chose the latter. Fifteen minutes later, they were back in the wards, tidying, filling water jugs, and serving afternoon tea.

At 4 pm, they collapsed into the hospital transport and were driven back to the hostel. They numbered ten but felt like the seven dwarves under the control of the wicked stepmother. The girls who were not on hospital duty were under the watchful eyes of Matron and the social worker, Hanna.

Matron called a meeting in the dayroom. The itinerary had changed for the following week. Each day, two females would be excused from the morning's work because they were to be registered with the hospital welfare department and examined by medics to determine their stage of pregnancy. After that, they would report to the ward sister and resume regular duties. Maggie was in the second group.

On Tuesday morning, Connie and Carol took over scrubbing the marble stairs. At the same time, Hanna shepherded Maggie and Wendy to the laundry, where they partially filled buckets with cold water, then carried them to the shower area. After undressing, and under Hannah's supervision, they sat on the edge of the chairs with their legs spread. They were to scrub their "not-so-private" parts with soap and a clean rag. Hanna would personally inspect. Wendy asked Hanna to turn her back and stop staring, then said it didn't matter because she wouldn't do this. It was vulgar, unnecessary and an insult. Hanna didn't say a word, left the room, and returned with a bucket of iced water. She spoke while pouring it over Wendy's head.

'Yes, Miss, you will see how necessary this cleansing is when you get to the hospital. Today's your day of inspection with decent doctors not used to dealing with your filth. Keep scrubbing till I tell you to stop.

Breakfast didn't happen, but on the bus, the girls who'd suffered Hannah's cleansing routine the day before showed compassion through light touches and gentle smiles. They knew that the girls' bodies were raw and numb, having been subjected to cold water and laundry soap for at least half an hour. They, too, had been belittled, made to feel common and unworthy vessels to carry a new life.

Maggie waited for her turn to see the welfare officer. She hoped to speak to the previous girl, who hadn't exited the way she'd entered. Instead, a hospital attendant pointed to an open door, which Maggie entered. A female seated at a desk looked up, nodded to a chair, then spoke.

'Hello, I am pleased to meet you. Please relax. I'm here to help with your situation. Have you been given previous advice?'

She looked down at her folder.

'Your name is Maggie?'

'Yes, Maggie. Advice? No.'

'Have you your family's support, Maggie?'

'No.'

'I'm so sorry. Then you have a great decision to make, my dear.'

'My family doesn't know I'm here.'

'Ah, then that makes it clear. You won't be taking your baby home. I'll mark your file with "B.F.A. which means baby for adoption.'

'I don't want my baby adopted.'

'Oh, but deep down, you do, my dear. Once you realise that you won't be able to provide your baby with all the things a child needs, clothing, food, toys, and a loving daddy?'

'I have a job lined up.'

And you can take a baby to work?'

'There are day nurseries for children with working mothers.'

'Maggie, I fear this will be too hard for you and most unfair to your baby. This child deserves constant love and care. Babies are helpless and so precious. I know a wealthy couple who cannot have a child of their own. Both parents will be home all day to pamper your baby. They will adore this child. Pity them; they have waited a long time for a baby like the one you'll have.'

'What do you mean by "a baby like the one I'll have?"'

'You don't know? My dear, we match babies by the natural mother's qualities with the adoptive parents' living standards. We take skin and hair colouring into account, as well as apparent intelligence and health. I assure you that your baby will want for nothing and will attend a private school. A standard of living you will never be able to afford as a single mother. There is another point which you must consider. A child with an unmarried mother is not socially acceptable; the poor thing is shunned at school and has no playmates. The married lady and gentleman eager to adore your baby are respectable.'

'Are you saying I am not respectable?'

'Maggie, you are young, very young and more than pretty. There is no doubt in my mind that you will, someday soon, meet your Prince Charming and have children, beautiful children of your own. The couple who want your baby is not so blessed.

'Then perhaps you can find them another baby.'

'You're not thinking clearly. I'll see you again as I'm your counsellor. I believe that you'll make an intelligent decision for the baby's sake and give happiness to the sad woman who cannot conceive. It is in your hands to either send these well-to-do people deeper into despair or to allow them to experience the joys of parenthood.'

She stood, so Maggie stood, and a curtain behind the welfare officer's desk slid open.

Maggie entered a room buzzing with a mixed-age group of men and women in white coats, stethoscopes hanging around their necks. Someone told her to replace her clothes with a front-opening hospital gown and lie on a bed. A female who introduced herself as a midwife in training pulled curtains around the bed. She rolled Maggie on her back, opened the gown displaying Maggie's body, then firmly bent her knees and spread her legs as far as they would go. She opened the curtains, then disappeared. Horrified at her naked, indecent exposure, Maggie lowered and closed her legs, then covered her body with the gown. The midwife stormed back and again positioned Maggie's body into humiliating vulnerability. She clenched her fist close to Maggie's face, saying.

'If you have my job, Miss, I'll have your disgraceful hide.'

Maggie froze. She turned her eyes from the fist. The room had many beds and just as many exhibiting females! She covered her face with the pillow and stayed immobile for what seemed an eternity. She was hoping for death when a soft voice whispered.

'I'm sorry, there is nothing I can do; instructions are to make single mothers feel the shame they've brought on themselves. It will be over soon. Students and midwives are coming now under the supervision of a senior male medic.'

Next, there was a nightmare of many sets of fingers poking inside her uterus and her anus. Then, palms were pressing her stomach and attempting to roll her breasts. Voices discussed her body as though she were a laboratory animal—then the sound of feet treading to the next bed. Her face was relieved of the pillow as a woman's voice said,

'Treat 'em rough, and they'll think before getting up the duff again.'

Hearing these words, Maggie realised she had no medical problem. Instead, there was a moral issue in a medical institution where morals shouldn't have any place. Putting this awful experience into perspective, the physical exposure and assault on her body outweighed the obscenity of rape by Greg Vasilakis, who had at least drugged her before enjoying her innocence.

Maggie dressed and slumped in a chair outside the ward. The welfare officer was passing; she paused, smiled, and touched Maggie's arm.

'There, that's over. For now. Not an experience you'd want to associate with your baby, was it?' A word of advice. Forget you have a baby there; instead, think of it as a lump you need to expel. Adoption is your best decision, and perhaps you won't be naughty again?'

To violate the sanctuary of a pregnant female's body was undoubtedly one of the greatest crimes. This morning, Hanna had degraded her in the hostel shower room. The saccharine-sweet welfare officer had laid guilt on her head to make her give her baby to a "respectable couple". She had endured unconscionable treatment from the same medical staff who had sworn on oath to respect life. What punishment would they mete out during birth?

According to the hostel girls, there was profit in the business of adoption. It seemed common knowledge that nuns stole babies from single mothers in their care for a nice donation. Yes, "stealing" was the correct term because it was done without the mother's permission. Human trafficking, even under the guise of a monetary gift for a religious cause, was inexcusable and a crime against humanity. The grief of a female parted from her child, and a future adult who will anguish over abandonment by his mother at birth are wounds that cannot heal.

While serving lunch in the wards, Maggie's mind entered a dark place. Confusion, desolation, loathing, and hate curdled with a growing love for her developing baby. She was overwhelmed by fear of the birthing process, and those letters, B.F.A., on her file, held by the welfare officer whose attitude had rekindled the hideous attack on Maggie's character by Margarite Vasilakis, the sister of her predator. Women like these betrayed other women.

Maggie was not overly religious, but she did believe the Bible was the cornerstone for a healthy society. She reminisced on words from Psalm 127:3, "Your children are a heritage, a reward from our Heavenly Father". What does this say of the mother who allows others to sell her child?

Maggie secured permission from Matron to attend a service in the church she'd found on her way to the hostel. Regrettably, Peter was on holiday, which was disappointing because she had decided to ask if she could consult with his welfare officer regarding options open to her and her baby after birth. Was there a single mother's support group? Perhaps a pension was available until she was on her feet?

Two weeks passed, and the marble stairs routine continued at the same time every morning. The hospital job amplified pain and tragedy, particularly for those who had signed their baby away. Day in and day out, they watched women feeding, holding, and cuddling their little ones. Insults were purposeful and constant. During visiting hours, they had to remain out of sight. They were socially offensive as immoral women. It was apparent that somebody had told the patients to ignore them. At first, when serving food or doing chores, the girls smiled, but the women stared straight through them or turned away.

One of the hostel girls peeped at a baby in a patient's arms. The woman rang the bell and started screaming,

'That creature tried to touch my baby! I won't have this. My husband is a major sponsor of this hospital, and we expect quality, not whores or prostitutes. She probably has a disease. Or worst still, she may be planning on killing or stealing my baby because she won't be allowed to keep her own. Her behaviour was scandalous. She was thinking of touching my innocent child with her vile hands. I know she comes from that house of shame.'

Someone grabbed the confused girl, bullied her out of the ward, and cautioned her never to return.

The girl at the hostel was named Daisy. She was sixteen. Her parents said she was too young to marry a man she fell in love with, so he arranged a secret marriage. She lived with him for four months and fell pregnant. He then told her that their marriage was a joke. She returned to her parents, who confronted his parents. They explained that their son couldn't marry their daughter because she didn't belong to their culture. Daisy's parents condemned her for being stupid enough to fall for a man who used her, then they forbade her from contacting them again for fear that the deeply shameful event would stain their name. They and the offending man's family each paid half her one-way fare from Sydney to Melbourne, but Daisy had no pocket money and nowhere to go after the birth.

She was not allowed to work at the hospital, which was her only way of earning her keep at the hostel. Daisy was in the last two months of confinement, but Matron made her scrub wooden floors from early morning till late afternoon.

Daisy was physically and emotionally bankrupt. She sobbed every night for a week. Nobody was allowed to console her as this was a 'house of regret and silence'. Later, in the evening, after lights out, if the forsaken girl cried, Hanna stood by the bottom of her bed, rang her bell and mocked Daisy.

'Tears are not always easy to come by, Miss, so save them for a rainy day!'

Matron separated Daisy from the other girls. She slept sitting on a chair in the dayroom with no blanket and, as was the custom in this hostel, no shoes, stockings, or socks. Daisy started to bleed; one could see the stain on the back of her clothing. Matron said it didn't matter if she lost her lump because the selfish girl had refused to put her thing up for adoption.

Hanna found some sympathy in her cold heart and sent Daisy to the hospital on the morning bus. They kept her there for three days, then sent her back. She lacked the strength to stand and peel vegetables, so Matron sent her to the dayroom without dinner.

In the morning, Daisy was missing. Her shoes and luggage were still under the bed. She had left in a nightgown. Nobody looked for her, and she didn't come back. Next, two days later, another expectant mother occupied Daisy's bed.

Matron's response to Daisy's demise made it evident to the remaining socially unacceptable, unofficial prisoners that this miserable hostel was an environmental hazard for "status offenders", which was the official social title for single mothers-in-waiting.

Weekends were less disciplined than weekdays. On Saturdays and Sundays, parties of five could sit in the nearby park for two hours.

Maggie made an appointment with Matron and asked permission for herself and others to attend the church regularly. Four girls came with her. Peter welcomed them from the pulpit and asked if they'd like to join his flock for tea after the service. The outcome was fantastic. Peter planned to talk to Matron about his intention to form a regular class on social adjustment.

Lily, the church's welfare officer, invited Matron to the social club's twelfth-day-before-Christmas luncheon, and of course, Matron accepted. Once there, Peter had Matron agree to the hostel girls helping to build a nativity scene.

Matron called a meeting and pretended it was her idea as a special event for her girls. She concluded the meeting by stating that Almighty God would well receive this effort.

On the following Sunday afternoon, Matron and the hostel girls joined the fellowship members. They made cardboard cut-out images of shepherds, angels, and animals. Joseph and Mary were fashioned from pegs, cardboard, wool, and paint. A halved ball made a cradle, and the manger was a redesigned slatted wooden box. The famous star was an artistically arranged bundle of sticks, generously sprinkled with glitter. Matron and Hanna had photographs taken beside it. They baked a gingerbread house, then enjoyed cakes and tea, after which the girls sang carols with the choir. Maggie found it interesting that the ladies, considered dregs of society and therefore unworthy to raise a child, were familiar with the praise of the Lord. She wondered how many "decent" women would be as versed.

Christmas came and went. There were no celebrations, although Matron did open her coffers to purchase dried fruit and candied peel. The girls made fruit scones that delighted Matron, so they were on the menu until the New Year.

Then the seesaw of existence fell to another low until Matron called Maggie to her office. She asked about Café Gerbeaud, whether it was a place of good repute, and whether Maggie knew the difference between afternoon and high tea.

'Matron, I shall tell you what I know and hope that my knowledge and ideas are suitable for the purpose you must have in mind.

In 1865, a member of the English aristocracy devised afternoon tea, typically served between 3.30 and 5.30 pm. The table holding the sweet and savoury dishes was lower than a dining table because the elite sat on comfortable chairs while chatting informally and partaking.

High tea was a copy of afternoon tea by the rural and working classes, but it quickly evolved into an early evening meal between 5 and 7 pm. Their menu usually consisted of a hot dish, followed by bread served on a tall table surrounded by stools or tall chairs, because high tea was popular at working men's drinking clubs.

Café Gerbeaud's specialty afternoon tea was famous. A sweet and sour cherry soup starter served with a dollop of sour cream, followed by thinly sliced bread spread with butter infused with herbs, wafer-thin cucumber sandwiches, lemon curd tarts, tiny cakes, and scones, jam and cream.'

'What did they drink?'

Teas of Mint or Chamomile, or a robust, fashionable variety. Sometimes coffee.'

'How much time would you need to prepare afternoon tea for six, Miss?'

'A full morning with at least one helper, Matron.'

'I don't have a low table.'

'Do you have a lovely tablecloth or perhaps a beautiful curtain or shawl?'

'I have a lacy cloth and hand-embroidered shawls.'

'Then we could disguise one or two wooden boxes.'

The invitation went out to Peter, Paul Bineham (Peter's Creative Master of Arts and philosophy), Matthew (the Choirmaster), and Lily (the church social worker).

Matron chose the two mature mothers-in-waiting, Elizabeth and Annie, to help set the scene, which allowed Maggie and Harriet the pleasant task of preparing the food. The remaining ladies became decorators and flower gatherers.

Four afternoons later, Matron and Hanna, dressed in their finest day clothes, gurgled words of delight as they inspected their dayroom. An impressive makeover masked its sterile, impersonal atmosphere.

Her servers were wearing smocks in matching colours, with their hair tied back.

Maggie suggested she and her waiting staff meet Matron's guests at the door. Matron and Hanna would be seated but would rise to greet when they entered the room.

It worked well, and Matron welcomed her first guests in fifteen years.

Lily brought flowers, deftly arranged in a large glass jar, and placed them in the Matron's view.

Paul Bineham mostly led the conversation. He said he preferred to be called Bineham. Maggie wondered if they would ever stop speaking about the weather and get to the reason for this meeting. Cherry soup received many compliments, with the church social worker asking if she could copy the recipe. Then Peter spoke in his well-modulated, mellow tones.

'Matron, I know you are a woman of empathy who has a challenging and heart-wrenching job. However, you stand alone against those who pressure you to cajole expectant mothers to put their children up for adoption. As a fellow female, this must destroy your faith and respect in social convention, let alone the fact that many of your mothers-in-waiting are too young to be worldly and therefore were either deceived or raped.

Matron wore an expression of concern.

'You are so right, Your Reverence Peter,'

Hanna nodded her agreement.

Peter continued.

'To them, afterbirth is not what medics term as the placenta and fetal membranes expelled from the uterus following the baby's birth. To these unfortunate mothers, afterbirth has another meaning; it is the ghost of inhumane treatment at a time most needed. It is also the breaking of the sacredness of blood ties.

Matron touched Peter's arm.

'You are alarmingly sympathetic and understanding. Yet you are a man. I praise you.'

Hanna smiled at Bineham, then Matthew.

Peter continued.

'As you well know, my dear Matron, the surrendering mother's loss is indeed even more irrevocable than the finality of death because she knows that her child is alive, somewhere. And worse still, if she knows where her child is and is forbidden to communicate with her. As a mother, it is and always will be her God-given job to protect her child. Therefore, she will continually wonder if her child is safe, well, and happy. Daily, she will suffer a sense of loss and agony.'

'A tragedy, yes, a sad, sorrowful happening.'

Hanna remarked to the choirmaster,

'Society has no tolerance.'

'It is evident, Matron, this is why you and your social worker, Hanna, have taken your much-appreciated positions. You are true females who carry the burden of protecting and nurturing those in need.'

The afternoon tea girls had been listening while serving. Peter had the sweetest tongue. He had such a way with words that the tough old boilers they knew as Merciless Matron and Hard-Hearted Hanna transformed into ghoulish spring chickens. Matron coyly smiled while tipping her head to one side. She'd put her weapon-like stick aside and held her hands loose over her crossed knees. Hanna responded to Bineham by patting her tightly coiled hair and eyeing him under her eyebrows.

Matron touched her chin with a finger and asked.

'Peter, apart from welcoming those in my care as part of your flock, you have another reason for visiting?'

'I have an idea which will lighten your load and at the same time give your ladies some direction as to how to adjust socially after their ordeal. But we cannot do this alone, dear Matron. We will need your professional help. May we meet again at your convenience?'

Matron flushed.

'We'd be delighted, Peter. Mr Bineham, Lily, and Matthew. Is this coming Saturday too early?'

The afternoon tea party was over. Matron claimed a win for Hanna, and they went for a walk while the dayroom was cleaned and returned to its sanitary self.

The girls chatted quietly. They found the afternoon fascinating. While being the centre of attention and hearing Peter's flattering description of her hidden character, Matron took on a new persona. She looked pretty in an offbeat way. Perhaps it was the flush of pink that had taken the place of her sallow complexion or her suppressed giggles that caused her facial muscles to soften.

When all was over, and the girls were leaving the dayroom, Elizabeth whispered.

'At least we know she's not a lesbian.'

For the first time in months, the four laughed until they became rag dolls with no stuffing, a state that made it easy to cry inside unnoticed.

# CHAPTER 16

*The Stolen White Generation explained.*

An ambulance was called to the hostel at 6 am. Harriet had fallen while scrubbing the marble stairs. Observing two exhausted females in advanced pregnancy surrounded by buckets, brushes and polishing clothes caused the medics to speak harshly to Hanna. They finished their lecture by asking if this was regular work or punishment—either way, they considered reporting it to the authorities. The ambulance men left after attending to grazes on Harriet's knees and elbows, checking both girls' health, and listening through stethoscopes pressed to their bellies. After which, Hanna told them to stop cleaning, tidy up, and then dress for hospital duties.

That same afternoon, Peter, Bineham, Lily and Matthew joined Matron and Hanna for tea. One of the ambulance attendants had gone home for lunch and told his wife, a friend of Lily, about the cruelty he witnessed at the hostel. His wife told Lily, who made a point of bringing the subject up as soon as the party were seated.

From the kitchen, Maggie and Harriet could hear Matron shifting the blame to Hanna. She explained that she had no idea Hanna had continued punishing the girls for something that happened three months before! Hanna objected to the shift of guilt and whined that Matron hadn't told her to relieve the unfortunate females. Then she asked if the girls didn't do this, then who would? Peter said there was no need to blame anyone, as this was a misunderstanding that happens to the best of us. Lily pointed out that as Hanna and Matron were the only people to tread this sacred elevation, daily cleansing was without justification; so perhaps, from now on, the cold stone should only be scrubbed and polished in the afternoon of every $7^{th}$ day and only by girls in early confinement.

Maggie and Harriet had proven to be good cooks, which prompted Matron to order omelettes for her and Hanna's breakfast. The girls were given a new work schedule for their minimum weekly duties of

60 hours. No more stair scrubbing, but they still suffered hospital duties until the early afternoon and returned to the hostel to prepare evening meals. Flavoursome food took much imagination because salt, spices, and all herbs except parsley were not allowed. Matron believed condiments, herbs and spices were not conducive to healthy babies. There was an open question: the girls wondered why Matron was so interested in healthy babies. Was she also a profiteer?

Maggie wished to eliminate meat, so she concentrated on egg-based dishes, veggies, and grains. Hurrah, the bland diet of boiled carrots, cabbage and sausages was gone forever, or at least while afternoon tea parties sweetened Matron's disposition.

Soufflés, quiches and paper-thin, rolled pancakes stuffed with vegetables simmered in their juices enjoyed high popularity. The savoury soufflé changed character on Saturday evening, replacing savoury elements with cocoa and sugar, and was served swimming in caramel sauce. For this, Hanna went berserk with desire, so Elizabeth always sneaked her an extra serving when Matron's eye was elsewhere.

On returning from church one Sunday, Harriet suggested she and Maggie rest on a park bench for a bit of conversation.

'Maggie, I know you're younger than me, but I think you have a better way of talking to people. Maybe because you've been working, and I haven't. Would you do me a great favour?

'I don't want to put my baby up for adoption. But the only way I can think of to keep my precious bundle is to tell my parents. So, would you tell them where I am?'

'Of course. Should I telephone or visit?'

'They live in Perth, so you'll need to telephone them.'

'Tell them what? That you're in Melbourne or tell them you're in Matron's hostel?'

'Both those things.'

'Where do they think you are?'

'I told them I've become religious and joined a convent and couldn't contact them until my training was over.'

'And they believed you? Do they know you're pregnant?'

'Yes, they believed me, and no, they don't know I'm pregnant.'

'What is their attitude regarding single mothers?'

'I don't know. We've never discussed it.'

'How do you want me to approach this?'

'Any way you want. I need to get out of here and keep my baby.'

'I'll do it, but we need to think up a plan that will not shock them.'

Maggie's mind raced; she was unsure about how to handle this problem. Maybe someone closer to Harriet's parents' age—possibly Lily, Peter's welfare officer, or Bineham—can help.

'Harriet, Lily was at the service this morning. Let's rush back now. We may catch her before she goes wherever she goes on Sundays.'

Lily listened carefully to their request, then questioned Harriet.

'Harriet, you didn't inform your parents about your predicament. Why?'

'They knew I was going out with a boy from the church social group but didn't know we were intimate.'

'Does the father of your child know you're having his baby?'

'No.'

'Why not Harriet?'

'His Grandfather was dying, so he and his family went to England to be by his side.'

'What does your father do for a living?'

'He's a surveyor with the council, and my mother is a kindergarten teacher.'

Then Maggie had an idea.

'Lily, would it help if Harriet wrote a letter to her parents? She need not give details of her well-being, but she could ask their forgiveness for saying she was training to be a nun when in truth, there was another reason for leaving the home she loves.

'Maggie, I believe a letter could cushion the unexpected news. Harriet, because your mother works with children, she may be more understanding than you think. Are you close to your parents?'

'Yes, I am a much-loved only child. They think I'm an angel, which is why I didn't tell them. I'm sure to be a disappointment.'

Maggie broke in, fearing the hostel Matron's punishment for returning late.'

'Lily and Harriet, I'm worried. We should be back at the hostel now.

'She can take it out on me because I think Mummy and Dad will stand by me. I'll tell Matron I felt a little ill, so I had to sit in the park for a while. Lily, will you talk to my parents, please? Maggie, please help me write the letter, will you?

Maggie replied, then stood.

'Of course, Harriet, we'll do it after finishing our chores this evening.'

Lily assured Harriet.

'I'll contact your parents, Harriet. Maggie, help her write the letter, then post it immediately. How long does it take the post to get to Perth? When is your baby expected?'

Harriet pondered.

'When we write to our Melbourne cousins, the letters take about four days. My baby is due in two months. Lily, I can't give my baby away. If my parents won't have me, is there somewhere I can stay—maybe another, nicer hostel—till I find a job? Is there anyone who can help me?'

Knowing the best possible help available to Harriet as a single mother was her family, Lily tried to be reassuring.

'Harriet, write your letter and post it as soon as you can. Peter won't mind if you use paper, an envelope and a stamp from his office. Come with me. I'll see you both next Sunday after the service. Then we'll put our plans into action immediately. Don't fret. I shall do my best. Maggie, I'm here for you, too.

*Dearest Mummy and Dad,*

*I am, without a doubt, going to prove a great disappointment.*

*I have told a purposeful lie because I didn't want to hurt you. I was confused about what to do in my predicament.*

*As I told you, I am in a Melbourne suburb, but I am not in a nunnery or a convent. I am not training to be a nun.*

*When David joined his parents for an extended holiday in England, you thought I was heartbroken, and that was why I left home. Yes, I was sad that I might never see him again.*

*But that is not why I left our loving family. I did something that made me afraid of soiling the family's reputation and perhaps hurting Mummy's job.*

*I am missing you both and need your support.*

*I need your love. I need your understanding.*

*I want to be in the safety of my home and family again.*

*I am too ashamed to contact you personally, so I have asked Lily Wilson, my church social worker and a trained welfare officer, to contact you.*

*I have given her your telephone number.*

*I am, as I always have been and always will be, your daughter.*

*I am not worthy of your love, but you are more than deserving of mine.*

*Enfolded in this envelope is my deepest love,*

*Harriet Lynnette Maison.*


Maggie found it thoughtful of Harriet to give Brown as her surname to Matron. She was protecting her family name. After receiving Lily's telephone call, Patricia and Bill Maison travelled to Melbourne and booked a hotel suite. Lily Wilson met them in her office at the Children's Welfare Department in Melbourne. Patricia Maison voiced gratitude to Lily for approaching the family.

'We can't thank you enough, Mrs Wilson. Where is our daughter? Is she poorly?'

'She's in good health physically, Mrs Maison, but Harriet needs to be in the bosom of her family. She needs your support.'

Bill Maison leaned forward and earnestly assured Lily.

'We plan on doing just that, Mrs Wilson. Where is our girl?'

'Mr Maison, Harriet is in a church hostel. But I fear arriving without warning may have a disastrous effect on the welfare of the other mothers-in-waiting. This Matron and her social worker are without empathy and will not take kindly to an unexpected loss. I have no doubt you want to rescue your loved one immediately, but I suggest a pleasant morning tea with Matron and her offsider, Hanna, beforehand.'

Patricia Maison jumped in.

'We are anxious, Mrs Wilson. I want to hold her in my arms and assure her that we welcome the birth of our grandchild and that we are proud of her bravery. We have spoken to Harriet's long-time boyfriend, who is the father of our baby. At this point, he is on a return flight from England to be by her side, as he put it, "for eternity". Please tell us about your plan.'

'You should meet over morning tea. I am sure that during that pleasantry, Matron will reunite you with Harriet. With your permission, I'll previously tell Matron that you are grateful for the care she has taken of your daughter, so appreciative that you couldn't possibly return Harriet to your family home before spending time thanking her personally.'

Bill Maison asked.

'You'd prefer not to tell us where she is for fear of reprisal on the other ladies if we do as our heart demands and just snatch her out of there?'

'Exactly. I'll set your heart at rest by telling you that your daughter is under the wing of another young lady called Maggie, who protects her.

'I'm amazed at the letter Harriet wrote to us; she has never been good at putting words on paper. Did you write that letter, Mrs Wilson?'

'Mrs Maison, I can't say for sure, but I believe Maggie helped her. The girls are close. Maggie suffered brutality as a child. Welfare placed her in safety at the age of thirteen. She has worked for two years and is a victim of rape.'

'How could we help Maggie? Is she keeping her baby?'

'I understand Maggie will keep her baby. She has an apprenticeship offer at a Sydney beauty salon upon her return. We can help find accommodation and child care, but there is nothing else we can do. The financial reality is that most of these girls have no choice but to give up their babies for adoption. Mrs Maison, how do you intend to spend the rest of today and tomorrow?'

'I'll make appointments for Harriet and me to have our hair styled, and I'll search out retailers to take her shopping for maternity and baby clothes. That said, I'm leaving now. Bill, shall we meet at the hotel at about 3 pm? Mrs Wilson, I look forward to meeting you again the day after tomorrow. I am beside myself with joy, knowing our girl will come home and present us with our first grandchild. Should we take flowers to Matron? A gift for Maggie? Shall we meet here and go together to the hostel?'

Lily smiled. The Maison's genuine love of their daughter was a triumph for humanity and, Lily hoped, the beginning of removing the stigma of single mothers from the remnants of Victorian society and institutional corruption. But Lily knew flowers would not be enough to compensate for Matron's loss because Harriet's baby, along with all babies born to hostel mothers, had been marked for adoption by the hospital welfare officer. So there was a likely bonus for an employee of the hostel, or perhaps for the hostel's treasury. Lily answered carefully.

'By law, a financial inducement is not necessary, but it is the way to go. Yes, we'll meet here at 9.30 am. Flowers for Matron and Hanna will soften the loss of a mother who is not far from giving birth. It would help Maggie if you left a monetary gift for her with me. I assure you, she will receive it. Maggie has put a little silk bag holding her savings in my safe.'

Harriet's mother left her husband with Lily. She knew him well, and he had something on his mind, likely some idea to discuss without fear of upsetting her.

Bill Maison had a lot on his mind.

'Mrs Wilson, I've heard there is a "white stolen generation" as well as a black one. Is there any truth to this?'

Lily replied.

'There are more stolen white babies than black babies. Regarding the Aboriginal, Mixed race and those of Torres Strait Island descent, initially, church missions, Federal Government agencies lawfully placed those children in suitable private foster homes and missionaries, fearing that the indigenous races were dying out. This action was meant to help them assimilate into modern society. Occasionally, some mothers of these children left them in the care of a mission while they went walkabout. But, for different reasons, many, many more white babies are stolen immediately after birth from helpless mothers. They are, as we speak, being sold, trafficked and adopted for underhand financial gain.'

Bill Maison asked.

'Why isn't the stolen white generation generally known?'

Lily explained.

'A public investigation would expose this massive and lucrative industry, which is baby farming in every sense of the word. Nationally, this illicit business involves religious institutions, adoption agencies, hospitals, medical and child welfare staff, and those in charge of homes and hostels for single and widowed mothers.

Mr Wilson, the Federal law had a secrecy act that allows government officials to seal an original birth certificate forever. They then issue an amended birth certificate establishing a child's identity with its adoptive parents. This deception is known as "Closed Adoption". It ensures that neither the natural mother nor her child will learn the other's identity. With incorrect parental information on a birth certificate, adult individuals risk intermarriage with close relatives and are oblivious to an incestual relationship.'

'Who adopts these stolen white babies?'

'Establishments have queues of infertile couples, lonely women too old to have a baby, families who want a child to work for them or look after their natural children and others who wish to collect child endowment.'

'Why do these ladies give their child for adoption?'

'They have little choice. A woman needs a hospital to give birth, and they must register with the hospital welfare officer before acceptance by a hospital. Without the mother's permission or knowledge, the initials B.A. or B.F.A. show on her form. This signals to the birthing staff that the baby is to be adopted. For months before birth, a welfare officer lacking ethics brainwashes the expectant mother, too inexperienced or distressed to understand the manipulation. She is shamed and told, "If you love your child, you'll give them up for adoption to a home with a respectable mother and father. Unmarried mothers, whether in this predicament because they were unworldly, widowed, raped, or who gullibly believed that the father was wearing protection when he wasn't, are deeply stigmatised. And Mr Maison, many families see their daughter's pregnancy as sinful, and therefore an immoral human, so they send her away and turn their backs indefinitely.'

'Mrs Wilson, why do you think there are so many females in these unfortunate circumstances?'

'Intimacy between young people has become commonplace. It was not long ago that someone was almost always present at a single woman's social occasions. Young females are generally romantic, while young men are often sexually adventurous. Many parents pretend that sexual relationships don't exist. Only yesterday, I overheard a woman informing her ten-year-old child that he was born in a cabbage. There should be, but never will be, education for parenthood, so we can't trust parents to tackle this task. Mr Maison, we can no longer afford to endanger our daughters through a lack of sex education. It should become a curriculum in schools.'

'Do laws exist to protect single expectant mothers?'

'Mr Maison, laws forbid brutality by midwives, nursing staff, and doctors to single women, yet they are mistreated and crushed mentally. They are refused pain relief during labour. They are prevented by any means, even shackled, from viewing their newborn. They suffer the painful after-effects of an injected carcinogenic hormone to stop the production of milk. That is the sadistic climax to months of slave labour, loneliness and degradation in homes, hostels, hospitals, and institutions. Laws do exist to protect these victims of fate, but whistle-blowers are afraid to come forward.'

'My last question, Mrs Wilson. At what stage do the single mothers leave the hospital after giving birth? Where do they go?'

'When they sign into the labour ward, they take their belongings with them. Then they are kicked out one or two days after birth.'

'Will you be Maggie's spokesperson, Mrs Wilson?'

'If I have the opportunity, Mr Maison.'

The next day, Matron asked Maggie, Wendy, and Harriet to make a light morning tea for seven people. She requested Harriet to pack her case and lodge it in the corner of the dayroom. Harriet was terrified. Was Matron forcing her to leave after they served tea? Where would she go? Maggie thought otherwise, but didn't dare give hope to her friend. Instead, she told Harriet to wait and stay calm, because Lily had everything under control. Matron didn't want the girls to greet the guests at the door; instead, they were to serve morning tea when Hanna rang her bell.

The dayroom had, as always at tea parties, a peaceful, inviting atmosphere. The flower-gathering girls had erased its harsh sanitary conditions. In the kitchen, Maggie, Harriet and Wendy were waiting to produce trays of citrus tarts, jam-filled doughnuts, pogácsa, tomato sandwiches, and black tea.

Guests entered and were seated. The conversation was quiet and voices indistinct. What was Harriet's fate? The bell rang. They could hardly believe it was Hanna's because it tinkled softly, having no resemblance to the clashing thunderbolt made in nights past to torture Daisy.

Maggie, Wendy, and Harriet entered. Matron, without her stick, Bineham and Hanna were seated, leaving four empty chairs. Hanna took Harriet's tray, put it on the table and told Harriet to sit. Maggie and Wendy placed their trays on the table. They were sent to the kitchen and told not to serve tea until Hanna used her bell again.

The doorbell chimed. Matron welcomed three people in her other voice, the honey-sweet one. The sound was hushed, as though a great secret were about to unfold. They heard Harriet scream with delight and a man's voice soothing her. Hanna's bell tinkled. Maggie and Wendy brought in the tea. They understood the strangers to be Harriet's parents. Mrs Maison was so engrossed with her daughter that Maggie couldn't see her face, but did notice her hands softly laid on Harriet's swollen belly. Matron was holding an exquisite bouquet, and Hanna a pot plant of bright red geraniums.

Before the girls returned to the kitchen, they overheard Mr Maison thanking Matron and Hanna for the care they'd given their daughter. He offered Matron a sizable donation for her hostel, which she coyly embraced with many thanks. Hanna saw the party out. When Maggie and Wendy came to clean, Harriet and her suitcase were gone.

## CHAPTER 17

*Year: 1955. Talent, decency, indecency, and an invisible feather.*

A widow arrived at the hostel. Through lowered conversations during transport back and forth from hospital duties, the girls learned that Shirley's husband and two children had died in a car accident. To add to the tragedy, the cost of their funerals left her destitute. She was in her third trimester, which meant she was about 8.5 months into her pregnancy. Shirley fascinated the first-time mothers-to-be with details of their baby's development in the womb, facts not offered by anyone else.

Her baby was about 18 inches long and weighed approximately five pounds. Being an experienced mother, Shirley thought she was carrying a boy because her bump was low. She called him Peanut. At this stage of development, he could close, open, blink his eyes and move his head. Peanut responded to light, touch and sound, so Shirley sang soft lullabies to win familiarity with her voice. When she knocked softly on her tummy, Peanut responded by kicking. The girls were enchanted but saddened for her. This baby was all Shirley had left of a once contented family unit. She was protected from Matron's passion for near-slavery because Matron knew Shirley was Hanna's cousin twice removed. That, plus her late stage of confinement, excused Peanut's mum from hard work, but she still carried out duties to cover her keep by folding linen in the hospital laundry and replacing Harriet in the hostel kitchen.

Shirley planned to keep Peanut. Having previously conferred with the Department of Social Security, she knew of a government monetary assistance program that had been purposefully hidden from the young mothers-to-be. They were now aware of their right as birth mothers to apply for and receive a weekly child endowment. With this knowledge, a plan evolved that would enable the ladies to keep their treasured babies. It was simple, workable, and straightforward. They would ask Lily to find a run-down farm to rent in Melbourne's outskirts. There, they could live communally and even grow much of their own food. Those who could work would pay the non-workers to mind their little ones. The only stumbling block was that, initially, money would dribble in according to when they gave birth and how soon someone would employ them. Shirley asked why they preferred Lily's help to that of Matron or Hanna. The girls swore her to secrecy, then told of Hanna and Matron's past vindictiveness.

When Matron called a meeting two days later, the girls asked Shirley if she'd dobbed them in or revealed their plans.

Shirley answered indignantly.

'Certainly not. I want to be part of this community group. As a mature widow, I have much life experience to offer and value to your cause. With my widow's pension and maturity, I have a greater chance of securing a rented property than a bunch of teenagers, each with only a child allowance. Alone, Peanut and I could live in misery through poverty. United with you, we will enjoy contentment and prosperity. Peanut should be the first baby born, and because I am destitute and as he is all I have left of my home and deceased family, the Salvation Army has promised to supply me with furniture at no cost or minimum cost. You may wonder why I am in this hostel. The "Sally" home for single mums was full; they placed me here. Hanna is a relative, yes, but she didn't lift a finger to help.'

Shirley's words were settling, so the mothers-in-waiting gathered in the dayroom to hear Matron out.

She and Bineham planned on staging a regular three-hour social adjustment and careers class. The first hour of the first day would be open discussions on mannerisms and how to present when applying for a job. During the following two hours, and from then on for the entire three hours, attendees could choose to learn bookkeeping, typing, sales register application or a facet of the arts. The classes will be in the dayroom on Saturdays beginning at 1 pm.

There was stunned silence when Matron had finished, so Maggie took it on herself to start the applause. A faint smile lit Matron's face.

'Thank you. I, too, am pleased. I wish to be a pioneer in changing society's views on single-parent families and childbirth methods. Starting with you, my girls, we have a Midwife Practitioner in this parish who has studied prenatal and painless birthing techniques in London and Germany. Karin Thomas has offered us workshops designed to prepare you for your coming labour. Furthermore, Karin will discuss those in early childcare who are keeping their babies.

Girls, I do not mean to frighten you, but the hospital may not offer pain relief. You can beat this, and so you should. It is safer and healthier for both mother and child if the birthing process is drug-free and occurs during a state of deep relaxation. Karin aims to familiarise you with exercise in a meditative state, so your body can behave as nature intended during the birthing process. With Karin's expertise, you will learn to release fear and use various methods to manage pain, from visualisation to stretches designed to strengthen muscles. She will put to bed old wives' tales that have conditioned us to believe that labour must be associated with excruciating pain.

Una, a friend of one of our girls, has sent me verbal affirmations and a recorded, pre-birthing visualisation which Karin has identified as a powerful meditation. It features dolphins and the ocean. Your first class with Karin Thomas is this coming Sunday at 9 am. I suggest you have a pot of tea and a snack on her table when she arrives.

You have tomorrow to turn your dayroom into a classroom for Bineham's Saturday business workshop and to prepare a quick change for Karin's Sunday prenatal. For the latter, you'll find rolled-up mats and cushions in the cupboard under the stairs. Maggie and Shirley, will you oversee this?'

Hanna spoke.

'Ladies, yes, I said, "Ladies", not "Misses". This hostel for pregnant females is changing its name to a Home for Mothers-In-Waiting. There is a new rule, one which must be honoured and not abused. Matron will tolerate whispered and lady-like conversations, but not in the dormitory or at the table.

Elizabeth whispered.

'Can we applaud, please, Hanna? Thank you, Matron, and thank you, Hanna.'

Stifled giggling, Hanna nodded, and applause almost blew the roof off the more appropriately named building.

The following Friday morning, Maggie was in session with one of the vipers as the girls called the hospital welfare officers.

'Hello, my dear. Not long now? I see by your papers that you're due about the end of March. Imagine how happy you'll be when this is over, your lump expelled. Of course, I know it's a baby, but we are better off thinking of it as a lump. No use getting fond of a lump, is it?'

Maggie didn't answer because she knew that if this woman was annoyed, she was capable of punishing Maggie by sending her for another examination, a lawful medical mass rape of a thousand fingers, fists, and palms. The welfare officer was playing a new psychological game.

'I am telling you something strictly off the record, and if you repeat this to anyone, I will brand you a liar. The couple waiting for your baby asked if you have enough money to begin your new life. They suspect you are in need; otherwise, you wouldn't be living at the hostel. Yes? They have opened their hearts and will open their wallets, that is, after you have signed the adoption papers. Think about it.'

'I have.

'I knew you were clever. I had no doubts you'd make the right decision. Of course, your baby will be so spoiled that they will be a bit naughty, but who cares? They will love your child over the moon and back. Now for your signature. The sooner, the better or they may change their minds and look for another baby. That would be a shame because, with your child, they will make a pretty family. The lady has exactly your reddish-blonde hair, and the gentleman has your blue eyes—a perfect match. The baby will resemble mummy and daddy.'

Maggie decided to play the viper's game.

'I'd like to meet this couple.'

'Good heavens, my dear Maggie, that is against the rules. I'm so sorry. If it were in my power to arrange a meet, I would. But, no, I can't. It would cost me my job, and you wouldn't want me to lose the only way I have of feeding my family, would you? Between you and me, my husband is incapable of work.'

'I have to think about this. What will my punishment be if I don't sign my baby away?

'We are not barbarians. Punishment is not this hospital's nature. Who has been feeding you false information? But I must ask this question. Do you believe an immoral female deserves punishment for not saving her virginity for marriage? Or for bringing a child into the world without a father? Or for not jumping at the chance to give an innocent child a life with respectable people?'

'I am not yet sixteen years old and not worldly, so I can't give an opinion. But I do consider it essential for you to know that I was drugged and then raped. I am not an immoral human.'

'Another one crying wolf! Maggie, they all claim to have been raped. I am sorry that you think I am so thick-witted as to swallow such a tale.'

'There are doctors' records and witnesses to prove it.'

'Do you know the father's name and where the police could contact him?'

'I do, and so do other people.'

'Then, after, or even before your confinement is over, the police will contact you for details to enable them to lay charges on this man. Maggie, you need to think this through. I see a drastic situation giving even more reason why you must sign these adoption papers. Do you honestly believe that you are mummy material? What type of mother would have her child carry the humiliation that they were the result of rape? I am sorry, but the fact remains that you need to sign adoption papers here and now to protect your baby's reputation. That way, nobody will ever know that their father was a criminal and their mother a survivor of a vile sexual assault.'

'I have heard stories about single mothers' unfair treatment by medical staff during the birthing process. If I sign the adoption papers, does this mean I will escape the cruelty?'

'I am shocked by your question. People tell horrid stories. There would be no difference to the medical help you receive if you do or don't sign the document, and if you were single or married.'

'Am I now in danger because you know what I know?'

'You are a brainy girl, but also foolish. Unless you sign this document, the medics will not examine your progress again before birthing. That could complicate your well-being and cause you to have a harrowing experience, particularly if the baby's head or shoulders become wedged against the bones of your pelvis.

'I am keeping my baby.'

'Beware of repeating our conversation. I wish you luck.'

'I will not put myself in danger by repeating this conversation.'

The viper moved her hands in a fashion that dismissed Maggie, who went straight to a toilet and vomited. It was almost time to catch the transport back to the hostel, so she waited at the entrance. As the little bus took off, Maggie decided to report this meeting with Lily, Bineham or Peter. That night, she lived in fear for her life because she didn't know how close the welfare officer, Hanna and Matron were or if Matron and Hanna were involved in baby trafficking. She whispered to Elizabeth that she should contact their church, Mrs Norris and Mrs Diana McLeod, whose addresses she provided, if anything happened to her.

Under Maggie and Hanna's supervision, the dayroom became a classroom. Chairs neatly lined up and a table set as a desk for Bineham; two chairs, one for him and the second for his helper. Hanna placed her pot of red geraniums on a stool next to the table.

All seated, and Bineham began.

'If you haven't met Matthew, he's the official choir-master at the church and unofficially my right hand. I'm sure you all know how to and how not to behave socially, but I doubt you've had much experience in the workforce. Most people believe that a family and a business are entirely different, but that is far from true. They are both families. In the family, the mother more often takes the role of Chief Executive Officer; her will is the law. In business, the Chief Executive Officer, or CEO, is in charge.

Much leniency is often given to a favoured apprentice, as seen in the family with the youngest child. The proof of my words will be in this gathering. Please raise your arm if you are the youngest in your family.'

There wasn't one show of hands.

'If you are the eldest in the family, please stand.'

All stood except one lady who lived in an orphanage until she turned fourteen.

'Sit, please. The eldest in a family is the least spoiled because as soon as that child begins walking, they must fetch their father's slippers, help in the garden and with housework. As the family grows, the eldest then shoulders the responsibility of looking after the younger children.

Business is the same as a family because it has the same construct: there is always a CEO answerable to no one at the top, who all others strive to please, particularly the Second in Command, commonly known as the 2ic. This latter individual is judgmental and often passive-aggressive. They guard their positions jealously and demand that others look up to them. In a small business, you may be interviewed for a position by the 2IC. We'll begin today's workshop with business manners, which will go far in gaining favour in your initial interview.'

Bineham divided the taller girls from the shorter girls.

'Trixie, Molly, Elizabeth, Maggie, you are the interviewer/Personnel Officer, and you are all small in stature. Will you sit? Shirley, Wendy, Suzie, and Daphne, you are the interviewees. Ladies, carefully review this situation and suggest changes that would have benefited the person interviewed. Will Matron introduce each girl to the Personnel Officer? I want you to show Matron some manners, then reintroduce yourself. Matthew will give an example.'

Matron spoke.

'Good morning, Miss Trixie. Mr Matthew Compton is here for his interview.'

Matthew looked at Matron and nodded his thanks. He took a couple of steps closer to Trixie, stopped, and spoke.

'Good morning, Miss Trixie. I'm pleased to meet you.'

Trixie stood, and it was strange to see that the boss was much smaller than Matthew. Bingham discontinued the interview.

'Think of the family; the parents are always taller than their children, which psychologically puts the parents in charge. In this case, the parent figure—the person taking the interview—is shorter than the child figure—the interviewee. Does anyone have ideas on how to make Trixie feel more important?'

Suzie.

'I'd bring myself to her size or lower; I'd ask if I may sit.'

Daphne.

'I'd say I'm quite tall. Perhaps we should both sit?'

Shirley.

'I'd just sit.'

Wendy.

'I'd say, Tiny lady, big job.'

Bineham.

All are correct, depending on the job, but not everyone would appreciate your sense of humour, Wendy. What if the interviewer doesn't appear to be friendly enough to ask if you can sit?'

Matron spoke.

'If I were interviewing, I would like the tall person to stand upright but show a decidedly unassuming but positive side to his/her nature.'

Throughout the first hour, Bineham put everyone through the interviewer and interviewee study. The girls were enthusiastic, gained confidence and a certain amount of elegance. Matthew called a fifteen-minute break while the church fellowship members carried in typewriters, registers, and official-looking books. At the same time, everyone quenched their thirst with a glass of water. Each lady chose what she'd like to learn for her future career and began practising. Matron had permitted the day room to permanently become a study library, much to Bineham's approval, so the machines stayed on-site on loan.

There was another study option: creativity. Maggie and Daphne signed up for that. Daphne wanted to become a tattoo artist, so Matthew gave her a physical anatomy book, a pad, a rubber, and pencils to begin her designs. Maggie produced the gift Mrs Norris had thoughtfully put together. On opening the box a second time, she reread the note.

*"Know your angel is with you. Believe in yourself, Maggie. Please find in this box jewellery wax, a carving toolset, and an instruction book. – Tea and biscuits are waiting when you come home. Sincerely, Mrs Norris."*

The tutors took their places with students who thirsted for their expertise. The church fellowship people instructed the typewriter and registered students. Matthew shared his artistic knowledge with Daphne while Bineham and Maggie settled into carving. She wanted to carve a seahorse because her baby would be born a Piscean. Bineham thought this a little ambitious for a first carving because of its complicated skeletal structure, so he suggested they work together on the form of a female torso —a less complex choice with flowing lines.

During the following month, talent exploded from Maggie's fingers. She completed the form she and Bineham had started together, and was working on her seahorse, which would one day be cast in gold to become a wearable pendant.

While carving, Bineham suggested that Maggie study an ancient treasure —a 5,000-year-old Chinese book of wisdom. It contained a tapestry of history, philosophy, morality, ethics, and science. Bineham introduced Confucius into the study because it was well known that Confucius lamented that if he had another fifty years to live, he would inquire more of the I. Ching to avoid error and become a living being without fault. Bineham vaulted Maggie's enquiring mind and insatiable appetite on natural forces and the cosmos.

Karin's workshops were attended by every mother-in-waiting, Matron, Bineham and Lily. They sat cross-legged on mats spread on the floor. Cushions supported legs not used to stretching. Karin explained that the method they were about to practice was as ancient as time, but Western medicine called it the new way. Children born through this method would be called Hypnobabes. Lily asked.

'Karin, the term hypnobabes suggests that somebody hypnotises the mother during the birthing process. Is that correct?'

'Good question, Lily. A professional hypnotist can be present, but it is mostly impractical and unnecessary. Instead, the mother learns to enter a state of light hypnosis, also called deep meditation. Self-hypnosis is a dream-like state that one can snap out of whenever one chooses. Initially, I will guide the meditation in which we shall practice relaxing the spine and deep breathing.'

'Miss Karin, my name is Trixie. How is self-hypnosis or meditation going to help us while we are suffering excruciating pain?'

'Hello, Trixie. Self-hypnosis and meditation can lift your mind to a level where you obliterate pain caused by anxiety through a state of tranquillity. The excruciating pain during childbirth is often, but not necessarily, an old wives' tale. Its roots are in ignorance of how a female should use her muscles during labour and delivery. Fear of the unknown causes a body to tense when it should be in a state of extreme relaxation. Self-hypnosis and meditation are tools that allow you to trust your body and let it function as nature intended. Shall we begin to understand meditation? Trixie, would you give everyone a candle holder and a candle from this box? Molly, will you take these matches and light each candle? Everyone, put your candle on a small table or something at eye level. You can lean against the wall for support if that gives you a sense of security. When you are settled and silent, I shall dim the lights in this room and lower my voice. I shall count to five.

One, concentrate on my voice and the flame.

Two, the flame is getting brighter.

Three, half-close your eyes, tilt your chin back, and watch the flame change shape. It is growing taller and pointed.

Four, breathe deeply and slowly, in and out, see the flame move slightly with your breath.

Five, concentrate on the flame and see that its light has expanded.

While watching the flame, stretch your fingers and your toes. Then relax them. Let your fingers and toes rest.

'Drop your chin, close your eyes and rest. I am going to count in reverse from five to one. Five, four, three, two, one. Open your eyes, blow out your candle. Stretch your hands, your fingers and your feet.' Talk among yourselves.'

There was silence, then Shirley asked.

'Karin, do you have time for us to repeat that exercise? I feel renewed, as though I've had a good sleep. I'm out to buy a candle as soon as possible.'

'Shirley, I understand and appreciate your enthusiasm, but please, everyone, do not do this exercise without my guidance until I give you the all-clear. We have a way to go; this is the beginning. Hands up those who had the same experience as Shirley, those who felt renewed?'

There was a show of all hands and excited chatter. Once more, their minds played with the candle's flame, but this time Karin led a guided meditation. She took them to the base of a stumpy hill. They wandered in the tall grass, searching for a gift they could touch, smell, or eat. They could hold it, wear it or ride on it. Then they thanked the gift, covered it with grass and walked back down the small hill to a shallow stream. They splashed their faces and washed their feet. Then, after the countdown from five to one. Karin asked each to recall their experience.

One person found a picnic basket, another a kitten and one an elephant. There was a moth that took Maggie for a ride on its back. Bineham found a Chinese coin tied to a Pekingese collar; Lily found an underground cavern, and Matron found a swan with a broken leg, which she healed with a touch! Karin was pleased, her pupils overjoyed.


Albert and Marj Piper were officially on holiday in Melbourne. They left Grandma Maggie in charge of the family in the Georges River house. Silva and Bertie were to attend to chores and care for Beth, Livia, and Lucy. The children thought Marj was expecting a baby for good reason. For months, she had been wearing a pillow stuffed under a maternity smock to fake pregnancy. Marj could now discard the pillow and go on a shopping spree for her new baby in the hotel suite that Albert had booked until approximately the end of March. A Sydney lawyer had previously secured an appointment with Matron under the pretence of enquiring about a particular female's wellbeing. But far from that, the Pipers wished to adopt her baby by any means, including donating a generous sum or settling on a predetermined cost. The female carrying the child was not to know of this appointment or a future arrangement.

Matron knew the many foul facets of the baby business, and she no longer wanted any part of it. If this had happened two months earlier, they would have met a woman with few ethics. But fate had put Matron on another path. Now reformed, she was a gladiatrix on the warpath against baby trafficking. She now firmly believed that every woman had a God-given right to be with her child and every child its natural mother. Matron shared the lawyer's letter with Matthew and took his advice on handling the situation.

Hanna met the Pipers at the door and guided them to Matron, seated in her office near the marble staircase. When the Pipers entered, Matron stood, asked them to sit, which they did. Their chairs were lower than hers, good, simple psychology. Matron had control of the conversation.

Good morning. I assume you are Mr and Mrs Piper?'

'A pleasure to meet you, Matron.'

'Mr and Mrs Piper, are you here to enquire about your daughter's health?'

Marj answered.

'And the baby. Is the baby due soon? Like in the next week, or do we have to wait till the end of the month?'

'Are you not interested in your daughter, Mrs Piper?'

Albert spoke apologetically.

'I'm sorry, Matron. My little wife loves babies. Of course, we're here to enquire about Peggy.'

"Why do you use the name, Peggy? Through conversing with her welfare officer in Sydney, we know that your daughter prefers Maggie, an accepted, short form of her birth name Magda. I have it on authority that you evicted her without a penny just before her thirteenth birthday.'

'She's always been a problem for my wife.'

'Strange because we have had no disagreements with her here, Mr Piper.'

Marj got impatient.

'I deserve a medal for taking her in. She was an unplanned love child, a Chanceling born to my widowed cousin, whom I never liked. As payment for my goodness, I must have that baby. Matron, you've received the letter from our lawyer; otherwise, we wouldn't be sitting here. Our children expect us to return with a new sibling. I've worn a pillow under a smock for months. She owes me that baby. We adopted her, clothed her, fed her and schooled her.'

'Not for long, it seems.'

Marj continued.

'The letter from our lawyer clearly states that as the parents of an underage mother and grandparents to this child, we are legal guardians of both.'

Matron felt repulsion for this woman.

'Any lawyer will tell you that a birth mother's right is to keep and nurture her child unless she chooses otherwise. Maggie is not putting her child up for adoption, Mrs Piper.'

Albert became assertive.

'She may want her way, Matron, but a court would show favour to us because we have the means and a home. She, as a single teenager, has neither. My wife and I prefer not to fight this in court. So perhaps we can come to an agreement which would benefit all?'

'I can't imagine what you're inferring, Mr Piper. Does this mean that I can tell Maggie that you will look after her and her child?'

'My wife only wants the baby. We ask that you or your staff contact us when the mother goes into labour. We are willing to pay for the inconvenience. Our lawyer advised us to speak to you rather than a hospital welfare officer who may have another couple selected for the adoption.'

Marj tried to be the concerned female.

'This baby is our flesh and blood.'

'Mrs Piper, I thought you said you adopted Maggie.'

'Well, yes, but she was born to my widowed cousin. There is a bloodline. She doesn't know she's not our child.'

'Mrs Piper, Mr Piper, are you here to help Maggie or purchase her baby?'

'That's a harsh accusation, Matron. My wife loves babies, and the child will have a good life.'

'And what of Maggie?'

Marj lost her temper.

'That baby is mine. And when we get it, she will not be allowed near it. She was born with the devil's imprint; we tried to beat it out of her, but failed. The proof is in her swollen belly.'

Matron stood, and so did Hanna, whom Matron had asked to witness the meeting.

'Maggie was drugged and raped. I am offended by your reference to underhanded money. Mr Piper, any morals you may have once possessed have been sucked out of you by this toxic woman, your wife. Our exchange has been most distasteful. Maggie has proven to be an outstanding individual and has contributed greatly to this hostel. Furthermore, it would be correct in the eyes of God if you did not break the maternal bond between mother and child. Good day, Mr and Mrs Piper.'

Matron turned her back, which sent them packing, but Hanna walked them up the street to their hired car. That night, Albert and Marj Piper were pleased with the secret arrangements they had made with Hanna. Life was easy when money spoke. Albert popped an invisible feather in the band of his Panama hat. Marj would have her baby.

# CHAPTER 18

*Dolphins, Dragons and a Man of The Cloth.*

Matron thought it unwise to upset a mother-in-waiting during her final weeks of confinement, so Maggie knew nothing of her parents' visit, nor was she aware they were in Melbourne waiting to pounce on her newborn. Matron was grateful that Mr Maison had handsomely paid Hanna to protect Maggie during labour and to ensure her babe was cradled in her arms. Then and only then would Matron inform Maggie of Marj and Albert Piper's callous behaviour.

The love Maggie felt for her baby was so intense that she was willing to adopt him out if those with life experience conceded it was correct. So, she had an in-depth discussion with Peter regarding his religious views, then called on Bineham's wisdom regarding the mental effects a child may endure without a father. She penned a note to Matron asking whether she may ask for her insight on single-parent social stigma and what exactly social stigma is. Matron invited Maggie to her office the following afternoon.

Matron didn't rise but asked Maggie to sit.

'I'm honoured that you desire my advice, Maggie. Social stigma is discrimination against any person with a lifestyle different from that of most other people. Through narrowed eyes, two parents, a man, and his wife, must be at the top of a family pyramid. Single parents, including widows and divorcees, are soft targets for those who criticise. These insufferable people have two weapons. Single women usually have less money to spend on their children because a woman's pay packet is smaller than a man's, even though they carry the same responsibilities. Secondly, employed mums have less free time to spend with their children than stay-at-home mums. Maggie, by the time your youngster will be of school age, professions previously thought exclusive to the male gender will engage females, and wages should begin to level.'

'Matron, I've heard that a child of an unwed woman is emotionally disadvantaged.'

'Disadvantaged? Maggie, they are more often doted on because there is no husband to compete with the woman's affection. I believe the single mum gives herself a hard time. She will worry that she hasn't had enough one-on-one time with her child, a worry with no substance because the child will be at school when the mother is working. Even stay-at-home mothers and children part at this time.'

'Matron, if I can't find a job within school hours?'

'You have been working for a few years, Maggie. Think back on your work hours. Would they fit your mother's schedule?' A couple of hours without a mother doesn't hurt, plus for little money or a favour, another mum will mind your child.'

'What can a man do that I can't?'

'Is there much difference between men and women? Think of bicycle riding, zoo trips, crossword puzzles, bird watching, studying the skies, our solar system, and the moon. You have had little practical education, so as your child progresses through schooling, you will learn too.'

'What if one day I meet a man my child doesn't like?'

'If that man doesn't win your child's heart, then he won't win your heart either.

Maggie, I'd like to take this opportunity to warn you against your parents influencing your child. You are at this hostel because Diana Page, who is now Mrs Austin-Webb, contacted me. She spoke highly of you and told me of the brutality you survived. She witnessed your development as a sympathetic person of integrity. I echo her judgment. You have decided to keep your baby, so I offer this advice: do not let Mr and Mrs Piper near your child. If you feel that grandparents would benefit, wait until the fifth birthday passes. By then, you will have established an unbreakable bond.'

'Thank you, Matron. One more question. Would you like to meet my baby? I'll understand if you say no.'

'Maggie, you are the first of my mothers-in-waiting to offer an introduction. With my heart, I answer yes. I shall cherish this honour.'

It was time for Maggie to plan her future. Until she and the baby settled, she wouldn't tell her Sydney friends or advise Miss Olessya in the beauty salon that she had decided to call Victoria her home state. She believed the community house was a great idea, so armed with money from gifts and savings, she made an appointment to meet with Lily.

'Lily, did you know the hostel girls plan to rent a small farm on the outskirts of Melbourne?'

'I do, and the idea has potential. I aim to locate the property and hopefully manage a deposit.'

'Lily, I have money in my silk bag.'

'Do you want to be part of the Community of Mothers? Think carefully; you have supportive friends in Sydney who will help find lodgings for you and your babe. A career with a future is in place.'

'If I stay in Melbourne and all goes well, I will have a ready-made home and nursery. As a chosen family, we will protect each other from the outside world. Would three hundred pounds help with a deposit?'

'Very much, but you may risk wasting your savings if the girls lose their babies in the system. Adoption without permission is not uncommon, nor is adoption with forced permission. Single mothers of newborns are harassed and threatened. Premature birth can cause death. Any of these would mean one housemate less, resulting in fewer mothers to carry household expenses.'

'Lily, I long to hold my baby, and so do the other girls. We have a purpose and an opportunity. I worry for Shirley, who has nothing. She must keep her baby as a memory of the family she lost. That makes at least two of us, counting the babies, four. Please accept my three hundred pounds. I shall still have money left to buy necessities. Shirley knows about second-hand shops and has a contact in the Salvation Army who may help us with furnishings.'

Lily was pleasantly amused.

'You're a stubborn lass. Shall I tell Shirley? Does Matron know of these plans?'

'Neither Matron nor Hanna has a clue, although I now believe we can trust Matron, but Hanna? Shirley, who's known Hanna for a long time, keeps clear of her, so I'm wary. Shirley will need a roof over her head before I do. Please put her heart at rest. I'm afraid to whisper in the hostel; the walls have ears.'


Karin Thomas, the Midwife Practitioner, held weekly workshops with the girls whose babies were imminent—Shirley, Elizabeth, Wendy, Maggie, and Daphne. They lay on flat tables in solid light. There was a recording of people chatting, occasional metal banging, and the disruptive sound of doors opening and closing.

'Ladies, this may be your harsh reality during labour and while birthing. Search the room and fix your eyes on a light. Imagine it to be the flame of a candle. Let your mind play with the flame, changing its shape, size, and colour. If you are distracted by the many noises, mentally gather them into a heap, cover them with a black cloth, and slide them under the table. Then return your attention to your light, see it as a flame and let it guide you to a place of your choice. Perhaps it is a mossy cave, a raft in the ocean, or a meadow.

Choose a voice to guide you through your meditation. Listen to that voice while you breathe rhythmically and deeply. Know you are safe. You are in a state of self-hypnosis. You are as light as a feather, free from worry and in a state of wonder. You have the honour of giving life to a child. You are in a pleasurable situation, safe and loved. You are now ready to accept guidance.'

Karin continued to make unexpected noises until all five pupils could eliminate them from their minds. She guided the ladies in techniques to relax muscles and gain personal power through breath and relaxation. Karin repeated training until all five were masters of their bodies and could enter and exit self-induced hypnotherapy.

Maggie was on hospital duty serving lunches when she felt the first pains of labour. In the bus returning to the hostel, it radiated down her legs. She changed, ran to the phone box, and spoke to Una.

'Una, you told me to call when it started. Una, I'm terrified.'

Una spoke with authority: 'During the Chinese occupation of Tibet, tortured Buddhist monks escaped extreme agony through meditation. Pain is part of birthing, but with Karin's training, yours will not be savage. My thoughts are with you, my sister in spirit. I'll begin a healing and birthing meditation in one hour and shall repeat it until I see all is well. The wind, the oceans and dolphins are at your service.'

Hanna accompanied Maggie to the hospital labour ward, where she signed her in, then left, saying she'd return in a trice. But Hanna telephoned Marj and Albert Piper to advise them that their baby was on the way.

In the ward, Maggie mentally called Una. She focused on a wall light, which became a candle that gradually faded into the background, leaving only the flame. Maggie asked White Feathers to send the desired energy her way and to protect her child from birthing forces that could cause harm. She breathed deep and slow, in and out, to gather her fear, compress it into a ball, wrap it in royal blue velvet and send the bundle to space. She then dissolved into deep meditation.   Una's voice came loud and clear.

> *'It is a pleasure to be working with you.*
> *We are not happy to see you on the verge of fear.*
> *Concentrate on our voices, they ride on the wind, the wind.*
> *The wind is at your back, supporting you as though you are on a raft in the sea.*

*The wind is from the sea, from the mineral-rich sea.*
*The raft is keeping you safe, the wind helping you breathe slowly and deeply.*
*Hear the soft lapping of the water against your raft.*
*Consciously match your intake and output of air to the pulse of the water.*
*Rhythmic breathing maximises the oxygen available to you and your baby.*
*Release all physical tension from your head to your toes.*
*Slow, controlled breathing, rhythmic breathing, focus on your breathing.*
*Your body is absorbing magnesium-rich seawater.*
*Magnesium is essential for pelvic muscle function.*
*Your muscles are getting ready for movement, contraction, and relaxation.*
*Your body is absorbing magnesium, which is vital for relaxing back muscles and reducing muscular tension.*
*You are on a raft in the ocean. The wind is rocking your raft.*
*Through your raft, you are absorbing the healing power of the sea.*
*Hear the soft, whooshing noise as water laps at your raft, your raft floating in the ocean.*
*Breathe deeply, inhale the smell of saltwater.*
*The essence of life is from the sea.*
*The wind whispers its secrets to help you relax.*
*Listen to the voices calling, calling your subconscious mind, your imagination, your body.*
*Sink into relaxation and follow our voice in this guided meditation.*
*Invite your higher self to help you follow instructions.*
*Continue your rhythmic breathing.*
*Dolphins are waiting, waiting for you to relax.*
*A family unit of Dolphins—an aquatic pre-birthing ring—is waiting.*
*You will know their tenderness.*
*Concentrate on your spine.*
*Focus on the lower half of your spine. Unroll each vertebra.*
*Breath in through your nose and out through your mouth,*
*Relax your jaw, part your lips, breath deep and slow.*
*Visualise your breath on a thread of gold, travelling to the distant horizon.*
*Close your lips and breathe deeply, deeply in through your nostrils.*
*Listen.*

*A pod of chattering dolphins gathers to prepare your body to give birth.*
*The leading dolphins approach your raft. Silently, purposely gliding through the water, two dolphins approach your raft.*
*You feel a soft nudge.*
*One dolphin is on your right, the other on your left.*
*They support your raft; dolphins are calling to other dolphins.*
*Dolphins to guard you and your baby against harm.*
*Breathe rhythmically, see the dolphins, and enjoy their unexpected smiles.*
*Inhale the healing properties of the ocean.*
*Seawater is rich in magnesium, zinc, iron, calcium, and potassium, Minerals to ensure fast recovery from the stress of childbirth.*
*Fine gossamer spray touches your body, kisses your face.*
*Feel your body absorb the moisture of fine sea spray.*
*The dolphins have circled your supportive raft, firmly held steady by the wind.*
*Water droplets lifted by the wind cool the heat in your belly.*
*The Dolphins have formed around you, a floating circle in the sea,*
*The gently pulsating sea.*
*You are secure in the ring of dolphins in the ocean.*
*They turn their bodies slowly, heads close to your raft, close to you.*
*Relax on your raft, floating.*
*Your raft is safe. The dolphins bring peace.*
*From the crown of your head, a purple thread spins to the crown of the dolphin on your right.*
*From that dolphin, the strand flies to the next dolphin's head, to the next, to the next, until the circle joins.*
*Together with you and bound to each other by a fine, purple thread.*
*Feel that colour feed your mind, your imagination.*
*Purple dislodges cobwebs, dissolves worry, and makes way for clarity of thought.*
*A royal-blue ribbon is spinning from the centre of your forehead.*
*The ribbon has attached itself to the centre of the forehead of the dolphin on your right.*
*From there, it travels to the next dolphin, to the next, to the next, clockwise, always clockwise.*
*The Royal blue thread continues its journey until the circle is closed.*
*Dolphin and man joined with dancing threads of royal blue and purple.*

*Enjoy the incredible feeling of being one with the unit of dolphins, beings who live in the sea.*

*You may wonder. Does a small dolphin have less sensitivity than a large dolphin?*
*Is a fish more critical to the planet than a bird?*
*Does a giant get hungrier than a dwarf?*
*Is the value of a child's mind less than that of an adult?*
*Should a lamb die to feed the mother of a human baby?*

*Breathe deeply and with rhythm, continue to spin the purple thread from your crown and the iridescent royal blue from the centre of your forehead.*

*From your throat, a strand of blue-green is searching for the throat of the dolphin on your right.*

*The wheeling, twisting turquoise thread* joins *dolphin to dolphin, and dolphin to you until the circle is closed. The softly coloured blue-green is aloft in the sea breeze, connecting all throats to throats, the seat of communication.*

*The dolphin on your left asks you to accept an emerald-green thread coiling from the centre of her chest.*

*Let the spidering thread anchor itself in the centre of your chest, then watch it fly clockwise to the dolphin on your right.*

*From the sea's healing circle, a bright emerald-green thread spirals clockwise from chest to chest, joining all at the heart energy point.*
*A sacred circle has created pure harmony.*

*Above you, threads of yellow, orange, and red* are *held aloft by the wind.*

*They are spinning and dancing to the lower half of the Dolphin bodies in the circle, then to you.*

*These colours do not stay long; the sea has strengthened these energy points so the red, orange and yellow are spinning back from whence they came.*

*Your healing is nearing its completion.*
*Purple to the centre of the crown at the top of the head.*
*Royal blue to the centre of the forehead,*
*Turquoise to the throat, emerald to the chest.*
*The purpose of the wind at your back, your raft, and the dolphins is complete.*
*Stay calm, breathe with purpose, with a slow, deep rhythm,*
*You are ready to accept the beginnings of birthing, and you have the honour of bringing a new life, spirit and soul into the world.*
*The wind has softened, but it remains at your back, supporting you.*

*The wind of change.*
*New life has had the privilege of forming in your womb.*
*Fire Dragon and Water Dragons accompany birth.*
*The Fire Dragon is your baby's guardian; the Water Dragon is the lord of your baby's world while in the womb.*
*Do not be afraid; your body is healthy; your mind is vital.*
*Your body is prepared, and your energy points are in balance.*
*It is time for the Fire and Water Dragons to prepare your baby for exit from his water-world and enter earth and air.*
*We, who have guided you through meditation, must leave you to motherhood.*
*We close with love, unconditional love.*
*We ask that you remain in your meditative state.*

  Maggie's belly became a cavern where a Fire Dragon was jealously guarding a large, perfect pearl. The pearl had an energy of its own and began rocking. The movement assumed the need for freedom. This caused flames to fly from the Dragon's eyes. Maggie's muscles contracted to escape the heat, which caused her stomach and groin to suffer intense cramps. Exhausted, she relaxed and breathed rhythmically.

Again and again, the pearl battled the Dragon for release, its struggle sending cramps shooting through her back and lower stomach, always ending in debility, but Maggie stubbornly kept breathing slowly and deeply.

The previously unseen Water Dragon showed itself coiled around the cavern's inner walls.

This Dragon wanted to help the pearl escape, so it discharged fluid that gathered momentum, forming waves. The Fire Dragon initiated combat. Still grasping the pearl, it darted, dropped to a low, then flew to a high. The pain was devouring Maggie's flesh; she heard herself scream. The Water Dragon doused the fire, causing the Fire Dragon to shrink, its body just able to secure its jewel.

At lightning speed, the Dragons changed places. Now the pearl was surrounded by water. It floated. It changed shape and pushed against Maggie's back. An ocean was in her belly, surging, causing waves to rush toward the entrance to the cavern, taking the pearl with it. The

Fire Dragon flew back, twisted its body around the pearl, then clutched it with clawed hands.

The Water Dragon slipped out of the cavern and dissolved. Maggie felt warm water rushing out of her. The Fire Dragon was still and content, holding its pearl in its belly. Fatigue took control. The mother allowed unconsciousness to take over because it was the closest thing to death without hurting her child within.

Maggie woke but didn't want to open her eyes or show any sign of life. Nearby, she could hear a woman begging to see her newborn baby—to know whether it was a boy or a girl and whether it was perfect and healthy. She prayed for her baby, and she cried for her baby. Maggie heard a sharp slap, and the new mother went into choking sobs, then fell silent. Maggie listened to a man's speech.

'This one had it tough. Great lesson, I'll bet we won't see her again. Has she got milk? You know what to do, then get her out of here. Stitch her, she's not married, so no pain relief.'

Maggie couldn't pretend to be asleep any longer. The pain was wracking her body. Between contractions, she sought the light, which became a candle. She once again concentrated on the flame, which expanded to show her womb as a cavern.

The Water Dragon had left a silvery trail around the walls, and the pearl seemed content in the tightly coiled body of the Fire Dragon. Something odd was happening. Although the Water Dragon had expelled its fluid when it left, deep waves, empty of water, began surging inside her belly, each slowly rising, oscillating to a peak, then gradually dropping to a lull. The pearl tried to escape the grip of the Fire Dragon. Together they pushed against her back, jerking, arresting her lower body. The Dragon stretched one of its clawed fingers, which stuck in her groin. Maggie heard herself scream, which brought her out of meditation. A human voice told her to shut up, that this was nothing to what was coming.

Maggie thought she was going to explode; she felt her belly, and it was rock hard. The Dragon rose and flared, consuming her insides, twisting while whizzing in eastward circles. The contractions were intense, radiating from her spine to the front of her core. Maggie redirected her mind to her baby and went deep into each contraction, matching each spasm with measured breath. She almost passed out, pulled herself back, located the pearl and the Dragon, found the energy that connected her to them and focused on her baby's health.

Her legs cramped, and she felt sick. The Fire Dragon was descending, exiting from the cavern face down, the pearl wrapped in its tail. She helped the Dragon push toward the exit and felt her body unfold and expand as the Dragon and the pearl forced a path through an impossible tunnel. She felt an injection, and all went dark. Parts of her body were burning—ice-cold burning.

Following the medically administered, mind-altering barbiturate that knocked her unconscious, Maggie regained awareness not in a hospital wing but in a cold, glassed-in veranda. She couldn't find her brain. She thought she was a sparrow but reasoned that she would have flown away if she were a real-live bird. Therefore, she must be a paper sparrow. She would have to wait for someone to open a window, then the wind could scoop her up and carry her to safety. But on concentration, she saw that the windows weren't the opening type because they were locked, and someone had stuck them with putty. Maggie closed her eyes and sank back into a state where there was no interruption, no noise of other females sobbing.

Matron worried because Hanna hadn't shown for dinner. She'd accompanied Maggie to the hospital labour ward, and eleven hours had passed. Perhaps Hanna was doing the job the Maison's had paid her to do. Or perhaps not. Matron remembered Hanna had escorted Albert and Marj Piper to their car. Hanna had taken her time returning and then carried a smug expression. Hanna had been present when Albert had hinted at the monetary reward for information on Maggie's birthing. Matron telephoned Bineham, who telephoned Peter.

The decision was unanimous. Peter, dressed in the cloth of a man of God, would hold more clout than anyone else entering a hospital in the early hours of the morning.

The nurses went into a flurry. In their wards before dawn, a church minister was demanding that he visit one of the single mothers held on the detention veranda, where only staff and police were allowed!

Lily had given Peter a detailed map of corridors to follow, so he didn't wait for a nursing guide; he began his journey through the labyrinth. He came to the glassed-in veranda and found the door locked and barred. Peering through the glass, he saw predominantly young women crying, praying, some restrained, others unconscious. They were wretched. Maggie was prone on a shabby bed half-covered with a rag blanket.

In the opposite ward, women were sleeping in comfortable beds, with cots beside them, either holding babies or ready to accept them from the morning staff.

A nurse tapped his arm.
'Do you know someone in there, Sir?'
'Open this door. Immediately. Why is it locked and barred?'
'They might escape, Sir, before they've signed adoption papers.'
'Open the door.'

Peter held his fury. It had been many years since he'd felt this emotion. Was it anger or disgust? This horrendous persecution was punishment for falling victim to the opposite sex. Yet, these women have honoured the life within because they did not abort their unwanted embryos. Instead, they courageously faced hardship and social injustice while carrying the child of a man who betrayed them. For the blameless child, they accepted the inescapable pain of birthing. Yet somebody stole the fruit of their womb for penance. That heinous act is beyond redemption. It is against the law of nature, which awards the mother and the newborn the pleasure of bonding. Why had uncivilised savagery in his parish been kept from him?

Peter contained himself. He cleared his head of thunder. The nurse standing beside him was not to blame. He thanked her with a nod, then went to Maggie. He took her hand. A nearby female pleaded with him for help. The police had told her that she would be locked up in an asylum if she didn't sign adoption papers. No woman had seen her baby or knew if she had given birth to a girl or a boy. Maggie stirred. Peter continued to hold her hand.

A man appeared beside Peter.

'Don't pity them, Sir. They are an immoral lot, a danger to society. There would be little doubt that their offspring have inherited unstable characteristics. The sexual activities of these Jezebels are a moral danger to themselves and others; they must be punished and separated from their babies.'

'I will go to the highest authority and report this fiendish barbarity. For the moment, I am particularly interested in Maggie and her newborn.'

'Are you the father? Of the baby, I mean, Sir.'

'Go away before I do something against my vocation. I demand that you immediately bring a hospital welfare officer, a doctor, and a nurse. Send warm blankets, and do not lock that door. Ladies, please stay where you are for your safety. I am Peter, a man of The Cloth.'

# CHAPTER 19

The Community of Mothers.

The three hundred pounds Maggie gave Lily enabled them to secure a small farm in the Yarra Valley. A stone's throw from Nellie Melba's Estate in *Coldstream*, 36 km northeast of Melbourne. Peter's parishioners gifted the "Community of Mothers" a cleverly thought-out living. It was a one-year lease on the local Railway Café with an option to renew. The ladies would supply home-grown fruits and veggies in pies and cakes, sold with non-alcoholic liquid refreshments to travellers.

As planned, Shirley and Peanut were the first to make it their home. Elizabeth, Daphne, and Wendy with babies were soon to join her in the rambling four-bedroom cottage. Maggie would take up residence in one of the small outbuildings.

Two days after Maggie gave birth, Albert Piper delivered an envelope for Maggie and another for Hanna. Maggie's envelope had a law firm logo; Hanna's showed the Piper Building Construction firm's stationery. To Matron, this was a red flag. Marj Piper wanted that baby, and Maggie's newborn was missing. Hanna was one of the few who knew Maggie had given birth, and she had previously spent time alone with the Pipers. Hanna must have been both informant and thief.

Matron called Lily, who told Matron that a hospital welfare officer had accused her of spiriting Maggie's baby away. According to the officer, a couple with a financial interest had previously booked him.

Matron knew Hanna had accepted a bonus from the Maisons, promising to stay with Maggie during labour and keep her little one safe. Now, Matron was certain that Hanna had taken another, and a more significant, cash reward for alerting Albert and Marj Piper to the birth. Probably more again for moving the newborn from the adoption cribs to the family nursery and marking Marj Piper's name on the little boy's identification tag. Hanna would have cut ties with the crime by employing an innocent midwife to deliver the baby to Marj and Albert Piper at their hotel.

Now, to Matron's surprise, Hanna returned to the Home for Mothers-In-Waiting to continue her trusted post as welfare officer. Matron confronted her. Hanna unconscionably complained that she didn't profit much because a significant amount went toward paying a hospital attendant and a labour nurse. She considered herself innocent because baby farming was a regular practice, a payment made to accept an infant's custody. Matron called the police and had Hanna physically removed from the building on a charge of human trafficking. After a discussion with Lily, Matron revealed Hanna's treachery to Maggie.

Maggie was strong enough to leave the nursing home where Peter had transferred her and the other veranda prisoners. She had become mentally close to Bineham, so Peter chose him to drive Maggie to the farm. Bineham was concerned because Maggie was the only mother Peter could not reunite with her baby, so he gladly picked her up, but remained on guard in case plans needed to change.

He worried as Maggie showed no signs of grief, yet Lily had informed her that the Pipers had her baby and were travelling to Sydney about a week after he was born, probably four days hence. Maggie was low-key but smiling, thankful to be looked after, and even asked him to help her choose and then purchase three personal changes of clothing, after which they bought a takeaway lunch and ate it while sitting on the banks of the Yarra. It was then that he handed her the officially stamped envelope Albert Piper had left with Matron.

Bineham observed Maggie closely as she absorbed the contents. She read it twice, showing no reaction, slowly folded it, returned it to the envelope, asked him to read it, stood up and walked to the edge of the bank.

Bineham was shocked. The tone and intentions of the document told him all he needed to know about her past. Bineham walked to her, then stopped short. She stood straight-backed, facing the river, arms raised, palms open to the sun, her fingers moving as though filtering the March wind. Softly, she spoke.

'White Feathers, lend me your wisdom. Send a guard to keep my baby safe. Thank you to the spirit beings who support me in my time of need. \*\**TathAstu*, so be it.'

Then she almost lost her balance. Bineham moved quickly, steadied, and lowered her to the grassy bank. Her eyes were wide and wet, but tears didn't flow. She repositioned herself in the Bhagavad Gita meditation pose, sitting straight, her spine aligned between heaven and earth, legs crossed, the soles of her feet open to the sky, palms open, middle fingers touching her thumbs.

Until now, he had wondered at her bravery. Now he knew that it wasn't bravery but acceptance —a condition that went hand in hand with the teachings of the Gita and those with a knowledge of Sanskrit. Someone had versed her in the ancient practice of Hinduism, Buddhism or Jainism. Bineham recalled a conversation they once had about God. Maggie did not believe that one deity had created everything. That ideology sprang from man's arrogant belief that God had created man in His form. The soul was not exclusive to humans; all things living have an immortal soul. The universe and its matter have always existed, and therefore Godliness, not God, was inherent in every organism. Maggie's intent to work towards Godliness was apparent as she refused to eat flesh or dairy. Bineham was pleased that he had followed his heart by introducing her to the I. Ching. He must take her studies further.

Maggie pulled out of her meditation, brushed the fringe back from her eyes and stood. She took his arm, and they strolled to his car.

'Thank you, Bineham. Do you have time to take me to the old farm? If not, I'll catch public transport.'

'No public transport for you, princess.

'Bineham, I need to consult the I. Ching and I need to put the finishing touches on my seahorse. Are you available in the coming two weeks?'

'Maggie, is this the calm before the storm?'

'I can see one shortly. I don't know what my baby boy looks like, so I may check when Sydney planes depart, then stake out the airport. Would it be too much to ask to speak to someone familiar with the law on these matters?'

The next day, Maggie travelled by public transport to Melbourne. She strolled through the botanical gardens before her appointment with Peter's lawyer.

'G'Day, Maggie Piper. I'm here to help. My name is Thomas. I believe you have a document. Thank you. Please take a seat while I review. Coffee?

Before Maggie could answer, coffee with biscuits arrived. Thomas took stock of the contents, considered it while doodling on paper with a pen, excused himself, then returned with a lady he introduced as Ellie, his secretary. She touched Maggie's arm, then sat reasonably close, showing female support.

Thomas began the conversation.

'Maggie, have you nursed your child?'

'No, a corrupt person separated us at birth. I don't even know if my baby has arms and legs or hair on his head.'

'I assume you have read and understood the threat in the letter attached to this document? If you do not legally sign your child to Mr and Mrs Piper, they plan to make it known to your child, his school, his classmates' parents, and neighbours that his father committed carnal knowledge, that he drugged and raped you. How important is this to you?'

'It is of significant concern; such information made public would cause social stigma and shovel shame on his head.'

'Regarding the violation you experienced, have the police approached you yet?'

'No. Perhaps because it happened in New South Wales.'

'It takes time and much red tape to mete justice when the victim and assailant are in different states. Could you have been sent to Victoria to aid the perpetrator's cause?'

'I hope not. The people who knew may have found it wise to shelve the matter for my sake. The doctors in Sydney told me that they would not report the case until I was strong enough to face possible accusations and embarrassing questions. The Pipers have cunningly chosen that injustice to blackmail me, so for my son's sake, I shall try to suppress charges. But, Thomas, I'd like to know what chance, if any, I have of retrieving my baby. Can these rotten people be jailed for conspiracy and for being receivers of human trafficking?'

'Your case would stand. Your parents could be found guilty but not jailed, as they are parents with dependent small children. Because they are your parents and your child's grandparents, and they own permanent housing and have a comfortable bank account, there is a fair chance the Pipers may gain custody. I have been informed that Mrs Piper wore a pillow under her dress to pretend she was pregnant to their family and neighbours. The idea being that their other children are eagerly expecting to have a new brother or sister.'

Maggie nodded.

'Matron at the hostel took note of that. My mother was pretending publicly.'

'Then Marj Piper's long-term planning and deceit would be in your favour if you have the financial means to fight them legally.'

'I do not.'

'How did your baby fall into the hands of your parents?'

'The hostel welfare officer accompanied me to the labour ward. Unbeknownst to myself and Matron, she had received payment from the Pipers to employ accomplices within the hospital to hide him, then a midwife to deliver him to their hotel. I'm referring to them as the Pipers because I cannot call them my parents.'

'Understandably. My duty as your lawyer is not to your parents or society. It is to you, my client. If I may offer advice?'

'Please, Thomas.'

'Maggie, it is evident that you have little choice, and it is equally apparent that there are future problems to consider if you sign this document. Marj and Albert Piper stipulate that you must never contact your child or visit their home or the school they will attend. You will have nothing to do with his upbringing. You will waive all rights as his mother. Maggie, understand they intend to cut you out of his life. If you agree to sign, these people will not only take your baby, but they will also take your child's first steps, birthdays, his ups, and his downs. His children will be their grandchildren. This document is airtight and ruthless. Its purpose is to curb your son from following instincts he may have toward his natural mother. Such people will poison his mind against you. You will lose him forever.

Maggie, they state they are your parents. You were born in 1939, a period when correct information on birth certificates was not mandatory. Some still believe that an adopted child should be ignorant of their true parentage. Are you the eldest child in their family?'

'Yes.'

I question whether Marj Piper is your birth mother. Some women have a greedy obsession for babies and no fondness for children. That being known, it is still inconceivable that one who has experienced the sacred bond between mother and newborn would plot to steal another's child. I also doubt Albert Piper is your natural father because a man's instinct is to protect his daughter, even against a controlling wife. These people show no moral compass, no empathy. By the sovereignty of the family, they should have offered to help you keep your baby. Yet they insist on legal adoption forbidding you to have any say in his life and robbing your son of his birthright to bond with his mother.'

'Thomas, I do not doubt the vindictiveness of Marj Piper nor of Albert Piper's ability to carry out her wishes. They have sworn to hurt my child by feeding him knowledge of his father's criminal actions if I do not sign him over to them. She is unrelenting, and he will obey her wishes. For my son's well-being, I have no choice.'

'Think carefully, Maggie. You have qualities that should take you far in life. You are not quite sixteen years old, yet you have clear communication and more wisdom than my grandmother; you need a career, perhaps an apprenticeship. I'm sure you could find your way even with your baby. Others will say that in time, the anguish and pain of losing your first child will diminish. They will tell you that you have your whole life ahead of you. Do you believe you will forget? I am asking you to think about yourself and your child, for your future, for his future. Whatever your decision, there is an immediate matter of his birth certificate.'

'I will name Greg Vasilakis as his father. That will give my son as an adult every chance to discover his Greek heritage.'

'Maggie, are you sure that you do not want that man charged with your violation?'

'If I proceed or let justice take its course, society will shame my son. I would rather him believe he was a child conceived through love. A baby in the womb is intuitive; they feel their mother's emotions, so I showered him with protection and love while carrying.'

'Maggie, that leaves the question of whether you sign this document.'

'Thomas, I see no alternative. I shall watch from afar. Information will come to me, and I shall take action, which will be hell-bound if they harm him as they have harmed me. Can you make it legally binding that government officials do not create a Closed Adoption record?'

'I shall do my best, Maggie, but the secrecy and deceit of closed adoption are still practised and allowed according to Federal law.'

'Thomas, I sign on the condition that I choose my son's two given names. He is Lincoln Pilgrim. I shall devote a greater part of my life to proving through actions that I am worthy of being his mother. I swear my son will know me.'

'I'm sure he will.'

***Coldstream** is a township 36 km northeast of Melbourne's central business district. The township developed around the railway station after the railway arrived in 1888. In 1909, Dame Nellie Melba bought Coombe Cottage at Coldstream.*

## CHAPTER 20

*The gifts, the gift, the wall and the sparrow.*

  Maggie stood at the converted barn entrance, watching Shirley arrange flowers in a glass bottle and Elizabeth hang a framed tapestry that read "Welcome home, Maggie". Their babies were sleeping in big wooden crates lined with soft blankets. The scene was domestic, the atmosphere blissful. They were oblivious to Maggie's presence because she wasn't expected to return for a few hours. She left the ladies to their thoughtful decor while she explored the property. Grandma Maggie used to look for signs that pointed to the possible outcome of a new venture. If she was correct, this Community of Mothers had to be a raging success. Lilies were one of Maggie's favourite flowers. Peter's welfare officer, whose name was Lily, secured the property with money from Maggie, who was always in a happy state when listening to the glorious voice of Nellie Melba, whose Victorian estate, titled Lilydale, was nearby. There was room for five expectant mothers to live here. The number five is unbreakable and holds strength and protection centred between the single-digit numbers one to nine.

In the far corner of the paddock, a hive of human activity was erecting a sizable wire enclosure. On closer inspection, it turned out to be a poultry pen. Nearby, brown feathered hens in holding cages were clucking to be released. Men were unloading a little truck that was buckling under the weight of building materials and straw.

Maggie continued to wander the paddocks while reflecting on the significance and outcome of her meeting with Peter's lawyer when a female voice shouted.

'Hey, watch it. I've just planted that.

'Sorry, I wasn't looking. What is it?'

A cherry tree. Are you doing anything? It won't hurt to get a bit of dirt on your hands. You've got a choice. Strawberries, they're easy, slip them out of their pots and pop them in a hole in the straw mound, or you can dig in cherry trees. You look a bit lean in muscle. Stick to the berries.'

A great idea. Maggie needed contact with *Gaia. She sat on the ground between two raked rows packed high with sweet-smelling straw and planted strawberries. Nobody knew her; she was just one of the workers.

'Where do you come from, cos you're not one of us. We're from Peter's church. Bineham, Matthew and Matron are in the house. Are you with them?'

'I like being with you now. My name is Maggie.'

'Maggie? Sweet Jesus, are you the one who lost her baby to a trafficker?'

The unexpected question and confronting reality took Maggie to the breaking point. The heavens opened, and buckets of tears streamed down her face, drenching her blouse and muddying her earth-covered hands. She sprang up, ran unthinkingly, reached the gate, and stopped. She almost bumped into a man as he entered.

His instinct was to hold her, but his calling curbed such action. Peter firmly took her elbow, then guided Maggie to a pile of fence posts stacked horizontally. They acted as a seat. He watched as the dishevelled, broken doll transformed into a tangible female. Maggie straightened from a slump, wiped her hands clean on the inside of her skirt, finger-combed her hair, held her head high and regained composure. It was touching and almost funny. But Peter didn't laugh; she was vulnerable.

'Thank you, Peter, for allowing me to consult with Thomas, your lawyer. I saw him this morning.'

'He's spoken to me.'

'I tried to think like you and Bineham when making my decision.'

'Your resolve was wise. Your only alternative was to plan a kidnapping, steal Lincoln back, hijack an aircraft, fly to Vienna, and disappear into the woods. You would have lived in a cave, slept on bracken, and killed wild animals for their skin and flesh. Messy business. My apologies, I forgot you don't wear leather or eat meat.'

Maggie was stunned until she saw Peter's eyes crinkle in a smile. She responded by feigning horror at his alternative solution. They both laughed, then walked towards the cottage. For precious moments, they were earth-freed spirits floating above the land.

The cottage was inviting, flooded by the aroma of freshly baked bread. Proof of its deliciousness, three almost-eaten loaves accompanied by a few slices of cucumbers on the trestle table. The mothers were fussing around their guests, Matron nursing Wendy's Alice, named after her, with Matthew standing close; they made an attractive couple. Bineham spoke.

'Maggie, I saw you sitting, playing gardener. You're wet and covered in dirt. Glad you've got a change of clothing. What happened?'

'I think it started to rain. I still don't know what my baby looks like, and I guess I never shall. But my heart is singing. This home for the Community of Mothers is more than wondrous. They will be happy with healthy babies, and in no time, shall earn a tidy living from café sales. Peter, these people — your church community — have godliness. And you, Matron, Matthew, Bineham and Peter, cancel society's wickedness through good deeds.'

Matron teased.

'Even me? I hope you truly include me, Maggie.'

Builders hadn't finished the bathroom in the barn, so that night, Maggie had a bush shower in a tiny makeshift room under the stars. Some inventive person had fashioned walls of bagging around four standing posts. Crossbeams stabilised them; flat stones flagged the floor. Showering happened after the person standing under a suspended bucket pulled a plug from its base. Not exactly elegant, but it did the job.

Bineham regularly came to Coldstream. His primary purpose was to teach Maggie I. Ching's decision-making guidance. "The Book of Changes", also titled the "I. Ching", had been used for centuries to forecast events. Bineham advised Maggie against using the text for this purpose until she fully understood the Characters' attributes. To demonstrate its accurate forecasting, Bineham asked the oracle if Maggie should stake out the airport. The ancient book advised strongly against this, warning that harm would come to her through confrontation. The likely result would be Maggie's innocence and youth being overpowered by dishonourable adults. Bineham had a hunch that her desire was overwhelming, and nothing would stop her. If so, she would learn the value of advice from The Book of Changes. Peter, always in the background, would be there for her.

Maggie made no secret of her return to Sydney. She was disturbed every time she heard a baby cry and knew that her misfortune called for the girls to tiptoe in her presence. She craved her recorded music. Beethoven's String Quartet was waiting on a disc, while Brunhilda's Ride of the Valkyries would encourage bravery. She longed to sup tea with Mrs Norris while marvelling at Nellie Melba singing Ave Maria. Benjie needed a walk, and Maria was waiting to tell her unique stories. Una would be in India, but her Yoga school was undoubtedly still in session. Maggie's resolve to leave Coldstream strengthened when Daphne arrived with Bonny, her baby girl. Maggie overheard Elizabeth ask Daphne to refrain from fussing in Maggie's presence or offering her baby a cuddle.

Staying in the company of mothers, being constantly charmed by the ever-smiling Peanut, whom Elizabeth named after Peter, Daphne's doll-like daughter, and Wendy's Alice with her ribboned shock of black hair, Maggie decided to do something she would regret. Against I. Ching's advice, against Bineham's wishes, Maggie found the hotel where Marj and Albert Piper held her baby hostage. Knowing they were travelling to Sydney when Lincoln had passed his first week out of her womb, she researched their outdate then waited at the airport two hours before they boarded the only scheduled flight.

Marj and Albert arrived, accompanied by Hanna and a midwife carrying Lincoln. They found seats, and the midwife put Lincoln in Marj's arms. Marj was in a state of complete happiness, once more the centre of attention; she played the little lady with her newborn, smiling at passing people and showing Maggie's baby's tiny feet and hands. Maggie heard Albert say that he was proud of his brave little woman who gave him their second son.

It was a downright lie and sickening. If Maggie had the power, she would have turned the man she once called father into a pillar of salt. Lincoln was her baby, and she was desperate to know his face, which medics had forcibly stopped her seeing at birth. Marj and Albert Piper had used every dirty trick to ensure possession. Hopefully, they would let her touch him; after all, Marj was a mother and should understand her need. Maggie walked toward them. Her baby was close, very close. Marj screamed, and Hanna laughed. Albert shouted for the police, who came in a trice. Albert pointed to Maggie and told them she was trying to kidnap their baby and that his wife needed protection.

Two burly police officers forced their open palms under Maggie's armpits and jerked her high in the air, her feet dangling above the ground. They lifted her to a holding room, then threatened to take her to jail after being charged with attempted abduction. She told them that she only wanted to look at her baby. Maggie began to shake uncontrollably. Her throat contracted, and she almost lost consciousness. She was half dragged to another room, shoved onto a bed, and left with a female in an airport uniform. When Maggie tried to sit up, the woman pushed her backward and then stood over her.

A knock, the door opened, and an officer appeared with the midwife. She remembered Maggie from the hospital. She didn't know for sure, but the timing was right. Maggie had given birth about a week ago, and the child had to be at least 1 week old before travelling. The Pipers had adopted, so perhaps it was Maggie's baby. One policeman asked Maggie for her surname. On hearing it, he wondered if they were her parents. The midwife saved Maggie by asking,

'Would your parents do that to you?'

The midwife had understood the situation. Her sympathy went to the young woman. She and her child had been victims of child trafficking. She drove Maggie to Coldstream, and the Community of Mothers gained a new and valuable supporter.

Bineham was refining the spiny plates on Maggie's wax seahorse when he realised its valuable purpose. She was creating a piece of custom jewellery. The wax shape was a pattern destined to form a mould. In time, a silversmith would pour molten silver or gold into it, wait until the metal had set, and voilà, the wax seahorse would transform into an exquisite pendant. Maggie had carved this water emblem while carrying a Piscean child. A perfect connection if they parted. Clever.

Following the airport disaster, Maggie was tragically private. Elizabeth reminded her housemates to follow Lily's advice. Do not handle Maggie with kid gloves, and keep fussing with your babes low-key. The new mums did baby stuff during the day while Maggie took lessons with Bineham. From early evening till about midnight, they included Maggie while creating a recipe book and five changes to the week's menu for the Railway Café customers. The business would thrive on Café Gerbeaud & Ruszwurm pogácsa, apple and apricot strudels, marzipan mice, jam-filled doughnuts, and cherry soup. They aimed to encourage travellers to become regulars and tempt them to place extra orders for their home table. Excitement and panic were on because, in two weeks, they would take over the lease. An almost new refrigerator and two ample kitchen cupboards arrived. The Salvation Army had come up trumps.

Again, following Lily's advice, they never mentioned that it was Maggie's money that had mainly secured their farm; instead, the ladies said they would always be thankful for her help and wished she'd stay part of their family. The barn would still have a "Welcome Home Maggie" at the entrance after fifty years.

Matron, Lily, and Maggie spent Maggie's second-to-last day visiting a nearby farm. There, Lily charmed a gentleman into offering his help if the ladies needed it. Maggie purchased a cow and her calf; Matron couldn't resist buying a goat and her two kids. The purpose of the mother animals was to supply milk after their babies were weaned, to act as living lawnmowers, and to have their babies as pets for the growing children. Matron promised the animals would live out their lives at Coldstream, even after they stopped producing milk. That day, Maggie asked Matron to give her Sydney's return train ticket to a mother in need. The Spirit of Progress was in Maggie's past, no part of which she wanted to repeat.

Maggie spent her final day in Melbourne. Not a hard thing to do. She found the interstate bus station, booked a seat on the 9 am departure the following day, and a hotel room to suit her budget for her evening arrival in Sydney.

She telephoned Aimee Norris, estate agent, whose books showed three suitable bedsits immediately available. She would expect Maggie in her office at 2 pm on Saturday. Aimee wanted to surprise her mother with Maggie's return, so she asked that Maggie keep it their secret.

Melbourne was buzzing. It was possibly the happiest and proudest city in the world. Officials were preparing to host the 1956 Olympic Games; street artists created commissioned works on selected walls. Landscaping was rife on street corners and public transport stations, while scaffolded buildings were cleaned and glorified.

Maggie had been yearning for art and music. She spent the morning in the Peter Bray Gallery, famous for mid-century Australian Contemporary art. On the wall, there was a poster advertising a brass band lunch-time concert in the Botanic Gardens, so while munching on a sandwich and an apple, Maggie indulged in sound. She was returning to herself.

Gifts were next on her list. Where to find creative goodies at a reasonable cost in this extravagant city? A lady told her that the place to shop and be seen was The Block Arcade and the shopping mall.

Maggie found her way to Collins Street, then to the Victorian-era Arcade, constructed between 1891 and 1893. It was riveting. Inspired by the Galleria Vittorio Emanuele in Milan, the arcade featured detailed mosaic-tiled floors, stained-glass windows, a glass canopy, skylights, wrought-iron fixtures, and carved stone finishes. Maggie stepped grandly on the mosaic tiles to survey an elegant array of boutiques; each entrance marked by an enormous Chinese pot crammed with growing flowers. She wandered the length, taking mental photographs of fashion, vintage and modern jewellery, art collections, hand-made shoes and a shop boasting maps from ancient mariners. Maggie wanted Melbourne souvenirs for her Sydney friends and keepsakes for those she'd leave behind. A window display combining European cakes and numerous beverages was reminiscent of Pippi and Elec's Café Gerbeaud. Maggie considered, but cakes would spoil in the outside heat. She bought a big bag of jellybeans for Matthew and, in a jewellery boutique, hand-sculpted bone China brooches with a silver backing for the Sydney girls. Tulips for Pippi, carnations for Mrs Norris, a rose for Maria, and for Aimee, rose earrings. In a mini-shop, an artist was pencil-sketching flannel flowers. Perfect for Lily and Matron. For the Community of Mothers, patterns and materials to make glass wind chimes.

Maggie decided not to tell the mothers she was leaving the next morning because goodbyes were complicated and full of promises impossible to keep. It was best to leave her gifts with a note on their doorstep, saying goodbye was too hard. Bineham knew when she was going. He was staying overnight with a friend nearby, so he offered to drive her to Melbourne. She asked to be on their way by 5 am.

Maggie waited at the gate for Bineham's car. The air was inviting, scented by flowering shrubs where calling Honeyeaters were flirting just as it had been many months before, the same day she had met Peter. Maggie had thought there was no part of her past she wanted to repeat until now, but something had changed.

An invisible envelope of silence surrounded Bineham and Maggie until they were in the city, approaching a corner with a van selling coffee and doughnuts. Maggie asked Bineham to stop. She invited him to join her for breakfast, adding that one should only share food with someone who has a beautiful mind. While finishing a jam doughnut, she looked him straight in the eyes and said,

'I thank you, Bineham and adore you. Your teachings and wisdom will influence my life decisions. My Grandma Maggie was a visionary. I have inherited some of her talents. Bineham, I am sure that in time our paths will cross. I have not said goodbye to Peter. I can't. I've asked you to bring me to Melbourne at this hour so that I may repeat one part of this journey. I am going to the church where I first met him. I shall sit there and meditate. What on I don't know until my guide, whom I named White Feathers, is with me.'

Bineham suspected this was coming. He wondered. Did Peter? He remembered a gift Peter entrusted to him —a ring featuring a sculptured gemstone scarab. He took Maggie's hand and slipped it on her finger.

'Come, Maggie, we'll check your luggage in at the terminal. Have you got your ticket? And you, my favourite student, are correct. I know we will enjoy the meeting of minds again. I will see your growth. I ask one thing of you. In a month, send a photograph of yourself and details of your good fortune, I'm certain you are about to experience.'

Maggie popped a small box into his shirt pocket. After they parted, he discovered it housed a wax seahorse, a miniature version of the one they both worked on.

The church door was open as it always was. Maggie sat in a pew and asked White Feathers to protect her child. She submitted to meditative prayer so profoundly that she didn't notice the man in a cassock who had taken place beside her. 'Were you a mother-in-waiting?'

'Yes.'

'I believe you were asking for protection for your child and perhaps physical and mental strength for your immediate future?'

'For my son, yes, but I do not know who I am or where I'm going.'

'Then pretend to be your secret self.'

'If you do the same.'

'That I wouldn't dare. I shall choose to be a talking wall.'

'Hello, Wall. I'm a bird. Have you heard anything worth repeating today?'

'Come to think of it, yes. I heard a young lady ask some white feathers to do something for her. Yesterday, a gentleman asked that a young lady visit him. He didn't say where, when or who.'

'Wall, do you ever wish you weren't a wall? I mean, do you wish you could change who you are or what you are? I ask because, as a bird, I can change location, dream, and sing. As a wall, you are fixed and cannot dream.'

'As a wall, I am and always will be a support, a shelter, a place to lean on, to divide, or enclose. That is my destiny.'

'In meditation, humans enjoy experiences unobtainable in the "now" world. Do you, Wall, travel in your mind? Do you wish to change your purpose?'

'Those, you naughty Bird, are tricky questions. I shall answer. I am a wall that can come to no harm because I am physically stable, so relatively safe. Unlike you, Bird, with plans to fly from a secured nest to face the unknown. Yes, I do astral travel to the fifth dimension, where I can temporarily be any wall I wish, and sometimes I dream of changing the material which formed me, but I cannot change my character. I enjoy being part of a building's foundations, one among many underpinning a great house. There are many aspects to being a wall, and many walls stretch for miles and miles. How could you believe a wall cannot dream? Some birds have no imagination. For the last four months, one of your kind landed in my vicinity and opened my eyes to a way of life that my station had previously blinded me to. Since then, I have been like the Great Wall of China, born with a purpose. I am now a wall with vision. I ask you, Bird, do you see all the implications and consequences of your actions? You once flew to this Wall for protection. You stayed for your season. Your song helped the Wall know its reason for becoming its divine self. You fly to your next location, but the Wall must stay.'

'I am curious as to what steps the Wall has taken in its new role.'

'Then I, the Wall, will retire and return you to Peter, who will reveal all while he walks you to your coach, little Bird.'

'Maggie, it is impossible for us not to speak about what we have seen and heard. Bineham, Matthew, Matron, Lily, Thomas, and I have formed a civic society to represent the needs of single parents. We aim to become strong enough that our raised voices will equalise educational standards for children, whether they come from single- or two-parent families. We invite all mothers, single and married, to attend committee meetings that we may group discuss means to stamp out baby farming, human trafficking, and honour all mothers' birthright as equals.'

Maggie answered.

'Peter, I don't understand how you will convince those haughty women who are sitting happily in marriage to join this purpose.'

Peter tapped his head with his forefinger.

We have employed the talents of celebrities and socialites as the face of our driving force because they are the Pied Pipers of social standards. Their influence is considerable. Many people clone their hairstyles, clothing, and way of life as financially allowed, and repeat their words. Celebrities have the clout to make or break popular opinions. They plant seeds in society, which their followers grow into forests.'

'Peter, should you be the face of this cause?'

'No, because I am only known to my parishioners. Strangers may see me as a minister of religion, as prejudiced against free-thinking. We've started a monthly magazine featuring photos of couples who have adopted a newborn. When interviewed and asked what their reaction would be if they discovered that their baby's natural mother parted with her child under duress and fear of social stigma, these people always pretend to be aghast. They all say they are against human trafficking, yet they directly cause that vile business. A Lest We Forget page features photographs of the graves of desperate women who have committed suicide after losing their babies to this government-condoned crime. Such information leaves a nasty taste in readers' mouths. Hopefully, shame will turn those who paid the piper for their child, and fewer will pay for an adoption. Without demand, there is no product to sell.

In each magazine, we feature a hero whistle-blower-medical-staff whose identity we hide for their protection. They admit to the routine practice of humiliating single mothers-to-be, making them suffer the pain of childbirth without medical relief, and refusing them the sight of their newborns. We are not pulling punches. Our people are infiltrating hospital boards, government departments, and medical and midwifery training schools.

Our young parishioners have opened a Baby Shop. Parents of children who've outgrown their clothing, blankets and cribs have donated. Goods are recycled for those in need, and the committee distributes profits from sales. Already two families have formed a creche to allow single mums to go to work.'

'Peter, you carry the name of a man who walked on water beside Jesus. Nothing is impossible for you.'

Passengers were boarding the bus. Peter took her face in his hands.

'My thoughts will ever warm you, woman from Magdala. Godspeed.'

Maggie took steps toward the boarding area, then turned.

'Peter, I couldn't find a suitable gift.'

'Maggie, you were the gift.

# PART 3

# CHAPTER 21

Sydney, The People's Palace and Potato Scallops.

Maggie paused on the steps of the Sydney-bound coach. She looked back at Peter, then complied with his hand movement, indicating that she should continue boarding. Once inside, she stood in the aisle near her allocated seat, but hesitated again. What was in Sydney for her? Lincoln, but the law forbade her from going near him. A trainee beautician job, but similar work opportunities would be available in Melbourne. Here, through shared life experience, she had a committed, supportive family in the Community of Mothers at Coldstream. In Sydney, she knew people dear to her, but what did she mean to them? Maggie's line of thought broke. A late passenger bawled her goodbyes at the top of her voice while racing up the steps. She threw her suitcase in the aisle and plopped herself on the first horizontal object, a gentleman's lap.

The bus driver blasted his horn, the doors closed, and a recording of Johnny Cash belted "Wide Open Road". As the gears meshed, passengers on the edge of their seats were pushed back, then jerked forward. The lady on the gentleman's lap tumbled to the floor. After which, the express to Sydney purred its way onward, having pulled away from the Melbourne terminal.

Passengers cheered, waved goodbye to those seeing them off, then introduced themselves to others by shouting above the music. There were two drivers, one actively picking up speed at the wheel, the other entertaining their guests on a public address system between songs on the road. Maggie's seat was comfortable, but people continued to be uncomfortably noisy, singing along or whooping with laughter at the stupid jokes told by either one of the two boisterous drivers. Passengers were a mixed lot of nationalities. Mostly Australian, Greek, Egyptian or Turkish, and all older than Maggie. Because she was young and travelling alone, people were curious and asked questions such as.

'Are you visiting family, dear? I'll bet my bottom boots it's your Grannie.'

She was subjected to tedious photo sessions of grandchildren, sons, daughters, and pets. There was a verbal competition about who had experienced the most operations or medical disasters. Women considered childbirth the most heroic. Men did not argue with that, so the ladies thought they had won until a man said his experience could beat the boots off childbirth, and he could prove it. He walked to the front of the bus, put his left arm up as though he was a policeman stopping traffic, and removed his left glove with his right hand to display a metal claw fitted and strapped to his wrist, proving he'd had an amputation. Everyone gasped. Then he demonstrated the claw's dexterity by grabbing a lady's hat and throwing it to another passenger, who hand-passed it to the people behind her. All but the almost bald lady retrieving her hat applauded. Maggie thought the action and passengers' response were weird but secretly hilarious. Then a family of four boasted about the numbers and sizes of fish they'd once murdered while on holiday at Tweed Heads in New South Wales, and an elderly couple took her into their confidence and whispered explicit details of family arguments. Maggie wondered why they'd think she'd be interested in such personal information about people she didn't know and would never meet. She decided not to divulge anything about herself because they could pass it along to strangers she might encounter in the future. So, whenever anyone asked a personal question, she answered by asking them about themselves. It worked every time.

Mid-morning, and all disembarked for tea and scones—all except Maggie, who took advantage of the peaceful vehicle. Three weeks ago, Maggie had been in the hospital labour ward; she'd given birth. Yearning for alone time, she curled up on the comfy seat and snuggled into the crocheted travel rug Matron had given her. She slept intermittently all day, kindly individuals waking her for lunch, afternoon tea, a stop at the border of Victoria and New South Wales, and supper.

Melbourne's bus company had organised an overnight stay at the Salvation Army hotel for Maggie's first night in Sydney. It sounded grand and was clean with friendly staff, but the People's Palace was not The Ritz. She found a shared bathroom and then returned to her room, cleansed but weary. She drank a glass of water, decided against sleeping in the bed, spread her coat on the chair, covered herself with Matron's rug and surrendered to sleep.

Daylight and a series of boat horns woke her. She was so stiff she could have been a statue, which didn't seem a bad idea. Maggie's bravery was a front; she was secretly afraid of what the future might bring. So far, life had been one battle after another. From her window, the city was still and cloaked in a sombre grey light. Two people were strolling in parallel, but far apart. A dog on a long lead was walking between them.

Downstairs, a gentleman at the reception desk nodded when Maggie showed her receipt.

Good morning. Do you have a timetable for the Manly ferry?

'And a perfect morning to you, Miss. We don't have ferry information, but I think the first one leaves the pier in about three hours. I suggest you take a stroll to the workers' cafe opposite the terminal, buy a sit-down or takeaway coffee and an egg buttie - they make the best in town - then look around the old Rocks area. New to Sydney? Here's a map of the streets. It's free.

Maggie noticed the receptionist pronounced it "cafe", not café.

'Thank you. Where on this map are The Rocks?'

'Here. It's a bit impoverished, but there is a lot of history. Its name comes from its location on the rocky headland that covers the western side of Sydney Cove. The Rocks were initially known as Tallawoladah by the sitting Aboriginal Cadigal clan, meaning 'many fish and seafood'. The Rocks became established as the convicts' side of town after the First Fleet arrived in 1788. These people were hard-working and creative. From scratch with few tools, men, women, and children constructed thatched-roof houses of wattle and daub. They carried earth from sites miles away to nourish fenced gardens on the sparse rocky outcrops. Extraordinary resilience. Women built bread ovens, and men built forges; some opened pubs, while others established craft businesses. And this, after they had been convicted of crimes they didn't commit, survived about 8 months of unimaginable hardship on the high seas, and were immediately put to work on a peninsula in Sydney Harbour, carving a chair out of rock and making a garden for the wife of Major-General Lachlan Macquarie! The Rocks isn't a rich man's area, but it's exciting and part of our history. Enjoy your day, Miss.'

Early morning breakfasters filled the terminal cafe. The clientele were men working on the new Sydney wharf, according to emblems on their overalls and jackets, and Ladies of the Night who looked dishevelled but seemed a happy-go-lucky lot. Maggie decided that some people might describe this café as "the place serving the other side of town". The walls reeked of salted bacon, sausages, and the bitter smell of hours-old, reheated coffee. Maggie took the receptionist's advice and ordered an egg bap to take away. She thought about coffee, but tea seemed more attractive.

The city was waking; trams were cranking along tracks; people with somewhere to go moved briskly, others dilly-dallied. Maggie followed her map from Circular Quay to The Rocks, a unique location that held many secrets. A hand-painted notice pointed the way to Church Hill. Here, there were numerous plaques boasting information of colonial importance. The latest billboard read: "On this site, under the tyranny of Governor Artur Phillip, his convicts, without tools, built the first church in Australia. Once completed, they were forced under mandatory law to attend services until, in 1798, they rebelled and burnt the building to the ground".

Looking away from Church Hill, Maggie saw a man sitting on a box. She headed towards him. A black dog with age-related white whiskers lay beside him. A puppy was asleep in a box next to her. The man looked cold. Maggie hadn't touched her warm takeaway tea, so she put it on the box next to him. She had walked on a few steps when she noticed the black dog trotting beside her.

'Stop, sweet thing; you can't come with me; I'll take you back to your dad.'

Maggie was so intent on steering the dog to her master that until she was upon him, she hadn't noticed that the man was now standing.

The right hand of his fingerless gloves held a book; his left hand signalled for the dog to lie on her mat. He started reading out loud. A small crowd gathered. One lady put a coin in the puppy's box. The man thanked her and asked which poem she wanted to start her day with. The lady replied.'

'One about love and passion, please, Sam.'

Sam flipped the pages until they stopped and stayed open.

*'It's too bad if a heart lacks fire,*
*And is deprived of the light of a heart ablaze.*
*The day on which you are without passionate love*
*is the most wasted day of your life.'*

The small audience clapped. A man put money in the box and asked. 'Can you read one on a bad relationship, please, Samuel?'
Again, Sam let the pages choose the verse.

*'To wisely live your life, you don't need to know much*
*Just remember two main rules for the beginning:*
*You better starve than eat whatever*
*And better be alone than with whoever.'*

More applause. Maggie took Matron's shawl from her bag and spread it over the elderly dog. She put a coin between the dog's paws, then asked.

'May I ask for an inspirational poem, please, Sam?'

For you, young lady, advise.
*'Dead yesterdays*
*and unborn tomorrows,*
*Why fret about it*
*If today is sweet.*
*From The Rubáiyát of Omar Khayyám'*

The other listeners had gone their way, so only Maggie clapped.

'Thank you, who is Omar Khayyam?'

'An eleventh-century Poet of Persia. The book I read is titled The Rubaiyat. It contains an English translation of Omar Khayyam's lyric poem written in four-line stanzas on life, death, love and religion.'

'Thank you, Samuel, you are a great teacher. I have enjoyed meeting you and your canine family.

Maggie found the nearest stone wall, sat down, took a pencil and pad from her bag, and wrote.

I should buy the book The Rubaiyat by the Persian poet Omer Khayyam for my sixteenth birthday. Look up the word "stanza".'

A clock struck the half-hour; it was time to head back to Circular Quay. Another plaque caught her eye. She was about to read it when she felt someone touch her arm. A child of about ten years old was beside her. He spoke in broken English.

'I am new.'

He put his hand on his chest and introduced himself.

'Pietro from Roma.'

Maggie reciprocated.

'Maggie from Sydney.'

Pietro put his hand behind one ear, pointed to Maggie with the other hand, touched his mouth with his finger, then pointed to the plaque. Maggie read slowly and precisely.

'Here lived Mary Reibey, born an orphan in Bury, Lancaster, England. She was transported to Australia in 1791, aged thirteen, for stealing a horse while dressed as a boy. She became a successful businesswoman, taking over her husband's commercial and shipping activities. Mary Reibey died in 1855, a pillar of the Church of England in Sydney.

Pietro ran off. Maggie walked as quickly as she could while carrying her suitcase. There was no way that ferry was going without her. Her mind remained busy. Pietro-Peter? Of the church? Coincidence? She decided to think of Pietro as a messenger, assuring her that all was well and as it should be. She touched her scarab ring.

Anyone will tell you that April in every part of the world tends to be warm, sunny, and seldom extreme. April is the beginning of Spring or Autumn, depending on which side of the planet you happen to be on. Likewise, the month heralds Summer or Winter. This allows the wind to change from the silken touch of an angel to a raging demon in the spin of a coin. On the upper deck of the Manly ferry, the wind was caressing Maggie's shoulder-length hair. She loved this journey; it brought back memories of a childhood birthday present from Grandma Maggie. They went to Manly, bought fried potato scallops wrapped in newspaper, and then walked to the ocean, where swooping seagulls stole their food. That day, the wind was heavy with salt water, and white horses thundered the waves, then turned to foam as they crashed on the shore.

While recollecting the affinity she and Grandma Maggie shared, the ferry had travelled the Harbour's spectacular coves and beaches. As Sydneyites called their famous bridge, the Coat Hanger was disappearing into the distance, and travelling across the heads in the open sea. Without warning, the wind became angry over whatever. It scuttled Maggie to the railings with every intention of pushing her overboard. She found her sea legs and turned her back to the force. She laughed at the antics of this air element as it tried to blow the hair off her head and clothes off her back. Once past the open sea, Mistress Wind once again played the gentile side of her character. Maggie dragged her tousled hair to one side, then plaited and fastened the end with an elastic band kept in her pocket for such an occasion. The engines stopped humming; the crew placed gangways joining the ferry to the pier. It was time to disembark.

While walking the Corso, Maggie bought fried potato scallops wrapped in yesterday's newspaper, then sat on the grassy strip between land and sea, sharing her meal with seagulls, when two police officers approached.

'Are you alone, girlie? Your name?'

'My name is Maggie Piper, and yes, I'm by myself, except for the gulls.'

'Funny. Why are you in Manly?'

'I wanted to enjoy the ferry ride and to relive a birthday outing.'

'Where do you live?'

'I don't live anywhere today, but I have an appointment with Aimee Norris, an estate agent who will give me a choice of three bedsits immediately available.'

'Maggie Piper, what age are you?'

'I'll be sixteen in three and a half weeks.'

'So, you're a runaway. You are homeless and underage. That's a good story about the estate agent. What time is she expecting you? Where is she?'

'I'm not without a home; I'm going to have one by this afternoon. My appointment is at 2 pm with Aimee Norris, Estate Agent at Kirribilli —well, we call it Kirribilli, but it's really Milsons Point. I haven't had time to find a home because I only arrived from Melbourne last night.'

'Where are your parents?'

'I understand that you are looking after me, but please check with Aimee Norris, my estate agent. I have never been homeless, and I have always had a job. I've worked since I was almost thirteen. I start an apprenticeship as a beautician in a salon on Tuesday. This coming Monday, they are styling my hair and fitting my uniform.'

'How were you getting to Kirribilli?'

'Back to Circular Quay by ferry and then by train to Milson's Point.'

'Where did you stay last night, Maggie Piper?'

'At the People's Palace in Sydney.'

'OK, we'll drive you to Kirribilli. You're in trouble if you've told a pack of untruths.'

'Have you any money?'

Bineham had advised her to carry a twenty-pound note to prove, in this unlikely scenario, that she was not a vagrant. Maggie opened her bag, found it tucked away and carefully unfolded the money. The female officer made a sound like "humph". The male officer smiled. Maggie had the feeling he believed she was truthful. But she was terrified. What if Aimee had forgotten their appointment and had gone out for the afternoon? Perhaps Aimee would be annoyed that the police had thought her a runaway and would pretend not to know her? Silence reigned during the journey in the police car to Milson's Point.

Aimee was waiting outside of her office as she had two years ago. The male officer opened her door, and Maggie bolted to Aimee, then burst into tears. Aimee stepped forward and pulled Maggie close.

'You're safe, my young friend.'

Then to the officers who were standing nearby,

'I thank you for delivering Maggie to me.'

The woman humphed again. Her victim had escaped. The male officer addressed Aimee.

'Just doing our job, Miss Norris. We didn't mean to upset her and didn't know we did till now. I wish her a good and rosy life.'

## CHAPTER 22

*A new start is a walk in the park.*

Maggie was hoping to find somewhere to live at Kirribilli or Milsons Point, but wasn't overly disappointed when Aimee Norris drove her to North Sydney. She viewed two large, airy bedsits with shared bathrooms and toilets, but they were a fair walk from public transport in poorly lit streets. Their rent was twelve pounds per fortnight, paid one month in advance.

The third choice was a room in a shared house with three others: a female art student, a nurse in her final year, and a male studying at the Conservatorium. The room on offer was tiny, almost bursting at the seams with a three-quarter bed, a wardrobe, a chair, and an oblong table that would comfortably seat eight. The lack of space was offset by double glass doors that opened to a large, roofed veranda with half walls and a gated entrance. Rent was eight pounds per fortnight, paid one month in advance, plus an extra two pounds per month for the services of a professional cleaner and the electricity bill.

There was much in favour here, including lower rent, a smaller deposit, and proximity to public transport. Maggie's savings had sizably diminished, but she knew her coming pay packet would cover living costs. Miss Olessya Frank's secretary had advised that her apprenticeship wages for the first three months would be fourteen pounds per fortnight, boosted by at least four pounds per week in tips. Finances were going to be tight; she would have to find work on Sundays or in the evenings.

Maggie wished to meet the other tenants before making a final decision. They were in the small garden at the back, playing a board game. The young man, Jerry, offered Aimee his seat. Linda and Nancy came forward to meet Maggie. Small talk was enough to feel a genial atmosphere. Maggie said she would be happy to fill their vacancy if she suited them. The young man gave a pantomime bow, and the girls a tiny clap. Aimee asked if Maggie could move in late this afternoon. All agreed.

On returning to the estate agent's office, Maggie saw her belongings and bicycle resting in a corner.

'Aimee, it's great to be reunited with my belongings. I left them with Maria. Has she moved?'

'Soon, but not yet. Maria is engaged to be married; she's been waiting for your return to hold the wedding.'

'Mind-blowing news, the best. Has Maria's fiancé met with your and Mrs Norris's approval?'

'Interestingly, yes. I say that because Noah is a great deal older than her, yet he's not a father figure.'

'So why are my possessions here?'

'I have three reasons. It would be best if you settled into your new digs and rested after your interstate journey. Secondly, you've only this evening and tomorrow before starting work. Am I correct in thinking Monday is the day a Hairdresser styles your hair? The third, I didn't want you to go to the house to find my mother missing.'

Maggie panicked.

'Aimee, what do you mean? Where is she? Is Benjie with her?'

'My mother is convalescing after a knee fracture. She's in great health otherwise, just taking time adjusting to a mobility walker.' She's coming home this Monday afternoon. I'm picking her up and driving her straight to Café Gerbeaud to choose the menu for High Tea.'

'To Pippi and Elec's Café Gerbeaud?'

'I thought it appropriate to celebrate your return, so I've booked a table for Monday at 4 pm, my shout.

About Benjie. After you went to Melbourne, he fretted. Apart from missing you, he needed energetic walks, which my mother couldn't manage. To give him some freedom and a change of scenery, Benjie came to the office daily. One day, Simon called in to ask about your well-being. He took Benjie to the park, played ball and put him through the puppy school's commands. Simon was impressed, and as it was evident that Benjie needed to be rehoused, he and Lorraine offered to keep him. Mummy decided that days spent guarding an expanding family, running in the orchard, and sleeping by a log fire on winter evenings had more appeal to a young dog than being bored with an elderly lady.'

Maggie noted, "expanding family", which suggested Lorraine was pregnant. She chose to ignore that and instead remarked.

'Here's that wind of change again.'

Aimee understood Maggie's psychological need to ignore her hint.

'Maggie, you're looking great. I'm about to ask a sensitive question, and based on your answer, I'll make sure everyone we know respects your wishes. Do you want to discuss your experiences in Melbourne openly?'

'Aimee, I value such thoughtfulness. The answer is no. I do not wish to share my negative pain with anyone. To my friends and all new people, that part of my life will remain hidden. To save me from having to verbalise events and outcomes, I have a lawyer's letter explaining everything. I want to share it with you, and whoever in our circle is interested, but not this afternoon. I've posted a copy to Diana and Rupert McLeod in Scotland. So far, I have no forwarding address for my precious Una. My instinct told me not to include Lorraine in the loop, even though her husband has been supportive of me.'

'Maggie, let's do a little shopping for immediate needs on the way to your new residence. You can leave your bike if you want, or take it with you after Café Gerbeaud. Be there, 4 pm Monday. I see your cycle has a headlight. Does it have rear and wheel reflectors? One last thing. I believe you should consider public transport across the harbour bridge and in the city until you have turned sixteen and are familiar with regulations and the lanes.'

On Monday morning, Maggie travelled by train across the Harbour Bridge, changed to another line, then alighted at St James station. It was a short and pleasant walk to the city building that housed the world-famous beauty salon. She hesitated in front of the big red door. Her heart was thumping. The lack of confidence regarding her character and appearance, drummed into her from childhood, reappeared. What if Miss Olessya had changed her mind? Why would they seriously employ her, a teenage nobody? Hopefully, it wasn't evident that she'd just given birth as an unmarried mother. How could a hairdresser fix her straggly hair? Maggie decided to leave before being told the position wasn't available. She turned her back on the door.

A tall, young man in a grey suit came sprinting up the stairs. His English had an accent.

'Good morning, allow me.'

He pushed the door open and offered her first entrance. Maggie, finding her confidence, thanked him.

'I am Rowbear, and you must be Maggie, our new apprentice. Maggie, welcome. We have arrived at the same good time. It will be my pleasure to style your hair. First, say hello to Juliette, our receptionist.'

Rowbear had guided her to the desk, then disappeared.

'Hello, I'm Maggie Piper.'

'Welcome to our house of beauty, Maggie Piper; I'm Juliette. I see you've met Robert. He is one of our two hairdressers from Germany; we have another from Rome and two from Paris.'

'I thought his name was Rowbear.'

'Can you roll your r's? If so, call him RRRowbear; otherwise, Robert will be fine.'

A demure young lady beckoned Maggie to follow, offered her a chair in front of a mirror, and draped a pink cape around her shoulders. This place was incredible. Maggie felt like the ugly duckling in the home of a majestic swan. The décor had an understated luxury that encouraged tranquillity. Careful lighting gave the person looking into the mirror a heavenly appearance. A narrow bench in front of her resembled pale marble-perhaps it was. Tall, crystal vases held two stems, each of budding and fully blown lilies, and the chair embraced her as if she were a child in her mother's arms.

Two hours later, Maggie hardly recognised herself. She still had her fringe and shoulder-length hair, but it was slightly shorter, cut to all one length, and as shiny as a copper penny. Robert held up a mirror, positioned to reflect his art from all sides and the back.

'Do you agree that your hair is now stunning? I think I must be the first hairdresser to style your locks, Maggie?'

She couldn't do anything but look. She finally found her voice.

'Robert, this is not a beauty salon. It is a house of wizards. Thank you, but how can I make it look like this after I wash it?'

'The style is easy. Because of my cut, it will fall back after you've shampooed it. It will turn out with a little help from a rounded brush and a blow dryer. Before, your flyaway hair looked like a thistle. Now it has a body and flows luxuriously. This style is suitable for your features and future. Now, Miss Maggie, it's Miss Suzanna for you. Working here, you'll have to wear more than that lipstick.'

Robert pulled a face as he said that, so Maggie guessed the shade was not to his approval.

She left the salon at 1 pm, shopped for a hairdryer and round brush, flat ballet pumps for work and wrapping for the gifts she'd purchased in Melbourne. Consequently, she was ten minutes late for her appointment at Café Gerbeaud.

From the street view, the Hungarian patisserie was as it always had been. The window display would beckon people, their mouths watering with the promise of gourmet delights. Maggie entered and approached the table where her friends were seated—her darling Mrs Norris with Dresden skin, lovely Maria, and Aimee. Elec had greeted her at the door, but Pippi remained behind the counter. Maggie's excitement had been overflowing, but now she was worried. Was Pippi not pleased to see her? After everyone stopped speaking at once and there was a lull, Maggie approached Pippi and saw that she discreetly kept her swollen belly out of sight. Maggie felt her eyes moisten.

'Pippi, dear Pippi, I'm happy for you. You are carrying a gift of love. Please understand that my past has nothing to do with your present. Our table is not complete without you and your little belly. Sit with us; I have gifts from Melbourne.'

Maggie was grateful that her sixteenth birthday went by unnoticed. Maria and Noah were married five days later, on the twenty-fourth of April. They left for New Zealand, where Noah's interests and livelihood revolved around the thoroughbred horse industry. As Maria, on the arm of her doting husband, was going to board the aircraft, Maggie could say no more than…

'Godspeed, my friend. May the road rise to meet you, may the wind be always at your back.'

Mrs Norris left Kirribilli to move in with her daughter, Aimee.

Maggie walked around the perimeter of the house that the three had once shared. It was empty, awaiting new occupants, yet it still exuded a sense of comradeship and safety. She was fortunate to have travelled part of her life's journey with Mrs Norris, her mentor, as was Mrs Loveday, and Maria the brave, who, as a child, evaded death camps, then travelled to and survived in a new world that spoke another language.

The big red door had become a regular part of Maggie's life five days a week for two months. She fitted in well at her posh workplace, both physically and mentally. Not one rude person, and everyone had something beautiful about them. Miss Olessya's manicurists trained Maggie to be proficient in both standard and the European style. She preferred the finish of the latter even though it was time-consuming. In the standard technique, she left the cuticle intact; in contrast, the European manicure wasn't complete until she had removed the cuticle, a mission accomplished after softening it with fruit acid, then coaxing its removal with a fine orange-wood stick. A soothing hand-and-arm massage was included in every treatment. When clients coupled manicures with hairstyling, Maggie worked from a portable table and stool while the hairdressers created. Others booked a manicure while enjoying a facial or body massage.

During the latter sessions, Maggie became doubtful about whether she wanted a career involving women who were so relaxed that they became verbally unchecked. During these hour-long treatments, she alternated between working on the client's nails and serving as the beautician's assistant. She soaked face towels in hot scented water, wrung them dry, filled tiny bottles with essential oils, and filled fingerbowls with creams. Then she removed used towels and empty containers, cleaning and disinfecting them for further use. As soft music accompanied these treatments, the atmosphere became soporific and very personable.

Many ladies gossiped in the room's privacy, spreading reputation-damaging information, directly or indirectly, about others. They indiscreetly exposed lurid details of their love life in and out of the sanctity of marriage. One outrageously identified her new lover as her husband's boss, and by chance, he was the next client's husband!

Manicuring was superior to waitressing, but only while the client was in the hands of her hairdresser or seated opposite Maggie at her table for two. Here, the client was interested in the elegant outcome and small talk. Hence, conversations took a different path —a pleasant, exciting forty-five minutes with ladies who oozed personality and had fascinating lives. Maggie quickly built her clientele. Two of these women were to influence her career and life decisions.

Googie Withers was a favourite with Maggie, not just because her birthday fell on the twelfth of March, the day after Lincoln's. She was born in India, where her Indian nanny affectionately nicknamed the little Georgette "Googie", meaning little pigeon. Googie's mother was Dutch-German, and her father was a Royal Navy captain. The family moved to England when Googie was twelve, and it was then that she began her acting career. Googie was an effortless beauty who owned the hypnotic weapon of a perfect speaking voice. Although an internationally acclaimed star of stage and film, she treated everyone equally and with respect.

During manicures, she intrigued Maggie with back-stage romps kept from the public. It was not gossip but real happenings that sparked light laughter. Once, Googie's left hand was most uncomfortable because a man had enthusiastically grabbed and shaken it so forcefully that her wedding and engagement rings were squashed into ovals!

Maggie's most exotic client was Tanya Sargent, a stunning blonde in mid-term pregnancy. Before Tanya married, she was a newspaper reporter, so curiosity was habitual. Tanya noticed that her manicurist, unlike other young females, didn't babble on about babies. After discovering Maggie's age, Tanya was taken aback by her maturity and wondered at her restraint if quizzed about herself. Tanya found that Maggie lived alone and had a great love for classical music, the arts and, of all things, the sacred mysteries of ancient gods. So, Tanya decided to introduce Maggie to the performing arts. She presented her with a gift of six tickets, two for a ballet, another set for a musical and two more to see a play in performance. Tanya expressed her opinion that Maggie should consider a career in the arts, perhaps as a trainee commercial artist or by attending a theatre school. She also told Maggie that, as she would not have the push and contacts of a theatrical family, she should keep her ears and eyes open for opportunities that may come her way.

Miss Olessya booked a manicure. While Maggie was massaging her slender hands, she asked.

'Maggie, would you have any objections to having your hair styled again and photographed? We won't take the length. It would be for an article in a glossy magazine to draw attention to our European hairstylists and broaden our image, since the public mainly associates us with our international cosmetic house and beauty treatments.

Once more, a session with Robert and Miss Suzanna, after which Robert's apprentice and Suzanna accompanied Maggie to a photographic studio.

A week later, Miss Olessya called Maggie to her office. Spread on her desk were large, glossy, and matte photographs of Maggie — nothing like Maggie. Miss Olessya asked her to sit.

'You look surprised, Maggie. Are you?'

'I'm dumbstruck. Robert's hairstyle is divine. The face is mine, but not me. My crooked nose looks straight, my fat, long neck is thinner and shorter, and my mouth is full. I'm guessing the makeup and photographic retouching did that.'

'These photographs were not retouched or altered, Maggie. They are as you are. Admittedly, you're incredibly photogenic. We chose you as our model because you have a long neck and a lovely profile. Be proud of who you are. Maggie, these photographs are to be published, which may bring work offers away from this salon. That could lead to a different career. How would you feel about that?'

'Miss Olessya, I'm a bit thick, but what do you mean? What type of career? Surely not modelling hairstyles.'

These stills are lovely. If photographic work comes your way, we will support you with casual manicuring until you decide on the path your career should follow. Please keep that in mind. Meanwhile, here's something for your bank account.'

Maggie's eyes almost popped out of her head. Fifty pounds!

A month later, she was photographed in hats for a leading department store and booked to appear in a fashion parade wearing the latest beachwear. A lady with a weekly column in a newspaper left an enveloped message with the beauty salon receptionist. It read that she would like to include Maggie in an exciting new venture. Maggie remembered Tanya Sargent's advice about taking advantage of offers that may come her way. Did she have something to do with this stroke of luck?

Maggie opened a bank account for Lincoln to build him a secret nest egg slowly. She kept her promise to Bineham and posted him an envelope stuffed with a glossy magazine, newspaper cuttings showing her wearing a golden seahorse pendant, details of her luck with work and the lovely veranda of her new home.

Marj Piper had done everything she could to convince everyone that Lincoln was her natural child. For months before his birth, she'd tied a pillow under a smock and feigned morning sickness. She knitted baby booties on the front porch and walked up and down the road while neighbours watered their gardens.

Marj's father, Charlie Pilgrim, had died, so her lifelong soldier was missing in action. Her mother openly disapproved of Marj trying to breastfeed Maggie's baby. And now, Albert brought home newspapers from which he cut out photos of Maggie in various hairstyles and hats. He was openly proud of her! On one occasion, Marj heard Albert on the telephone boasting to a masonic mate that he had a new shot of Maggie nursing a white cat on the southeast pylon lookout of the Harbour Bridge. Now that would get him in because Albert loved cats. Then another two newspaper cuttings appeared. Maggie was modelling a new hairstyle called 'Luna Touche' and, in the other, was wearing a mink bikini, sky-scraper wedgy shoes, and a giant Mexican sombrero.

When Marj demanded that Albert burn the clippings or toss them in the garbage, he laughingly refused. Before Marj could confiscate them, he gathered them up, then, with Marj hot on his heels, raced to his workshop and locked the door. She saw him through the window, sticking them on the wall. Marj threatened from the outside that if the other children saw any of these photos, she would divorce him.

Albert had gone against her wishes and found a mind of his own. Marj decided there was only one thing to do to break off any future communication. Sell up and move to a new location. But how to influence such a decision? He loved this house; Albert and the children had cleared the land, handmade every brick and set them in place. And more, much more.

Recently, there was lousy publicity about hospital staff selling babies belonging to single mothers who had not given their permission. Shameful, charitable nuns asked for large donations in exchange for newborns stolen from unsuspecting widows in their care while birthing. At the bus stop, somebody posted a photograph of a welfare officer who took money from a couple who wanted to adopt. She was wearing a dunce hat with "shame' written on the band. The subject was on everyone's lips.

Marj had to hatch a plan to protect her secret. It hinged on moving to a new location. She sat in a big chair and waited for Albert to return from work. Lincoln was in a cradle beside her. When her husband entered the room, Marj was rocking and sobbing.

'My darling little wifey, who has upset you? Is something wrong with Lincoln?'

'There is something wrong with our world, Albert. The neighbours are suspicious that Lincoln is not our baby. I know that because the children visiting next door told Livia that her new brother came from a baby farm because his hair is different.

'But that is ridiculous. Lincoln's hair is dark, and so is mine. Did you tell Livia to tell the children that?'

'Then, Albert, I heard our children whispering. They think we killed Maggie and buried her in the bush, somewhere near her cat.'

'Marj, I haven't heard any of this nonsense, but I did get suspicious that the butcher had suspicions. He asked after Maggie's welfare the other day and then asked why we had travelled to Melbourne. He added that because you were expecting a baby, travelling could have endangered your health. He added that a woman carrying a child and travelling could haemorrhage and die. He finished by asking me to say hello to our eldest.'

'What did you say to that?'

'I said we were visiting my brother in Victoria, who was not well, and that Maggie went with us and decided to stay.'

'You fool, Albert; he would smell a dead fish a mile away because I kicked her out two years ago. They know she hasn't lived here for yonks. What else have you not told me?'

'Nothing, Marj. Please calm down. It doesn't matter what people think; we are a family.'

'It doesn't matter, and we're not all family. She isn't. You haven't told me everything.'

'Well, I can remember something amusing. It will make you laugh. When I had Lincoln out in the stroller, a couple asked if he was my grandchild. They said he looked like me! I replied that it was impossible because we adopted him.'

'You said what?'

'I couldn't tell them a lie; his mother was not my child; we adopted her. Apart from that, they were visitors to the district, so it didn't matter.'

'You stupid man, what if that information got back to our children? We have told Silva, Bertie, Beth, Livia, and Lucy that Lincoln is their brother, that I am his mother, and that you are his father. How could you have been so bloody stupid to tell strangers we adopted him?'

'They caught me off guard, Marj. I didn't want to tell an outright lie or say Lincoln was my grandson, because then the cat would be out of the bag and people would know he was Maggie's child. They would wonder why he wasn't with her.'

'Get out of my sight, you drongo. You don't deserve me, Albert Piper. Because of your big mouth, we must move to a new address. This place means so much to me. I am so unhappy because my blood and tears have gone into making this our forever home. But sacrificed it must be; it is the only thing to do. Sell this house and move to a neighbourhood where nobody knows us. We will be a new family with our children and my baby.'

## CHAPTER 23

*Ave Maria, an answered prayer.*

Loraine heard the postie's whistle. It always accompanied the mail. She walked to the gate where the bespoke wine-barrel mailbox sat on the frame of an old bicycle. Simon said it lent character and a visual introduction to their orchard cum vineyard.

The letter addressed to Simon and Mrs Norris had been sent by somebody she didn't know, called Margaret Pilgrim. It might have something to do with Maggie. Lorraine returned to the cane rocker on the veranda. Benjie followed, sat, and waited until she looked settled, then offered his paw, his eyes fixed on her belly. She knew what her dog wanted.

Four months ago, he was present when she felt the first tiny flutter. Benjie had sensed new life. He sat bolt upright, head and ears slightly forward, eyes concentrating on her belly, leaning his head from one side to the other, appraising the situation.

In quiet times, the ever-gentle Benjie wanted to touch the area after it bulged. He liked to lay his ear against her tummy and feel the baby wriggle in response. Lorraine mentioned this to her midwife, who wasn't surprised. She told Lorraine to encourage the dog to protect and to love the newborn. He should sleep near the bassinet, the cot, and the playpen as soon as they set the furniture in place. Then, after Loraine gave birth, Simon was to let Benjie smell their baby's clothing before laundering it to strengthen the bond that had developed not long after conception.

Knowing the close relationship Benjie had shared with Maggie brought regrets. Loraine had selfishly decided it was none of her business that her friend was carrying the child of a neighbouring rapist while living in dire circumstances. But since Loraine was carrying a baby of her own, she felt remorse at her lack of support and for cutting their sistership. If there were ever a chance to make amends, she would, but if she reached out now, what would Maggie's reaction be to her?

Loraine took the letter in both hands. She was itching to open it, but she and Simon had a family rule. Her mail was hers, and Simon's was his. Anyway, Margaret Pilgrim had also addressed it to Mrs Norris. Lorraine casually let Benjie smell the envelope.

'Benjie, is this about our estranged young friend?'

Loraine thought he nodded the affirmative, so to curb herself from opening the mail, which was not hers, she stood and picked up the vintage flower gathering basket she'd found in a Brick-a-brack shop in *Katoomba.

She and Benjie roamed their property, collecting long stems of lavender for vases and fallen camomile flowers to sweeten Simon's bathwater. They then waited in the shade of a tree near the gate for her husband and Benjie's master to return.

Benjie heard the distinct hum of the Panel Van before it showed.

Loraine handed Simon the letter, then, wanting praise, smiled.

'Simon, my darling, praise me. I've shown great restraint. I didn't open it, even though my instinct told me it had something to do with Maggie. If it has Simon, there may be a chance of her accepting me as her friend again.'

Simon answered while absently caressing Loraine's tummy.

'You'd have to learn diplomacy, Lorrie.'


Simon telephoned Mrs Norris, who didn't answer. He called Aimee, and yes, her mother was there. Mrs Norris came to the phone, asked him to open the letter, read it, and then call her back.

Lorraine and Simon read it together.

*Dear Mrs Norris and Simon,*

*I thank you for leaving your contact.*

*Simon, I write because Marj has hatched a plan to break all possible contact between Lincoln and Maggie. She's moving the family to a new location, then lodging a private forwarding address at the post office.*

*As Maggie's Grandmother, and as a person who has fought injustice since my daughter was old enough to manipulate the men in our lives, I have an intense and heartfelt concern that Maggie's child may never know his birth mother. I worry that if he does meet her later, Marj will have poisoned his mind beyond repair.*

*It is a mother's eternal tragedy to be denied the sight of her child and not know where he is or of his well-being. It is against the rules of heaven for others to break the spiritual umbilical cord that binds them.*

*Mrs Norris and Simon, I believe we can remedy this.*

*Albert told me that he had Maggie arrested at Melbourne airport. She approached him, asking to see her child. Maggie only wanted a memory of Lincoln's face, which medical staff had denied her on the birthing table. Albert added that Marj wanted the little girl's baby so desperately that he donated copious cash to the hostel welfare officer, who arranged for the child to be stolen from the hospital and then delivered to them in a hotel.*

*Mrs Norris and Simon, I suspect Albert has found his moral compass. I have seen him putting wildflowers on Maggie's cat's grave, which she would have done if she were able. This action points to an apology to Maggie. Against Marj's wishes, Albert keeps newspaper cuttings of Maggie and is the toast of his friends at the Masonic Lodge since one of the men's wives found a photograph of her in a glossy magazine.*

*I can arrange favourable circumstances for Maggie to play Marj at her own game, in which she will meet Lincoln and, at the same time, form a relationship with Albert, which will pay dividends for future contact.*

*Jenolan Caves is about an hour's drive beyond the Blue Mountains. Within the Lucas Cave complex is the acoustically perfect Cathedral Chamber. The tour guide usually asks if someone in the group can sing. Albert has a golden voice and will perform when asked. Maggie loves Jenolan Caves; she enjoyed a school excursion there as a child.*

*Marj will celebrate her birthday in March. One week later, Lincoln will turn one year old. To commemorate the double occasion, I plan to arrange a three-day vacation in Jenolan Caves House for Marj, Albert and Lincoln. Albert could promise Marj that he would put their home up for sale if she allowed him to sing in the Cathedral Chamber while he was still young enough to have a melodious voice.*

*Marj will cooperate because she cannot put the Georges River property on the market without Albert's signature, and he is, at this time, standing firm against the idea. But he knows he will eventually do as his wife pleases.*

*Maggie must not be told of the surprise in case it backfires.*

*You may ask: How will the meeting between Maggie and Lincoln take place?*

*Mrs Norris and Simon, Marj is a lazy female, so she will stay in Caves House, filling in crossword puzzles while Albert takes Lincoln out in the stroller. Maggie will be walking with whoever accompanies her. Maggie and Lincoln meet. Albert returns Lincoln to Marj, then joins Maggie for the guided Lucas Cave tour, which will* allow *bonding.*

*Albert is a god-fearing man, so he needs Maggie's forgiveness. He has a childish sense of humour, and the mischief will appeal.*

*Mrs Norris and Simon, I ask this favour of you because you thought enough of my granddaughter to approach the Pipers for financial help, hoping to ease the hardship she could not avoid. Forgive me if I ask too much of you; I can see no other way to grant her dearest wish. If my plan is out of the question, please let me know, and I'll find an alternative. I will not be part of robbing Maggie of her child's whereabouts.*

*The cruelty of my daughter's decision to change location brings my time with this family to an end. I am not well and choose to spend my remaining days in a rest home. When I have an address, I will forward it to you for Maggie.*

*I have had the honour and privilege of being part of Maggie's life. She was born to my niece, who, in early pregnancy, was widowed during the war. For Maggie's future and to escape social stigma for both mother and daughter, Emma bowed to her family's wishes and allowed Marj and Albert to adopt Maggie legally.*

*Magda Joy is a direct descendant of Robbie Burns, the National Bard of Scotland. To my knowledge, my granddaughter, as I shall always think of her, is unaware that she is not the natural child of Marj and Albert Piper. I have never found the opportunity to tell her, and I consider it unwise at this time. She has been through more than the average body could endure.*

*I am pleased that Lincoln carries the name of my musically talented and beautiful son, who died in his early twenties.*

*Mrs Norris and Simon, I write with sincerity. Heartfelt thanks for the opportunity to contact you, who has my Maggie's trust. Her weapons are courage, intelligence, and clarity of thought.*

*The return address is that of the church Maggie attended before her departure. A member of the fellowship will personally deliver your mailed answer to me.*

*May the wind be always at your backs and the road rise to meet you,*

*Margaret Pilgrim, nee Burns.*

Lorraine and Simon decided that if Mrs Norris found the plan too much of a hassle, they'd carry it without her. If Mrs Norris wanted to come, the more, the merrier.

Mrs Norris agreed, but thought that Lorraine should break the ice with Maggie first. Maggie hadn't voiced it, but her disappointment in Lorraine's lack of support and bewilderment regarding their broken friendship was evident. Perhaps Lorraine needed a manicure?

Maggie almost tripped on the salon's deep carpet when the client she greeted at the reception desk was Lorraine. They instantly forgave each other: one for not keeping the other in the loop, and the other for cutting their relationship for the sake of a business opportunity. One did not mention her current pregnancy, and the other did not mention her past one. Instead, Maggie asked for details of life in the Blue Mountains and about Benjie. That allowed Lorraine the opportunity to invite Maggie to a travel party to the *Jenolan Caves*. Mrs Norris, Pippi, and Benji would come, and Benji loves car rides.

Maggie Pilgrim (nee Burns), Mrs Norris, and Simon met privately with Albert. As predicted, Albert played the man who needed to right his wrong; he agreed he had no chance of keeping the Georges River property and thought it remarkable to have the upper hand for once. He beamed at the thought of singing in the acoustically perfect Cathedral Chamber.

On a balmy Friday evening, Maggie, Pippi and Mrs Norris drove to Katoomba to stay at the heritage-listed **Carrington Hotel*. That same evening, Simon picked up Grandma Maggie in Lorraine's ***Fairlane Crown Vic*. She visited the farm and slept in a comfy bed for the first time in many years. Grandma Maggie still slept on a single couch in the lounge room in the Georges River house, even though she had financed much of the building materials from the sale of her ****Sans Souci* home.

The first Lucas Cave tour began at 11.30 am, so the Katoomba trio climbed into Lorraine and Simon's elegant six-seater vehicle at 7 am.

It was a bit squashed but great fun as Benji played musical chairs between Mrs Norris, Maggie, and Lorraine. The two Maggies were almost speechless at seeing each other again, but within seconds, they settled into their old togetherness as though they'd never parted.

Albert, Marj and Lincoln had been at Caves House for two days and an evening. Marj enjoyed being fussed over by the staff as the lady with a baby. Albert already had her in the habit of sitting in the reading room, working on crossword puzzles, and gobbling ham sandwiches while he took Lincoln for regular strolls.

Maggie was unaware of her probable meeting with Albert and Lincoln. Her friends planned to walk with her at the appointed time, intending to be her army if need be. All wanted to witness the uniting of mother and child. During the journey from Katoomba to Jenolan, Pippi kept glancing at Lorraine, their excitement almost reaching its zenith at times. In contrast, Mrs Norris and Margaret Pilgrim kept the atmosphere as level as possible. In the plot, Simon's part was to speak calmly to Albert and praise him for his good deed. Margaret Pilgrim knew Albert would eventually confess to Marj, but who cared? By then, Maggie will have had direct contact with her child, and Margaret Pilgrim, nee Burns, would either be in a hospital, a rest home, or in the arms of an angel.

The drive from Katoomba included dramatic stretches of road winding down into a deep valley. A bit further on, looming ahead, was the imposing entrance to Jenolan Caves.

Simon pulled over, and the girls tumbled out with Benjie on a lead. A notice informed them that this was the Grand Arch, the largest open cave in Australia, perhaps globally. It measured close to 80 feet high, 180 feet wide and over 400 feet long. From the edge of the road, looking down, a pond was fed by a stream. The water was incredibly blue — bluer than lightning — an unforgettable introduction to their destination. They piled back into the Crown Vic, and Simon drove a short distance to park near the Tudor-style Jenolan Caves House.

All went as planned. The travellers entered the iconic building, freshened up, then met in the tearoom to enjoy a second breakfast.

Albert had previously taken Marj on a morning stroll. She was happy to rest while he entertained Lincoln.

After satisfying genteel appetites on an early High Tea, Margaret Pilgrim and Mrs Norris waited in the foyer to curb any possible unexpected appearance of Marj while Pippi and Lorraine went on an adventure walk with Maggie. The area around the caves was extraordinarily serene. A giant lizard was sunbathing; multi-coloured birds were busy doing whatever birds do, and indigenous wildlife peeped shyly from bushes.

Albert stepped into the crisp air to be joined by Simon, who made light conversation. They strolled with baby Lincoln in the direction of the three young ladies.

Pippi turned and saw Simon, Albert and the stroller catching up with them. She feigned tiredness and begged to stop walking so that she could sit on a bench to rest. Maggie and Lorraine joined her. Lorraine kept Maggie's head turned in conversation so she couldn't see Albert approaching. Then Albert did something unplanned.

He stopped, lifted little Lincoln out of the stroller and stood him on his feet. Simon automatically took one hand and Albert the other. They walked him to the seated girls, then, when only a few steps away, the men let him approach alone.

The silver cord between mother and child was not severed. Lincoln toddled straight to Maggie and stood in front of her. She was amazed and delighted.

'Where did this unexpected little pixie come from, and why are you alone?'

Lincoln held her gaze. She laughed lightly, then offered her outstretched fingers, which he grasped.

'Look who found me. I have a boyfriend.'

She glanced up as she spoke, saw Simon standing beside Albert and stopped laughing. She looked back at the toddler.

'Lincoln? You are my Lincoln.'

On hearing his name, Maggie's baby broke into a wide smile that showed some tiny white teeth in his generous mouth.

Albert and Simon noted Lorraine and Pippi's tears. The magnetism between mother and child was riveting. Albert found words.

'Maggie, he loves you before he knows you. Walk with him. Lincoln has strong little legs and sure feet. He has a curious mind, so he may suddenly stop to investigate something.'

'Are you taking him away?'

Silence. A long, hellish silence. All eyes were on Albert. He hung his head and replied.

'I am reluctant but must. Please walk with your baby; we cannot stay long.'

Throughout the conversation, the gaze between Lincoln and Maggie had locked. Then, with Lincoln tightly gripping the fingers of Maggie's left hand, she carefully stood. They walked together, Pippi and Lorraine, a few steps behind.

A short walk further, Maggie halted, turned to face her beloved child, crouched down and spoke directly.

'My son, I love you and always will. Mirror clear, I see you, your blue eyes reflecting mine. You will be the driving force in my life. I promise you, Lincoln Pilgrim Piper, that I shall become a mother whom you will be proud of. You have a powerful brain, and you are beautiful.'

Lincoln repeated the word.

'Bootiful.'

Maggie stood, turned her child carefully, and they walked as one to Albert Piper. Simon swooped Lincoln up and secured him in the stroller. According to Albert, Lincoln looked at Maggie and spoke his first word for the second time while stretching an arm out to Maggie.

'Bootiful.'

Lorraine swiftly put her arm around Maggie and guided her back to the seat. Pippi stood firm and addressed Albert.

'Hello, Mr Piper. I'm Pippi; Lorraine is with Maggie. We are Lincoln's mother's close friends. I believe you and Maggie are touring Lucas Cave. Maggie wants to hear you sing again. Please oblige her.'

Simon spoke.

'Yes, Albert, Maggie, and Mrs Pilgrim praise your baritone. I'll purchase tickets and meet you and Maggie where the tour begins.'

Simon pointed.

'At that little building. If I'm welcome, I'll join you. I have driven a long way, so I refuse to miss this once-in-a-lifetime experience. These caves are estimated to be at least 340 million years old. Albert, please turn your back and disappear fast. Pippi and Lorrie, I know you'll take care of Maggie. Neither of you is in any condition to clamber through the Lucas Cave. There are 910 steps to negotiate at the start, and the tour is strenuous. It lasts about 1.5 hours. While we're away, don't wander far. The ladies Norris and Pilgrim are in the downstairs tearoom waiting to hear the mother meets babe details.'

The tour began at the Grand Arch. Their guide was waiting, finger to lips, indicating no noise. He turned his head and nodded towards a family of wild wallabies in the longish grass. He then warned.

Good morning. I'm Ray. Yep, like the sunshine, Ray. I ask that you stay within the light of my torch. Jenolan Caves consist of at least 25 miles of multi-level tunnels. A large section of the system is so deep and narrow that humans have never explored it. If you wander inadvertently into the labyrinth, a search party may or may not recover your skeleton someday in the distant future.

Be afraid, very afraid of the dark. Authorities will extinguish the guide-lights dotted throughout the limestone formations ten minutes after the last tour exits. If you linger and are left behind, you will know the suffocating darkness that will envelop the Lucas Cave, and you will imagine falling with every blind step. You may last forty-five terrifying minutes before you lose all sense of balance, then your brain will fumble. You will drop and freeze solid on the cold, damp floor.'

A headcount of the party, names checked against paperwork, then Ray, pointing to an everlasting set of stairs.

'Anyone here not fit enough to climb 252 stairs throughout our journey should retreat to the tearooms and enjoy scones, jam, cream and a cuppa with the old ladies. Ahead is the longest flight. If you're game.'

Some gulped, but all answered in the affirmative. Ray reprimanded three people who pretended to slow-motion run up the steps.

'Stop larking around.'

A controlled group assembled on the landing at the top.

'OK, from now on, it's easy-going. Let's do another headcount.'

Another warning.

'No smoking, no eating, no sneaking samples of Limestone, and please refrain from touching anything. Oil from human bodies discolours the pristine crystals.'

Ray pulled a switch, and the Lucas cave was subtly lit but ablaze with heavenly magnificence—stunning snow-white columns, shimmering in the glow of carefully placed spotlights. Stalagmites were growing up, and stalactites were growing down—the guide explained how to remember which was which.

'Stalagmites grow up. Like stockings on a modest lady's leg, whereas Stalactites come down. Like a shameless lady's tights.'

An unexpected, dubious joke, but they all appreciated the effort and applauded.

'Some time ago, perhaps near the beginning of time, at least millions of years ago, eruptions lifted limestone covered with debris from the sea, so numerous marine fossils have been found. The network of these caves follows an underground section of the Jenolan River. The Gundungurra Indigenous people penetrated the caves as far as the underground river, carrying sick people to bathe in the curative water, as did visitors in Victorian times. They, too, believed in the healing power of Jenolan Caves water.'

The party moved to another platform and had another headcount; Ray was a careful man. Nature's imagination had come to fruition. A master sculptor had been at work, carving numerous art objects in unfamiliar shapes to please Gaia and numb the brains of humans who dared to enter this hidden sanctuary. The colossal columns, composed of crystal upon crystal, demanded veneration for their grandeur. Maggie thought it fun to consider that a team of aliens had fashioned this landscape for the eyes of gods who resided in this subterranean Valhalla. She was annoyed that humans had given common names to these otherworldly structures based on earth-like resemblance. Inappropriately, there were the bride and groom, the mother-in-law, the witch's cauldron, the old lady's shawl, and the farmer's boots.

Too soon, they entered a massive Chamber that measured 164 feet from floor to ceiling. The guide positioned his followers in an area he described as an auditorium.

'Famous people have been singing in the Cathedral Chamber since Settlers discovered it in 1860. The acoustics here rival the world's grandest opera houses, and many famous voices have blessed this glorious space. Our own Dame Nelly Melba arrived by horse and cart to sing and experience the phonics. The Vienna Boys Choir sang here, and John Denver sang in this natural auditorium.

On reliable authority, we have, in our party, a talented baritone. I ask Mr Albert Piper to put his name alongside the many famous performers today. Mr Piper, would you do us the honour? We thank you.'

Scanty applause because nobody knew if they should. The air was pregnant as the group crept to seating, and the guide escorted Albert to a platform. Echoes of whispering from the audience hushed as the first note of Ave Maria filled the world's most acoustically perfect auditorium.

Could an angel emit a more sacred sound? Sublime amplification showed the purity of Albert's voice. Schubert's well-loved melody, with only the human voice as its instrument, was an eerie agent of creation. Maggie wondered how a man with this gift could have been so brutal in her childhood. Albert's voice continued to enrapture his audience. Maggie asked White Feathers to help her control her negative thoughts, to live in awe of the moment.

She became one with the sound as she stared into a crystal formation and saw the images of Peter, the man of honour and faith, and her mentors—Bineham, Una, Mrs Loveday, and Mrs Norris. She astral travelled to the blue pond and looked into Lincoln's blue eyes. She returned to the present by a change of sound, thunderous applause. The guide asked Albert for another song. Tiny Grey Home in the West was an excellent second choice. It was lyrical and light.

The tour over, Simon drove from the jagged Jenolan mountains, from concealed rivers in chambers and anterooms decorated with mineral deposits and limestone arches to Katoomba. The early supper was delicious. The air enveloping the party was vibrant, yet the conversation didn't happen. Bleeding hearts do not speak; they bleed.

Outside, Simon hugged Maggie, Pippi and Mrs Norris all at once, then offered Maggie Pilgrim and his wife an arm. Benjie rolled his eyes from Lorraine to Mrs Norris, to Maggie, who kissed him between his ears and then led him to the Crown Vic. The two Maggies physically touched for the last time. Goodbyes had no meaning because memory will not allow itself to be snuffed.

Margaret Pilgrim, nee Burns, had bequeathed to her chosen few an ethereal experience. That night, she slept once more in the comfort of the big, soft bed at Lorraine and Simon's, enjoyed a shared country breakfast, and then asked them to take her to the hospital, knowing she would rest in peace.

***Katoomba** is the City of Blue Mountains' chief town, situated on the Great Western Highway, 110 km west of Sydney. Elevation: 1,017 m. Founded: 1879*

***The Carrington Hotel** is in Katoomba Street, Katoomba, in the Blue Mountains. Constructed in 1883 by Harry George Rowell and by a proceeding series of prominent families over the next century, it was added to the New South Wales State Heritage Register on 2 April 1999.*

****The Fairlane Crown** Victoria, nicknamed the "Crown Vic", was the pick of the Ford Motor Company's 1955 to 1956 cars. The 2-door, 6-seat coupe differed from the "Victoria" model because of a stainless-steel band that 'crowned' the hard-top roof.*

*****Sans Souci** is a southern Sydney suburb in the state of New South Wales, Australia, 17 kilometres south of the Sydney central business district.*

******The **Jenolan Caves** are located within the Jenolan Karst Conservation Reserve in the Central Tablelands region, west of the Blue Mountains, in Jenolan, New South Wales, Australia.*

## CHAPTER 24

*A cat in a hat, Gaia's lullaby, and Scheherazade.*

The bicycle stand at Neutral Bay pier was a great idea. No doubt the brainchild of some local politician who needed votes from health-loving constituents. Maggie wasn't old enough to have her say in the ballot box, but her body appreciated the free-wheeling, fifteen-minute exercise from her digs in North Sydney to the ferry terminal.

Onboard, she took her favourite spot on the upper deck where she could feel the wind in her hair, fill her lungs with the scent of the aromatic ocean, and be entertained by the playfulness of passengers boarding. The same people travelled this water transport every day of the week, so many knew each other by name. Maggie classified them as "the ferry-clubbers".

This morning, a stranger was on board, an older man sleeping on the main deck. Maggie was directly above him, studying his face. She'd like to sketch it using the dry, dusty medium of charcoal on her recently purchased roll of toothed paper. The man was in deep slumber, so profoundly that he didn't stir when the ferry pitched as it undocked. He must have endured a wakeful night.

Maggie relished this short trip across the harbour to Circular Quay. It was a refreshing start to a heady day of perfumes, face creams, body lotions, nail polish, hairsprays, and coffee. The late-afternoon return trip was even better, as it marked the end of another day. This thought caused Maggie to ponder her future in the workforce.

As a child, she had dreams of being a trapeze artist or a spy. The first fizzled out on discovering that trapeze artists began training before they could walk, and thoughts of a spying career ended on the sure possibility of torture on capture. In her final year in primary school, she decided on Archaeology, but now, that was out of the question.

Without parental backing and no savings, Maggie had to choose from the best fate offered. Although working in a beauty salon was the dream of many a female, she found it tedious. Fortunately, a fashion photographer had listed her in his books, bringing diversity and building her bank account. But an inquiring mind needed more. Maggie was yearning for something to educate her and to give vent to her creativity.

Next week, she was meeting with a lady named Martina Morre. She wanted Maggie to make pen-and-ink sketches of fashion items for her newspaper column, learn journalism, and serve as a teenage model for her upcoming television show. That could lead to an exciting career, but Maggie saw limited opportunities in that field because employers in journalism require degrees in education.

There were cheers from the deck below. Passengers were raising their takeaway coffee cups to toast a couple who had announced their intention to marry. The girl's fiancé was holding her left hand high to show the newly placed engagement ring.

Even applause and whistles didn't wake the stranger. An Asian passenger noted the man's head was uncomfortable. He removed his jacket, rolled it up, then cupped it under the sleeping head, imitating a soft nest that offers fledglings security. Amber fingers from the rising sun caressed time-worn furrows on the man's face. A perfect study. A homeless man with his kitten asleep in his hat beside his rolled-up blanket. The Asian man disappeared, then returned with one of the ferry crew who bent, stroked the kitten, picked it up while still in the hat and carried it to the captain's cabin.

The boat saw-sawed in the wake of another ferry, and the watchful young man steadied the body with his shins when it reacted to the rolling swell.

Then Maggie understood. It was fitting that the ocean had rocked the homeless man to eternal sleep in the joyous company of celebrations. There was no announcement, but an ambulance and police officers surreptitiously waited for passengers to disembark at the Quay. Yes, she would sketch the repose of that face alongside his kitten in the hat.

Maggie had lived in North Sydney for five months. Although the four shared one house, they were all working or studying. Consequently, they greeted each other briefly when paths crossed but knew little about each other apart from first names.

That changed after Linda spotted a photo of Maggie in a hairdressing magazine. Her final exams were on the horizon, so she asked Maggie to be her comb-up and colour model. Tanya Sargent's gift of two tickets to the ballet was about to go obsolete, so Maggie asked Linda if she would be her guest.

After the performance, they shared a late supper in the house kitchen. Nancy came home exhausted after working an eight-hour stint as a duty nurse in the emergency department. She said she'd never seen a live show. Hence, Maggie and Nancy enjoyed Tanya's second gift: two tickets to a musical.

Jerry's dream was to conduct open-air classical concerts or operas or to be an artistic director of a dance company. Although he shone in instrument knowledge and interpretation, he was too shy to stand alone and give it his all. When he did find the courage to do so, he embarrassingly went way over the top. The audience almost fell out of their seats, laughing, which sent Jerry into a near state of depression. Maggie decided to make him happy, so Jerry accompanied her to the play.

Following that, the four housemates were sitting in the garden, playing a board game, when Nancy came up with a solution.

'Jerry, I think you need acting lessons.'

'Why?'

'I've heard that actors put on an invisible hat to become the person they're portraying. I don't see why you couldn't put on the hat of some famous conductor and become that character.'

Nancy thought deeply, then said.

Herbert Von Karajan is a legendary conductor of the Berlin Philharmonic. My uncle says, "Once seen, never forgotten", because he is confident, assertive, and sensual. Uncle has a photo of him in a top hat.'

Linda had another contender on whom Jerry could fashion himself.

'Sir Eugene Goossens. He is a man who likes a little magic in his life. The Queen of England has recently knighted him for services to Australian music. He's even written an opera. He's friendly with *Rosaleen Norton*, the Witch of Kings Cross, who mixes a potent brew of sex and magic in her artwork.'

'I believe you're about to say I should wear a wizard's hat.'

Jerry liked his wisecrack, but nobody laughed. Instead, Maggie remembered something.

'You could take acting lessons here in North Sydney.'

'And where in North Sydney, Clever Pants?'

Linda joined the conversation.

'Maggie's right. I know someone who regularly goes to live performances at the ***Independent Theatre*. Maybe someone there gives private tuition.'

'Wonder at what cost? I'm going to have to find work soon; my parents have hinted at it. But Lindy-Lou, I think you've got something; I'll check it out.'

The Independent Theatre at North Sydney did have a school for actors, and Jerry had already decided that was the way to reach his goal.


Late November that same year, Jerry waited with Maggie in a hall attached to the Independent. He had prepped for an audition. She was there to lend courage. Maggie had listened to Jerry's assessment piece at least ten times, a Heracles speech from the play "The Rape of the Belt".

The young man who was ushering candidates to the adjudicator approached Maggie.

'Hello. I believe your name isn't listed?'

'For an audition? No, it's not. I'm here to support a friend.'

'Miss Annabel Howard wants you to audition.'

'Why?'

'I don't know. Maybe you'll be lucky.'

'I can't. I don't know how to audition. I came to champion Jerry.'

'Miss Howard is a goddess around here. I'd do as she wants if I were you.'

'I don't see the point because I couldn't afford the lessons.'

Jerry whispered.

'Go, this could be fate.'

The young man led Maggie to a big room, almost devoid of furniture. A lady with large, soft eyes and short, smooth hair sat casually on the desk, preferring it to the accompanying chair. She reminded Maggie of a seal. Miss Annabel Howard's smile was reassuring. Then she spoke. If a voice could sound like brown velvet, it was hers.

Good afternoon. I'm Annabel Howard. And you are?'

'Good afternoon, Mis Howard, I'm Maggie Piper. I'm not here to audition; I'm supporting a friend.'

'Well, you're going to audition now. I gather you haven't prepared a piece, so I'll ask you to take this sheet of paper and study the words as you walk to the opposite wall. While reading, imagine you are the very royal Queen of the Fairies. You are not in a perfect mood because the bisexual King, Oberon, desires your changeling child for his purpose. In the speech, you refuse the child in no uncertain manner. Maggie, when you reach that wall, turn, and I shall read. You shall listen and watch, then copy what you have seen. You're on. Start walking.'

Maggie did as instructed. She remembered the hat, so she secretly put on an invisible crown. On reaching the wall, she turned to face the lovely seal.

Miss Howard slid off the table, stood and balanced her book on the palm of one hand. She stretched her body and stood tall. In swift, successive movements, she flung her free arm sideways at shoulder height, then hesitated while lengthening her neck and blazing her eyes. The hand on her free arm scooped the air as she raised it above her head. Miss Howard's voice was firm. Her tone reinforced the meaning of each word, and as small as Miss Howard was, if Maggie had been Oberon, there would have been no way she would have crossed this Queen of the fairies.

*'Set your heart at rest.*
*The fairyland buys not the child of me.*
*His mother was a votress of my order.*
*And in the spiced Indian air by night,*
*Full often hath she gossiped by my side,*
*And sat with me on Neptune's yellow sands.*
*She, being mortal, of that boy did die.*
*And for her sake, I do rear up her boy,*
*And for her sake, I will not part with him.*
*Not for thy Fairy Kingdom.'*

Now it was Maggie's turn. She mentally replaced the changeling child for Lincoln and substituted Oberon with Marj and Albert. After she read, Miss Howard smiled, then beckoned her to approach. She took her chair behind the desk while Maggie stood in front of it.

'As a student, you need to attend classes four days a week and some evenings. Would your parents support you and provide finances to purchase books?'

'They wouldn't. I am an apprentice in a beauty salon. Our manager allows me time off to model hairstyles and hats. Miss Martina Morre has offered me a full-time job sketching for her newspaper column and modelling for a new TV afternoon segment which begins next year. I will be paid, not handsomely, but well enough.'

'Does a career in theatre interest you? If so, why?'

'This is a new idea to consider. Working in the salon, I meet interesting women. Googie Withers is one of my favourites. She exudes the energy of the sun, and, like you, she has a divine voice honed over the years through training. Am I right in thinking that learning to use your voice as a musical instrument is part of theatre school?'

'Very much so, an actor's voice is a vehicle, no less than an opera singer. The art is called Voice Modulation. Speaking should be a musical passage in which you shift from one key to another, adjusting your pitch and volume without straining your vocal cords. Speaking is a form of singing with less range but with a definite rhythm and melody. An innovative public speaker would study voice modulation.

Our school trains individuals in the obvious areas of acting, directing, painting scenery, and backstage work. On a personal level, you would learn presentation, organisation, memorisation, speaking and listening skills. Would you consider attending four days weekly?'

'I got carried away, Miss Howard. I apologise. I'm wasting your time because I don't see how I could do that and work.'

'If you won a scholarship?'

'What would that do for me?'

'Pay for your books and a year's tuition. A study such as this would prepare you for a wide choice of careers in communication.'

'Really? Perhaps I could manage if I took evening work in a café.'

'If you were financially able to finish three years at this school, would you plan to act full-time?'

'How would I know? Perhaps I'd do it for fun, part-time.'

'What? Part-time? Acting is a full-time occupation. You live it; you breathe it. Theatre becomes your reason for being. Theatre is the heart and soul of literature that you bring to the public to educate and spread joy. The theatre is everything. An actor cannot and does not want to be anything for hours each day other than live the character she portrays.

Go away, Maggie Piper and think about a possible three years of solid training in the classics and contemporary work and voice production. If you have luck, you may be an accepted student.'

The following Sunday, Mrs Norris was Maggie's lunch guest: chilled cherry soup, cucumber sandwiches, iced jasmine tea, and Beethoven String Quartet. Tummies satisfied, they then retired to Maggie's veranda, where they lay on separate sofas listening to Rimsky Korsakov's Scheherazade, a gift from Jerry. Mrs Norris was familiar with the story woven into the composition. Maggie heard her guest speaking in rhythm with the music.

'Once upon a time, a Sultan who ruled over India and China went on a hunting trip. He returned to his palace earlier than expected to find his wife making love with a servant. At sunrise, she was executed. Fuelled by mixed emotions of betrayal and injured pride, the Sultan vowed to avenge all women. He took a new wife every night, made passionate love to her, then had her publicly beheaded the following day while he raged that, being dead, she would never have an opportunity to cheat on her husband. In little time, the kingdom became a hostile place for young women.

The Vizier had two daughters, Scheherazade and Dunyazad. He begged them to flee the country, but Scheherazade asked to become the Sultan's next wife.

The bridegroom was amused when Scheherazade asked that her sister join them in the bridal chamber as the last wish on their wedding night. The sisters charmed the Sultan, and with his approval, Scheherazade began telling a long and mesmerising tale. As it was about to climax, she fell asleep. So did the Sultan because Dunyazad had dipped his fruit in a sleeping draft. In the morning, the Sultan woke and wanted to hear the end of the story, but Dunyazad told him that Scheherazade had lost her voice and that it would return in the cool of the evening. So, the Sultan allowed his bride to live an extra night to finish it.

That night, Scheherazade finished her story. The night was young, so she began another, but again fell into a deep sleep at a tantalising twist. Dunyazad beguiled the Sultan, who again delayed Scheherazade's beheading until the story finished. Many nights later, love for Scheherazade, her beauty, and his addiction to her storytelling cancelled the Sultan's need for revenge. He and Scheherazade married, and the Vizier declared peace in the kingdom.'

The friends dozed for a short time, waking when Jerry arrived with a small bouquet that suspiciously resembled flowers growing in the nearby park. He stayed long enough to tell Mrs Norris about their theatre audition adventure, then left. Mrs Norris was very interested. There was an opportunity. For some time, she had wanted to discuss her young friend's future in the workforce.

'Maggie, can you see yourself working in a beauty salon for the rest of your life?'

'I'd rather not. It seems an empty profession, even though it offers a luxurious atmosphere. I meet interesting people and am groomed free of charge by the best from exotic countries.'

'Apart from meeting with your friends, what are your favourite things in life?'

'Writing poetry, painting, drawing, singing, listening to music, learning about ancient cultures, their gods and goddesses, racing the wind from one lamppost to the next.'

'Maggie, I also know you're very good with people. You ask questions that make them feel comfortable. Have you always been interested in others?'

'Not unless they are creative or unusual, Mrs Norris. The main reason I ask questions is to stop them from asking about me. Through their answers, I learn much. I also feel it sometimes relieves them of hidden pain.'

'What do you want from life?'

'I would like to have my son by my side. But as that can't happen, I want to be the best person I can be. I want to spread beauty. Perhaps through writing, painting.'

'What is your attitude towards money?'

'I haven't thought much about it, except to earn enough to stay alive. If I were a millionaire, I'd use it to change people's view of animals. They have as much right to a free life on the planet as humans.'

'If you had a dream career, what would it be? Before you answer, pretend money doesn't come into this. Imagine you can have any job you want.'

'I'd be an archaeologist. Mrs Norris, did you have a career?'

'Maggie, I trained as a classical singer. I was a Mezzo-Soprano and was rising in the world of performances when I married and had two children.'

'I thought Aimee was an only child, Mrs Norris. Perhaps I shouldn't ask?'

'You didn't ask, and I'm happy to tell you. I had a son who died from diarrhoea aged two years, so I understand the void left in a mother's life without her son. It was my pleasure to stand with your Grandma Maggie in arranging your time with Lincoln. A clear memory of his face is important for the female who loses her child.'

'I'm sorry, Mrs Norris.'

'No sorrier than I, my dear Maggie. Let's get back to finding a suitable career for you, one that will take advantage of your talents, give satisfaction and a reasonable income. Theatre training could lead to an exciting life. But there is a negative side. I imagine that there may not be enough acting jobs for all the actors in the world. The most successful people in the entertainment industry have family connections that keep them in directors' sights. You haven't. That means you would have to subsidise your income. But why would you worry about that? You already have hospitality experience and qualifications from a leading beauty salon, whose reputation will stand out to future employers. Maggie, do you enjoy photographic modelling?'

'I like working with a camera, Mrs Norris; it's probably like a toned-down version of stage acting, but I don't have to learn lines, which means I don't have to speak. The camera is better than a catwalk because I can't see their eyes. I pretend the camera is somebody I know. Mrs Norris, I'll bet you didn't guess that when you see a picture of me in the newspaper wearing a funny hat or hairstyle, I was probably looking at you. Another thing, people don't recognise me because I look ten times better in photographs than in the flesh, so I remain private.

I had fun when buying shoes the other day. The salesgirl remarked that I looked like the model Herbert Henry Salon used for their latest hairstyles. Then she added, but of course, these models have wheelbarrows full of money to afford all sorts of plastic surgery and beauty treatments, but you do have some resemblance to that model.

Mrs Norris, after a parade, I hang about in the dressing room until the guests leave. I do not enjoy the limelight; people ask questions and say things that would upset anyone.'

'Like what, Maggie?'

'Mainly, they ask if my parents are proud of me, what product I use to colour my hair and if I have a boyfriend. Insultingly, one lady said she'd like to introduce me to her son because he needs experience with girls! I put on a happy face and do the job because I need money, but an attack of nerves is waiting in the wings. Live modelling is scary because models are ruthless. They are hungry for contacts that would get them more work. I would prefer to forget all modelling. Anyway, nobody will want to employ me when I get a few wrinkles. Should I think about theatre training?'

'Don't make a decision yet. Wait to see what the wind blows. It may be the scholarship.'

'Not likely. The lady who auditioned me was furious because I told her I'd probably do acting part-time.'

Mrs Norris laughed.

'Maggie, Maggie, Maggie, you're sometimes too truthful. I love our times together, but now I'm tired. Go telephone Aimee to pick me up.'

That evening, Maggie was weary but found sleep hard to come by. The air was sticky, and she was restless. Her mind flew from one subject to another. From one uncertainty to another. To the people who had been her transitory family in Melbourne and the Community of Mothers and their children. She was glad Shirley chose to name her Peanut after Peter. Will Lincoln remember her? Then she had a silent conversation with White Feathers during which he informed her that she'd stepped on a path of many forks.

Maggie decided to leave her bed and return to the veranda. Here she had a clear view of the heavens. So few Stars, but sky-ship-shaped clouds chased panicked cloudlets across a cosmic ocean. Annabel Howard's question regarding financial help from her parents recalled hints from intelligent people in her past. Could they have adopted her? But wait. If Marj and Albert Piper were not her parents, then they were not Lincoln's grandparents, yet this was one of the legalities they had abused to acquire possession of her son! If only she had the money to employ a lawyer.

The stench of an old, idling car parked directly outside was trying to override a strolling female's obnoxious perfume. Both were polluting the air. Then a passerby said to another that a family was important —everything. Were the Pipers her natural family? If not, who were her parents? Did she have siblings?

*Rosaleen Miriam Norton (2 October 1917 – 5 December 1979), nicknamed Thorn. She was a New Zealand-born Australian artist and occultist, known as the "Witch of Kings Cross" because she lived in the bohemian area of Kings Cross, Sydney. As an occultist, she was devoted to the mythological Greek god Pan.

**The Independent Theatre Ltd. was an Australian dramatic society founded in 1930 by Dame Doris Fitton. The death of Doris Fitton's co-producer, Peter Summerton, in 1969 put a strain on her deteriorating health, and with no one able or willing to fill her shoes, the Theatre closed in 1977. It reopened in 1998 as a training ground and showcase for actors and playwrights. In 2013, Wenona Girls Boarding School purchased this gem and now uses the 303-seat theatre as an educational and performance venue for students and as a venue for public hire.

# CHAPTER 25

*Year, 1958. Magical memories.*

Maggie had been navigating through a world of business, commercial art, and study for five years. Although she'd connected with many people, she felt divorced from those dear to her. Mrs Norris needed more and more sleep time, Pippa and Lorraine had settled into married life, and darling Benjie didn't need her to walk him. Their once common interests were in the past. Una had played a significant part in Maggie's life, but she was in India continuing her studies on yogic scripture. So far from Australia, yet Una's teachings remained an intensely luminous, wise counsel in times of need.

Maggie chose to celebrate her nineteenth birthday with her favourite energy boost—a ferry ride from Sydney to Manly. Onboard passengers were entertained by a pod of wild dolphins fearlessly investigating the turbulence of the wake. They frolicked in the churning channel, then hitch-hiked below the surface to conserve energy before spinning high above the rushing river in the sea until airborne. While looping their bodies and tail-dancing, they offered smiling countenances to their applauding audience: the more ovation, the more boisterous their aerial behaviour. Keeping a safe distance from the frantic theatre calves, they were moving in concert with mothers and aunties to avoid danger. Maggie paired the pod's collective intelligence with Gita teachings on malleability. In times of war, one should become a messenger if there is something to convey, but when there is beauty to record, one should become an artist.

After disembarking, Maggie's birthday treat to herself was nine hot potato scallops she purchased while strolling the Corso. She reached the grassy verge between pavement and sand. The beach was deserted. Great, alone times were medicine for the soul. She slipped from her sandals and danced from dry to wet sand with an invisible partner. They moved to the passion of the tango; he, the leader; she, the follower. Her feet kicked up shiny grains of sand, sending sunbursts into the air. She turned too quickly, lost balance and sat breathlessly laughing.

Not wanting to miss the fun, the wind came to play. It formed a tunnel by spinning along the surface, scooping up sand as it rolled towards the ocean, then disappeared into invisibility. Maggie was ready for morning tea. Her feet were touch-sensitive on the hot sand, so she looked to the cool water of the Pacific Ocean. Teased by breaking waves, a bobbing red bucket begged for rescue.

Maggie moved towards it, jumping over wriggly lines carved by worms that could be mistaken for delicate red strings. This sand artistry, if stuck to a canvas, could sell for thousands of pounds. Happily, marine animals have no use for money, so nature here would remain untouched. A Ghost Crab, named for its colour matching its habitat, disappeared down a deep hole, dislodging uneven, hardened lumps of lining from its underworld chamber, hidden and protected from drying out till evening. Then it would adventure, scavenging for food. Maggie reached the bucket, shook it dry, stuffed her wrapped food into it, then cradled its handle in her arm. She wandered the water's edge, picked up a stick, scored MJP in the wet sand and watched receding waves journey her initials out to sea. Maybe, when carried to a kinder country, the tiny, impregnated grains will call her to join them. She crouched down and wrote Lincoln.

Her potato scallops were 265eting cold. Maggie found her discarded sandals, sat and placed her unopened parcel on the upended bucket. In a few seconds, an epic battle of the birds exploded around her. Whizzing gulls were tearing the wrapping and making off with her potato scallops. Their behaviour was insane, considering the amount of fresh food in the sea. She needed to escape, so she wriggled on her bottom far enough for safety but close enough to enjoy the antics of the airborne thieves. Still, their wings were fanning too close for comfort. She heard a voice shout.

'Got her.'

It came from a small group of elderly citizens scoring hits on the squabbling birds. Lumps of bread were their ammunition, and she was their sitting target! A chunk landed on her lap, followed swiftly by a gull that decided to tread air rather than risk a human's swipe. The bird was very close. Maggie was afraid of a creature for the first time in her life; its sharp beak wanted the prize. If she touched it, the bird might attack, and the same if she moved. Then she heard a police siren and a man's voice.

'Scallywags, give me your bread.'

A great bundle of broken bread flopped on the sand a fair distance from Maggie.

'Off with you, elderly delinquents. If I didn't know better, I'd think you were in second childhood. Are you OK, Miss?'

Maggie faced the same policeman who had been on the verge of arresting her for vagrancy just before her sixteenth birthday! He burst out laughing.

'G'Day, Miss. Was it how many years ago? Are you celebrating your birthday again? Here at Manly? It seems the gulls were enjoying the party, as were your uninvited guests in their second childhood.'

Using a gentler tone, he walked to the sand and bent, offering his hands to help her stand.

'You're a unique young lady. Are you doing anything special for your birthday?'

'Believe it or not, tomorrow, the same estate agent you met, and my other friends have planned a surprise picnic. But, of course, I'm not supposed to know about it.'

'Do you still live near Kirribilli?'

North Sydney. Thank you for remembering my special day.'

'I'm guessing you've had enough of our Manley for today. I'm still on duty, so I shan't drive you home. Can I take you to the ferry terminal?'

'Can you turn on your siren?'

'Sure can. Happy birthday. Maggie Piper, isn't it?'

With the culinary satisfaction of freshly baked pogácsa and coffee for breakfast, Aimee drove Mrs Norris and Maggie to the *Gordon Falls Reserve* in the Blue Mountains.

The vicinity honoured valuable memories and ongoing friendships that began six years previously, when Lorraine took Maggie, aged thirteen, under her wing at the Nursing home. She introduced her to the Deri family-Pippi, Elec, Pippi's brother Andras and his wife, Karine.

Pippi and Elec had owned Cafés Gerbeaud & Ruszwurm, and Andras was their Pâtissier of fine sweets. The family had recently moved from Sydney to Leura, where a prominent hotel had contracted Elec and Andras to supply Hungarian and French pastries, specialty bread, and sweets, including Turkish Delight. Lorraine, Pippi and Karine were planning a creperie stand at the local once-monthly markets after the three had given birth to their second children, all due this year, sometime in September or October.

For Maggie, the eucalyptus-scented air, epic views, and the picnic were a much-needed healing experience away from work and study. She stuffed herself on yummies for her tummy and a Gerbeaud birthday cake. She pretended not to watch as the children poked their little fingers between the pastry layers and scooped out the soft almond filling. Innocence was at play in the weak April sunshine. Autumn breezes tussled Sebastian's golden mop and Zaba's charcoal curls as their tiny feet blazed around the solid trunks of trees, chased by Elec and Simon. Maggie shifted her gaze. Andras and Karine's little Jazmin was piling fallen leaves on Benjie's compliant head. If the world stood still, here would be two perfect paintings to grace a Victorian chocolate box.

The beauty of creation actively blessed the bond between her friends' children, and here was positive proof that love between parents and their children did exist. Maggie's concentration was interrupted by Mrs Norris and Aimee, who had seen Maggie's expression cloud and wisely decided to take her mind off children. Mrs Norris hugged Maggie.

'It's time for a stroll before we leave this idyllic place. Let's go for a happy birthday walk. I remember well that it was in the Blue Mountains, where we took leave of your Grandma Maggie. Margaret Pilgrim, nee Burns.'

'She's always with me. I feel her in a capricious wind, in a teasing breeze, and when I look at tea leaves in an empty cup.'

Nobody mentioned the sweetest memory of all when Maggie set eyes on Lincoln for the first time, and when he repeated the word 'bootiful' looking at Maggie. But it was on everyone's mind at some time during that day of enduring fellowship.

Maggie's life had changed for the better. Annabel Howard, of the brown velvet vocal cords and Principal Tutor at the Independent Theatre School, fervently believed that everyone was born with a potentially beautiful speaking voice. It was a prime communication method, a fundamental part of every individual's identity and a vital acting component. To fine-tune this art, students participated in "blind acting" for two half-days weekly.

Three students at a time stood behind a screen and conversed in voices ranging from youthful to aging, from feeble to powerful, from persuasive to melodious, from terrifying to soothing. Listening students took notes and then gave critiques on characterisation. As a future stage, film or radio actor, newsreader, or presenter, it was their duty to develop the full potential of voice for the sake of their audience, for playwrights and producers.

David Dallimore gave individual lessons to those with singing potential. He often coupled vocal technique with advanced studies on stagecraft movement. Annabel threw a spanner in the works at the beginning of the second year by introducing another tutor and stage director, Miss Colleen Whitehouse. She gave a different slant to character acting than Annabel Howard taught. Both tutors preferred the classics but utilised other methods. For instance, when portraying Shylock, a wealthy Jewish moneylender and the principal antagonist in Shakespeare's The Merchant of Venice, Annabel wanted him to be raw, greedy, and somewhat vulgar. Colleen preferred Shylock to be a whining victim of his greed and a slyly vengeful figure, with a pretence of gentlemanly mannerisms. The choices from the directors' analysis were fascinating.

Maggie had proved her dedication to Annabel's cause by constant attendance four days a week, learning lines and sonnets, and singing. But to pay for lessons plus living expenses, her workload was extreme. She spent evenings sketching the latest fashion trends in pen and ink for Martina's newspaper column and rose with the sun to return those items and collect more for the following week's art. One day each week was spent flat-out preparing Martina's television segment, and another on the TV show itself. Then she sometimes managed to squash in a photoshoot of a new hairstyle, hat, or sportswear.

Martina was intelligent, elegant, creative, and a great boss. Her sixty-minute show attracted high ratings and was fun. Its format was steady. The highlight was a guest-celebrity interview discussing a fascinating subject, such as the release of a new book, a film, or a live theatre performance. Maggie modelled hairstyles, hats, and clothing, and Martina advertised what she was wearing, be it a handbag, jewellery, or shoes. A guest musician opened and played for an hour off-air.

One day, after the show and while Maggie was still in the building, the receptionist called her. Albert was on the telephone.

'Sorry to bother you, Maggie, but my little wife watches Martina's TV show and wants you to put Lucy on it. Lucy wants to meet ***Roger Climpson,* the newsreader.'

'Roger is not in Martina's segment, and why would a little girl want to meet an adult male newsreader? Does an eight-year-old listen to the news?'

'I don't know. Your mother says so. She wants Lucy to go on TV.'

'There's nothing for children in the show, and I'm just Martina's teenage employee. I'm genuinely sorry, but I can't help. It's not my television show.'

'Marj says Lucy also wants to meet *** *Chuck Faulkner*, the other newsreader.'

'Daddy, Chuck Faulkner works the evening news, and I'm not in a position to do this. I've seen both men around, but I don't know them. I repeat, I'm just Martina's teenage employee.'

'Ask her, tell her it's a favour for your mother.'

'My mother? Am I supposed to recognise her as my mother? Forget that she has stolen my son? That you had me arrested in Melbourne for trying to see his face? That she put me out in the world aged twelve with no money, clothes, or anywhere to sleep? My mother deserves no favours, and I can't risk losing my job. I need to work to stay alive.'

'OK, if you won't do it, I'll write a letter to Martina care of the channel and ask if she'll introduce our little Lucy to Roger and Chuck. I'll introduce myself as your father.'

'That will make you just another person wanting fame for their child, and you'll put me in danger of losing my job. Please, please don't do this.'

Marj wants to see Lucy on television. Lucy wants to meet the newsreaders.'

'I don't believe you. It's your wife who plans to meet them by accompanying Lucy to the TV station. Is that correct?'

'I don't know. I haven't discussed who'll bring Lucy. But of course, I'd have to drive; my wifey is too delicate to learn.'

'You've had my telephone number for two years. You promised you'd give me news of Lincoln every three months, which you haven't. You blackmailed me into signing my son to you, and now you are threatening to do something that may lose my job. Are you proud of yourself?'

'Please try for my sake. Lucy is beautiful, and she would do as you ask. She won't ruin Martina's show.'

'Martina knows little about me. I am a private person. You are forcing me to let people know about my god-fearing, devilish parents and how they have treated me. Do as you like. I will not risk my job. You carry the shame of being a weak man who will destroy his eldest daughter to please his spoiled wife. Until you keep your promise and contact me with news of Lincoln, I want nothing to say to you.

Maggie hung up. Jerry came by and found her sobbing on the veranda. She told him as little as possible about her past and about her conversations with Albert. Jerry came up with an idea.

'Linda could do with publicity now that she's opening her hairdressing salon. I wonder if she'd like to do a mother-daughter hairstyle duo? Martina might like the idea, and she's known to interview beginners starting a new business.'

'That's a clever idea, particularly if it helps Linda. There would be no need to tell Martina that Lucy is my sister. Do you think Linda would approach Martina?'

'I think we may have to fill Linda in a little bit. But I'm sure it would be good publicity, and Linda's a creative hairdresser.'

Albert telephoned again. This time, Maggie wasn't caught off guard. She told him that on condition that he or Marj would not approach Martina or visit the television channel, a hairdresser she knew would speak to Martina about featuring the latest little sister, big sister hairstyles. First, Albert was to take Lucy to meet Linda; then, if Linda thought Lucy suitable, she would contact Martina and put the idea to her. If Martina went for the concept, Lucy should be delivered and picked up from Linda's salon. Albert whooped with joy.

'The boys at the lodge will love this. Two of my girls are on TV at the same time. When will it be on?'

'That is up to Linda and Martina. And it is a one-off, never to be repeated.'

Martina thought the mother-and-daughter hairstyles were a fabulous idea and immediately contacted a fashion house to supply mother-and-daughter clothing: Blue, Maggie's favourite colour.

Annabel Howard hadn't lost patience with Maggie because she wasn't that type of tutor. But after two years of training, Maggie, a powerful force in rehearsals, suffered debilitating stage fright so much so that Annabel had a colossal uphill battle to keep her in the school after the near catastrophe she caused during the previous year's adjudication performances.

Annabel had cast Maggie as Titania opposite Jerry's Oberon from Shakespeare's "A Midsummer Night's Dream". Maggie should have successfully advanced to the following year, as the speech was the same; she had initially won entrance. But no. At the very last minute, Maggie suffered a panic attack and refused to step on stage. Annabel announced Titania was indisposed and read the speech. Stage fright did not justify inexcusable, unprofessional behaviour. In a double audition, she failed her fellow actor, and if that had been a public performance, she would have ruined the play and shamed the playhouse.

Annabelle's exemplary reputation as a fine tutor and judge of talent stood in Maggie's stead. Miss Fitton granted Maggie the benefit of the doubt only after they had worked together for two weeks. Then, during a professional rehearsal directed by the famous lady, Maggie took notes and verbally repeated them to the cast while standing on stage. This innovative exercise gave Maggie confidence to use her voice with authority and to learn about technique, artistic consciousness, and directing.

Maggie managed her second-year fees by paying each term in advance. She bought used textbooks from those who moved on or up and hired plays from the library. But how to conquer fear?

Annabel noticed that although Maggie and Jerry were close, their relationship was platonic. The teenager kept people at a distance, unusual for someone with an infectious personality. She appeared to be outgoing but was hideously shy. There was no doubt that photographers found Maggie easy to work with; she strutted with confidence on the catwalk, and when playing a character, readily took on the persona, but it disappeared faster than a frog confronted with a snake when she stepped on stage. Why? Annabel realised the problem. In Maggie's daily work, she didn't have to speak! OK, at the end of this year's adjudication, Maggie would play a non-vocal character.

Annabel chose William Inge's play titled "Bus Stop".

The author had set his play in a small restaurant situated at a bus stop in rural Kansas, thirty miles west of Kansas City. The restaurant owner and her teenage daughter were waiting for a bus with passengers to arrive. The sheriff had advised them that due to an expected blizzard, all roads were closed. The passengers scheduled to ride the bus would remain in their diner until further notice. The ensuing drama featured several romantic entanglements and dark comedy. Characters included an alcoholic, a cowboy, the sheriff, the bus driver, and a few others. Annabel took the director's licence and added a deaf and dumb female who lip-read conversations, then tried to communicate in sign language, which nobody understood—a part made to order for Maggie. Annabel distributed scripts to the cast, and rehearsals were to begin in a month.

****Gordon Falls*** *in Leura, the Blue Mountains, New South Wales, offers sweeping views, excellent birdwatching, and bushwalks. A short track leads into the national park and lookout from the picnic area, with breathtaking views of Gordon Falls' water plunging 200m into the valley.*

** ***Roger Climpson OAM- Medal of the Order of Australia*** *(born 18 October 1932) is a retired English-born Australian media personality who served a lengthy career in radio and television as a journalist and announcer, newsreader, and presenter.*

*** ***Charles Stephen Faulkner*** *(21 October 1922 – 4 December 2000), professionally Chuck. One of the first news presenters at the Nine Network with studio TCN from 1956 to 1964.*

**** ***Dame Doris Alice Lucy Walkden Fitton, DBE*** *(3 November 1897 – 2 April 1985) Born in Santa Ana, Manila, Philippines, the five-year-old Doris relocated to Australia with her mother and sister after her father's death. Doris Fitton was a much-sought-after actress and a talented dancer on stage and in film. As a stage theatrical director and producer, she founded and, for 35 years,* *headed The **Independent Theatre Ltd.** In Sydney, New South Wales, staging over 400 productions. North Sydney Council commissioned a plaque in her honour in the pavement at the theatre's entrance on 17 December 1986. The council named a nearby park in her honour; there is a Fitton Close in the Canberra suburb of Dunlop, and her name is in the Live Performance Australia Hall of Fame.*

## CHAPTER 26

*The Beanfest to end all Bean fests.*

Martina Moore was a person of defined vision. She had the power to see, imagine what could be, and create a strategy to fulfil her dreams. Martina wished to float a company that organised conferences, exhibitions, and society events. She had everything it took to do well in a fast-paced environment: personally, grace and style; good connections; organisational and marketing skills; and the ability to lead and work as part of a team. But the final jewel in her crown was missing. Martina needed just one more stepping stone, so she decided to sponsor a candidate to compete in the annual Miss Australia and Charity Queen Quests.

This powerful fundraising medium for the Spastic Centres was arguably the most popular event in Australia's social history. In each state, a panel of judges, chosen by the lingerie manufacturer Hickory, selected semi-finalists from submitted photographs. On meeting their chosen contestants, the judges would search for more than just a pretty face. She certainly had to be good-looking, but more importantly, the new Miss Australia had to be the ideal Australian woman, capable of conversing intelligently and holding her own in all walks of life. She was to be an ambassador representing her country diplomatically abroad and promoting charity fundraising at home.

The Miss Australia Quest encouraged contestants to prove their worthiness to the community by demonstrating an ability to raise enormous swags of money for the Cerebral Palsy Foundation. But the judges discovered that the contestant who raised the most money was not always the absolute material to wear the crown. This gave rise to additional titles within the Miss Australia Quest: Territory and State Charity Queens and Miss Australia Charity Queen.

Martina was aware of Maggie's public reticence but was confident that, handled carefully, she could change that. If Maggie, who regularly appeared on her TV show, were an entrant in the Miss Australia contest, its weekly ratings would soar. In addition, interviews with connected people would be accessible, fashion items would be more exclusive, and Martina would gain an excellent reputation as an organiser of charity events.

Maggie was an appropriate choice from all angles. She was used to the camera, was obscenely photogenic, a natural on the catwalk and could handle people. Martina had often amused herself watching Maggie turn potential lovers into brothers within a few minutes. Interesting for one of the tender years. Martina decided to probe.

'Maggie, how many boyfriends have you had?'

'None, Martina. I haven't met anyone fanciable. There was one man, but we met in circumstances that disallowed union. Sometimes I look at husbands and wives with a baby in a stroller and wonder if I will ever marry and be loved in that special way.'

'Would you help me give a charity party for a worthy cause? I'd like us to raise money for the Spastic Centre. But to gain the publicity we need to attract donations, we will have to enter you in the Miss Australia Quest. I'd do it myself, but as you know, I've been married.'

Maggie laughed.

'Martina, no way. I've seen the event on TV. The contestants are almost always beautiful, and they have money behind them. They are like gemstones polished to perfection and are not afraid to speak in public.'

'But you wouldn't have to continue with the Miss Australia stuff; we'd only have to register you as an entrant. Did you know there is another contest alongside the Miss Australia Quest? Miss Charity Queen. Have you heard of that?'

'Vaguely.'

All we have to do is raise more money than any other contestant. That would be easy. We'll hold events where people will buy raffle tickets to win donated prizes. It won't cost us a thing, and we'd make money for a needy cause. You would be doing me a favour because raising money for charity is a great desire I've had for years, and it would certainly help your career as an actress if you became a Miss Charity Queen. You'd be featured in street parades sitting on a floral float, piped in by Scottish bands, introduced by marching girls, protected by uniformed police on horseback, followed by clowns on stilts and painted elephants dripping with golden decorations. Once crowned Charity Queen, you would promote Australia's export products and the Spastic Centre for a year and then boom, your acting career is off the ground. God knows such a worthy cause needs as much help as it can muster.'

Maggie was hardly convinced.

'But must I enter the Miss Australia Quest to help you raise money for the Spastic Centre?'

'I see no other way, but as I said earlier, you wouldn't have to compete for the national title because the state Charity Queen is decided beforehand according to the amount of money raised by individual contestants.'

'Martina, are you saying that I wouldn't have to speak to a panel of judges and compete with beautiful beings?'

'You would be crowned Charity Queen because we raised more money than the other contestants. Of course, the judges want you to look pretty, but frankly, you don't have to be drop-dead gorgeous.'

'I'm not afraid in front of a camera or on a catwalk, and I've been practising walking and talking on stage, but Martina, I'm terrified of crowds if they get close to me.'

'They won't get close; you'd be on a stage surrounded by people guarding you. To show you how easy it is, let's have a fundraising Beanfest and see what you think. Then you can change your mind if you want. I'll arrange for raffles, door prizes and lucky dips.'

'And you want me to help? I'm good at catering but know little about cooking beans.'

Martina laughed.

A Beanfest is an informal, come-as-you-are social event where people dress to the nines, drink alcohol, and pig out on nibbles. We'll have professional caterers. You could help me sell raffle tickets; you know how. Generally, charm the pants off wealthy men, so they buy oodles of tickets at a time.'

'Do you think I'd be good at that?'

'You could rake in thousands of pounds with a smile, and you're a natural flirt.'

'What would I wear?'

'Maggie, you know me and my contacts. I'll find you a deliciously sexy dress, not too revealing. Linda will do your hair, and the channel's make-up artists will do their bit. I promise you'll look like a movie star.'

It was a good plan, but Martina did not know about Maggie's whopping social problem. Having been drugged, she had no recollection of being ravished. Maggie had never been to an adult party and was utterly unaccustomed to alcohol and its effect on individuals. She came across as a tad naughty, so men could think she'd be an easy pushover, but that was far from the truth because Maggie knew the consequences of sexual intercourse. The unsuspecting did not realise intimacy was off her radar.

Maggie shared lunch with Martina on her balcony overlooking the harbour, discussing the potential benefits of a financial boost for the Spastic Centre, but Maggie got cold feet.

'Martina, I can't do this. I wouldn't have a chance of winning; I'd make a fool of you and myself.'

'Ah, but Maggie, you could always change your mind at this early stage. Let's see how you feel after our first fundraising party.'

Maggie settled, so Martina continued.

'A newspaper reporter may interview you. It would be in our favour to tell them that you are a cadet journalist, an Australian by birth, and that you were brought up in NSW. You are attending acting school to better your communication and voice production. Your hobby is learning about and becoming an expert in Australian history. Your great love is Australian poetry. Then you could name Dorothea Mackellar, Banjo Paterson, Henry Lawson and Mary Hannay Foott.'

Maggie nodded because this was true. Martina added the last, not-so-well-known poet to see how Maggie handled it. Maggie answered by reciting some Mary Hannay Foott she learned at school, titled;

**"Where the Pelican Builds.**
*The horses were ready; the rails were down,*
*But the riders lingered still –*
*One had a parting word to say,*
*And one had his pipe to fill.*
*Then they mounted, one with a granted prayer,*
*And one with a grief unguessed.*
*"We are going," they said, as they rode away –*
*"Where the pelican builds her nest!"'*


Martina was taken off guard, but being Martina regained composure and gave an encouraging light applause. Then they got down to detailed arrangements. Martina said it would carry more weight if each letter requesting a raffle donation were handwritten and accompanied by a glamour shot of Maggie, so she dictated. At the same time, Maggie wrote the template and a press release. They could display the prizes on Martina's mezzanine floor, which would act as a stage. Martina's son, Norman, would sit at the Baby Grande playing light musical numbers throughout the evening.

The response was generous. The raffle trophy was a "Tin Lizzie" Ford T. Model car worth a small fortune. They would display it on Martina's driveway, adorned with balloons. Then came a tropical getaway for two on the Gold Coast, Queensland; a Hot Air Balloon experience over the Hunter Valley; four indulgent gift hampers; two pedigreed Persian kittens, to go strictly to the same household; and an Afghan puppy. Martina thought it a great idea to add a bundle of housekeeping goods—a broom, a mop, rubber gloves, and an outsized feather duster—for the person who volunteered to provide three hours of housework.

Small firms and individuals donated lucky dip and door prizes, a gift certificate worth one hundred pounds of costume jewellery, a local travel voucher worth seventy-five pounds, monthly subscription packages for a year, one home-baked cake each week for two months and a fifty-pound voucher from the local Chinese takeaway.

Maggie's dress arrived. A fabric artist had covered heavy silk with hand-painted autumn leaves. Fashionably, it had no sleeves, a low, scooped neckline and a full quilted skirt that flattered her waist. Accompanying that were silk leaves for her hair and Cinderella's glass-heeled shoes.

The evening of the event, Maggie dressed in the outside powder room next to Martina's unit entrance, leaving her day clothes in her bicycle basket. The idea was that she could slip out unnoticed after she drew the raffles. She had to be fresh the next day for a 3 pm read-through of the end-of-the-year adjudication play.

Norman was on the mezzanine at the baby grand. Martina and Maggie greeted guests who began streaming through the open double doors at 6 pm. Immediately, each was offered a Whiskey Sour from a silver tray by a smartly dressed waiter. The early Beanfesters were in subtle colours and tailored styles, but then came a parade of outrageously garbed individuals who seemed more suited to courtiers in Marie Antoinette's entourage. Maggie had to stifle giggles. They were decidedly overdressed, and their diction would have been termed "over-the-top" by Miss Howard.

First to arrive was a weedy gentleman on the arm of a buxom lady whose hat had a brim so large she could have fitted another two insipid men under it, then entered a man dressed as a lady. He teetered on stilettos, saving himself from falling by leaning against the weedy man who was still attached to the buxom lady in the big hat. The cross-dresser straightened up, released the clasp of the necklace he'd been swinging when he made his grand entrance, threaded the stilettos on it and strung the lot around his neck. He declared they deserved to be worn as jewellery because he'd picked them up in Paris for the same price as a red spinel pendant that dangled on his forehead!

Numerous couples and singles swung through the doors, followed by a hunting team, each wearing one exquisite earring of a pair of enamelled and bejewelled ocelots. They took the mezzanine stage, explaining to all that they were conservationists who wore hunting gear while wearing animal motifs to make others aware that one should not murder animals. One should instead pursue those offered by the global design house Tiffany & Co.

More highly scented, beautiful individuals sashayed into Martina's apartment, occasionally standing on tiptoes, one arm lifted high to catch another's attention across the room. They purred and yoo-hoo-ed messages such as 'Hello Darhhhling, must give you a smooch' or 'love Yoh, Dear Heart'. One man teased another by threatening him with a live snake curled around his upper arm. A woman with twin boys posed at the entrance. The children were each assisted by a nanny carrying their violin cases. After a warm welcome from Martina, the lady announced that her virtuoso twins would play a duet for whoever held the winning raffle ticket. She produced a bowl with booklets and began selling while the virtuosos sat dangling their legs off the stage.

Marina's guests wore brocades, laces, jewelled sleeves, feathers, and leather. One lady had a very long ponytail. A cheeky man pulled it for a joke, and the whole thing came off in his hand. The mortified woman screamed. Her assailant leapt up to the mezzanine floor and danced wildly, stretching the ponytail across his top lip to imitate a very long moustache. Two hours in, a female decided to lie down across a human's lap, sitting on a crowded settee because her dress had drawn her waist in too tightly, and she was about to faint. Someone else made an ass of himself by sitting astride a giant pouffe imitating his dog's love-making movements. People applauded politely, then left him to it.

Maggie laughed; this Beanfest was silly and exhilarating. She felt as though someone had opened the door of a cage, and she'd flown free.

As the evening wore on and guests consumed copious amounts of alcohol, Maggie noticed a change in the partygoers' expressions and movements. They looked strange. Men put their heads in weird positions, looking like birds of prey and leading with their noses, which looked penile. They reminded Maggie of rough drawings on public toilet walls of men with enlarged penises in the centre of their faces, instead of noses. Two men approached Maggie. They introduced themselves.

'We are lecherous lawyers. We work to live and live to party. Hello Party Girl.'

'Hello, Party Boys. I'm selling raffle tickets. All proceeds to the Spastic Centre. Will you buy a book? Please. Pretty please?'

'What's the prize?'

'Three hours of housework.'

The men were interested.

'Any housework? Scrubbing, cleaning cupboards, making beds?'

Maggie smiled and shrugged.

'Housework is housework, so my guess is as good as yours. Probably anything you want, as long as it's not too strenuous. It was donated by one of the beautiful ladies here this evening. I don't know who, but they're all lovely. If you win, you shouldn't be too hard on her.'

One man looked at her earnestly.

'I'd never be too hard on a beautiful lady.'

Maggie wondered why they snickered and looked at her intently; she felt decidedly uncomfortable.

One asked.

'How many books have you got?'

Maggie picked up the bundle and answered.

'Ten.'

The other offered.

'I'll buy eleven.'

The first added.

'I'll buy one more.'

Maggie had a fleeting thought. The two men resembled jumbo spiders about to pounce. She took their money while saying.

'As you've bought all the tickets and more, I truly thank you. Please write both your names on the box, not on the stubs. I'm sure you'll win. Wonder what chores you'll give the lady?'

She glanced at the two men before moving on. Alcohol would never be her thing. It changed people. Maggie noted these men when they arrived. They were flirty but refined before they started drinking. Now they were gross and offensive. She moved on to the next raffle to sell its books. Martina was right; she could sell raffle tickets. Easy to make money for charity.

But the party and the guests wore thin. They were mostly a pretentious lot. Maggie wondered if this was the correct way to help the Spastic Centre. It seemed more like a way to clamber up the social ladder. To where? For what? Nothing and nobody looked real.

Martina called Maggie to the mezzanine to help draw the raffles. Looking down at them, Maggie became scared, vulnerable. They and she lived on different planets. She didn't speak their language — English, yes, but the usage was unlike anything she had encountered. It seemed that life had little value to them except for gaining connections that came about through exchanges of promises, sensuality, sex and money.

Norman stopped his background music to explode party poppers that showered thin paper streamers, which attached themselves to anything protruding —hair mostly. Maggie drew the tickets, and Martina called the winning numbers. The crowd howled and whooped amid thunderous applause as the prizes were accepted. It was an assault on her ears. When the lawyers won the winner of three hours of housework by a lovely lady, they leapt up on the stage and flanked Maggie. Everyone cheered and whistled. They clapped as the men put one hand under each of her elbows. She stiffened in fear; they lifted her feet off the ground. She heard voices yelling.

'All for the sake of charity, rumpy-pumpy for charity, the more, the merrier. Twosomes or threesomes? No *Brownies* allowed. Wonder who'll do the washing? Uh oh, the diddly oh, celebrate the little housemaid!'

They put Maggie down, she jumped off the stage and tried to escape, but one of the men lifted her to his shoulder and started to fireman carry her through the jeering, cheering odd bodies. Maggie kicked him, he dropped her, and she got up and ran, pushing her way through the crowd.

She reached outside and heard loud booing and shouted accusations of 'party pooper' coming from the drunken mass. 'Party pooper, party pooper. ' She ran to the outside powder room, where she's left her day clothes in her bicycle basket. She tore off the beautiful gown, threw the shoes into the washbasin and the dress on top of them, donned her daywear, then jumped on her bicycle.

With the wind behind her back, her feet spun the pedals faster than a milling storm. She turned a corner in the road, and the wind dropped. Her legs felt heavy, and the peddling slowed to a walking pace. Maggie dismounted not far from her bedsit and wheeled her bicycle forward—just one more house to pass. A car stopped a short way ahead. Three men sprang out and stood firm in her path. One made a gesture for Maggie to keep coming towards them. She extended her arms, pretending to accept him, then found the strength to run forward, dash between them, and speed through the open gate of her veranda. She slumped on her bed and sobbed herself to sleep.

Jerry's morning at the academy finished early, so he decided to check whether Maggie was home and planned to read through the adjudication play. He was surprised to find her bicycle on its side a short distance from the house. He secured it to its stand near her veranda entrance, then saw her gate open. Jerry knocked, but there was no answer. He panicked, entered, and saw her sleeping, fully dressed. Maggie's face was make-up streaked, her clothes crumpled, her shoes missing, her feet dirty, and her hair tangled with crumpled autumn leaves. But she looked peaceful, and her sleep was deep. He touched her hand; she responded gently. Jerry knew she'd been to a party, so he automatically thought she'd had a wild evening. He decided it would be nice for her to have music, so, sorting through her records, he stacked Tchaikovsky's Sleeping Beauty Suite and Nellie Melba's Ave Maria, then set them spinning on the record player. Maggie's soft, white blanket was on the floor, so he threw it over her and left. If she didn't make the read-through, he'd cover for her.

Maggie woke to the last strains of Ave Maria. She stood up, grabbed a white feather from her collection, threw on a skirt and top, wrapped a scarf around her head and slipped sandals on her feet. She rode her bike to Neutral Bay wharf and crossed on the little boat to Circular Quay, making it just in time to catch the afternoon ferry to Manly.

The top deck was almost empty. Maggie stood against the wind. It loosened her scarf, then stole it. She watched it fly high, dip low and skip over waves, then lift to seek adventure beyond.

The Community of Mothers popped into her head. Although far away, Maggie was spiritually bound to those brave women and their babes. Her thoughts went to Matron, who had changed from devil to angel; Bineham, her mentor; Lily, the pure in heart; and Peter, the man of the cloth, the embodiment of moral concept. Maggie had left that family of circumstance to be close to her son, Lincoln.

Not long ago, she'd been waiting to pick herself and Lucy up from Linda's hairdressing salon. They were to appear together, modelling sister hairstyles on Martina's TV show. Outside, she noted Marj seated on a bench near the bus stop with little Lincoln. She spotted Maggie, said something to Lincoln, put him down and pointed. Lincoln ran to her. Excited and full of yearning, she feasted her eyes on this child who vaguely resembled his Greek father, except for his blue eyes. When nearly at touching distance, she opened her arms to him. Her child stopped, spat with all his might on the ground at her feet, then ran back to Marj, who swept him up in her arms, spinning in circles while kissing his face.

It had been challenging to smile into studio cameras after that. And harder still to face the future when alone at night. The Melbourne Lawyer's warning rang in her ears.

*"Maggie, it is evident that you have little choice, and it is equally apparent that there are future problems to consider if you sign this document. Marj and Albert Piper stipulate that you must never contact your child or visit their home or the school they will attend. You will have nothing to do with his upbringing. You will waive all rights as his mother. Maggie, understand they intend to cut you out of his life. If you agree to sign, these people will not only take your baby, but they will also take your child's first steps, birthdays, his ups and his downs. His children will be their grandchildren. This document is airtight and ruthless. Their purpose is to curb your son from following instincts he may have toward you, his natural mother. Such people will poison his mind against you. You will lose him forever."*

Today, before leaving home, she'd placed two bank books with two open notes asking that Albert Piper keep and honour the account in Lincoln's name and present the letter addressed to him when he turned fifteen. That letter read.

*To Lincoln Pilgrim Piper, the son I never had.*

*For the first time on your* first *birthday, I saw your face and your eyes. I felt your fingers entwined in mine. I heard your voice when you repeated the word "beautiful". I desire a time machine that would return me to those precious minutes.*

*My short but extraordinary life experience and knowledge of spiritual stuff would never have happened if you had not been born. Thank you for being. I am happy. There is nowhere to go but the horizon. Know that you are beautiful.*

The second note to Mrs Norris was folded around Maggie's scarab ring.

*Mrs Norris, thank you for being my trusted friend and mentor. Miracles don't just happen. Well, perhaps they do for the righteous and the wealthy, but I am neither. Off to the sea for baptism. M. x*

After the ferry berthed at Manly, Maggie followed the Corso to the beachfront. She discarded her sandals at the edge of the grassy verge. Dry sand separated her toes and caressed the soles of her moving feet. Eyes fixed on the line where sea and sky met, she surrendered to its hypnotic call. Cool clouds of foam carried by pulsating water circled her feet and caressed her legs.

Further in, water lifted the hem of her skirt to partner, then dance with white horses capping the incoming tide. She flexed her body on one side, then the other. She was a fish; her feet were nowhere. She prayed that this baptism would dissolve the pain of the past and her fear of the future. Her soul joined a chorus of gulls playing at ballet's seven basic movements-bend, stretch, glide, lift and turn. Happiness welled inside her. She had no weight; the water and she were one. The lovely Ave Maria flowed through her blood as a euphoric tonic. The release was hers, and she was in the now. Her being was coloured with happiness never experienced. Her bruised spirit hovered in a universal womb of darkness while the pacifying water allowed her buoyant body to drift. Then the forceful current of the rising tide tossed it as flotsam to the arms of the prevailing wind.

\* *The* **Brownie** *was a long-running popular series of simple and inexpensive cameras made by Eastman Kodak and introduced in 1900. The Brownie 127 sold in the millions between 1952 and 1967. It was a Bakelite camera with a simple meniscus lens and a curved film plane to compensate for the lens's deficiencies.*

## CHAPTER 27

*Place: North Sydney Hospital. "Begin with the end in mind"*

Maggie lay on her back studying the sky. From an artistic understanding, it lacked tone and depth. She'd heard someone say it was midday. Usually, at noon and near vision, an unclouded sky was bright and bold as though it reflected a metallic surface, fading to a powdery blue in the distance—but this sky was different. A puzzle to be solved another time. She succumbed to sleep.

'Wake up, Maggie. It's time to know yourself.'

The voice had urgency, but Maggie couldn't open her eyes.

'Rouse, Maggie, stretch your toes, circle your ankles, move your thigh muscles, straighten your legs, now your arms, bend your arms. Shake your hands, your feet, your brain.'

Who said that? She remembered offering herself for baptism in the ocean, then floating weightless in an inky space. Her head was throbbing with faint drumming, reminiscent of the inaudible sound of a cat pushing in and out with its front paws, alternating left and right on a soft surface. Lub-dub, lub-dub, lub-dub. Perhaps she was dead. But that was silly because dead people don't think. Then again, they may; nobody has returned to tell. One thing was sure. She was now in a strange place surrounded by blue, the colour of God's country. An amusing turn of events. She couldn't believe she had a place in this domain; she'd done nothing to deserve entry. The topography was strangely monotonous. Confused, Maggie decided it didn't matter where she was; her eyelids were heavy, and she'd work it out later.

Nancy, one of the three people with whom Maggie house-shared, was on Trauma Nurse duty in the North Sydney Hospital when ambulance officers admitted an unconscious, bedraggled female found on a sandbank at Shelly Beach. Off duty, Nancy had sat by Maggie's bed for two full evenings, speaking softly, working her muscles, holding her hand. Although her patient woke on occasions and sat steadily for intermittent sponging, Maggie failed to recognise Nancy. Today was different. Maggie's face had colour in it, and Nancy felt consistent strength in her fingers. The slight rasp in her throat had dulled to almost nothing, and her breathing was regular. Physically, she was on the mend, and there were no post-complications after entering an involuntary state of unconsciousness. Medics concluded Maggie's body had floated on the incoming tide, and the high wind had hammered out any water that had found its way into her airway, saving her from suffocation.

'Maggie, do you know who I am?'

Maggie opened her eyes.

'You're Nancy.'

'I am, and this is your third day in the hospital. How do you feel?'

No immediate answer, but Nancy noted a questionable expression. She helped Maggie sit by propping pillows behind her back for support.

'Nancy, something's wrong. I can't remember coming here. I woke earlier and thought I must be in heaven.

The nurse laughed.

'I know why. Look.'

Nancy stood and drew the curtains around the bed, then pointed to the ceiling. They were matching blue, sky-blue.

'You almost drowned. Was that your intention, my friend? You didn't go for a swim. You were fully dressed.'

'I wanted to be cleansed, to be baptised.'

'Maggie, people commit suicide doing exactly what you did. Psychiatrists will interview you in time, maybe very soon. If you don't respond as I believe you must, you could end up in a psych ward. You must sharpen your wits and get out of here. We'll look after you back at the house. Gerry and Linda have agreed, and they send their love. We decided not to contact Mrs Norris or Aimee without your permission. I've put a magazine on your bed. Can you hold it?'

Maggie's fingers had trouble doing what she wanted, but her stubborn nature forced the issue. She leafed through a few pages, stopped, and tried to read.

'The words are fuzzy.'

'And so is your brain. Concentrate, and heed my advice.'

'Maggie, the circumstances leading to your admittance automatically led doctors to assess you as a possible suicide case. You are to be interviewed by the mental health team. It would be best if you remain calm. Do not show your bubbly personality; stay low-key, speak softly, but show clarity of thought and speech. Do not cry; it will weaken your case. Do not offer information. Only speak when spoken to, and if they ask if you have a job, provide positive information. You are a cadet journalist who co-writes and illustrates a monthly column on new fashion items in a national newspaper. Say you are about to start your solo column, but do not mention that it targets individuals born under the influence of astrological signs.'

'And why this magazine, Nancy?'

'Find a subject of interest. You're a budding actress. Prove your worth. Memorise as much as you can from one page. Mark it by turning an obscure corner at the bottom. Flip to that page if required to read clearly.

The analysts will most certainly ask if you have tried to commit suicide before. Answer that you didn't try to commit suicide but were drawn into the ocean by its calm water, as the day was hot. They may ask if there are mental health issues in your family. Answer not what you know. That may lead to an adoption issue. Answer that your parents told you that you are their child. Maggie, I viewed the two letters you left in your room. I have a suspicion that Lincoln is your child and that social circumstances forced you to adopt him out. I ask you no questions, but if he is, this may be an opportunity to speak with a psychiatrist about your deep sadness. That will satisfy those assessing your behaviour as not erratic but usual from a particular Christian view of cleansing by baptism. They may then drop the idea that you are suicidal. Attempted suicide is considered a mental state which often needs correcting by hospitalisation and drugs.'

Maggie's mind had gone on alert, fully aware and attentive.

'Nancy, the Buddha said, "Three things cannot hide for long: The Moon, the Sun and the Truth." Suicide didn't enter my mind.'

A doctor and nurse appeared at the end of Maggie's bed. Nancy excused herself, thrusting the magazine into Maggie's hands.

'Look on your bedside table; I've brought your vase of white feathers. In the cupboard, fresh clothing. Be positive and attentive. I'll wait outside, hoping to take you home.'

The doctor flipped Maggie's medical chart while speaking.

'Hello, Maggie. Lucky for you, your friend Nancy identified you on admittance and has offered to care for you on discharge.'

'Am I being discharged now?'

He investigated her face.

'Almost. But first, a general physical and mental assessment. How are you feeling?'

'Slightly light-headed and a bit lazy. While I dozed, I thought I heard a cat making dough on my blanket, lub-dub, lub-dub, dub-dub.'

The doctor listened to Maggie's heart, then smiled.

'We don't have cats in this hospital. It's common to sense the beat of your heart while lying in bed. I'm guessing you were a little anxious when you woke because you didn't recognise your surroundings. Maggie, your ticker is diamond strong, and although your blood pressure is low, I have no concerns. Nurse, would you help Maggie out of bed, please? I need to see her balance.'

While walking a few steps, Maggie felt woozy but kept going, hoping she didn't give herself away. Nancy was right; she must get out of here. Maggie felt unsafe, unprotected, even with White Feathers nearby. Her prior experience in Melbourne put her off hospitals for life, so as soon as the nurse and doctor left, she planned to change into her clothing and stuff a lucky feather into her bra.

'OK, Maggie, rest now. I think you're of sound mind, but a suicide assessment consultation is part of our clinical guidelines.'

Maggie was about to object, then remembered Nancy's warnings: remain calm, stay low-key, speak softly, do not cry, or offer information. The doctor and nurse left, and Maggie picked up the magazine, chose a page with clear writing, donned her invisible actress hat, and did as Nancy advised. She read, memorised, and dressed. Maggie asked White Feathers for strength and clarity. She recited the memorised paragraphs into the bathroom mirror to ensure she knew her script, a trick she learned in drama class.

She was taken, in a wheelchair, to a sitting room in another wing of the hospital. The attendant placed her facing a seated man and a woman dressed in staid yet fashionable streetwear. They were studying papers on their laps. Both looked up briefly as she entered, then returned to their documents as though she wasn't there.

Maggie sat in the chair and said nothing—an irritating situation.

Were they obnoxiously rude or testing her patience and ability to sit until they were ready to speak? Was she supposed to say hello, introduce herself or ask who they were? It was safer to sit and wait. The man finally looked up and smiled. Maggie smiled back and held his gaze softly. He looked vaguely amused, then went back to his papers. Maggie started to think of funny things to do. Her mind went to Pietro from Rome, the boy at the Rocks. What if she were to tap on their desk, then mime saying hello and shake hands with them? No, she'd best not do that; it might put her in the lunatic asylum. Maggie longed to break the silence but sat and waited, repressing the desire to scream by pressing her tongue to the roof of her mouth. She amused herself by looking past them, scrutinising the static scene through the window. Suddenly, a book fell to the floor. Maggie jumped up, picked it up, placed it back on the small table, then returned to the wheelchair. The woman broke the silence.

'Thank you. Why did you pick it up?'

'Instinct, I guess. Its place was not on the floor, and some pages were creasing. Hello, I'm Maggie Piper.'

The man introduced himself and his colleague. Maggie was so frightened that she instantly forgot their names. She decided to refer to them both as "doctors," but felt they could be the Spanish Inquisition's arresting officers incarnate. The female had sharp eyes that darted before she spoke. The male was laid-back and loose. Maggie thought of a cat she once knew who used to roll over and beg to have his tummy rubbed, but heaven needed to help the person who fell for this lark. Dr He smiled faintly, encouraging Maggie to speak.

'Why did you think about suicide?'

'I didn't.'

Dr She leaned back in her chair, the glint in her eyes making Maggie think of icicles hanging from a Christmas tree.

'I'm in a mind that you wanted to kill yourself. Do you hear voices telling you to harm or cut yourself? Have you made a will?'

'Gosh. No to death, to voices, and to writing a will.'

Dr He gave silent permission for Dr She to lead the interrogation.

'You were found washed up on the beach at Manly. Surely you didn't go for a swim fully dressed.'

'No. The day was hot. The water was cool, and the horizon beckoned me. I thought it was an opportunity to be baptised.'

'So, you are a Christian, Maggie Piper? Was this the first time you wished for religious cleansing?'

'I think I'm still a Christian, and yes, I'd never considered baptism before. It was a spur-of-the-moment need, not a decision.'

'Any particular reason?'

Maggie thought it best to provide an excuse.

'Perhaps those obnoxious men at the fundraiser party, or the men who tried to grab me on my way home, or because I was born with the stain of original sin. I don't know.'

Maggie felt she'd said too much, but she couldn't take it back. Dr She glanced at Dr He, who took over.

'Have you recently experienced any significant losses (such as losing a job, your home, experiencing a death or losing a financial investment?'

'I have a few different jobs, and as far as I know, they are secure. As a cadet journalist, I co-write and illustrate a monthly fashion column in a national newspaper.

'Are you a regular churchgoer?'

'No. But yes. I mean, I don't purposely attend a service. But I do like the atmosphere a holy place offers if its energy draws me in. So, I enter, sit in a pew and meditate.'

'Before entering the ocean, were you under the influence of alcohol or other substances? Do you use alcohol or drugs frequently?'

'Alcohol doesn't attract me. Those who drink it are vulgar. I've never thought of taking a drug, and neither do the people I know.'

Dr She stood. She was tall and forbidding.

'Maggie, we know you live in rented accommodation, so you are no doubt estranged from your family. Do you have friends?'

'Yes.'

'But you don't trust them to confide in them?

'Would anyone want to hear my thoughts about myself? Should I offload on other people?'

'You should not feel ashamed of sharing or feeling suicidal.'

'I'm not suicidal. My wish was to cleanse myself by baptism.

'I don't believe you, Maggie Piper. Have you ever felt that way before? If so, what did you do to avoid suicide previously?'

'No. I wasn't trying to commit suicide. That would be a sin. It is in the doctrine that successful suicide cases go to hell for eternity.'

The woman shrugged, turned her back and looked out of the window as though dismissing Maggie from further interrogation. If the decision were up to Dr She, Maggie was sure she'd find herself in a psych ward. Dr He moved his chair closer to the wheelchair.

'Maggie, do you have a boyfriend?'

'Do you mean a lover? No.'

'Have you had a lover?'

'No, I haven't, and I don't want one. I am aware of pregnancy through rape.'

'I feel your need to purge spiritually has much to do with toxic experiences beyond your control.'

'True. It has become apparent that I was born to be a willing wench to wealthy drunk men or used as a sex object.'

'Unlike my colleague, whom I respect, I believe that you did have intentions of baptism, not suicide.'

Maggie hesitated for a moment, then said.

'I now know that I didn't need cleansing. I made a mistake. Negative circumstances caused a mental return to childhood. My parents believed I was born carrying the original sin.'

Dr She turned swiftly. Dr He continued.

'Will you attempt baptism again?'

'No. Although strangely, I feel clear and clean, as though I am a new me. Perhaps the ocean washed my brain.'

'Your appearance and personality will not have altered through this experience, so you need to think of a crisis plan. What will you do to cope with the same problems?'

My crisis plan is easy. I want to be close to a dog and a cat again. I would never let a being in my care down; there is no way I'd leave them to an unknown fate. I accidentally won a scholarship to train at the Independent School of Acting in North Sydney. I discovered the wonder of being another character, of studying how to be that person. This training gave me insight and enhanced my understanding of individuals. On stage, all worries are non-existent, and one is safe from harm.'

Dr He became solidly sincere.

'Maggie, no therapist or doctor wishes to hospitalise their patient. Rather, it is our goal to help our patients remain as high functioning as possible, standing on their own two feet.'

'Am I a psychiatric patient now?'

'If you feel that you need our help, you are welcome as an out-patient. Otherwise, you are your own counsel.'

Dr She stepped toward Maggie; her demeanour softened. Maggie had witnessed this personality change before- Matron in Melbourne. Dr She was much like Matron. She bent and offered her hands, which Maggie gratefully took.

'If you feel strong and can walk without help, you are free to go home. But we recommend another night's sleepover in this hospital, then on with your life. I'm almost one hundred per cent sure that you don't need us, but we could and will act as advisors rather than as psychiatrists. What are your plans for your future?'

'To nurture a career through which I can teach empathy, justice and respect regardless of colour, race, religion or physical differences.'

Dr He stood.

'They're social values which call for a public figure.'

Dr She showed interest.

'Do you want to become famous?'

'And make my private life publicly known? No. I believe I can work in live theatre, avoiding publicity that seems part and parcel of acting associated with films.'

'How could the stage encourage community conduct?'

'The marriage of the many arts which birth a brilliant play subliminally draws an audience to consider their lifestyle through grandeur, history, mystery, magic, and laughter. Have you not noted the joy on the faces of an audience, the fellowship as strangers nod to each other at intervals and bid farewell at the end of the performance? The equality of the rich and poor, of children and adults at a pantomime? Theatre is the only affordable career that offers to build and convey my message of harmony through communication. I shall never stop refining my art.

'Maggie, I am certain you will put your heart and soul into your purpose. But the most important thing for you to remember is that what happens in your head, fuelled by the cruelty of others, doesn't have to stay there.'

Dr He walked to the door, held it open and waited for Dr She, who hesitated before leaving, turned and took on the facial features of Grandma Maggie.

'From me, a Gaelic blessing. May the wind be always at your back.'

Maggie stood, nodding thanks to the departing Doctors. She felt the white feather against her skin; Ku-ah-Lee, her guide, was with her. She touched the scarab ring Nancy had returned to her finger and pledged.

'I have refused to purchase fame and position in society with the violation of my integrity and have survived baptism in deep water. I have endured torment and degradation for carrying the child of a rapist and suffered the brutality of my newborn being torn from me on the birthing table. Yet, Ku-ah-Lee, thanks to your energy, I stand tall and know that all will be well. I have faith that my life will be as it should be, beautiful and without fear. Like the Moringa tree, I shall offer shade, nourishment, and healing. And prove to my son that I am a worthy person, yet he shall never hear from my lips that his beginning was non-consensual. Lincoln must never know that shame. I will immerse myself in the knowledge of the ancients and the arts. I shall mentally live like a Bedouin and settle where the wise winds rest, allowing no moss to gather to hinder my cause. Like the eldest daughter in a Chinese household, I shall mirror early summer and live with gentle penetration and flexibility. I am whole. I fervently believe.'

## ABOUT THE AUTHOR

Magda Palmer Cordingley is a multidisciplinary artist and author with a creative career spanning the United Kingdom and Australia. She has worked in theatre, broadcast media, visual arts, and education.

Her prior publications include The Healing Power of Crystals (an international bestseller translated into German and Spanish), My Feng Shui, plays, scripts, and poetry collections. Trained in theatre at Dame Doris Fitton's Independent Theatre School and voice production under Jean Wynne Scott, Magda has performed in London's Young Vic and Newcastle Theatre Royal, and hosted cultural events for the Australian High Commission in London.

Magda's artistry has always championed those who have been mistreated, in both the human and animal kingdoms. Paper Sparrow is her most personal and courageous work yet—designed to inform, inspire, and confront the historical injustices that shaped future generations.

Magda's code of conduct is rooted in Ahimsa, the key virtue of the ancient Indian principle of causing no harm to other beings and living without malice, greed or gluttony.

Printed in Dunstable, United Kingdom